MY MIND WAS THE GASOLINE AND MY BODY THE MATCH. THOSE THAT
HURT ME WERE THE KINDLING TO WATCH THE WORLD BURN...

the consumed trilogy book one

Burn

FOR ME

BROOKLYN CROSS

BROOKLYN CROSS

Copyright © June 2022

Burn For Me
Book One
The Consumed Trilogy

Written by: Brooklyn Cross

FIRST EDITION.

ASIN: B09XM4XHNK

ISBN: 978-1-998015-01-6

ALL RIGHTS RESERVED.

Edited by: Rebecca Colvin from JustAskHer Productions In House Editing Team

Cover Art: Dazed Designs

Book Cover Disclaimer: Individuals depicted in the images on the cover and anywhere are models and solely used for illustrative purposes.

This book may not be reproduced or used in whole or in part by any means existing without the author's written permission. Author Brooklyn Cross.

This book is a work of fiction, and any resemblance to persons, living or dead, or places, events, or locales is purely coincidental. The characters, incidents, and dialogues in this book are productions of the author's imagination and are not to be construed as real.

The ideas represented in this book are not factual representations of anyone's thoughts affiliated with Author Brooklyn Cross, or of any of the trademarked acknowledgments mentioned in this story. This story is simply a work of fiction.

Trademark Acknowledgements

The author Brooklyn Cross acknowledges the trademarked status and trademark owners of familiar wordmarks, products, actors' names, television shows, books, characters, video games, and films mentioned in this fiction work.

❀ Created with Vellum

Also by BROOKLYN CROSS

Lost Souls

(Motorcycle/Rock Star Romance/Enemies to Lovers/Friends to Lovers - Dark
4-5 Spice 3.5-4.5

Malice - Snake Duet Book 1

Surrender - Snake Duet Book 2

The Righteous Series

(Vigilante/Ex Military Romance - Dark 3-4 Spice 3-4)

Dark Side of the Cloth

Ravaged by the Dark

Sleeping with the Dark

Hiding in the Dark

Redemption in the Dark

Crucified by the Dark (Coming Soon)

Dark Reunion (Coming Soon)

The Consumed Trilogy

(Suspense/Thriller/Anti-Hero Romance - Dark 4-5 Spice 3-4)

Burn for Me

Burn with Me

Burn me Down (Coming Soon)

The Buchanan Brother Duet

(Serial Killer/Captive Romance - Dark 4-5 Spice 3-4)

Unhinged Cain by Brooklyn

Twisted Abel by T.L Hodel

The Battered Souls World

(Standalone Books Shared World Romance- Dark 2-3 Spice 2-3)

The Girl That Would Be Lost

The Boy That Learned To Swim (Coming Soon)

The Girl That Would Not Break (Coming Soon)

The Brothers of Shadow and Death Series

(Dystopian/Cult/Occult/MFM Romance - Dark 3-4 Spice 3-4)

Anywhere (Coming Soon)

Seven Sin Series

(Multi Author/PNR/Angel and Demons/Redemption - Dark 2-5 Spice 3-5)

Greed by Brooklyn Cross

Lust by Drethi Anis

Envy by Dylan Page

Gluttony by Marissa Honeycutt

Wrath by Billie Blue

Sloth by Talli Wyndham

Pride by T.L. Hodel

W A R N I N G

This is a dark novel and is intended for mature audiences only.
This book is for sale to adults ONLY, as defined by the country's laws in which you made your purchase.
This book may contain violence, course language, graphic content that includes dubious consensual sexual scenes, alcohol, tobacco and drug use, and scenses that deal with mature subject matter and that some readers may find disturbing.
For a complete breakdown of the trigger warnings, please see Brooklyn Cross's website

Playlist

Burn For You - Jace Everett

Stranger In My House - Ronnie Milsap

Nothing - Bruno Major

Carry On Wayward Son - Kansas

Flowers On The Wall - The Statler Brothers

What A Wonderful World - Sam Cooke

Inner Ninja - Classified

Watch Me Burn - Michele Morrone

Hot In Herre - Nelly

Heat Waves - Glass Animals

Basket Case - Green Day

Light Em Up - Fall Out Boy

Play With Fire - Sam Tinnesz

That's Not My Name - The Ting Tings

Super Freak - Rick James

Love The Way You Lie - Eminem

Fireball - PitBull

Demons - Joel Plaskett

Shout Out

I would like to say a huge thank you to T.L. Hodel for allowing me to cameo a few of her beloved characters in this novel.

Aknowledgement

I would like to say a huge thank you to Julia Murray PA for always being there when I need her, and for going above and beyond to help make this book launch special. I'd like to take a moment to thank Just Ask Her Productions for all their hard work and for putting up with me and my impossible deadlines. I would also like to thank my Beta, Arc, Street and Blogger team. Your support means the world to me. For a book is but a dream without a team like you.

Not
even the
Devil could burn
the world like
I could

CHAPTER 1

Four Years Ago

My whole life boiled down to a split second in time. What I was before that moment and who I became after hinged on one pivotal act that shaped me into the *thing* I am now. I'm a thing—I can admit that. I'm not sure if I'm quite a monster but simply calling me a man wasn't accurate either. Normal men didn't enjoy the screams of people in pain as they burned while watching them reduced to nothing more than ash, but I did.

I didn't just enjoy it—I fucking loved it. I craved it, and I wanted to fuck to the sound of their dying wails. Well, at least I fantasized about what it would be like to kill more. In reality I'd only ever killed four people that all deserved it, and only got to see my mother burn alive.

I screamed, my voice a high-pitched screech that sounded more animal than human as the excruciating pain matched the stench of my flesh burning. Pushing on the front of the stove with my shaking arms, I strug-

gled against the hold that held me by the neck. Another terror-filled cry left my mouth as the flame licked toward my eye, and I kicked out with my legs, not caring what I hit.

I heard a yell and then we were falling.

With a hard bang, I crumpled to the floor and went to touch my face, but Asher grabbed my hand and shook his head no. His eyes were wide as he stared at my face. Unable to stop myself, I glanced at the glass in the front of the oven and saw the bubbled and ruined skin.

"Come on," he said and yanked on my arm.

My father was yelling and struggling, his hand reaching for me, but my brother pulled hard and got me to my feet. I slipped on the tiled floor of the kitchen, the cheap linoleum not giving any traction. Asher kept his arm around my waist as we stumbled into the front hallway and pushed out through the front door into the night. My father was bellowing for us to get back there, his words slurred. I looked over my shoulder once to make sure our father wasn't following and never looked back again.

I barely remembered the sequence of events but remembered every tiny detail about how my parents paid for what they did. The screams, the blood, and the burning awakened a demon in me. It awakened my true self, and I liked the new me, or I did until my butt landed in this fucking place.

What was it about an asylum where builders and caretakers of said building thought everything inside the place needed to be white and smell like cheap bleach? The scent aside, I thought white was the most lifeless and depressing color they could've chosen. Then again, maybe that was the point. Maybe they were trying to kill us with boredom and exasperate our depression.

Shifting my shoulders from side to side working at the itch that was driving my shoulder blade crazy. All I could feel was a tingly sensation like something was crawling on my skin and grew in persistence the longer it was left there. Fucking straight jackets were such a pain.

"Ahhh, no, no, get it away from me!"

Sighing, I looked away from the view of the back garden to stare at the patient in the middle of a psychotic breakdown. I didn't know the name of this guy, he'd only been here like three weeks, but he sure liked to scream. All fucking hours of the day or night, and now he was ruining the only time of day that I got to pretend that I was still part of society.

"Hey! Fucknut, shut up!"

The guy blinked and stared at me, his eyes wide like I was going to jump up out of this wheelchair and beat him as if I weren't tied to it.

"Yeah, I'm fucking talking to you. I have fifteen minutes left. Shut the fuck up, and then you can scream the place down."

The guy looked like he might start screaming again, and I glared at him and growled low in my chest. I pulled up my gums snarling at him as I pictured ripping his throat out, so he bled all over this bleached white hospital outfit. The guy spun around so his back was to me and hunched over as he mumbled softly to himself.

A rule I'd picked up while being here, look like the baddest mother fucking crazy around, and the other nutjobs would leave you alone. Five years, three months, and twenty-one days...I glanced at the clock...and sixteen minutes. That's how long it had been since I was first brought to this place. My life had become a rhythm of the same crap over and over. How they expected people to get better when they stuck them in this hole and then not give them anything to do was beyond me. Well, that wasn't true. They gave you things like arts, crafts, or books. I'd never been a big sit back and relax with a novel kind of reader, but I figured out quickly that there was a lot of very useful information in books.

I'd learned that someone can survive a whole three minutes without breathable air. I glanced over again at the fidgeting man, who was being quiet but was giving off some serious nervous energy. That energy was filling the room and felt like nails on a chalkboard. Something else I learned was that it usually wasn't the flame of a fire that killed most people. It was the hot gases that a person inhaled into their lungs as the body burned that killed them. This fact was particularly fascinating to me. It meant that, in theory, there was opportunity out in the world where I could slowly burn people for hours or days, and they wouldn't die. The idea of prolonging the thrill was exciting. I might even be able to get them to live for months. I wiggled in my seat as the thought stirred a darker desire in my gut.

"Hi, you're Derek, right?" a soft and pleasant voice said from behind me.

The reflection of whoever stood a few feet away was feminine and smelled like citrus. Bottom line, whoever she was, this person was new, which meant a new play-toy for me.

"What the fuck is it to you," I snarled at the voice.

The woman stepped around into my line of sight, a stethoscope around her neck and a wide smile on her face. Her blue eyes weren't like the rest of those that worked here. There was a sweetness that glowed inside of them. She also didn't seem to care about my abruptness, which instantly made me skeptical of her.

What did she want from me?

"Well, I'm asking because if so, then I'm your new nurse, but if not, I'll move on." There was no way someone, especially me, wouldn't notice how pretty she was.

She was going to be a walking target in this place, and my eyes glanced around to see what other guys had already caught sight of her. Her smile pulled at the rubble surrounding my heart as she turned to walk away, and I found myself calling out to her.

"Yeah, I'm Derek," I mumbled and slumped into the wheelchair.

For the first time in a long time, I felt humiliated that I was strapped into a rolling chair. It had taken me a whole month to gain the privilege of being strapped into the wheelchair whenever they wanted to move my ass around. Initially, I fought it and spent the first couple of months confined to my room. I'd never been much for people as a whole, especially the crazy lot in this place. Yet, that much solitude even had me talking to myself for the sound of anything other than the screaming of my own mind.

The woman, who appeared not to be much older than myself smiled as she looked over her shoulder at me. "You sure about that?"

I could tell she was teasing. Her eyes sparkled with mischief that felt immediately addictive. The tiniest spark of 'I wasn't sure what this emotion was' lit inside of me.

"Yeah, I'm sure."

With a flourish, she turned toward me and opened her arms up wide. "Well, in that case, how about we make it our first priority to not have you in that stupid white jacket? Wouldn't it be nice to sit out here of your own volition?"

I snorted at the pipe dream she was painting.

"Spare me. They'll never let me out of my room without this thing on. It's like they think I'm a wizard or some shit, and if I have my hands, I can magically burn the place down." Rolling my eyes, I turned my head away. No one needed to know I'd already figured out a couple of ways out of this hell and all of them involved burning it to the ground.

"Well, I'm a fountain of hope and optimism, so I'll see what I can do." She stepped up behind the wheelchair and placed her hand on my shoulder. "But unfortunately, that doesn't stop me from having to take you back to your room now."

"Don't have enough pull to let me stay another five minutes?"

"Sadly, no. Hey, can I borrow you?" She waved to one of the orderlies guarding the sitting area. "Don't worry. We'll get you sorted out."

She gave my shoulder a gentle squeeze, and I stared at her hand. Long after she let go of my shoulder, I could still feel the heat and impression of where her hand had been touching me.

I had rarely been touched with kindness in my life, but I hadn't been touched here at all unless it was to beat me or torture me with one of their "therapy sessions." It had been so long that I'd forgotten what it was like to be touched in any other way. My eyes found hers again. "What's your name?"

"Oh, yes, sorry about that. My name is Adalyn, and I'm very happy to meet you, Derek."She gave me a wink, and I had to wonder if Dr. Wallace decided to torture me with a whole new mastermind trick. I wouldn't put it past him to screw with me like that. He took great pride in building me up, only to tear me down. He didn't say it, but he didn't have to acknowledge it verbally. I knew what lived under the disguise of the prim and proper glasses he had on his face, and none of it was good or kind.

"Adalyn, yeah, I guess that name will do," I said, making her laugh.

It was too painful to think that there could actually be a little sunshine after all the rain? Adalyn hummed a soft tune as she pushed me toward my room, and even though I knew it was dangerous, I still couldn't help hoping. I was a glutton for punishment, I guess.

Not
even the
Devil could burn
the world like
I could

CHAPTER 2

Present Day

I smiled as the screams echoed in my mind, the flames dancing before my eyes as those inside the random building ran frantically like a bunch of mice. Hands pulled on doors that refused to open and banged on windows that wouldn't break. I sucked in a deep breath relishing in the scent of burning wood and other things that would curl another person's nose.

"Mr. West, stop that right this moment."

I blinked as I was pulled out of the vision that felt so real. I could still feel the heat dancing along my skin. As my eyes focused on the man on the opposite side of the desk, I remembered where I was. The doctor's hair had a mottling of salt and pepper in it, and his half-cut styled glasses made him look like my fifth-grade science teacher. Dr. Wallace pointedly glanced toward my lap, and I followed his line of sight. My hand was down the front of the white cotton pants they made us wear in this shithole.

I smirked, my lip curling up as my eyes flicked up to Dr. Wallace again.

"What's the matter? Don't you like to see a cock being stroked?" Instead of stopping, I made my movement more exaggerated. "I always took you for the voyeur type. I mean, you like to watch everything else."

One of the small pleasures I got in this place was pissing off all the humans that worked here. They liked to pretend they were there to help me but 'pretend' was the optimal word. I didn't need or want their kind of help. It always led to tons of pills, white jackets, and other forms of fun that the doctor liked to cook up. What they failed to see was that they were not breaking me or curing me, not in the way they thought. No, they were molding me into what they prayed I'd never become. Their ignorance only fueled the anger that burned as bright as the flames of the fires I liked to set. The more they tried, the more I wanted their flesh to taste the lick of my brand of punishment.

"I said stop that," Dr. Wallace barked out as he bolted up from his chair and slammed his hands on his desk. His reaction was fucking fantastic and spurred me on. I pulled the semi-hard cock out of my white pants to waggle it in the air at him. "Orderlies!"

"You like it don't you? Admit it," I yelled.

The door opened, but before they could get to me, I jumped up and smacked my cock off his desk. There was a sweet sting to the act as it banged off his desk, and I laughed hysterically at the horrified look on the doctor's face. It was truly a beautiful moment and one that I would savor until I was able to end him permanently. The two large men each grabbed an arm and dragged me back from Dr. Wallace, my pants slipping around my ankles as I growled and pretended to bite at the men's faces.

"What the fuck is wrong with you," Dave, the orderly, said and gave me a hard shot to my ribs. The air pushed out of my lungs with the sharp pain, but I laughed and fought harder in their hold. I was not their puppet. I'd never conform to the bullshit they spewed.

Those lingering in the corridor stared at the commotion, their matching outfits, a reminder that I'd end up just like them unless I took action. I refused to end up as an old man with a limp dick and dreams unfulfilled, and all personality wiped away by depression and heavy doses of medication.

As we reached my special padded space, I fought harder. I didn't really care if I went into my room. In fact, I preferred the area more than anywhere else in this fucking place, but I wanted them to work for it. The orderly I deemed Jumbo Jim was gripping my right arm, and I wrenched hard away from him and unloaded my fist into his abnormally large nose. Jim stumbled backward, his hands going to his face as blood exploded like a miniature geyser from his twisted broken nose.

"Fuck, you fucking prick," Jim yelled, but the confusion allowed me to get ahold of the back of Dave's shirt and yank back hard. I twisted the material in my fist, pulling it tight against his throat. He slapped at my hand as I cut off his air supply and used him as a shield from Jim as he regained his senses.

Backing up into my room, I kicked my door closed in Jim's face before he could walk through it. The joyful mania pumped through my blood until I took an elbow from Dave to the gut. I groaned as the air was knocked out of me for the second time, but I took him with me as I dropped to the ground. Dave struggled like a turtle on his back, his arms and legs flailing around as I held him firm to my chest in a choke hold.

Jim got the door unlocked, and a fist found the side of my face a moment before a third orderly, whose face I couldn't see, stuck me with a needle in the arm. I knew they would give me whatever tranq. they deemed necessary, but I didn't care anymore. I used to at one point, but that died the first year I was here. The strong drugs and little skirmishes were the only real excitement I got in this place.

Within seconds my arms felt heavy and weak, and Dave was pulled off of me and out of my hold. I couldn't help it. I smiled up at Jim with the knowledge that I got one up on him. It was as delicious as the memory of sweet candy in my mouth.

Jim loomed over me, blocking out the light. "Put him on the bed and strap the fucker down. I'm so sick of you, West. I'll be happy when they finally decide to move you to prison."

I didn't know what he meant by that. I'd been here nine years, and I was never leaving unless I broke out as far as I was concerned. The drugs made it too hard to concentrate, and the delightful buzz swirling in a steady stream of colorful sparkles made every muscle feel heavy. I assumed this was what it felt like to drink—not that I had a ton of experience with alcohol. Not seeing outside these walls since I was seventeen made it impossible to experience pretty much everything. It was always the stupid shit that I never thought I'd miss that I ended up longing for the most. I was trapped in a groundhog day of cafeteria food, crap coffee, no new movies, no phone, no friends, no sex, no anything new and only a few moments of the sun by a window. What the fuck was a normal conversation? I could barely remember what that was like without being told I was a sick fuck, punched in the face, or strapped down and drugged.

There were more voices and talking. My eyes slowly traveled around the room as my head swam around in the little sea of foggy bliss.

Dr. Wallace was speaking to someone that I couldn't see, but then all the men left, and the room became quiet. The only voices left were mine and the ghosts that haunted the place, or maybe they were in my mind. I wasn't sure, but I voted for this place being haunted because what I was seeing now...would creep anyone out.

I was used to this show, and calmly watched 'them' crawling across the floor, their twisted and mangled bodies leaving wet, bloody streaks as they pulled themselves closer. I always wondered why they looked wet. Did we all die and look wet forever, or was it just these tortured souls that were trapped in this fucking place?

They used to scare me, but now I realized they were the versions of me that never got to leave. They were the sad souls that this place broke and discarded as trash.

No, I wouldn't become one of those disturbing images that lingered along the halls. They wanted me to. They wanted me to break and take my own life, they didn't say it to my face, but their eyes said more than words could. What they failed to see was that I was stronger than that. I was stronger than all of them. I'd been conditioned from a young age to withstand whatever they decided to do to me. I had plans—plans that would see me outside of these walls sooner rather than later.

My eyes fluttered closed as I relaxed into the out-of-body lightness that made me feel free of the bed I was strapped to and the restraints that held me to it. The door made a loud clang, and I wasn't sure if it was Jim on his way back to teach me another lesson or someone else. My head lulled to the side, and I peeled my eyelids open enough to see the approaching person's legs and petite running shoes.

Hints of sweet lavender and tangy citrus filled my nose and made me sigh, the scent giving away who it was. I slowly turned my head to look up into the face of the only person inside these stark white walls that I liked.

"Hey you," Adalyn whispered, her small hand brushing back the unruly mop my hair had become. "Why do you like to agitate Jim and the others so much? His nose is broken, you know. He will file a complaint that you're violent and say you should never be released. He's already pushing to have you found competently sound. If that goes through, they will move you to prison."

My lips pulled up into as much of a smile as I could muster. I smacked my lips and tried to rid it of the dryness that made my tongue feel thick. "Assss hoesss," I managed, proud that I could say anything.

"Well yes, they are, but that's beside the point. Isn't nine years long enough to be in this place let alone go to prison?" Her fingers trailed over the scars that lined the right side of my face.

I'd been so ashamed of them until she started working here, but her kind voice and eyes that never looked at me with disgust had melted the hardness surrounding my heart and made me feel like my scars were a badge of honor. I survived a childhood that most wouldn't have and lived to tell the tale.

My head fell from side to side. "Thhhhy nooo mee oout."

Adalyn shook her head no, and her brown wavy short hair bounced as she did. "I had a good case going that you were changing, that you felt bad for what you'd done, and that you should be given a chance to speak at your next hearing."

She took a deep breath, gripped my strapped hand with her small one, and linked our fingers together. I shuddered with the connection. It was prohibited to have a relationship with patients, but she was the one thing that didn't make me see red. She was kindness personified, and I marveled every second that someone as beautiful as she could like me.

"Whyyy soooo saaad?" I stumbled over my fat tongue, and like a miniature magician, she held a cup with a straw up to my mouth. She giggled as my tongue swirled around the straw, but the look I gave her was heated as I pictured her nipple in my mouth.

A pink blush crept across her cheeks as she cleared her throat and looked down. Her blue eyes shined from under her thick lashes. "I'm sad because they're serious about having you transferred to prison to finish serving out your time. I was arguing that you were a changed man, but Derek, Dr. Wallace has all the ammunition he needs now to force you to leave, and then I'd never see you again."

I could see the sadness as clearly in her eyes as I felt the pang of panic in my gut. I wouldn't let them take me away from her.

I gave her hand a soft squeeze. "Nevvver."

"You may not have a choice in the matter." She bit her lip and looked toward the door as Jim yelled out in the hall about something. She slipped her hand out of mine and stood just before Jim burst through the door.

"What are you doing in here? You know you can't be in here alone. He's dangerous," Jim yelled at Adalyn, and I could feel the rage that simmered bubble to the surface once more.

"Jim, look at him. He's drugged to the gills and strapped down to a bed. What exactly do you think he will do to me? Besides, I still have to do my job, and no one was available to come in with me to check his vitals and give him some water."

Jim shook his head, and I wanted to laugh as I stared at the white tape that was across his nose. It made me childishly giddy inside to know that I did that.

"I don't know why you're nice to him. He's a monster, Ady...a fucking menace." He pointed to his face. "Look what the bastard did to my face. What do you think he could and would do to you if given a chance?"

"Yuuze," I mumbled and glared at Jim, his face going in and out of focus. I hated that Jim shortened her name. It was beautiful the way it was. "Woozzar."

"What the fuck did you just call me?" Jim balled his fists and took a step further into the room, making me laugh.

"Jim, that's enough. He's only acting like this to get under your skin. You must see that?" Adalyn held up her hand and stood between Jim and me.

"Whatever, the guy is a piece of shit."

He wouldn't have dared to say that to me if I was free. The anger flared like a lump of red-hot coal and throbbed in my chest as I tried to stay focused on his face.

"I'm nice because I'm nice, Jim. Now I'm almost done here. If you don't mind giving me a moment, he always gets agitated when you're in the room. It makes it difficult to get a proper heart rate."

"Three minutes, and I'll be right outside the door." Jim and the testosterone cloud surrounding him marched out the door.

Adalyn took the stethoscope off and put the little buds in her ears as she leaned over. I licked my lips as I stared down at the slim gap of her modest scrubs.

"I wish I had more time," she whispered in my ear, and even in my drugged state, my cock twitched. "I see you, Derek. You're more than they keep saying you are. There's so much more to you." She laid her hand on my cheek as she stood. "Try to behave. I don't want you to leave."

I wanted to lean into her touch and savor the sensation, but she pulled away before I could get my head to move.

Our eyes locked, and she smiled. It was the sweetest smile in the world. "Nevvver," I said again, and she bit her lip, the action gaining another twitch from my cock.

"I hope you're right. I'd miss you." Giving me a wink, she walked out, and I let my eyes close once more.

My heart felt a little lighter just having her near me. When she first started working here, I hadn't been very nice to her. I hadn't been nice to anyone, but their response was always the same. They thought that if they'd beat me, I'd submit. When I growled at her like a grizzly, she would smile and act the same.

The shadows on the walls looked like they were dancing and spinning with little sparkles floating around. I gave my head a little shake to clear my vision.

For the first time in my life, I wished that I could offer her more than the four walls that kept me confined. She made me crave normal. I didn't know what normal looked like, but whatever it was, I wanted it with her.

Whatever they gave me was a shit ton stronger than normal. One of the hauntling things pulled itself up onto the bed and sat on my legs.

"Ett daa ffff ooofff ooo mee," I slurred at the ghostly thing, but it ignored me. Its long, wet-like hair brushed along my pants, making them wet.

Or did I pee myself?

I didn't give a fuck either way.

I closed my eyes and swallowed hard as the words Adalyn said bounced around like a ping pong ball in my head. There was no way I'd let them take me to prison. I'd find a way to burn them all down before they did that to me. They wouldn't take me away from her. I'd never let that happen.

"Riiigghtt," I asked, the thing still perched on my legs. "Iiii buurrn iit dowwwn." The thing looked at me then. Its wide lips looked odd on the smallish head pulled up in a grin. My eyes fluttered closed, the world slipping away as the drug finally yanked me under into the dark.

Not
even the
Devil could burn
the world like
I could

CHAPTER 3

I slowly shuffled my way down the hall with the orderly chaperoning me. My stupid pants were caught under my sock-covered feet, making it slow going. And the stoned-faced orderly didn't seem to give a fuck if I fell on my face or not. He had his hand wrapped around my bicep with my wrists in fun leather cuffs so I couldn't break another nose. I mean, I could, but what good would it do? I'd worn the full gear before, which was annoying. However, I didn't want to go back to that, so I was playing the part of a dutiful patient today.

I preferred to stare out at the garden or read a book in the corner, but it was group therapy time. *Yay!* I rolled my eyes at the concept.

I fucking hated group therapy which was run by a different doctor or therapist, or whatever the hell she was. It wasn't Dr. Wallace, but she wasn't much better. I dubbed her Twit because she was an idiot. Only an idiot did the same thing day in and day out and expected a different result. She genuinely thought that the people in this place could be reha-bilitated. If she only knew that most had fantasies about her death or fucking her. For some, it was fucking her as they killed her, and they craved it. They smiled their fake ass smiles and nodded their heads at her every word as they dutifully agreed with the crap she spewed.

A wide grin spread across her face when she saw me. Her tight blonde bun on the top of her head made her look like one of those weird Teletubby things. Every now and then, one of the orderlies would find it amusing to put that shit on in the entertainment room.

Bunch of sadistic fuckers.

I wasn't allowed in there, but it blasted down the halls louder than the screams of some of the patient's night terrors. I genuinely liked to watch television. It sort of allowed me to feel like I was a part of what was going on outside these walls, but I never got to go in that room or spend time with the other patients. I was a bad influence, and apparently, throwing food at the shit on the television was not very nice. Boo-fucking-hoo. So, they had to clean up a little porridge off the screen and floor. I mean, any reasonable adult would've thrown something after listening to children's shows for hours. I thought I'd shown restraint, but the food fight that erupted might have been the real cause for my ban. I smirked.

"I'm so happy you could join us today," the Twit said.

Like I fucking had another choice, was what I wanted to say, but I kept my mouth shut. I was guided to one of the six chairs in the room and plopped down, stretching out my legs.

"You gonna be good, or do I need to leave those on you," the orderly asked.

Sighing, I held up my hands so that he could undo the restraints. As soon as my wrists were free, I rubbed at the spots where the cuffs sat. You'd think that after so many times of having to be strapped to one object or another that I'd be used to it, but I still hated them.

The last of the group arrived, and I knew who it was. He made a distinct short shuffling sound due to the cuffs around his ankles and wrists that were attached together. I'd worn those a few times, but this guy never had them off when he was outside his room. Sometimes I wondered if they kept them on all day just to be safe, and I wouldn't have blamed them if they did.

Adam was the most unassuming of the group. His small stature and weathered face had many of the orderlies pegging him for a genteel older man. I looked over at Adam as they sat him beside me. He smiled, the corners of his mouth turning up, but it was the look in his eyes that could make even someone like me shiver. I could feel the darkness that lived in Adam as surely as I could feel the itchy cotton material against my skin. I hadn't believed in ghosts and demons until I was brought to this place, but what lived inside Adam wasn't normal.

"Welcome, group. Thank you all for being here with me today. Who would like to start," the Twit said. She smoothed out the simple blue dress she was wearing and took her seat as she clutched the electronic notepad. The nympho looked around the room and then slowly raised her hand. Her room was across from mine, and I heard her screams of release more than once as she either touched herself or talked an orderly into fucking her. It amazed me how there was a double standard even in a place like this.

If a male orderly wanted to fuck a patient, everyone looked the other way, but if one of the nurses wanted to get it on with a patient, it was sacrilege. The women were branded as lustful whores who broke hospital protocol and immediately fired.

"Marylynn, go right ahead." The Twit smiled and pushed her fake-ass glasses up her nose.

"I only touched myself once this morning, but I have the urge again now. May I please be excused," Marylynn asked, proving my point that those in this wing were unfixable. Marylynn wasn't in here because she liked to have too much sex, although that was the root cause of her issue. No, she was here because she preferred public displays of attention, and the Governor of Florida got quite the show as she stripped and jumped on his lap at a five-star restaurant. It caused quite the scandal and took three people to peel her off him. Impressively, she managed to get his cock out for the whole world to see before she was yanked off his lap. I had to admit the girl had balls and went after what she wanted.

"No, Marylynn, you may not. Did you have anything else you would like to share?"

"Only that I really want to fuck that guy. He's hot." She pointed to the orderly standing guard at the far side of the room. Her eyes found the Twit again. "Did you want to join? That would be a hot threesome. You're really pretty."

Twit's nostrils flared, and she tapped at the notepad before moving on and dismissing Marylynn. "Derek, would you like to share today?" Her shit brown eyes found mine, and I lifted my shoulders in a half-hearted shrug.

"Sure, I'd like to get a better fucking meal in this place and scrubs that don't itch my ball sac. And how about a rope to hang myself, so I don't have to keep coming to these fucking share sessions?"

Twit gave me one of those disapproving scowls that parents liked to give. "I meant about your past, Derek. There's no need to be sarcastic. This is our safe space."

"Safe space for who exactly? You? Cause it certainly isn't my safe space, and I doubt it is for anyone else. Besides, no matter what I say, nothing is ever going to get me out of here, so why bother?" I pointed a thumb at Adam. "He's been in here seventeen years and counting. I don't think sharing his feelings has gotten him any closer to getting out or feeling healed."

I made little air quotes with my fingers. With each word I said, her face puckered into a sour and annoyed expression.

"So, back to your original question. Would I like to share? No, and if I have to, then it's to complain about the bullshit treatment the patients get in this place. Don't believe me? You eat the food or spend one night in a room here. Share my feelings. What a crock of shit."

"I'd have to agree with Mr. West. These scrubs do chafe the boys. Something in a higher thread count would be nice for sheets as well. I do like to feel the softness against my skin," Adam said quietly, drawing the attention of the entire room. That one innocent sentence made my skin crawl. Where others would picture silk or some shit like that, the look on Adam's face said he was picturing skin and not in the way anyone would want.

"I third that," one of the other patients said, and all those sitting around nodded their agreement. Twit looked at the group, whose attention she was losing quickly.

"Okay, that's enough of that, moving on. Adam, would you like to share?"

A shiver raced up my spine as Adam straightened in his chair. I knew this was going to be good before he opened his mouth. Every now and then, this fucker showed his other side, which was so different than the tranquil appearance he wore most of the time.

"Well, I was sitting here thinking how much I'd like to hear you scream as I take the pen that's in your pocket and stab you through the eye. And, how much I want to ride your writhing body to the ground, driving the pen in until it meets the back of your skull. Then how delightful it would be to use my bare hands to rip your stomach open like a wild animal and roll around in your blood while playing with your internal organs."

Twit's hand went to her heart, her mouth dropping open into a silent 'oh' as Adam leaned a little forward.

"And, how amazing it would feel to try and fit my body inside yours like you were a second skin. Of course, that is all before I stuff my cock into your eye socket and fuck it until I come. Gives a whole new meaning to impregnating your mind, don't you think?"

His maniacal laugh filled the suddenly quiet room as the Twit jumped up from her plastic chair, sending it clattering backward.

She comically yelped as it banged behind her. I laughed hysterically as Adam took the distracted moment to leap from his chair for her. All hell broke loose, and for once, I just sat back and watched this shit show ride out. Even the fights couldn't compare to this entertainment. The fact that I wasn't involved or getting punched in the face only added to the thrill of the drama.

The orderlies rushed in and grabbed Adam as he tried to bite off Twit's nose. His teeth narrowly missed as she held him off while thrashing and screaming wildly for him to get away.

The others must have decided this was a good time to get into the fray. I couldn't really blame them. The staff never did anything with us other than let our brains melt down and fry from boredom and drugs. What did they think would happen? Did they picture everyone holding hands and singing Kumbaya?

The only one that didn't leave their seat was Marylynn, who shoved her hand into her pants and was in the middle of rubbing one out. I smirked and crossed my arms over my chest. Then as more orderlies arrived, I pushed my chair back to give them room like a good little soldier.

I didn't think Twit would be back after this session. It had become a bit of a sport to see how long it took to drive the next therapist away. I had to hand it to Adam. He was going to end up in solitary for that performance, and yet I'd pay money to see it again.

"Let's go West," an orderly said, laying a hand on my shoulder.

Normally, that would piss me the fuck off, but nothing could upset me right now. I slowly stood and walked out, and my smile grew wider as I spotted Adalyn in the hallway. She gave me a shy smile as she continued to fill the little paper cups with medications. I watched her out of the corner of my eye as I passed and noticed her shifting around her stand so she could do the same. She was this ray of sunshine in a very dark place that would steal your soul and leave you bleeding in its wake.

"For once, it wasn't you starting shit," the orderly said as we got to my door. I made my way inside the small room that I called home.

"And you guys think I'm the sick fuck," I said and turned to face the orderly who hadn't bothered to put the cuffs back on me. If I'd been in a different mood, that would've been an error that could've cost him his life.

He let out a little laugh. "You don't fool me, West. You are a sick fuck, but on the fucked-scale, you're more bright orange than red."

As the door locked in place, I pondered that thought, and I was left watching Marylynn through the small window. She was struggling and screaming hysterically as they dragged her into her room.

"Fuck me! I need to come! Please fuck me! No, don't tie me up! No, no, don't leave. Please don't leave," she wailed as they left her room and closed the door with a bang. The vibration from the metal door was loud, but she was louder. She shrieked so harshly that I could hear her as easily as if she were inside my four walls.

Shaking my head, I wandered over to my bed and flopped down to stare at the ceiling. I had no idea how long I'd laid there in the quiet, the minutes ticking past, when the lock on my door softly clicked. I assumed it was an orderly but sat up as Adalyn slipped through the narrow opening and closed the door softly behind her.

"You shouldn't be in here, you keep doing this, and they're going to get you in trouble," I whispered as I stood.

"I don't care," she whispered as she wrapped her arms around my waist.

I buried my nose in her hair, loving the sweet fresh scent of her citrus shampoo. For four years, I'd been smelling this shampoo. Its scent brought me a tingly sense of relief like I'd taken a deep breath for the first time after the air had been stolen from my chest.

"I don't know what you see in me." I stepped back and moved to the only spot in the room where we wouldn't be seen if someone looked through the window.

"That's because you see yourself as a monster, but all I see is the man you are now, holding me." Adalyn laid her hands on my chest, and I sucked in a ragged breath.

"You're too good to me. If you knew what I've done, you wouldn't be saying these things. If you understood how much I enjoyed them...." I shook my head back and forth, but her eyes didn't change. There was no fear or disgust.

"I want to be naughty if you're up for it," she whispered and bit her lip. I sucked in a gasp as her hand cupped my cock.

This wasn't the first time we'd messed around, but every time I was caught between really wanting it to happen and worrying about her getting caught. If she did, I'd never see her face again.

"We can't keep doing this. We're going to get caught," I said and then groaned as her hand expertly stroked me through the pants.

"Does that mean you don't want me to help you relax," she asked, her hand as seductive as her voice.

"Of course, I want it. I'd like to finally fuck you for real, push you up against this wall and make you scream. But I don't want to see you get fired. I'd be really upset, and then there is no telling what I might do." I ran my hand through her short hair, loving the soft feel in my fingers.

"I love it when you talk dirty to me." She bit her lip as her big blue eyes looked up at me, and my cock surged in her hand at the thought of her lips wrapping around my shaft.

The memory of how her tongue liked to swirl around the tip had another groan leaving my mouth.

"I'll only get fired if they catch me, but Jim's on lunch." She looked at her watch. "I still have twenty-five minutes before I need to leave. Let me do this. I need to do this."

I licked my lips and nodded. Apparently, I was easily swayed when it came to her, as the want for gratification overrode logic.

"You know how to twist my rubber arm," I teased.

She smiled wide and pulled the string on the scrubs I was wearing. The material pooled around my feet as she knelt in front of me. Grabbing the bottom of my shirt, I held it up and out of the way to watch as her dainty hand wrapped around my shaft.

"Oh fuck," I whispered as her tongue did that hot as hell thing where she pretened I was her fucking lollipop. She giggled, and it sounded sweet and wicked at the same time. As her mouth bobbed on the sensitive head, I had to lean my back into the wall. Adalyn was moaning loudly as her lips slid around the thick shaft spreading her mouth wide. It was beyond hot to watch my cock disappear into her mouth and then re-emerge. She got into a rhythm, and as she did, my body shuddered with immense pleasure.

I didn't have any experience other than her, but as far as I was concerned, she was the best anyone could pray to have. Maybe Marylynn had a point. Maybe it was better to fuck all the pain and hatred out of my system.

Unable to help myself, I let go of my shirt and grabbed her hair. Fisting the softness of her I silky strands in my hand, she gagged a little as I added some pressure to the back of her head. The only sound in the room was my heavy breathing, a soft slurping, and a slight choking noise that sent a tingle right to the tip of my cock. The need to find release throbbed at the base of my dick, and with every twist of her hand and hollowing of her cheeks, I could feel it pulling closer. Desperation overcame me as she slowed slightly.

"Don't stop. I'm gonna come," I said through gritted teeth, and Adalyn moaned. Like I'd hit a switch, she sucked faster and harder, her nose softly brushing against my stomach as my cock pushed down her throat.

"Holy fuck," I growled, my muscles tensing.

The sensation was like pulling a lever and opening the flood gates. I bit my lip hard to keep from yelling out as the first shot of my come sailed from the tip of my cock. Adalyn moaned and sucked remarkably faster. It was like she was sucking on a straw and drawing out the liquid inside until she took every last drop I had to offer. Panting hard, I slumped against the wall. There were no words to describe how it felt to watch her lick me clean before licking off her fingers.

She laid a gentle kiss on the tip of my cock, and grabbed the forgotten scrubs pulling them up my legs as she stood.

"That is the sexiest thing I've ever seen. You're incredible," I said and pulled her in for a hug.

"I don't want to, but I better go."

Cupping her face, I kissed her softly on the lips. "Thank you, that was fucking amazing."

"No, thank you," she teased and made her way to my door. She was stealthy as she opened it a crack. She listened before giving me a wink and slipped out into the hall.

Wow, this had been the best day I'd had in this place. I thought Adam's stunt had made my night. No. Adalyn made me feel connected by weaving in a thread of normal. When I was with her, I didn't think about hurting anyone. I didn't dream about death or fire consuming everything in its path. All that existed was the ounce of happiness that my soul latched onto. Her. With a smirk on my face, I fell asleep with the image of Adalyn on her knees in front of me.

Not
even the
Devil could burn
the world like
I could

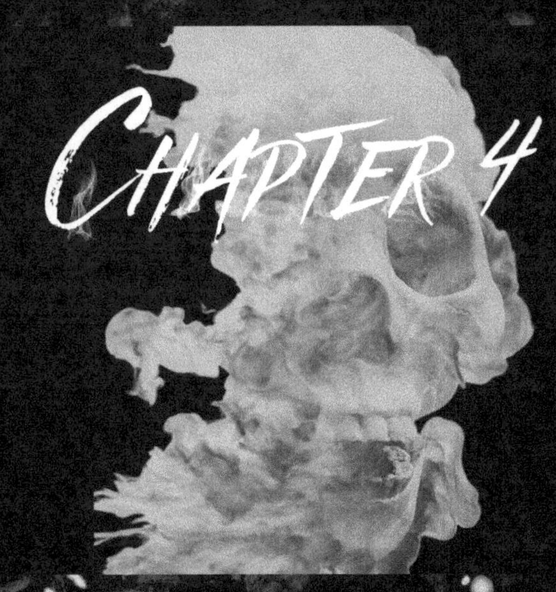

CHAPTER 4

I had no idea why I had to go to school, I hated it there, and it was stupid. They never taught us anything useful, information that we'd actually need. No, they made us do useless kiddy crap like build something out of popsicle sticks. Really? Like that was a life skill that I needed. How in the hell was building a popsicle stick castle going to help me figure out how to stop my dad from hitting my mom or stop my mom from drinking so much? How was learning the state's names in alphabetical order or how to play an instrument going to help me?

I sat at the edge of the playground, tossed a small pebble along the sidewalk, and watched it roll into the grass and disappear. I wanted to be that pebble. I wanted to disappear. Other kids ran around with a football or tossing a baseball, their smiling and laughing faces irritating. I'd bet the idea of not going home was the furthest thing on their minds. No, those lucky dicks had parents buy them ice cream and asked if they were okay when they fell. Not me, not in a very long time.

Sighing, I hooked my thumbs into the straps of the backpack and knew I had to get going, and yet I would've preferred to sleep on the bench that my ass was sitting on. The problem was I knew what *happened to kids like me—a twelve-year-old with no home, no family, no money, and no place to stay ended up dead or sucking dick for old men to make a buck.*

I wasn't stupid. I knew it was a cycle that would never end, one that you thought was an escape. Only to realize too late that it was a different kind of hell all on its own, one in a different beer-stained shirt. I'd thought about it, and even spent a night in the shelter pretending to be mute to investigate, but at least at my house I knew all the escape routes. A place like that was a different kind of danger. My hand rubbed at the sore spot on my arm under my long-sleeve T-shirt. The area was now a black bruise from the hand that had gripped me last night and wrenched my arm behind my back because I hadn't cut the lawn the way 'dad' liked. I'd made the mistake of asking him how I was supposed to know when he didn't tell me, but that only angered him more. The handprint—that I had to hold an ice pack against to make sure it was gone to come to school— told that story.

I'd finally got up my nerve to tell my teacher about the abuse, but nothing was done. Social workers called before coming to the house. They looked around, staring at empty rooms filled with emotionless items. Like that would tell them all the secrets they needed to know.

Of course, my dad lied and said, "he'd been known to yell."

But then he placed a hand over his chest and swore to god that he'd never hurt his kids. My mom nodded and lied right along with him. My little brother looked up to me, his eyes asking what his voice didn't, 'What should we do?'

What the hell was I supposed to do?

I couldn't say in front of my parents that my dad was an asshole that liked to hit me. If they didn't cart him away and lock him up, I would end up with more than a few bruises, I'd end up buried in the backyard. So, like the chump, I shook my head and said that my dad had never touched me.

The idiot woman left, and as she drove away. I wanted to pound my fists on the door and scream, 'Come back!'

Why couldn't she see that we didn't dare open our mouths? Couldn't she feel the tension or see the fear in my eyes?

"Who the hell do you think called Social Services," my dad asked my mom and grabbed her arm, shaking her hard.

"I don't know."

"Was it you, you bitch?" His hand cracked across my mother's cheek.

"It wasn't me, I swear, I didn't call. I'd never call."

My dad grabbed his keys and jacket. "I'm going out."

He stormed past me and knocked me aside like I didn't exist. Hitting the wall, I fell along with the small decorative picture and crashed to the floor helpless as I watched, the screen door slam in my face.

I rubbed my eyes at the memory and knew it would come up again. My dad would ask something like this repeatedly until he got the answer he wanted, whether it was the truth or a lie. We'd have to blame a neighbor or the school at some point, but I couldn't say it was me. No, I didn't dare do that, or he would kill me for sure or punish me so much that I'd wish he'd kill me.

Pushing myself off the bench, I made my way along the path and tried to imagine what it would be like to be one of those kids with great parents. Would I smile and laugh like they did? Would I picture a future that didn't include killing my father before he killed me?

Someone was yelling, and of course the voice was coming from my house. The sound bounded up the driveway, and the old woman who lived next door gave me a sad look, but she turned and walked away like everyone else. That's all anyone ever did was walk away.

The yell sounded again, and it wasn't from my mom. Oh god, it was my little brother. Bursting into a run, I yanked open the front door. My dad had Asher on the ground, his big fist hitting his little body so hard that I thought he was going to kill him. Asher must have done something really bad to upset him because Asher was Dad's 'golden child' and never got hit.

"Hey, asshole," I yelled, not even giving it a second thought until my dad's bloodshot, livid stare found mine.

He ran at me like a charging bull, and I sucked in a breath just before he slammed me into the wall.

As I awoke to a dark room, the screams that I heard were coming from me, and they only got worse when I looked to the side of the bed. The twisted and contorted images of my father's body, face, and eyes stared back at me. Blood was dripping from his bulging eyeballs as he crawled toward me, his back arched over in an unnatural position.

"Get away from me, stay away!"

The door to my room burst open, allowing light to pool in. My terrified wails only increased as I yanked my arms away from the men who grabbed for my arms and legs.

"No, stop. He'll get me," I yelled and pulled harder, but soon there were too many men to fight. They were going to trap me in this room, defenseless and unable to move with the thing that looked like my father.

My father's head poked through the body of one of the men as it stared at me with its black eyes and mouth hanging open. A cool breeze brushed over my skin as one pale fist pressed into the mattress, and a gurgling hiss left the thing's mouth.

I could hear swearing as my foot connected with something solid, but it only registered as something sharp was stuck into my arm.

"No, don't drug me. He's going to get me!"

My heart hammered in my chest, and I fought the restraints like a wild man as my body thrashed like a worm. The men didn't listen, and the deformed shape of my father crawled onto the bed and sat on my chest, staring down at me. It got so close that our noses were touching and every hair on my body rose on end. The door to my room was closed and locked, bathing the room in an unearthly darkness. I couldn't breathe, and gulped at the air trying to fill my lungs.

"Go away! Just go away," I whispered.

Paralysis set in, and I froze in position with the thing making gurgling and rasping noises. "Go away, please go away," I said over and over until the tranquilizer took control and my eyes were too heavy to hold open any longer.

"You did this to me, son," it whispered in my ear. "I'll always be with you." I heard and passed out.

Not
even the
Devil could burn
the world like
I could

Chapter 5

"Are you ready to co-operate today, Mr. West?"

I couldn't even be bothered glaring. I simply stared into his eyes and wondered what they would look like melting inside of his head... The fear that would fill them just before they disappeared forever.

"Mr. West, this is your final chance to work with me. I'm not going to waste my time with you when you clearly do not want to participate in the sessions."

He closed the file on his desk, and I could see Adalyn's sad face floating in the air. She clutched her hands together and mouthed, "Please."

Sighing, I did something I hadn't done since arriving, and that was to try and make an effort to appease this piece of shit.

"I don't know what you want from me," I said, and Dr. Wallace paused, his hand on the way to the phone to call and have me carted away.

"You need to open up about the pain that triggered your rage and set you on the path to killing four people."

I squirmed in my seat. I never talked about that shit with anyone, and I certainly didn't want to talk about it with this pompous windbag that thought he could "fix me." I shook my head and crossed my arms over my chest.

"Start with why you dislike authority, Mr. West. It's clear that you have issues with any form of it."

I fixed my stare on the man across the desk and loved that he shifted in his seat. It was subtle, but I knew I made him nervous. Truth be told, I made everyone nervous but Adalyn. She saw something else other than the demon they all deemed me to be. I might have been what they thought, but only her opinion mattered.

"What have authority figures ever done for me," I asked, sitting a little straighter.

"I'm not sure what you mean."

"Let me recap." I held up a finger. "My father was a drunk that liked to knock my mother around and then went after me." I held up a second finger as I counted. "My mother let him do it." A third lifted. "Teachers turned a blind eye." A fourth finger. "Social services walked away saying that there wasn't enough evidence of abuse and didn't do fuck all to help. Like the bruises that lined my mother's face under her makeup and the cigarette scars on my body weren't enough?"

Angry now, I slid to the front of my seat, and Dr. Wallace slid further back in his.

"And the government doesn't really give a flying fuck about what happens to the kids from abusive homes as long as they still get to smile and wave to the adoring fans while they kiss the cheeks of babies that they would sooner run over with their car like a speedbump than bother to help."

I stood but walked away to stare out the grated window that over-looked the parking lot and a small sitting area where those deemed less dangerous could sit.

"The system is broken, doctor...." I looked over my shoulder at him.

"And you, are no different. You come here every day to collect your paycheck and fuck some new naive nurse before you go home and pretend to love your wife and daughter. All the while, you can't stand your life and wish there was some way out. And since you can't see one that doesn't require you killing her or costing you a fortune, you take your anger and emotional issues out on those you treat, myself included. So before you decide to tell me I'm wrong, would you like me to list off all the shit you've done to me since I arrived here nine years ago?"

Dr. Wallace's mouth was hanging open, but no words came out. "Ah...."

"Ah, ah, ah, what? Not true, or are you simply shocked that I know your secret of what you do in this office or the nurses' station when you think no one is around and paying attention?"

He licked his lips, smacking them together like a motor trying to get going. "That...that's preposterous," he stammered but looked away, unable to hold my stare.

"Is it? Are all the things you've done to me over the years preposterous as well? I know all your secrets, Dr. Wallace. The walls are not as soundproof as you think, and those that have died on your watch whisper in my ear." I tapped the side of my head. "They don't like you very much and want to see you burn."

The conversation had taken a sideways turn, but I was so sick of this man and his unfair assessment of right and wrong. He had a God complex that needed to be snuffed out and I was the man for the job.

Dr. Wallace stood so fast that his rolling chair banged into the wall and made him jump. "That's it. You've proven that you can't be rehabilitated enough to move down to the less-secure wards, let alone out into society. My official recommendation is for you to spend the rest of your sentence in prison, which in your case will hopefully be until you die." I clasped my hands in front of me and smiled wide. "Why are you smiling? I'm serious."

"If you make that call, then your world is going to burn down around you. And if you're not careful, you'll go up in smoke with it."

"Is that a threat?"

"Simply a truth. Have you known me to lie, Wallace?" He knew I never lied, if anything I was too loose with a truthful tongue. That's what terrified Dr. Wallace the most. I knew him better than he knew himself and he didn't like to be analyzed the way he did to others. "Of all the notes you have in that thick folder, have you ever jotted down pathological liar?" He looked at the folder. The phone shaking in his hand was still only halfway to his ear. "I don't make idle threats, doctor, and always have a contingency plan. The truth is that I'm conflicted. That's the only reason why I didn't leave this place a long time ago."

"What do you mean?"

"I mean, that on some level buried deep inside me, I don't want to kill dozens or maybe even hundreds of people, but on the other hand, I crave to see them burn and smell their charred flesh smolder off them as they scream. So I've stayed, but believe me when I tell you, I could've left a long time ago because if I had—"

As I stepped close to the desk, the sweat on his brow and the terror in his eyes were there even though he was trying his best to cover it up with a calm façade.

"Your house will be the first I find on Marigold Lane." A smirk tugged at my lips as his eyes bugged out. "You will experience firsthand what I'm capable of."

"You're bluffing."

Staying quiet, I rolled out my shoulders and cracked my neck. The tremble in his arm and the sweat on his upper lip told me that he was not just scared, he was terrified.

"I don't believe you, Mr. West. If you could've left, you would have. You're not the type to stay someplace simply because—"

"Who said I don't have a reason for staying? Maybe that reason is you."

He sucked in a sharp breath before his finger jabbed down hard onto the button to summon an orderly. Jim opened the door so quickly it banged into the wall like he expected me to have the doctor down on the ground killing him.

"Jim, please see that Mr. West makes it back to his room. Our session is done for the day."

I gave the good doctor a wink, a warm gleeful excitement flowing through my body as he shivered. Turning my attention toward the door as Jim grabbed my arm, I felt pretty damn superior to that arrogant, fucking douche.

The television was blaring, and those inside the social room were cheering loudly at whatever show they were watching. I glanced at them as I passed and realized that I'd never fit in—not at home, not a school, and not here. Predictably, Jim gave me a shove inside when we reached my door, but I had no intentions of fighting tonight.

Once inside, I stripped my shirt and got down on the floor to do my workout. Every day, it was the same thing, two hundred push-ups, and squats followed by as many burpees as I could manage until I wanted to throw up and then finished it off with either an ab workout or some Pilates.

Panting as I stood from my last burpee, there were two new books on the small corner seat in my room, and I knew Adalyn had left them for me. I'd read every book that the library had to offer, but the book I lifted up was one I'd never seen.

Bringing it to my nose, I breathed in the scent of the new book and smiled. I'd read everything from how to complete relaxing workouts, meditation techniques, and cooking recipes. But most importantly, I learned all the different ways that one could start a fire or create a bomb.

I'd memorized the exact ingredients needed to create a combustible explosive, and out of all the ingredients in this hospital, there were plenty at my disposal. I'd also learned a great deal about architecture and engineering, which not only made me an arsonist and a passionate one at that—I was one that was armed with all the knowledge I needed to get myself out of this joint.

Adalyn really was amazing, and I may have fucked it up.

"Shit," I mumbled, putting the book down and wiping the sweat from my eyes. Why did I let my anger get the best of me? Why did I have to push Dr. Wallace's buttons? It had felt so good to get under his skin and reveal what a snake he was and that I knew it, but a man backed into a corner in fear was dangerous. There was no doubt in my mind that I terrified the good doctor.

I took a small whore bath using the sink in my room and then laid down to plot. There were still a few minor issues I needed to work out, but I could almost taste my freedom. I hadn't lied to the man, I had three different scenarios planned, and each one was more devastating than the next. Smiling, I closed my eyes.

My door clicked, and my eyes snapped open. The sweet scent of Adalyn filled the room before she quietly closed it and rushed to my side.

She ran at me, and I grabbed her shoulders. "What is it? What's wrong?"

"Take this. You need to get out of here," she said, grabbing my hand and slipping one of the key cards into my palm.

"Is this?"

"Yes, and you have to get out of here tonight. They're planning on hurting you and then shipping you off to the prison as soon as your hearing is complete. I don't know how long this card will be good for, they keep changing the code on them."

She was shaking as she spoke, her words blending together.

"I heard them, Derek. They are going to try and break you. Please, you have to hurry. I left a bag for you at the end of the hall with a change of clothing inside. A new guy that was supposed to be on this shift called in sick. His name is Mark. Just say you're him and keep the side of your face hidden. The guards won't know you either way."

Adalyn looked at the door as we heard voices approaching.

"No, they can't be coming now. They said midnight," she whispered and looked at her wrist, the little numbers glowing.

I quickly stuffed the security pass under my mattress and turned to face the door as it was pushed open. Four of the orderlies walked in, and even with my size and strength, I knew I wasn't going to be able to get through them.

"What the hell are you doing here," Jim asked, his glare fixated on Adalyn.

"I came to give Derek his meds."

"Bullshit, where's the cup?" Adalyn hesitated a breath, and Jim's face morphed into pure rage. "You like this psycho...like actually like him." Jim took a couple of steps further into the room, and Adalyn held her head high as she squared off with the head orderly.

"Jim, you're being an asshole, and I don't appreciate...."

Jim's arm was as quick as a whip, his hand cracking Adalyn across her face. She cried out as she grabbed her cheek and fell to the floor. The ball of white-hot fury was instant in my chest, and all common sense and logic flew out the window.

Leaping for Jim, my fist connected like a sledgehammer to the side of his face. He stumbled back, his head snapping to the side as a tooth flew from his mouth. Ignoring the pain in my hand, I turned to the next man closest to me and ducked under his right hook. Then landed a hard jab to his kidneys before driving my elbow into his chin. The man doubled over, so I grabbed the back of his head, forcing his face down into my knee. A distinct crunch sound reached my ears with the force of bone meeting bone. The blow knocked him out and I dropped him to the floor. My knee pinched with pain as I took a blow to the leg just before I was tackled to the ground by dipshit number four. We landed hard and his weight knocked the wind out of me as my head cracked hard against the bed frame.

Wincing at the pain in my head, I managed to get a few short jabs in at his ear as we wrestled along the ground like a pair of bears. We rolled into one of the other guys, and he yelled out as our combined body weight sent him into the wall. The crash rang through my ears.

If they'd been hoping this would be a quiet beat down, they'd been mistaken. My blood coursed through my veins, spurring me on as my elbow caught the guy I was wrestling with in the jaw.

Oh, how my energy fed off this shit.

Two more quick jabs to the dipshit hanging onto my waist, and he let go. He scrambled to control the blood from his now very broken nose. As I jumped to my feet, the room spun like I'd been stuck with drugs but didn't remember getting jabbed. Touching the spot where I hit my head, it was moist. I stared at the red on my fingers.

That's fucking great.

The guy I thought I knocked out was stumbling to his feet. We were all breathing hard as we stared at one another in a standoff.

"Fuck, grab him already." I heard Jim yell, and a fist came out of nowhere to slam into my gut.

I suddenly couldn't breathe. Tackled to the floor once more, I couldn't get up with the weight of three of the men pressing down on me. Jim walked around the guys and stared at me as I snarled and struggled to free myself.

He smirked, his eyes showing the true man that lived under his skin as he slammed one of his boots down onto the scarred side of my face. The pain was excruciating as the tread scraped along the side of the old injury. Warm drops of blood splattered my cheek.

The instant fog made it hard to fight, and I could feel myself being dragged. My body was forcefully flopped onto the shitty mattress. Like a wildling, I thrashed and yelled, managing to hit the guy I didn't know in the crotch. He hollered and fell backward. Two of the guys, both of them bloody, flopped their weight onto me as Jim grabbed my feet. He strapped them tight faster than I could yank them away.

"Don't hurt him!" I heard Adalyn yell, my rage mounting.

"Grab her," Jim growled.

I was still pulling hard on my arms, my workout regime coming in handy as I fought with everything I had. With sheer will alone, I managed to get in another cheap shot to the solar plexus of one of the guys I did recognize. My eyes met his, my stare promising death as he groaned.

I'd kill them. I'd kill them all.

Jim marched around to the other side of the bed and leaned all two hundred and fifty pounds of his muscled form down on my shoulder and arm.

Breathing hard, I roared as I continued to battle the straps hoping they would miraculously give way. I really did love seeing the blood pouring out of Jim's nose and a bruise already forming by his eye. He was breathing just as hard as I was. Our hatred matched as we stared at one another.

Jim wiped the blood off with the back of his hand and snarled down at me. "I was just going to come in here and rough you up, but I've changed my mind. I'm going to take something from you that's a whole lot sweeter."

Jim stood straight, his height exaggerated by my now horizontal posi-tion. He held a wild menacing look on his face.

"Let go of me," Adalyn yelled.

My eyes searched for her by the sound of her voice and found her struggling in one of the large orderly's grip. He had his arms wrapped around her small body like a vice, holding her off the ground until her feet dangled.

As Jim waved to the man holding her over the floor, panic gripped my heart.

She'd never make it out of the room.

Why hadn't she run? Why hadn't she gone to get help?

The guy I didn't know finally put her on her feet and held her by her arms. She was impressive as she twisted and fought against the grip that was leaving red handprints on the bare skin of her arms. She managed to get an arm free and cracked her hand across the side of Jim's face. I would've cheered if Jim hadn't smacked her back. He knocked her head to the side so hard that her hair splayed over her face.

"Don't touch her," I roared and hauled on the straps so hard that the bed they were attached to groaned.

"Want me to tranq him," one of the other men asked.

"No, I want him wide awake to see this." Jim grabbed Adalyn, and I knew what he was going to do even before he pulled her cotton scrubs down. My muscles strained as I fought again, and I'd never wanted superpowers more in my life than in that moment. My back bowed off the bed, and the cuff's edges were cutting into my wrists, but I didn't care.

"Let go of me." Adalyn fought hard, her nails connecting with more than one spot on Jim's face and body before he simply overpowered her. Tears streamed down her beautiful face as her arms were wrenched behind her back. Her eyes found mine, and I didn't look away, even though I wanted to, even though it gutted me that she was going through this because of me.

"You think he's great, do you? Let's see if you still feel that way when I'm done with you."

"Hey, hold up man, you never said anything about raping a nurse," the one I'd labeled dipshit said. I had to give him points that even after I smashed his face in, he was trying to do the right thing.

My respect for dipshit notched up slightly as Jim ignored him and he yanked on his arm, trying to pull him away from Adalyn. Jim's elbow came up fast, connecting with dipshit's jaw and making a loud crack. He stumbled back and landed on his ass. His face was taking a real beating, and I wondered how he was able to stand at all as he pushed himself up. He earned more cred in my book.

"Don't fucking do this man, she's not who you're mad at, not to mention it's fucked up," dipshit said, his words slurring through the blood pouring from his mouth.

"Get him out of here, and then come back for your piece of this little peach." Jim smacked Adalyn's bare ass hard. She cried out as he pushed her face-first up against the wall.

"Get off of me! I'll have you fired, Jim," she yelled, her voice muffled with her face pressed at the odd angle into the wall.

"You can try, but who's going to believe the nurse that fell in love with a murdering pyro? He's a fucking nut job."

"Yeah, you're one to talk!" I yanked again on the straps. "Look what you're about to do, so much better than I am," I taunted, hoping that he would turn his attention on me instead of her. I didn't care what they did to me, not anymore.

"You shut the fuck up. This is your fault."

"Don't do this, Jim. Your issue is with me. Take it out on me instead," I tried to reason, but I understood the darkness that stared back at me from Jim's eyes. I got the same look in my eyes when I watched something burn. It filled me with a desire that I couldn't control. He'd wanted to do this to her, and I'd given him the excuse to push his mind over the edge. Jim planned on taking what he wanted, and right now, that was Adalyn.

"That's the thing with you, Derek. You don't care what happens to you, but what happens to her...." Jim reached inside his scrubs and pulled out his cock. "You care a whole lot about, and I'm going to take that from you. I'll take the only thing you have left and then ship you off, so you'll never see her again."

Adalyn fought hard as Jim stared at me. He lifted Adalyn up and forced her to stop fighting. Soon, she just took whatever he gave.

With each sob she made, a coldness gripped my heart and fury burned in my gut. The remaining two men took their turns, and I never looked away from her eyes. If she were going through this, I would endure it with her, and then I would find a way to kill each of them for touching her. She was like a spring flower, sweet and bright and fresh, and they were destroyers of beauty, smashing the delicate flower into the ground. The last bit of my humanity broke with each one of Adalyn's whimpers.

Jim stuffed his cock into his scrubs after his second round with Adalyn and smirked as he stared down at me. "Remember, West, this was all your fault. Let's go," Jim said as he made his way to the door.

"What about her? What if she fucking reports this shit?" The guy ran a hand through his hair. "I mean, should we take her with us?"

Jim turned his stare on Adalyn, who was curled up into a ball, her body shaking as she buried her head into her knees.

"And do what, kill her?"

My blood ran ice cold with the thought of them dragging her from this room and not knowing what they would do to her. Jim shook his head, the feral man now calm.

"No one would believe her. Everyone knows she's hot after West, and he's fucking crazy enough to do this himself." Jim gave me a vicious look as if daring me to speak, but I kept my mouth closed.

I didn't want them to have another reason to go after Adalyn again.

"Besides, even if they did believe we did it, we could always say she asked for it. Bitches like her are always asking to be used and punished and then cry wolf. Flirting and teasing and then acting all innocent is her specialty. Trust me. The doctor will have our backs."

"I don't know, man. This seems like a bad idea. I can toss her over a bridge or some shit."

Jim's face screwed up, and he pushed the guy in the chest. "Don't be so fucking stupid. They have cameras everywhere in here. How are you going to explain dragging her out of the building all bloody and her disappearing? Like that doesn't look suspicious. Fucking idiot. No, we'll leave her for now. I want West here to remember forever what he caused to happen."

Jim looked down at Adalyn, who still hadn't lifted her head from her knees. "I think she liked it. She got good and wet. Maybe she'll come begging for more."

The door slammed closed as they all filed out, and all I could hear was the soft, muffled sobs of the sweetest creature I'd ever met, and my battered soul was crushed into dust.

I stared up at the white ceiling, and a line of tears slowly trickled down my cheek. I hadn't cried since I was a child. There was no point in crying. It never made anything better, but I cried now. Jim was right about one thing—I'd done this.

"Adalyn, I'm sorry," I whispered.

There was nothing I could say that would make this better. My eyes closed, unable to take staring at the white of the ceiling any longer and wished that I had some of that tranq now. Anything to wipe away the pain that was flowing throughout my body would be welcomed.

I startled as a cool hand touched my arm, and I thought for a moment one of the ghosts from the room had finally reached me. Eyes snapping open, I looked at the hand and then into the red eyes and bruised face of Adalyn.

Her hands shook as she reached for the buckle holding my arm. Small sobs left her mouth as she got the strap undone. With my one hand free, I quickly pulled on the strap and undid my other arm before sitting up to do the same to the ones holding my ankles.

Finally free, I leaped from the bed and grabbed her discarded top, but it was torn down the middle. I walked over and pulled the top off the spare set of scrubs they had in the room for me and squatted down in front of Adalyn. Handprints lined her arms and her neck, and the dark bruises were a stark contrast on her skin. She had her arm across her chest, her body shivering as she stared at nothing.

I held up the shirt.

"I don't want to hurt you," I said, unsure how to get it on her without touching her.

Those soft blue eyes found mine, and they held so much agony, but she lifted her arms slowly above her head. As gently as I could, I slipped the material over her head and then helped her sit on the edge of the bed to get her pants back up into position. I cupped her face, and this time she leaned into my touch. "I'm so sorry."

She nodded and then yelped as the door clicked and banged open. Adalyn jumped and cried out as she tucked herself behind me. Her small arms wrapped around my waist, and I could feel her body shaking uncontrollably. This time Dr. Wallace was leading the charge and with him were six orderlies. The only one I recognized was the youngest one that had left the room.

This wasn't happening again. If I had to break every one of their necks, I'd make sure they all died in this room before a single hair was hurt on her head again.

Dr. Wallace held up his hands like he was trying to ward off an animal, and maybe he was. I'd always felt more like an animal than a human. My soul was broken and stamped down into something that no longer fit into society.

"Easy Derek, we came to help," Dr. Wallace said.

I pointed my finger at him.

"You did this. You sent those men in here to teach me a lesson, and they did this to her. You'll pay for it as much as they will. I'll make sure of it," my voice was low and sinister, and I could see the men shifting uncomfortably from foot to foot. I fixed each of them with a glare as I memorized their faces.

"Come on, Adalyn, let's get you to the hospital," Dr. Wallace said and held out his hand.

My body instantly went rigid and ready for the fight. "She's not going anywhere with you."

Adalyn's small hands slipped away from my body, and she stepped up to my side. I looked down at her and knew if she wanted to go, I'd let her. But in truth, I didn't want her to leave my sight. I didn't trust the doctor or a single word that came out of his mouth.

"I'll go. This will only escalate if I don't," she said.

I searched her face, and all I saw was fear, but she was acting brave to save me from another round of beating and drugs.

"Don't do this for me," I whispered.

"I'm not." She looked down, her hair covering the side of her face. "I need to see a doctor."

"Okay, only if you feel safe going with them."

She looked up at me again, and there was so much in her eyes that I couldn't decipher. "I don't know if I do, but I have to go," she said so softly that I barely heard her before she stepped away from my arm. She limped over to Dr. Wallace, and at least he had the decency to look horrified by what happened.

As the procession left and the door closed, I was once more alone with the demons in my head. My hands balled into fists, my heart still pounding hard. They would all pay for what they had done. Every single person in this place would pay with the only thing that mattered —their life.

Not
even the
Devil could burn
the world like
I could

CHAPTER 6

Unsurprisingly, over the next few days, I didn't see Dr. Wallace, Jim, or the other two men that had hurt Adalyn. What tore at my heart was that I didn't get to see her either. I didn't hear her voice in the halls or see any sign of her with another patient as I was moved from one area to another for my daily activity or medication distribution. My hearing had been pushed out by a week, which I was happy about because it gave me more time to plan. I was the grim reaper walking the halls. Every face I passed was another hauntling just waiting to be made, and I was going to set them all free.

I'd made sure that I was uncharacteristically calm and made myself look near-catatonic with the trauma of what Jim and his friends had done. It took a week, but the first phase of my plan started to take shape. All those who worked around me were lulled into a false sense of security, so I used my time wisely. Cameras were a constant issue, but I quickly found ways and reasons to be in the areas where I needed to stash items. I'd gone so far as to stand in the corner of the men's changing room and stare at the wall until two orderlies guided me back to my room.

I needed a fucking award for the acting job I'd been pulling off.

"Mr. West, please come in and sit down." The orderly that had my arm moved me across the floor, and I waited until he gave me a push before I sat.

I focused on the exotic bird painting that was on the wall behind the doctor.

"Mr. West, can you hear me?" He waved his hand in the air, and I slowly moved my eyes from the wall to his face but stared at the silver streak in his hair. "Do you feel like talking about what happened?"

It was a baiting question, and I wasn't falling for his shit.

"Mr. West, it concerns me that you're acting like this. That is what you're doing, isn't it, acting?" I was tempted to say something sarcastic, a sentence on the tip of my tongue.

Instead, I let my eyes flutter closed, blocking out the doctor completely as I began humming the same song that Adalyn usually sang as she worked. If he'd said anything more, I couldn't say what it had been. My mind floated around in a darkness that contained a strange combination of Adalyn's beautiful face and Dr. Wallace screaming as he died. Both images brought me peace.

Dr. Wallace must have given up at some point because the orderly came to escort me out. It wasn't until we were out in the hall that I realized the guy was the same one that had left the room the night of Adalyn's attack. His face still had a bruise from where Jim had laid him out.

Loud screaming erupted, and one of the patients ran out of his room, screaming and pushing people to the ground as the demons chased him in his mind.

"Shit. West, can you wait here?" I didn't respond as the guy let go of my arm and took off after the man that was now accosting a nurse. I couldn't have planned this any better. This moment was exactly what I needed.

Scanning the area, I slowly slipped into the men's changing room. No one was inside, and I ran to the lockers reading the little white labels that announced who's locker belonged to whom. There were three of the guys that visited Marylynn on a regular basis, so they were my first stop to find what I needed.

I yanked open the first locker and grinned wide as I stared at the jumbo box of condoms. Emptying the condoms into my pants pockets of the scrubs, I pulled my shirt down into place and tossed the boxes into the garbage. Hunching over, I stared at my reflection in the mirror, and staring back at me was the image that everyone else saw, but what they missed was the evil that swam behind my eyes.

I sprinted across the floor and resumed my meek look as I slipped out into the hall and leaned against the door. Whoever had been cleaning had left the mop and bucket, and I gripped the handle and then closed my eyes.

"Come on, Derek, I have to get you back to your room," the same orderly said as he touched my arm. "Why are you hanging onto the mop."

I opened my eyes and looked at the man like I'd just woken up from a long nap.

"I'm done," I said and held out the mop for him to take. I would've laughed at the look he gave me if I hadn't been keeping up appearances.

"Thanks." He took the handle and pushed the bucket out of the way. He didn't hold my arm like the others did when they were escorting me back to my room. I looked at him out of the corner of my eye. He was only a couple of years younger than me, but I felt far older than my twenty-six years. We reached my open door, but before I stepped inside, I looked into the young man's eyes as my gaze drifted over his face. He had butterfly bandages holding together all the cuts from the fight closed on his face, and on a whim, I did something unexpected.

Leaning in a little closer, I whispered. "The devil dances in flames, you know. You'd be wise to make sure you're snug in your bed before that happens, or the devil's plaything will consume you."

His eyes grew wide, and I could hear him swallow hard. I smirked as I stepped into my room and turned to look out the small glass pane as the door was locked in place. As he looked at me through the glass, I mouthed the word, "Run."

I had no idea if he would understand the warning or even believe it after the act I'd put on for days, but it was all I could do. The rest was up to him.

My moment came when my last set of pills for the night arrived. The orderly that walked in was not the same young man as earlier, and it gave me a glimmer of hope that he'd wisely taken off. I'd seen this guy a few times, he'd administered medication and stood outside my door on a few occasions when Jim had to subdue me in his not-so-pleasant ways, but he'd never been personally cruel. I did exactly what I had done since the attack on Adalyn and lay perfectly still while staring at nothing. He asked me to sit up and held out two small paper cups, so I moved slowly like I was out of it.

I couldn't afford an error and took the pills, pretended to swallow them with the mouthful of water, and waited for the moment the man stood and turned his back. There was one thing Jim was right about— you should never turn your back on me. I was on the man in the span of a heartbeat, my vise-like grip around his neck, and like a python squeezing its prey, I pulled him back onto the bed, cutting off his air supply.

He smacked at my arms with as much success as a child swatting at a fly. Kicking his legs his white sneakers softly squeezing on the floor, but hitting nothing, and then all was quiet. I hung on longer than needed, he was passed out, but my gift to him was killing him before what came next. This was at least a peaceful death. The others wouldn't be so lucky. I pushed his lifeless form off my body and felt for a pulse, but there wasn't one to be found.

Rolling him onto his side, I placed the guy into a sleeping position on the bed and pulled the sheet up, so just the top of his head was showing. Taking the patients' room keys off his waist, I removed the access card that Adalyn gave me from my safe-keeping spot. Poking my head out of the door, I could hear other orderlies in patients' bedrooms as they completed their rounds for the night. Slipping into the hall, I locked my room before darting down the hall in my sock feet.

The card pass gave me access to the now locked men's changing room, and I slipped inside and listened for anyone milling around. All was quiet, so I immediately got to work. The chemical had been filled and stashed a couple of days earlier, and I grabbed the hidden jug from a locker that wasn't in use. I'd managed to save all my medication and even stole some from other patients and carts whenever there was a distraction. The furthest shower stall was the best place to work, so I took all the tools I needed into the square space and pulled the curtain across.

The excitement was beginning to brim inside me. The level of danger was intoxicating all on its own. Blood pumped hard through my veins because it meant I was free if I pulled this off. Nine years...nine fucking years in this place, and I wasn't staying one more night. I didn't care if I had to live out of a garbage dumpster. Anything was better than here.

I tore open all the condom packages and blew into them before laying them down in a line. Then carefully filled each one and tied off the end before poking a small hole through the excess material at the top for a makeshift hook.

Sweat beaded on my forehead because I had to work fast. The mixture I was creating with the pills and the chemical had already begun the process of combusting inside each condom. Each latex-filled balloon would act like a miniature bomb.

Finally finished, I placed a couple of my bombs behind the backs of toilets and in lockers, then quickly pulled on one of the orderly's jackets, shoes, backpack, and baseball cap. I casually made my way down the hall like I was leaving my shift when an idea came to me, and I changed course. I headed to the end of the wing, where no one liked to be placed. Pulling out the universal key I'd stolen off the dead orderly, I turned the lock and pushed open the door of the monster's cage.

Adam stood at the back, his hands clasped neatly in front of him and his emotionless eyes trained on the door like he'd been expecting me. I wasn't sure this was a smart idea, but it would most certainly add some much-needed searching in another direction other than on myself.

"You wanna get out of this place?" I said in a shushed voice.

"West, my goodness, I was not expecting you." Adam stepped forward, and as he did, a voice in my head yelled, 'what the fuck are you doing?' It was too late now. I was going to see this through.

"Here's the deal, we get out of here, and then I never see you again. You go your way, and I go mine."

"Why are you helping me?" He twisted his head to the side as he inspected me like some lizard, and I almost expected him to stick out his tongue, maybe catch an insect from the air.

Every nerve ending in my body was on high alert. Funny, my nerves hadn't bothered me when I was killing and setting bombs, but this man was not right. Something deep inside me sensed it.

"I don't have time for this, you either take the deal, or you stay here and burn alive."

Adam's eyebrows raised, and a sadistic smile curled his lips. "As much as I'm looking forward to meeting my maker, there are a few things I'd like to accomplish first. It's a deal. Lead the way."

Opening the backpack, I pulled out a spare sweater and hat I'd taken. "Put these on and act normal. Or as normal as you can anyway. That means don't try to kill or eat anyone."

"I like you, West. You have potential." I blinked and stared at him.

Didn't think that was the compliment I ever wanted to hear, yet it felt good to have a serial killer with over fifty known kills tell me that I had potential.

Rolling out my shoulders, I stood straight and marched toward the exit. Dumping a handful of condoms down the laundry shoot and another in a hamper on my way toward the exit. Adam was a silent ghost beside me, his head down and a slight limp to his normally even gate gave him a whole new appearance. The man was a chameleon, and I wanted to learn to be like that, but not from him, never from him.

I swiped the card to open the first set of doors, and the little lock box clicked green, unlocking the metal lock. Taking a deep breath, I felt an electrical charge race through my body as the door clicked shut behind me. In front of us, there was a short corridor and a set of double doors with a security guard station being managed by one male.

"If he gives us any trouble, I will take care of him," Adam said softly, and I swallowed hard at the tone in his voice.

I made sure the burnt side of my face stayed hidden from his view as I said goodnight and unlocked the door the guard was manning. He obviously didn't know or care about the orderlies because he didn't even pay us any attention. In fact, he never lifted his eyes from the tablet he held that had a show on he was watching.

As soon as the doors were closed behind me, I made my way over to the fire hose they kept locked up and broke the glass pulling it free. I always knew memorizing the building map would come in handy.

Adam watched me slip the thick hose through the pair of handles on the doors and then use the fire extinguisher as the center of my tourniquet-type knot that I twisted tight.

"I like your style, West." I looked at Adam over my shoulder and wished I had eyes in the back of my head. If people thought they shouldn't turn their back on me, they hadn't met this man.

This time of night was a beauty and a curse because of the skeleton crew staff. On one hand, I wanted to kill as many the people here that had hurt me as possible, but I wanted to escape more. Looking around to make sure there was not a soul in sight, an evil grin spread across my face when I saw the coast was clear. Leaving the remaining condoms in the backpack, I dropped the whole bag into the trash by the front exit. I stopped with my hand on the door, glanced at the empty administration area, and sighed with relief.

We'd only made it to the parking lot when the first explosion erupted inside, setting off a chain reaction of events. The bombs themselves were relatively harmless, but miniature annoying fires, but I knew that the fire sprinklers would come on, and that was the key. Anticipation vibrated through my body as I waited, and I almost cheered with triumph as the spray could be seen flicking on through the windows and dousing the floors. I'd specifically chosen that combination of chemicals because they spread with water and spread like a wildfire in a dray forest with a gentle breeze, they did. Within a moment, the entire building was a bright orange glow that filled me with a sadistic desire that was as loud in my ears as the screams.

"I must admit that is quite impressive, my boy," Adam said and turned to face me.

The shadows from the blazing fire danced across his face, and the normally disturbing eyes practically glowed an unearthly shade. He looked like he belonged among the flames, and as I stared into his eyes that seemed black, I wondered if I'd regret this moment. Had I just made a deal with the devil?

"I owe you one favor for setting me free. If we meet again, be sure to use it, and then we will be even." Slipping his hands into the sweater, Adam whistled a tune that I didn't know as he casually strolled out of sight.

I turned my attention back to the flames that were now out of control. They sprouted out of the top of the building in turrets that reached for the sky like arms grasping for something only it could see.

I wanted to stay here all night and watch as the people still stuck inside ran past windows, trying to find a way out before the whole building came down. But they were realizing by now that they were trapped. The same safety measures specifically designed to keep us horrifying members of society in the building now prevented those trying to escape from getting out. They reminded me of fleeing rats in a flood. I could picture that terror in their eyes as my creation fed on their flesh as it devoured them.

"Too bad those windows aren't breakable huh," I said to myself as more than one chair began beating on the panes of re-enforced glass.

The fire trucks in the distance were closing in and a giggle snuck out. Until they realized what kind of fire it was, they were only going to make it worse with their water hoses. As my cock stirred in my pants, I knew it was time to get going even though every instinct screamed to stay and watch. Fighting the internal battle, I turned and jogged a few feet away and froze in front of a small yellow car.

"No, no, no." My eyes roamed over the brightly colored Volkswagen with the pink flower on the dash. How many times had Adalyn joked about how silly I'd look driving her bright yellow Bug? Jogging around to the passenger side, I slammed my foot into the window two or three times until the glass finally shattered.

Reaching inside, I unlocked the door and opened the glove compartment in search of what my racing mind needed to know. My hands shook as I grabbed the little folded piece of plastic and opened it to stare at the name: Adalyn Cooper.

"No, no, no." The only words my mouth could form as my eyes shot back up to the building—no one was getting out of there. "No, she hadn't been to work. She can't be inside."

But the voice in the back of my head understood one thing. It wasn't that she hadn't been back to work. It was that the good doctor had assigned her to a different wing, one that was far away from me. With the car ownership record clenched in my fist, I ran for the building as the firetrucks came screaming up the driveway.

The front entrance was fully engulfed in the bright flames, so I ran around the side of the building, searching every window on the lower level to find a way inside. Even though I had no idea where she would be, I found none that weren't already on fire and the windows groaning with the heat of the flames. I'd done too good of a job. The fire had used the water as a mode of transportation and had spread faster than even I could have fathomed.

The water turned from savior to weapon as it rained down on all those inside.

As I reached the backside of the two-story building for the second time, I stopped and stared up at the place I'd lived in for the last nine years.

There was a creak and a deep groan as the fire and building fought with one another, but the fire won as the top floor exploded outward. With glass raining down on me, I ducked and covered my head. The blaze was so hot that it had me backing away until I stood among the tall trees at the edge of the property. It was my only option.

With each new explosion and the crumbling walls from the force of the blasts, my soul crumbled with them.

I'd killed her.

I'd killed the only person to pull out the best parts of me, I killed the last ray of hope I had in my life. My hands clenched, my nails digging into my palm as I pictured her sweet face. I'd always dreamed about Adalyn and my orange dancing flames, but I hadn't meant for the dream to turn into this. I saw her as the one person that could twirl with them and not be burnt because she was with me. The knowledge left an emptiness in my soul, an emptiness that would only ever be filled by the monster that I'd just set loose.

Adam was right about me. I was like him.

A peacefulness washed over me at that realization. This was what I was, what I'd always been, and this was a fitting punishment for my actions. Those like me never found happiness or love and if they did then we always found a way to crush it and snuff it out.

The firefighters worked with a white chemical on the blaze, but it was too late. I knew that all those inside the building were already dancing with the devil and his flames.

Not
even the
Devil could burn
the world like
I could

CHAPTER 7

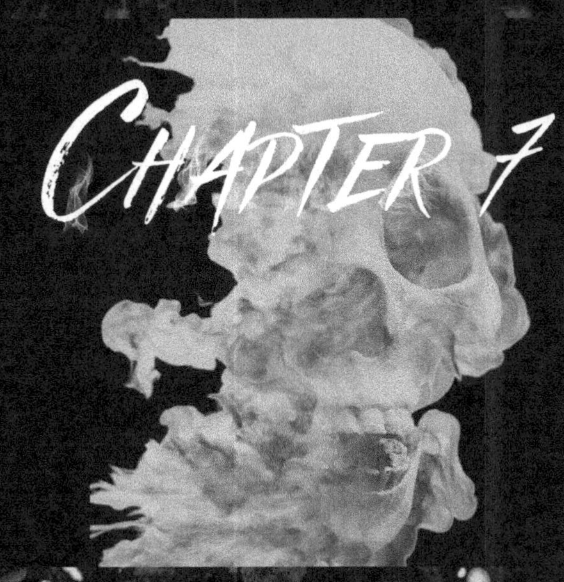

One foot in front of the other I walked until the sun came up. There hadn't been a larger plan after escaping. No grand place to disappear to, friend that could be called, or bag of hidden money to dig up. As the hours stretched on, there was only one place my mind could come up with to go until I figured out my next move. As I rounded the corner to the dusty road that led to my destination, everything felt the same, but the longer I stared, it felt like I was seeing it for the first time. The trees were taller. A couple more homes had been built while others had been torn down while I was locked up.

My feet hurt because the running shoes I stole from the orderly were just a bit too small, but it was a sweet pain. It was a pain that said I was free and alive, or as much alive as someone like me could be. Pausing, I looked up the long driveway toward the old farmhouse, which my brother and I had used to hide in for a few years. The farmer told me that he and his wife had taken pity on us when he found us curled up in the straw together and hadn't called the authorities. So, I'd bargained with the farmer. I'd work in exchange for allowing us to sleep in the barn and have two meals a day to eat.

Getting on in age and not having any children, they took the opportunity to have us there. We happily carried on like that until I couldn't take it anymore. The fire that burned in my gut grew into an inferno of uncontrollable rage despite their kindness. It had been a little too late for my soul to forgive and forget. Asher wanted us to take the opportunity and gain back the innocence stolen from us. I envied the hope I saw in his eyes—the keenness to wipe the memory slate clean and move on, but I just couldn't do it.

As I neared the old farmhouse, I took in the peeling paint and unattended garden that had spread out of the decorative confines. Their old truck looked like it had years' worth of dirt and grime on it and the front door banged in the breeze, but no one came out to stop it. The steps leading up to the front of the farmhouse groaned loudly under my foot, making it easy to tell that the wood was soft and rotting out. Reaching the top of the rickety porch, I peered through the dirty window to see if anyone was inside.

Taking a deep breath, my fist raised and knocked loudly on the door. I had no idea what I was going to say to them. What did one say after being dragged away by police in the middle of the night and then find yourself being sentenced to an asylum? I knocked again and put my ear to the door.

When no one answered, I tried one last time. Still, no one came. Wandering around the wrap-around porch to the back of the house, I noticed the barn was also in rough shape. Part of the roof had caved in from what looked like water damage, and the fencing surrounding the fields wasn't much better.

There wasn't an animal to be found, and this time I didn't bother knocking as I tried the back door handle and found it unlocked. I stuck my head inside, and my nose crinkled at the stench of mold in the stale air.

"Hello, is anyone home?"

As I made my way inside, everything was too quiet, like the house was frozen in time. Nothing hummed or moved, not the fridge or the old radio that still sat on the counter. It was exactly as I'd remembered. A shiver raced down my back. I felt the side of the fridge as I passed, and it was warm. Continuing into the hallway, I flicked the light switch, and nothing happened, so there was definitely no power.

As I slowly made my way around the first floor of the two-story home, everything creaked and complained about the weight and movement like it wasn't used to the abuse anymore. Reaching out, I pushed on the wall, and half expected it to fall down, but it seemed stable enough. It was a serious trip how everything was still an identical match to the last time that I'd been here. From the pillows on the couch to the curtains on the windows to where the pictures hung on the walls, the place was an ultimate time capsule. If it hadn't been for the fact that I vividly remembered all the shit that was done to me at the asylum, I would have wondered if I'd ever left at all.

The hardwood stairs squeaked like an animal wailing in pain. If someone was still here, they couldn't miss that noise. I grabbed the handrail, hoping it would hold if I fell through one of the stairs, but it pulled free of the wall in multiple locations, even with a light touch.

"Well, that's fucking useless," I muttered.

"Hello," I called out as I reached the top. My eyes flicked to the three closed doors. Like this wasn't already freaky as fuck, now I had to guess what was behind each door? Why close them?

"This has to be what it's like in a zombie apocalypse," I whispered and wished I had a weapon. There was a decorative canister in the corner with an assortment of umbrellas, and even though it was ridiculous, I grabbed the curved handle of one and spun it in my hand. It would do.

Cracking my neck, I opened the first door and found the little knitting room. Mrs. Giltbert loved to sew and knit and had made Asher and me more than our fair share of uncomfortable sweaters, but it was the sentiment behind it that we loved. We hadn't received a birthday or

Christmas gift for years before coming here. The sewing machine looked to still be intact, but like everything else in the house, it was coated in a layer of dust so thick you could write your name on it.

The next door would be the bathroom. In horror movie fashion the door squeaked as it opened inward, but the room was empty. The candy pink flower pattern on the tile had faded, but it was the same as I remembered. The sun shining in the small window showed off the number of spiders that had made decorative webs in the corners. I slowly walked to the last door, and my knuckle echoed loud against the wood as I knocked.

My hand paused before wrapping it around the tarnished brass knob. Taking a deep breath, I turned the noisy handle and pushed the door open. There were the Giltberts. They always said they didn't want to live without the other, and I guess they'd gotten their wish. The Giltberts were laying under the covers, but they'd died so long ago that they'd fully decayed and been ravaged by maggots and other insects, leaving behind dried-out skin and bones. There was something about the way they held onto one another like they'd died at the same time that clogged my throat with emotion. They'd been willing to give me and Ash a new start, a new beginning. No matter how things ended, I'd always be thankful for the kindness they'd showed us.

Mrs. Giltbert had a warm smile and smelt like jasmine, while Mr. Giltbert always had the scent of diesel and fresh dirt on him no matter how much he washed. Taking a deep breath, I could almost smell the remnants of the jasmine in the air. For just a moment, they weren't the dried-out husks on the bed—I could clearly see them laughing and smiling. She looked toward me at the door and lifted her hand in a wave. I returned the gesture as the image faded, and I was left with the old bones and the lonely memories of a time long passed. The door softly clicked as it shut behind me, leaving them to their peaceful rest once more.

First things first, if I was going to stay here, I needed water.

Gingerly, I tiptoed down the stairs and made my way out the back door to the old handpump well. There was still a metal bucket hanging under the spout. Grabbing the long metal handle, I started to pull down and push up. One, two...ten pumps later, I could hear the subtle gurgle of water. Thirteen, fourteen...a splash of water hit the bottom of the bucket. Stopping momentarily, I quickly cleaned out the bucket with my bare hand to remove the age-old dirt before beginning to fill again. I was sweating by the time I managed to get the pump to pull up clear water from the well and couldn't stop the smile that spread across my face.

Some of the water splashed as I pulled the bucket out from under the spout and the cool wetness felt good against my heated skin. I had this sudden urge to laugh, and I did just that as I wiped the sweat from my brow and looked around at the wide-open space of possibility.

Putting the bucket to my lips, I drank and let the water pour over my shirt, soaking it all the way through. It was the sweetest water that had ever touched my tongue. Filling another bucket, I was making my way toward the house when I heard a noise and stopped, looking over my shoulder to see a chicken wandering around on the far side of the barn. A sly grin spread across my face at the sight of the small feathered beast.

It didn't take as long as I thought it would to clean the living room out so I could sleep on the couch. The oversized rodents were pretty pissed that I'd evicted them, but I was done with unwanted housemates. Humming as I moved through the house, my next task was to empty the fridge and then get the generator set up to run electricity.

The sun was setting by the time I got to the tractor. Giving it a look over, I quickly determined that it needed an oil change, and I had to drain the fuel and add some from the sealed jerry can, but the old girl still fired up with a sputtering roar.

"Ya!" I said and smacked my hand on the steering wheel of the rumbling old piece of equipment. "You always were a good old girl."

It took a little rocking, but the tractor pulled out of the ruts it had sunk into, and I slowly pulled her around to the back of the house and under the only structure that still looked to be in decent condition. There was still work that needed to be done before I attacked the fields, and I needed to get my hands on more fuel, but this was a huge win.

A sense of real accomplishment washed over me by the time I flopped down with my plucked chicken. Putting my feet up on a stump, I watched my chicken cook on the open fire spit I'd created. It felt like camping, or at least what I figured camping would feel like if I'd ever gone.

Trips like that were for other families, normal families, but that was not mine. The only trips I could remember were going to the casino, racetrack and the smoke-filled bar that let me and Ash sit in the corner while my father got wasted. We'd also been left in a dirty motel room with bags of snacks from the vending machine all day instead of going to the amusement park like promised. Later that night, we were forced to listen to my drunk parents fuck in the bed beside us. Not exactly the excitement we'd been looking forward to.

My fist clenched tighter on the knife I was using to whittle a piece of wood. Some of the anger that always burned bright in my chest rose in time to the fire in the pit.

My eyes were trained on the dancing orange flames that felt like family. The light sensation in my chest faded as I thought of another fire, more specifically, who'd been inside that fire. My hand stilled from working on the wood, and I looked down at the piece I was whittling.

I hadn't intentionally carved Adalyn, but it was her eye that stared up at me from the chunk I'd chosen to work with. The earlier sadness gripped my throat, and I had to push that emotion aside. The shadow of death slithered over my body like a blanket and seeped into my skin as it once more consumed my soul.

"They will pay Adalyn. I'll make them all pay, I promise you."

I was going to need money to complete my plans, and my lip curled when the realization hit that I had the answer all along.

Not
even the
Devil could burn
the world like
I could

CHAPTER 8

A bright light was shining in my eyes and bathing me in warmth. Confused, I blinked and sat up straight, gasping as I tried to piece together where I was and why. Staring around at all the items that I'd known as a young teen and then out the window, which had been the source of the bright light, I pieced together where I was. How long had it been since I'd woken up to sunlight on my face? It must have happened before the asylum, but the memory was so faded it felt impossibly out of reach.

Taking a steadying breath, I pieced together about the last couple of days. The attack on Adalyn, the fire, Adalyn's death, and my walk here to find the Giltberts dead.

The sun was so bright unbelievably bright. Had it always been this bright? Holding out my hand I let it filter through my fingers, and it looked like glittering dust against my skin.

"Are you my sunshine now, Adalyn?"

My heart rate began to even out, and I stood to stretch. Last night, my search of the house had yielded only stale or out-of-date food. There were some very helpful granola bars, cans of soup, beans, fruit, and vegetables. There was also a single can of peaches that I planned on coveting as dessert for a few days.

Yawning I made my way outside and rekindled the fire pit, which didn't take much coaxing. A fire was never really dead. It only lay dormant until it seized the opportunity to re-ignite and spread once more.

Marching back inside, I aimed for the massive pantry with all of its little canned treasures. Grabbing a can of beans, I made my way back out with the hand crank can opener, and with a few short twists of the wrist, the top was free. Dumping the can into a metal pot I'd used last night to boil water and set it on the small makeshift grate to heat up.

The one thing that we learned by living in my house and taking off with my brother at such a young age was survival skills. We could live off the land for months if need be, but this was like finding the Ritz and all the rooms vacant for the taking.

The ability to eat breakfast when and how I wanted...made the meager meal taste as good as any gourmet meal. The farm needed a lot of work, but as long as no one filed a death certificate for Mr. and Mrs. Giltbert, I could live here as long as I wanted. A flutter of something unexpected rose in my chest. Even in death, these were still the two nicest people other than Adalyn I'd ever met.

After I washed my pot, my next adventure was to see if the generator was strong enough to run the shower. Cold or not, my body needed a good scrub. Then lists needed to be made—three lists, actually. I needed one for what I planned to do next around the farm, a list of what supplies were necessary to make that possible. Finally, there was the kill list. At the moment it held four names, but there was a decent possibility of more names being added. The shit list was what I'd deemed it. The corner of my mouth pulled up at the thought. It was my sarcastic homage to my father. He liked to call me a worthless piece of shit so the name of the list seemed fitting. But first I was determined to make this a functioning farm again, resurrect the dead, so to speak.

By two o'clock, I had a massive old phone book on my lap and was going through the pages and pages of Davises. I drew a line through the next four that I knew couldn't be Jim. I didn't know if he'd been caught in the fire, but I did know I hadn't seen him at work.

It was amazing what you picked up on if you bothered to listen. And it was equally amazing the things people would say when they thought that those around them either weren't listening or couldn't hurt them with that information. Simple things really, like what buildings and restaurants were near their house or what side the sun rose and set on. Jim had been nice enough to mention that he hated how the name of his road, Slipper something, sounded girly.

I circled all the places that I could find with the word Slipper that could potentially be Jim's. Looking through this phone book was a long shot since the clunky thing was a few years old, but at the moment it was all I had. The internet would be very helpful right about now.

Tearing the page out, I folded it up and stuffed it in the pocket of the pair of jeans that I'd found upstairs. Mr. Giltbert hadn't been as broad as I was, but he'd been roughly the same height. I was officially a grave robber on top of all my other sins. If I was going to hell anyway, I might as well make the ticket worthwhile.

Florida was beautiful. I hadn't appreciated it growing up, but after seeing nothing but white walls for so long, the colors were almost too bright for my eyes, especially the vibrant greens and blues. The swaying palm trees and white puffy clouds reminded me that no matter how dark my soul had become, a small part of me still craved normal. Whatever the fuck that meant.

I wheeled the old bicycle I found out of the shed and around to the front of the house. Pulling the hood of my hoodie up over the top of the baseball cap made me feel safer. Couldn't take the chance of being recognized.

It felt good to peddle and use my legs for a purpose again. The first street I was paying a visit to was most certainly not Jim's place. Jim always said he didn't have neighbors, and this place was in the middle of a massive subdivision, so I peddled on past it.

By the time I found houses number two and three, which were close together, the hot afternoon sun was beating down on my back. House number two had been a total bust with the gated community and locked gate, and house number three wasn't looking much better. The name on the mailbox was completely different, and the letters looked new. The gold and black didn't have a scratch on them, which told me that if this had been Jim's house, he'd moved.

It took another hour to get to the fourth house. As I made my way up the street that turned into a dirt road, the hair stood up on my body like it already knew we were at the right place—the energy, the kind that only happened when I burned something down, coursed through my body. I stopped at the end of the driveway, and I could barely see the house from the road. Biking on a little further, I found a slim path that animals had created through the surrounding bushes and trees.

I stood among the shadows of the dusky sky and tall trees and stared at the black pickup truck that was near the small garage. Unfortunately, I couldn't remember if that was what Jim drove. It wasn't like I could see him arrive or leave at the asylum.

The lawn was pristine, manicured grass with a line of sunflowers that added warmth, which was a real contrast to the man that I'd seen almost every day. The longer I stared at the pretty home, the angrier I became until I was the scariest garden gnome ever.

Gone were the good feels from earlier as the beast that lived in my mind stood tall and reminded me why I was here. This man had tormented me and hurt Adalyn in the most humiliating way possible. My fists clenched as the image of the house engulfed in flames swirled around in my mind while those living inside screamed for help.

The door opened, and the man himself stepped outside and jogged down to his truck. I watched the taillights come on and glow a bright red as he put the vehicle in gear and backed up. I ducked down low as the truck turned in my direction and then around the small roundabout to head out to the road.

I waited until I couldn't hear the truck any longer before walking around to the back door and peering through the windows. A light was on in the house, so I kept expecting to see someone else, but every window I passed didn't show another living being inside. Jim mentioned a girlfriend a couple of times, but I wouldn't be surprised if it had already ended badly. He couldn't seem to hang onto a woman. Then again, it takes a special kind of human to put up with a narcissistic cheater.

The back of the house was simple. It had a single door that was locked and a couple of windows. A smile crept across my face as I spotted a window that was a little higher up than my six-six frame, but it didn't matter. It was open a few inches.

"Naughty mistake Jimbo, that will cost you." I chuckled.

He had some old crates near the small tool shed, so I grabbed one and dropped it under the window. The little bit of extra height was all I needed to push open the window. With a heave, I managed to get myself up and into the space. Looking around, I had dropped into a dining room.

Rising to my feet like a demon from my night terrors, I moved around the small, darkened space and made my way through the kitchen and into the laundry room. After a very quick inspection, there were lots of toys I could play with, but I wanted to see what else this treasure trove of a house would reveal.

I slipped from room to room and dug through drawers, stuffing anything of value into my pockets—money, watches, and anything else small that I could pawn, I took. At the back of his sock drawer proved the most fruitful. There was a single stock stuffed full with a thick roll of cash.

"Fuck," I whispered, my thumb running across the wad of bills. Smoothing out the contents in the drawer, I closed it and made my way to the garage.

A giddiness washed over me, and I laughed aloud as I lifted the three heavy gasoline cans. I sniffed it to make sure it wasn't diesel and found it to be exactly what I needed. He also had a large toolbox, but it was full of fishing equipment. I started to close the lid when an idea occurred to me, and I dug around inside, pulling out what I needed.

I was about to step back into the house when a long crowbar hanging from a hook on the wall caught my attention. I slowly walked toward the curved-end piece of metal. Picking it up, I rolled it around in my hand, balancing the weight before I squeezed it tight. Now that brought back memories.

I opened the trunk of my father's car and dug around in the mess until I found the crowbar I knew he kept in there. Picking it up, I stared at the piece, a snarl curling my lip. Tonight was the night. They would pay for what they did to me, for what they cost me.

There was no fear, no regret inside me as I marched for the front door of the house and yanked open the screen door and closed it softly behind me. As quiet as I had when I lived in this shit hole, I snuck down the short hallway, and peered into the living room. There he was in all his drunken glory, the man who claimed to be my dad. He was as I'd seen him a hundred times before—shirtless, with his standard navy work pants on and a beer in one hand and the remote in the other. He had the football game blaring and didn't even notice that his death was standing in the doorway.

I marched across the dirty old carpet, and he didn't look up until he could see my reflection in the television screen. Turning his head to look up at me, he frowned.

"What the fuck do you want," he spat out as he started to stand.

Those were the only words that left his mouth as I brought the crowbar around with a devastating whack to the chest. He fell back into his chair with a thud, dropping the can of beer on the floor as he clutched at his chest. I twirled the bar around in my hand and changed position to stare into his eyes. I wanted to see him die, experience his soul being ripped from his body. Every fiber of my being craved to see the man in excruciating pain.

"How did you like that...dad?"

I brought the curved end of the metal around again like I was playing T-ball. The loud crack his jaw made and the way it shifted left no doubt that I'd broken it and almost ripped it off his face. The fear and pain in the muffled scream only fueled the darkness that had been cultivated in my soul like a little sapling that was now growing into a tree. A tree that could stand on its own with bark thicker than any other.

As the crowbar found its mark, again and again, blood flew across the room and pooled on the floor like a red oil slick. Even as my dad's body went limp, I kept swinging even though I knew he was no longer breathing. But I wanted this feeling to continue for as long as I could milk it. Each blow represented every time his fist had touched me, hurt me and ruined me.

I heard a muffled scream and looked down the hall toward my mother. She stood there like a deer with wide and terrified eyes. The shock seemed to have rendered her motionless, but as my eyes found hers, she screamed and ran into the bedroom. No door was stopping me tonight.

The sound of gravel moving as a vehicle pulled up to the garage outside had me shaking off the old memory and darting into Jim's house and flicking off the light. Taking the crowbar with me, I darted into the house and looked around as I made my way to the front hall. Comfortable that everything was as clean as when I first arrived, I opened the front hall closet and closed the door behind me.

It was a perfectly deep space with areas off to either side that Jim wasn't using. Quietly, I pushed my way through the jackets to the far corner and sat my crowbar down. It was going to be difficult to build what I wanted inside the dark, small space, but I didn't need to see to complete my creation. So many nights hiding in small dark spaces had given me the skills needed to see by touch.

Slowly, I pulled the heavy gauge fishing line from my pocket.

The front door opened and closed, and I could hear the keys drop in a glass-like dish before Jim pulled open the door to the closet I was in. My body tingled with his nearness and the anticipation of my kill. His hand reached in, grabbed a hanger, and put it back with a jacket hanging on it.

The front door opened again, and a woman's voice yelled at Jim. "What the fuck? You leave me to carry all the shit in from the truck by myself and then can't even hold the door open?"

"I brought in the case of beer. What more do you want from me," Jim yelled back.

"You could've come back and helped me. I'm loaded down like a pack mule."

"You always look like a mule. What's the difference?" Jim laughed, an arrogant sound I'd heard so many times that I could picture his face. "Besides, you could handle it, and if I held open the door, it would just let in a shit ton of bugs. Shit, you left the window open from your fucking smoke earlier."

"I told you I went into the garage," the woman argued as the cupboards were opened and then banged closed.

"Bullshit, I could smell the shit as soon as I came in the house, and I never leave a window open."

"Ah yes, how could I forget how fucking perfect you are? You're such a goddam prince charming that you ended up getting fired for misconduct and roughing up a patient. Now we are living off my income only."

So, Jim had been fired for what he'd done, but it didn't sound like this woman, whoever she was, knew the whole truth of it.

"Don't fucking give me side-eye, woman. I'll smack that shit off your face." My nose flared, and every muscle flexed as Jim yelled. The memory of that tone used on me stirring all my inner demons.

Keep your shit together, Derek.

"I told you I was set up. I was ordered to go knock that guy around for being a fucking asshole in his therapy session, and then my boss gets pissed when I do my job too well."

"Whatever you say," she said as a cupboard door closed, and I smirked at her sass. It was too bad she was going to die as well.

"And what the fuck are you complaining for, woman? If I hadn't been fired, I would've died in that fire. So fucking appropriate that West died in a fire if you ask me."

I shivered with excitement as I pictured the look on his face when he realized that I wasn't dead. A joyful giddiness filled my body, and I almost chuckled out loud.

Now I get to make sure you suffer longer.

My dick came to life with the images of his burning body. It was so wrong, yet I rubbed my cock through my jeans. To get my urges under control, I ended up giving my cock a hard squeeze that almost made me gasp at the bite of pain.

"I guess that's Murphy's Law for you," the woman said, her voice flat as she agreed with Jim.

"When Dr. Wallace called to tell me about West being dead, I didn't believe him until he said they found his body locked in his room. Honestly, he deserved to die like that if you ask me."

That was one thing I'd been banking on. The fire needed to burn hot enough to make it difficult to pull any DNA. They may not have even tried with the door locked, but hearing that Dr. Wallace was convinced made me smile. The flames had shimmered a vibrant blue and white before I forced myself to leave.

The sound of the fridge closing pulled my attention. "As you keep mentioning."

"Why are you acting like such a bitch?"

"I'm not."

"Yeah, you are." There was the distinct sound of feet moving around, and I pictured the dance of where they were in the home based on the heavy and light footfalls.

"Long day at work, I guess. I'm going to go shower and then head to bed. I'm beat."

"What about this window?"

Um, how about you fucking close it? I thought at the same time the unknown woman yelled, "fucking close it yourself."

I would've laughed if I wasn't trying to keep as quiet as a church mouse. It really was kind of a shame that I was going to kill this woman. She seemed as genuinely annoyed and pissed off with fuck-face-Jim as I was.

Reaching inside my jacket pocket I pulled out a long screw and continued to work on my little craft project. Jim mumbled a bunch of swear words as the window closed with a thud. The television flicked on, and what sounded like a sports channel blared.

I waited, and then waited some more and stayed inside the closet until I heard soft snoring. Daring to move from my hiding spot, I cracked open the door. The darkened room flickered with the flash of light from the sport's commentary that was now playing on a loop.

The door was silent as it slowly opened enough for me to stand in the shadows of the hallway and stare at the man in the living room. So many parallels to my past life, and like my dad, this man was going to meet his end and never see it coming. Like a deadly shadow, I slipped along the hallway into the kitchen to listen for any sound of the woman. All was quiet from the other end of the house, and no lights were on, so chances were she was asleep as well.

I felt like a tight rope walker as I made sure to land one well-placed step after the next, and I snuck up behind Jim as he slept in the chair. He really couldn't have fallen asleep in any better position. His cue bald head tilted down and to the right. If he'd been drunk, that was a good position for him to suffocate and die. His arms were relaxed at his sides, and his breathing was even. Every time his breath pushed out with a little woosh sound, the harder my cock became.

I stretched out my special little tool and smiled wickedly. I hadn't lost my touch. It was going to work perfectly.

"Psst Jim, it's time to die," I whispered in his ear.

The man jerked awake and stared straight ahead. Confusion turned into shock and then roared into fear as our eyes locked. Before he could think to move, I brought the line over his head and around his neck, pulling back hard and fast. A gurgling gasp was the only sound he made before the line pressed deep into the tissue of his neck. Pretty sure this wasn't what the manufacture meant when the packaging said it could hold any big fish.

The fight was instantaneous, a mass of flailing arms and socked feet as Jim tried to pull at the thin-lined garrote contraption pressing him into the chair and cutting off his air supply. Using all my strength, I pulled the two ends together and gave myself a pat on the back for the ingenious work of creating a deadly version of a toggle clasp.

I walked back to the closet, grabbed the crowbar from its hiding spot, and then stood again in front of Jim. The line was so tight I could see it creating a deep indent in Jim's throat. He could barely breathe. The sound of the air leaving his lungs was nothing more than a wheeze. If Jim struggled at all, it would continue to cut his throat open. It was really quite ingenious and my pride notched up a rung. Jim was damned if he did and damned if he didn't. His face was red and his eyes wild, but his shit brown eyes still held the same hatred they always had, which was good. That look only encouraged the monster.

"I need a minute to get a few more things, Jim. You picked up the girlfriend and groceries quicker than I thought you would be back. So rude not to give me enough time to prepare fully for your arrival," I whispered.

The man grumbled something through the line that sounded like a fuck you, but I wasn't a hundred percent sure.

"So, just to make sure you don't move while I finish setting things up, I'm going to play a little *Misery* on your ass. That was a really good Stephen King book, by the way. Thanks for bringing it to me from the library."

A smile pulled up the corners of my mouth at the wide-eyed look of panic that crossed his face as I lifted the crowbar like I was out for a round of golf. The curved metal edge of the crowbar cracked into Jim's knee, and a strangled scream left his lips. The only thing missing was me yelling, 'fore.'

"Did you know that I'm ambidextrous?" I switched the bar to the other hand. "Those who are, are supposed to be highly intelligent."

I brought the crowbar down from the new angle, and this time tears and high-pitched whimpering came from Jim. His second knee made a loud cracking sound as the kneecap shot off to the side under his skin, making it look deformed.

"Yet, you assumed I was crazy, and that crazy meant stupid. Big mistake Jimbo, big mistake." I took a step back to assess my work. "That should keep you there."

I loved the pained look on his face and how tears silently slid down his cheeks as he gulped, trying to yell or get air. The horror filling his body would create an extra adrenaline boost making it hard for him to breathe. It should feel like a boulder was sitting on his chest. I knew because I knew that kind of fear and pain, but no one came to help me, and no one would come to Jim's rescue now.

I made my way to the dining room to grab one of the tall-back chairs when I spotted a black phone. Now that would be handy. I picked it up, but it said to put a finger on the screen.

I tried to keep up with the quickly changing technology while locked up, but my knowledge was limited to what I could overhear others talk about and the glimpses of the tablets the doctors wandered around with and used. Chair and phone in hand, I walked into the living room and sat the chair down to face Jim.

"Is this yours?" I watched his reaction carefully, but he continued to glare as he made strange noises through his compressed airway. "Not going to tell me? That's okay."

Walking forward, Jim's breathing and panic reached another level. It was delightful to see the shoe on the other foot for a change. Jim's hand was in a fist by the side of his recliner chair. Kneeling I, peeked at his clenched hand, and sighed.

"You have two choices here, Jim. The easy way, or I go get your pliers and cut one finger off at a time until I find the one needed." There was only a moment of hesitation before his hand opened flat, and I slipped the phone under his fingers until it lit up and opened with the right one.

It was like finding candy in a candy store. There were so many little glowing squares. Some were labeled games, and others appeared to be work-related, but it was a miniature treasure trove. First to change the password. It took me more time than I would've liked to find the settings for the phone. Finally, a grin spread across my face as I found the needed area and once again slid Jim's finger into the correct spot and changed the password to my own.

"Thanks for your help, I'm very excited to see what you have saved in here. Some kinky porn, perhaps? Maybe a list of all your favorite things that you'll never get to do again, or maybe the names and numbers of all the men who raped Adalyn?"

As I said her name, Jim's eyes grew wide, more tears brimming in the bottom of them as he silently begged. How many times had I begged? How many times did Adalyn beg to be let go?

Jim tried to scream as I lunged forward until our noses were almost touching.

"It's a terrible thing to feel helpless, isn't it? While you wait here, I want you to remember every time you strapped me down, every time you forced pills down my throat, and every time you beat me until I couldn't stand. I want you to remember everything and then...." I held up my finger. "I want you to wonder what I'm going to do to you."

A soft whimper escaped Jim's mouth, and the defiant look was wiped clean from his face. Standing straight, I smiled wide as I stared at the phone once more. I'd never been allowed to have a phone. My parents said it was too much money, and the closest thing to modern technology the Giltberts had was a color television that still had rabbit ears and a static-filled radio. I'd always been envious of the kids that came to school with their fancy phones that played music and could look shit up like naked girls.

I was going to need a charger for it and quickly wandered around until I found the charger plugged into a kitchen outlet. Digging around in the cupboards until I found an empty grocery bag, I put all of my newfound treasures inside and sat it near the sliding glass door, my planned exit. Taking a deep breath, I needed to focus and went back to the living room and stood behind the chair I'd brought in to stare down at Jim.

"I need you to understand, Jim, that you took the small thread of kindness from my life, the little piece of happiness that kept me on the non-murdering side of sanity." Locking eyes with the man my hands squeezed the metal back of the fancy dining room chair. "Do you know what happens to a man like me when you destroy the only thing that was keeping him from killing?"

Jim didn't say anything, but the tears and his deadpan stare said it all.

"Yeah, you really did fuck up good this time. Does your little honey know that you raped a nurse for sport and fucked the nympho patient, Marylynn, as often as you could get it up?" Pleading eyes found mine, and I just shrugged. "I didn't think so, but she's about to find out. I believe that truth and confession are good for the soul before you die."

I took a step toward the hallway and stopped to stare over at Jim.

"You're a power-hungry hypocrite, Jim. Adalyn never fucked me, and you treated her like a whore for being nice to me while you were fucking around on your girl. Was it guilt or maybe jealousy that drove you to do what you did? Or had you always wanted a piece of her, and the opportunity simply presented itself?" I shrugged. "Guess it doesn't matter now."

Walking away, I shook my head. I didn't want to hear his excuses or reasoning because no matter what he said, it wouldn't take us back in time to fix what had been done.

Making a trip to the garage, I found two bungee cords and a tow rope and then made my way to the bedroom where the woman was still comfortably sleeping and none the wiser to what was going on a few rooms away. Walking around the bed, I stared down at her face and didn't recognize her.

"Sorry, my dear, but you're going to need to pay for Jim's sins."

In one swift move I picked her up, blanket and all. She was trapped like a caterpillar in a cocoon, and I tossed her over my shoulder like a sack of cattle feed. The screaming started immediately after I began to walk. The confused yelling turned into a high-pitched alarm sound as I slammed her ass down into the chair. Before she wiggled free of the makeshift cocoon, I grabbed a bungee, wrapped it around her body, and secured it to the back of the chair.

"Who are you? What do you want?"

I ignored her questions because she'd find out the answers in due time. The second bungee was wrapped around her legs and hooked behind the chair too. Then picking up the rope, I wrapped it around her body as well, tying it securely in place before laying out the rest and binding it around Jim in his recliner.

"Why are you doing this?" the woman repeatedly asked as she blubbered.

With a heavy sigh, I flopped down on the couch and stared at them.

"You want to know why," I asked, and she nodded so hard I thought her head was going to snap off. "How long have you been with him?" I tossed a thumb in Jim's direction. Jim's nostrils flared as he continued to struggle to breathe.

"We've been together just over a year."

"You put up with this piece of shit that long? Kind of impressive in a pathetic way, I guess." I sat forward and leaned my elbows on my knees. "Haven't you ever looked at him and thought to yourself, what the fuck am I doing with this guy?"

She looked at Jim and then back to me. "Sometimes."

"Only sometimes? Jim here has been cheating on you regularly. You had to know that it was going on. If not, you're a fucking idiot." I stood as she shot daggers at me and then at Jim.

"That's what this is about, some girl you screwed?" Jim tried to say something, but the words were too quiet to make out. "I don't even want to know." She looked up at me. "So what are you, some boyfriend coming to get revenge for screwing with your girl?"

I walked around Jim's chair to stand behind him and pulled back the hood on my hoodie. It had been shadowing my face and had hidden the scar from her view, but as I turned my head so she could see the mark, she whimpered.

"I bet you know who I am now," I said calmly and then walked around and loved how she tried to jerk away from me as I squatted down between the two. "Did he tell you what he did to piss me off or why he really got fired?"

Her eyes flicked up to Jim again.

"I bet he didn't. So let me tell you. Your boyfriend Jim here did come to my room to rough me up. That part of the story is true. Not that it's okay or anything, but it's beside the point. When he arrived with the other men, a sweet little nurse that wouldn't sleep with him, I might add, was in my room trying to warn me that she'd overheard Jim and a few of the other orderlies saying that they were planning on hurting me. You see..." I paused as I realized I didn't know her name and didn't really care, but asked anyway. "Sorry, what is your name?"

"Nancy."

"Well, you see, Nancy, Jim decided to rape the sweet nurse in front of me." I raised my hand, and she winced away like I was going to hurt her. "Don't worry. I'm not like him. I'm a different kind of sick."

I snickered as the monster inside took a firmer hold of the reins. Nancy's tears turned into blubbering as I went into graphic detail. I explained everything her precious Jim did and used my hands to demonstrate the positions he'd held Adalyn in.

"So, as you can see, Nancy, things are a bit more serious than him simply sleeping with my girlfriend."

I took the lighter out of my pocket and flicked the metal lid open. The little rowel was loud in the sudden silence as the flame clicked to life. Jim jerked at the sound. Walking around the chair, I knelt down in front of Jim, his eyes watching my every move. Grabbing the front of my hoodie, I pulled it to show off my collar bone and the small cigarette burn.

"Did you ever wonder if this hurt? What it felt like to have your skin and nerve endings slowly burnt away while you screamed and struggled to get away?" Stuffing my hand in the pocket of the hoodie, I pulled out the pack of smokes I'd found in the garage. "Found your hidden stash." My eyes swung to Nancy. "I bet he told you he quit for good. It was another lie."

I put the end of the smoke between my lips and lit it up, drawing the smoke into my lungs. It had been a long time since I tasted the sweetness of tobacco on my tongue.

"I quit before I came to the asylum, you know." I took another pull and let the smoke travel out my nose as I stared at Jim. "I will again. These things will kill you." Smirking, I stood and leaned on the chair, getting close to Jim's face once more. "Let me know how this feels," I said and placed the glowing end of the smoke against the side of his neck.

There was a slight sizzle sound, and Jim's eyes snapped open wide as a strangled scream was ripped from his throat. Nancy was bawling hysterically from the other chair, and I looked over at her.

"Do you think he likes this?"

She didn't say anything but shook her head no.

"Neither do I. You think I'm sick, Jim?" I pulled the hot little end away from his neck. "Did you ever wonder how I was made? What it took to make me kill four people? No, I bet you didn't. You were too consumed with judging me and making me feel small while you held all the power." I turned my head, so he had to stare at the scar on my cheek. "How do you think this felt?" I pointed to it, and his lower lip trembled. "No answer? Well lucky you, you're going to find out."

"What are you going to do," Nancy asked through her sobs.

Taking one last inhale, I tossed the rest of the pack in Jim's lap. "Now that right there is the million-dollar question, isn't it?" Standing, I marched away to grab two of the heavy containers of gasoline.

"Oh my god, no," Nancy yelled.

With her eyes wide, she looked at Jim, who was now showing his true cowardly nature. Tears ran down his cheeks as piss filled the front of his pants. Nancy struggled so much that the chair fell and crashed down onto her arm. She screamed in pain and I blocked out her begging. Slowly humming a song, I poured the first jug of gasoline on the couch and the living room walls and made my way over to the front door. The second jug allowed me to complete the circle. Nancy began to cough at the strong fumes, but I took a deep breath of the sweet scent I loved.

I opened the sliding glass door and then picked up the last of the red jugs and walked back to Nancy and Jim. Staring between the two it was hard to decide who looked more pathetic.

"I want you to know, Nancy, that if Jim here had only hit me, I would've only made Jim pay, but since he is the cause for my Adalyn dying in the fire, I think it's only fair that I return the favor."

"No, please, I'll do anything you want. I didn't have anything to do with this. Pleeeese," she begged, and I looked to Jim.

"You see this? She's willing to throw you under the bus to save herself. Great choice, Nancy, but it's too late for that." I looked back down at Nancy, who was banging her head off the floor as she continued to beg. "I guess you really shoulda left him when you had the chance. You always knew he was going to hurt you."

Using my foot, I knocked over the last can, so it slowly dumped out onto the floor between them. I leaned on the arms of Jim's chair and got close to his face.

"You shouldn't have touched Adalyn, and someone should have warned you never to play with fire."

His body shook as he succumbed to the same sobbing as Nancy. Walking to the open door, I held up the lighter I'd swiped from the hidden stash of smokes in Jim's fishing equipment and lit the little flame. I watched it dance for a moment and then sighed as I tossed it onto the liquid trail I'd made. Turning, I walked away, and the screams started before I reached the edge of the bush, making me shudder with desire.

Reaching the old bicycle, I turned to appreciate the tall billow of smoke and then laughed like the devil himself as the house exploded with a thundering roar that rustled the treetops. With a happy tune on my lips, I mounted my old bike and peddled down the long dirt road for my home.

Not
even the
Devil could burn
the world like
I could

Chapter 9

My throat worked at chugging down the cold water as I took a well-deserved breather. Tearing out the rotten deck boards was hot work and the pile I was tossing them in was getting taller. The sound of a car reached me before I could see the white car slowly roll up the long driveway. Putting on a baseball cap, and a pair of sunglasses I leaned against the post with the good side of my face pointed toward the newcomer.

An older woman stepped out carrying a package that looked like a casserole dish.

"What the heck," I whispered under my breath.

She waved and smiled wide as she shuffled closer. "Hi there, I'm Dora. Are the Giltberts back? I brought them a chicken casserole. Made it just this morning."

Well, that wasn't what I expected the woman to ask, but I might as well make the most of it. "No, I'm sorry they're not. I was hired to get the place back in order." It was a perfectly crafted lie and one that I'd been thinking about since arriving.

Her face fell, but she nodded with a sad little smile and took another step forward. "Would you like the casserole then? I could never eat this all myself."

I slowly made my way down the steps to greet the woman, still leery about her true intentions. It seemed strange that the couple laid upstairs dead for years, and she came over today, only two days after I arrived.

"Do you know the Giltbert's well," I asked as I reached the dirt driveway.

"Oh yes, once we were very close, but they wanted to see the world and took off on a trip. I haven't seen them since." Dora pointed down the road. "I live that way and saw smoke the other night and thought they were back."

"I'll take it you don't see much action out here," I said, debating whether she needed to be eliminated as I took the casserole from her weathered hands.

"No, my Rupert passed away years ago, and all my friends are moved or dead now too. Truth is, I haven't seen another soul except my mailman in...." She paused and tapped her chin. "I don't know how long." Dora shaded her eyes, and as her eyes found the ruined side of my face.

I braced myself for the usual reaction. Pity or horror was what I was always greeted with by others. Adalyn was the only one that looked at me like I was a person, well, her and my brother, but I never saw him. He was the one that had me locked up, and as soon as I was out of his sight and the key tossed away, I never saw him again.

Taking me by surprise, she reached up and snatched my chin in her bony hand that had more strength than I thought those fingers could. She pushed on my head until I turned it so she could see the full devastation.

"My boy, what happened," she asked, but her expression was more concern or maybe anger. I wasn't quite sure.

"Burnt as a child. It was a bad accident," I said, telling the patented lie I'd been telling everyone since it happened.

She clucked her tongue at me and narrowed her eyes. "Well, whatever got you, boy, it did a fine job, but you're still as handsome as sin. Don't think I didn't see you trying to hide your face like you should be ashamed."

My mouth fell open not knowing what to say. She'd taken me completely by surprise with the statement and the accurate observation.

"I better be off. I don't like to stay out past dark. These eyes don't see as well as they once did." Dora shuffled toward her open car door.

"Dora, my name is Derek," I called out and wasn't sure why I offered over the information.

She put her hand in the air and waved as she got in her car. "Nice to meet you, Derek. Drop by some time. I always have fresh baked goods that get thrown out."

"Then why do you bake it," I called out.

"What else is an old lady going to do? I can only knit so much before I want to strangle myself with the yarn." Dora closed her door and waved as she drove around the small circle to head out the driveway.

Shaking my head, I brought the casserole to my nose and sniffed. My stomach rumbled as I groaned. Little old Dora just made my night. In all my productivity today, the one thing that hadn't been completed was buying some groceries. I was waiting until the cooling element was fixed in the fridge before purchasing anything perishable. Stupid mice had made a home in the bottom of it.

Making my way up the stairs, I was about to go inside when I looked over my shoulder to see the little white car still sitting at the end of the driveway. It continued to sit there, and curiosity had me jogging back down the steps and toward the road. Dora was sitting staring straight ahead, her hands tight on the wheel.

I wasn't sure what she was looking at as she stared across the road at the open field of nothing. "Dora, are you okay?"

She looked out the window at me and nodded. "I...I...I...." Confusion was shining from her eyes as her head turned to look up and down the road. "This is so embarrassing, but I don't remember which way to go to get to my home." Her lower lip trembled, and she looked completely lost.

"Why don't I get in, and then I can help you?"

"You don't have to do that, my boy. I'm good. Just getting a little forgetful in my old age. It will come back to me. I just need a minute," she said, but her body language told me she was really terrified and who could blame her. To leave your home for five minutes and not remember how to get back had to be scary. When I was a kid, there were times I wished I could've forgotten which way was home, but I couldn't leave my brother. Then again, maybe I would've been better off if I had.

"It's no problem, Dora. If it makes you feel better, I can eat this with you. The fridge is not working. It's on my list of items to fix, so there's no good way to store this, and I don't want it to go to waste. I can always come back and eat more if you insist." I smiled wide and had no idea why I was being so nice to her, but it felt right, so I was going with it.

She waggled her finger at me. "You're not planning on taking advantage of an old woman, now are you? I don't think I could bend the way you young fellas like to during hanky panky."

I laughed, and then I laughed harder. I couldn't remember a time when I'd laughed until tears rolled down my cheeks. "No hanky panky, I promise."

"Alright, then come on and get in. I can't remember if I ate, but I'm hungry. Not like I can't put on a pound or two." She patted her stomach, which looked like she'd missed more than one meal despite her claims of cooking so much. I walked around the front of her car and hopped in.

"I think you said you lived that way." I pointed the way she had earlier.

Grinning wide, she pulled the car out onto the road, and then I wondered if I should've gotten in a vehicle with someone that couldn't remember where they lived. I shrugged. Well, I was in the car now. Couldn't be any more dangerous than the asylum had been.

Not
even the
Devil could burn
the world like
I could

Chapter 10

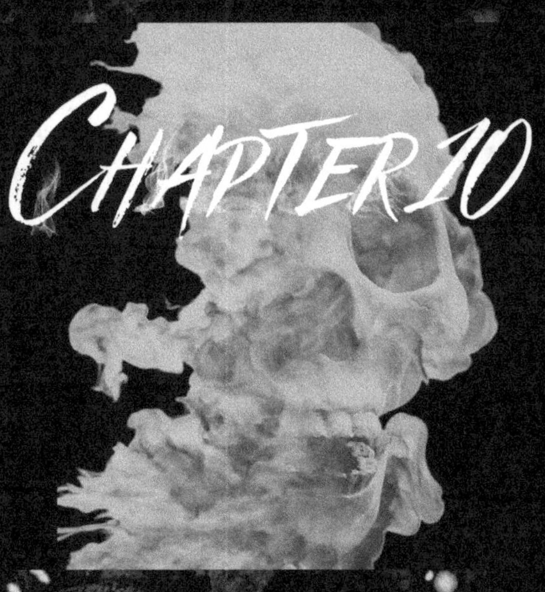

D rip.

I shook my head.

Drip.

I wiped at my face and opened my eyes to stare up into the black eyes of a creature, its saliva dripping on my forehead. I froze with the thing mere inches from my own face as I tried to make sense of what looked too solid to be a ghost yet couldn't be living either.

Its face had a distinctly human shape but had been distorted by lopsided eyes and a mouth. It looked like it was melting on one side. Wide-open holes were the only thing left where a nose once used to be, and it whistled with every breath. Rags of white hung off the boney body that was as twisted with the joints pointing in the wrong direction.

I swallowed loudly as more liquid dripped from the gaping jowl that held an unusual amount of teeth.

"They want to be consumed," it said, its voice coming out like a wheeze. A low rumble that seemed more like a growl rippled out from trembling lips. When it reared back and opened its mouth wide like it was going to attack, I put my arms over my face, but only a hot flash flowed over my skin.

Looking over my arms, I saw that the living room was on fire, the bright flames weaving back and forth like they were moving in time to a drum that only they could hear. I jumped up and looked down at the fire on the floor, but it didn't burn me.

"What the hell is going on?"

The sound of laughter sent a shiver up my spine, but even as dread settled in my chest, another sensation emerged from the darkness that lived in my mind. I could see the people from the asylum in the flames. Their screams rang in my ears as they ran down the hallway, their faces like wax figurines. Taking a deep breath, I allowed the scene to fill me with its sensations. The pleasure coursing through my body as steady as the blood in my veins. I reached down and grabbed my cock and yelled as it jerked in my hand.

Like a light being switched off, all went dark, and the image that had been playing out like a movie for my own personal viewing pleasure was gone.

"No, don't go."

I rushed over to the wall and ran my hands all over it, but it was cold to the touch. My hands clenched into fists, and I began banging them off the peeling blue wallpaper covering the cold plaster.

Laughter filled the room. As I turned my head, I realized there was a light on in the kitchen. Peering into the adjoining hallway, I sucked in a sharp breath as a much younger version of myself and my brother came running down the stairs, laughing as we chased one another.

"Hey, you two, no running in the house," Mrs. Giltbert's voice called out from the kitchen. I followed the younger version of myself, and warmth spread throughout my chest as I watched the dinner preparations that were now underway. "Don't eat too much too fast. It will give you a stomachache."

"Oh, let them be boys, sweetie. They're growing and need to eat.

Don't listen to her. You eat all you want," Mr. Giltbert said and gave us a wink from the head of the table. I smiled at the sight of those faded blue overalls that he always wore.

"Ash," I whispered at the sight of my brother's smiling face, his hair a mop of sandy blond exactly like I remembered. Ash looked up and smiled before holding out his hand and beckoning me over as if he could hear me. I took a few small steps toward the table, and the image wavered and then spun around the room.

"No, stop, don't go," I cried out as the figures began to fade. I leaped for the image of my brother, but my arms wrapped around nothing. Collapsing to my knees in the middle of the kitchen, clutching nothing to my chest, the tears poured down my cheeks like they had when they dragged me away from Ash to lock me up.

I could clearly remember how his face was twisted in agony as he yelled he was sorry and fought the unknown woman holding him back from running to me. Even as my hands were pulled behind my back, I watched Ash disappear into a tiny speck from the back window of the police car. The sound of his yelling still echoed in my mind.

"What are you doing?"

My head jerked up with the sweet sound of Adalyn's voice.

"I'm..." I looked around and jumped to my feet. "How are you here?" I smiled wide and pulled her into a hug, sighing as her arms wrapped around my waist.

"You killed me," she whispered, and my body stilled.

"I didn't mean to...I didn't know you were there." I pulled back and cupped her beautiful face in my hands. "I'm so sorry."

"What are you doing here," she asked and looked around the old kitchen.

"I needed a place to stay."

"No, I mean, why are you not avenging me? Did you not care about me at all?" She shook her head as she stepped further away.

"I'm working at it. I killed Jim, and I made sure he suffered." I tried *to take a step toward her, but she held up her hands to ward me off.*

"It's not enough. It's their fault I died in that fire, and it's the reason I'm not here with you right now." Her eyes filled with tears, and I took *another step wanting to hold her and offer any comfort I could. "No, I can't be with you until you've made this right. They need to die. They all need to die."* Her beautiful blue eyes started to darken until they were *black and pupilless. "Make it right,"* she said and then disappeared.

"No, don't go!" I jumped at her, trying to get her to stay for a little *longer.*

With a thud, I landed hard, face-first on the hard wood floor.

"Ugh, what the fuck?" Arms shaking, I pushed myself up and turned to sit on the living room floor, leaning against the old couch.

The sun was just starting to filter through the window, but I could tell I was alone even in the dim light. I ran my hand through my hair and stared around at the blue wallpaper that was peeling and water damaged. All was still the same as when I'd fallen asleep. It was all a dream.

Make it right.

I sat up straight and looked around as the cool breeze passed over my neck like a soft caress.

"I'll make it right," I said through gritted teeth as I rose to my feet. "They'll all die."

Not
even the
Devil could burn
the world like
I could

CHAPTER 11

I promised Dora butter tarts for the use of her car, but it was well worth it over having to bike hours to get to all the spots I needed and pick up the supplies necessary to move forward.

Thanks to Jim and the unscrupulous pawn shop I found, I had more than enough money to purchase the items needed for tonight's surprise, as well as a new fridge coil and Dora's butter tarts. Definitely had to make good on my promise, or she may not let me use her car again. Then again, I could always burn her in the backyard with the lawn garbage, but I kinda liked the old woman. She didn't treat me like a victim or a monster.

I'd figured out very quickly that Dora was the straightforward no-bullshit type. She had a dry wit that was funny, and the woman could cook. Before I left with her vehicle, I'd eaten half of a casserole she'd offered me and then managed to stuff a piece of key lime pie in somewhere.

Deciding to park a few blocks away from my target, I pulled into the mall parking lot that currently had no lights and one car.

Fucking perfect.

I liked this area of the city. Okay, so 'like' may be too strong of a word, but it was the shit part of town where there were more criminals than hardworking everyday people. Drunks wandered the street like lost dogs looking for a meal, while junkies stared at walls as if the pissed-on bricks held the key to the universe. There was a constant supply of screaming and crashing inside the tiny shoebox homes and rundown apartments where fighting and beating one another was the rule and not the exception.

My home had been fake. It wasn't like the homes in this area, where people expected abuse to happen because it was as common as taking a shit. Nope, my home had been smack in the middle of suburbia hell. We'd been the exception in our neighborhood, yet I quickly found out that those on my street had been just as willing to turn a blind eye to what went on inside our walls as those from this side of town. At one point, I thought maybe they didn't know, but they did...they all did. I stared up at the small apartment building that was only four stories tall. Keeping my head down and hood up, I jogged up the steps to the front door.

I highly doubted the place had regular running water, let alone video cameras, but it was better to be safe. It had taken a bit of time to figure out the fancy new phone I'd taken from Jim, but once I had, I found a chat with Jim and two of the orderlies. They had been messaging back and forth.

Dave: This is bullshit that we got fired. This is your fault Jim. You promised no one would get in trouble.

Jason: How am I going to find a new job with rape on my record?

Jim: Relax, and stick to the story.

Rage swirled in my gut as I found the stairwell, the messages playing over in my mind. I heard a door open above me and kept my head down as a man passed, talking on his phone. I wasn't positive, but he sounded like he was in a gang and getting ready to roll out for a hit by the way the man was talking. Not that I was up on my slang anymore, but I was pretty sure there would be two major news stories before the night was over. The question became which one would make the front page? This place was filled with human rats, an infestation of depravity that I was all too happy to exterminate. They were nothing more than a different version of the same useless bag of skin my mother had been.

I almost yanked the door off the shitty hinges as I reached my floor. My breathing evened out, and the walls narrowed in as I marched toward my target. Reaching the door, I smirked as I texted the man inside.

Derek Typing as Jim: I'm here. Open the fuck up.

I turned my back to the door, so Dave wouldn't see my face and listened carefully. I could feel the heavy footfalls, and with each one, the anticipation in my body grew. Excitement flared in my chest as the click of the lock and chain on the door rattled behind me.

"It's about time you showed up," Dave growled.

There had been very few instances in my life that I wished I could freeze a moment in time, but this was one of them. As I turned to face Dave, his eyes went wide, and his mouth dropped open in a comedic display.

"Hello, Dave," I said and let my fist fly before the man had time to recover. My knuckles collided squarely in the center of Dave's face, the crunch of his nose breaking, warming my heart. I was getting good at breaking noses.

The beauty of breaking the nose was the incapacitating and instant blindness that takes over for a few moments as the body registers what the fuck just happened. Well, unless the person was a professional fighter, then that rule didn't apply, but Dave was not so lucky.

He was still stumbling backward and falling toward the floor as I stepped over the threshold and locked the two of us in together.

"I'm guessing you weren't expecting me." I smiled and dropped the duffel I'd been carrying.

Grabbing the front of his shirt, I let him have it again and again. His arms came up as he tried to protect his face from the vicious blows, but nothing was going to stop my fist from finding its mark.

I didn't stop until my leather glove was slick with blood, and he went slack in my hold. Making sure he was indeed knocked out, I dropped his body like it was a hot potato before I killed him. I was planning on killing him anyway, but snapping his neck would've been too easy and far too kind for him.

I was panting hard but felt alive and invigorated with the exertion. Wandering over to the blinds, I pulled them closed to make sure someone didn't call the police and say, "There is a man tied to a chair from a building across the way." That would just never do.

Dragging Dave over to one of the kitchen chairs, I propped his heavy ass up like a bloody, decorative rag doll. His head lulled back and forth as a soft moan escaped his lips.

Whistling the little tune that was becoming my own personal anthem, I snagged what I needed from my duffel, zip-tied Dave's hands, and then attached them to the metal chair legs before doing the same thing to his feet. With a heave, I pulled the oven away from the recessed area and glared down at the dirt and grease that covered the floor.

Gross.

"Really, Dave, I think you could have cleaned your home a little better. There's even mouse shit behind here," I said. "Don't you know this is very unhealthy let alone a fire hazard?" I looked at the limp skin sac in the chair, but there was no response from the man.

Moving the oven as far as the gas connection would let me, I'd take care of finishing that part of the job in a second. The farm was a treasure trove of long-forgotten supplies. I'd still had to buy a few things to make my little white phosphorus bomb, but Mr. Giltbert had ordered a large amount of bagged fertilizer for the fields that never had been used. It was the number one ingredient that was needed, and now I had enough cooking to take out all of Miami if I wanted. I hadn't planned on doing anything quite that extreme, but the thought of watching it all burn to the ground did have its appeal.

Pulling out my homemade toy I smiled wide. I'd had a moment of brilliance, and with a few tweaks and a time-release canister, I'd proudly made my first bomb. I held it up and admired the work. It was still rough and not close to what I'd planned to learn when it came to bomb-making, but it was a fucking fantastic start.

With a smirk on my lips, I placed the canister on the kitchen counter covered with takeout containers. Once dipshit Dave regained consciousness, I was going to need to cover the sound of his screams, so I made my way to the television. Grabbing the remote, I clicked on the television, and it was already set on the sports channel.

It was currently playing a basketball game, so I turned up the volume. The crowd picked that moment to cheer, but it wasn't quite what I needed. I was really starting to resent all these fucking technological advancements as it took a few minutes to figure out how to use the guide on the television remote.

"Oh, that's perfect," I mumbled as I clicked on the channel that was doing something called live streaming. A guy was talking, but what he was playing intrigued me. It was some sort of war game with gunshots, explosions, and screams.

A soft groan had me looking over my shoulder, and Dave was starting to come around. I tossed the remote onto the couch and stalked toward my prey.

"Dave, so nice of you to wake up." It was easy to tell it took him effort, but Dave managed to lift his head up and look at me through his squinted eyes.

"Look, man, I'm sorry," Dave panted out.

"For what exactly," I asked and pulled open his fridge door. Grabbing the carton of milk, I opened it and gagged. "Man, that's disgusting. Are you trying to give yourself food poisoning?" I tossed the carton into the sink and watched the chunks glob out into the drain as the stench made my stomch turn.

"You know what I'm sorry for," Dave mumbled and then spat blood onto the floor.

"You're going to need to do better than that."

I looked over my shoulder at him as I bent down to see what else was in the fridge. There was an unopened bottle of orange juice. Snagging it, I chugged half the bottle. Leaning against the counter, I stared at Dave and waited for him to continue.

"I'm sorry I hurt Adalyn. She was always nice to me."

My hand stilled with the bottle of juice touching my lips. A sound close to a growl left my mouth.

"Don't say her name. You don't get to say her name to me." Dave looked down to the ground, and his shame angered me.

Dave flinched back as I stepped forward and grabbed his battered jaw. I forced him to look at me as I got in his face.

"You can't even say what you did, can you? You can't say the word rape," I said, my voice low as my hand shook with rage. Dave winced as if the word hurt him. "If you were man enough to do the act, you should be man enough to own up to what you did. You're pathetic."

Dave jerked his head away from my grip and glared up at me. "Man, you don't understand. Jim is a real fucker, he...." Dave stopped, and I could almost see the wheels turning. "Wait, how do you have Jim's phone?"

My lip curled up. "Jim had a very unfortunate accident, but he was nice enough to donate his phone to my cause."

"Oh shit, oh shit." Dave swallowed, the gears kicking in and turning the lightbulb on in his dim brain. "No, man, please...I'm begging you. Don't kill me."

"That's funny. That's the exact same thing Jim said right before his house blew up." I reached into the duffel and pulled out a roll of thick tape, and ripped off a large piece as Dave began to scream for help.

"Well now, Dave, screaming like you're crazy will never do." It took a bit to get the tape on Dave's mouth as he thrashed his head back and forth, screaming like he was Tarzan, but I won out.

"Let me ask you something, Dave. Do you really think there is anything you can say to change my mind?" Dave nodded furiously. "Nope, I'm not removing the tape. Just think about it. Let's pretend roles were reversed, and you were forced to watch as I held down, say...your mother or sister as I did this...." I mimicked wrapping my hand around someone's neck, and slammed my hips forward. "Like this, as I raped them."

I looked around the apartment.

"I doubt with this shithole left the way you have it that you have a girlfriend, but if you did, how would you react?"

Dave's eyes shifted from terrified to anger and then back to horrified. Point made, I stood straight and finished off the juice before tossing the plastic bottle in the sink. Smacking my lips, I savored the sweet taste that reminded me of Adalyn.

"See what I mean, Dave? You'd want me dead. Now pretend you really are me, the me that everyone is terrified of, the me that wishes I could stick around here to watch your skin melt off your body as you scream."

Dave's muffled scream made me chuckle. I watched as he rocked back and forth helplessly, trying to free himself from the tight bindings. Dave's fight or flight was kicking into gear, and I could almost smell the adrenaline permeating the air. I was enjoying his struggle and wished I could savor this moment a little longer, but each second here was a second more that I could be discovered. Sighing with disappointment, I pried my eyes off Dave. It was time to get this show on the road.

I did a quick walk-through of his meager apartment and took anything else I could sell. I conveniently found Dave's phone, and he didn't have a password.

"Thanks, Dave," I said and waved the phone in his direction. He also had a tablet lying on the coffee table, and I picked it up and turned it on.

Perfect.

With my search complete, I stuffed all the found items in my duffel and grabbed the large bolt cutters. I'd hoped that this building had a gas hookup, but I had other options if not. My new motto was to be prepared for any situation before going after my prey.

Reaching behind the oven, I severed the gas hose with one squeeze. I sniffed and smiled as a steady hiss of sweet fumes began to pour into the room. I put my tools away and picked up my homemade little gem.

"Do you know what this is, Dave?" Tears ran down his cheeks in long streams over the wide tape. "No?" I waved my hand. "Of course, you don't. This is...oh, never mind, you're going to be dead, so it's not like you'll appreciate the genius."

Kneeling down, I flicked on the timer and set the device right in front of the hissing hose.

"That should do it. Dave, I'd say it has been a pleasure, but I'd be lying. You have nine minutes and twenty-three seconds left to live. I'd take the time to pray for someone to care enough to forgive your soul."

The muffled screams got louder as I grabbed my bag to leave. Dave thrashed around so hard that the light kitchen chair fell over.

"Why do you people keep doing that? It's not going to help."

Shrugging, I made sure my hat and hood were in place as I opened his door and headed toward the stairs at the opposite side of the building. Keeping a close eye on the time on my wristwatch, I slipped out the side door into the night and kept a casual pace. As far as anyone else would be concerned, I was enjoying the evening as I walked across the road toward the alley. The narrow lane was the perfect spot simply to disappear. It was well away from any cameras, and it popped out into an alley where only rodents of all sizes lived.

I wasn't going to stay, but the urge to watch, to see the fire I created, was too much to resist. Taking a deep breath, I turned around and hid among the deep shadows until I melted in with them and waited. I was Dave's reaper and he'd signed the papers the night he touched Adalyn.

Boom.

The apartment that would've been Dave's exploded, but so did the one on either side of his. Glass rained down on the few people on the street as they screamed and scattered. It didn't take long for more explosions to follow suit, and soon, people were running from the building, but I smiled as others banged on windows trying to free themselves of my creation.

My cock was rock hard by the time I pried myself away from the scene as the sound of sirens blared down the street. There was nothing sweeter than this. A dark warmth of desire rose from deep within and wrapped me up in its golden light. I was complete. The flames would dance in my mind all night, but that wasn't good enough. I needed to find a way to be able to watch this over and over again. It was too good to only experience once.

Tossing the duffel into the backseat of Dora's little sedan, I drove away feeling like the cat that had caught the canary. My work was just beginning, and that thought warmed my blood. My body shuddered as a shiver traveled down my spine, with the image of the burning apartment replaying in my mind like a porno. Fuck I wanted that next kill—Jason was next on my list. I wanted to save the good doctor for last. I was really going to enjoy watching him burn.

Not
even the
Devil could burn
the world like
I could

Chapter 12

*B*ang, bang, bang.

Plucking a nail from the few I had gripped between my lips, I placed it in the needed spot on the post and gave it a few taps before banging the nail in harder. I wiped the sweat away with the back of my arm and looked around the paddock that I'd been working on all day. It still needed a bit of fixing, but it would be able to hold a few animals soon. Based on the planting books and time schedule Mr. Giltbert kept in the house, it was too late for most crops to be planted this season, but there was a couple I could try cultivating in a small area.

The crunching of rocks under the tires of a vehicle announced the white sedan pulling into the driveway. Leaning against the fence, I waved to Dora as she got out of the car.

"I have some food for you," she called out.

Slipping through the fence boards, I hooked the hammer on the leather belt and made my way toward the older woman.

"Hey there, I hope I'm not being a pest," she said but didn't give me a chance to answer before reaching into the backseat of her car. "I made some deep-fried gator bites and potato salad."

"I thought you said you don't get out much," I said, leaning against the open car door. Dora turned and handed me a still-warm tray that I had to admit smelled fucking amazing.

"Who said anything about going anywhere?"

"Where did you get the gator," I asked—my eyebrow lifting at the woman that was no more than a hundred pounds soaking wet.

"The shithead was trying to get into my rabbit pen for a snack, so he found himself shot and skinned." My mouth fell open, unable to hold back the surprise. "Don't look so shocked. This old bird still has a few tricks up her sleeve. Besides, I don't like gators gettin that bold with my property. The next thing ya know, the buggers will be wanting to be in my sitting room and watch television. Don't trust those bastards. They're cagy."

Dora headed for the house, but I jogged a couple of steps ahead to steer her the other way.

"Why don't we eat out here on the deck," I said, taking the bowl of potato salad from her hands. "I just finished laying the new boards so it's good and sturdy and besides, I don't have the inside cleaned."

"I guess so. It's kinda hot, though."

I didn't want her heading upstairs to the only bathroom in the place and accidentally coming across the Giltberts. The thought of killing the older woman didn't sit well in my stomach like the rest of my kills.

"I have an idea." Sitting the food down on the small table I wandered into the house, the screen door bang closed as I made my way toward the fan. I'd been using it to help me stay relatively cool at night. Not that it helped much with the humidity making your ass crack sweat doing nothing. The fan had cleaned up surprisingly well, with only a few spots of rust on the thin spokes. It had a slight rattle but still worked like a charm.

"Here you go."

I plugged the fan into the extension cord I had lying on the porch and turned it to face Dora before I sat down. Dora continued to stare off into the distance, her eyes trained on something behind me. The hair on my arms stood on end as I turned to look over my shoulder. All I saw was the pair of rocking chairs that were moving slightly in the breeze and the fields and trees beyond.

"Spirits of the dead follow you around and are tied to you like an anchor. They'll drag you to an early grave if you let them," Dora's said softly, her voice wispy with a strange edge. My head whipped back to her direction, and she blinked and then smiled wide. "Are you not going to eat? I'm starved."

"What was that, Dora?"

"What was what?" She licked her finger and stared at me in confusion.

"Nothing. I thought I heard something." Swallowing hard, I nodded to the food.

What was the point in questioning her? Obviously, whatever disease was crawling around in her brain was eating it away in a way I couldn't comprehend.

The food was fantastic. I could get used to this. I threw together a half-decent meal, but this was different. You could taste the emotion she'd poured into the food. Every mouthful told a story, and sometimes it felt sad, but today it was full of positivity.

As soon as we were finished eating, I helped Dora back to her car. She linked her hand through my arm as we made our way down the stairs and didn't let go until we reached the small white sedan. I still couldn't figure out why in the hell I was letting her drop by like we were old friends. The thing was, she was the closest thing I'd ever had to a real friend, and it felt good to talk to her about random, pointless things. She reminded me that maybe there was still a spark of humanity left in me.

"Thank you for the company, my boy." Dora patted my arm before she got into her car. "Do you mind coming by once in a wee while? You know, just to make sure I'm not dead on the floor?"

The irony of the question was not lost on me, but I gave her a little smirk. "Sure, I can do that."

She stuck her arm out of the window and waved as she pulled away. Shaking my head, I wandered over to the fence to continue my work. The goal was to house cows in here in a few weeks. The less I had to go to town, the better and that meant raising and growing as much of my own food as possible.

It was dark by the time I made my way back to the house and grabbed a soda from the fridge. There was a storm on the horizon. The dark clouds were not far off, and I could hear the gentle rumble of thunder rolling in. The bright, wild flashes of lightning in the distance that hit the ground and screamed that it was going to be a bad one.

The lone bulb in the kitchen flickered above my head, swinging slightly, as I grabbed Jim's phone and a paper map I'd created. There were a few red circles on it, two of them that had an X through them, but there were still two that needed to be marked off.

Boom.

Thunder shook the bones of the house, little bits of dirt raining down on my head. I turned my gaze back to the two circles on the map, and my thoughts began to swirl. The house shook again, the light blinking, but it was the shadow that moved at the end of the kitchen that had me standing. My eyes searched the darkness beyond the door that led to the cellar, and my hands balled into fists. Anger rolled around inside me, as the thought that someone had invaded my space. Grabbing the large knife off the counter, I spun it in my hand as my gaze flicked from one shadowed corner to the next.

"Unless you want to die, I'd show yourself," I growled.

My eyes flicked between the hallway, the cellar, and the open doorway that led to the living room. A soft laugh echoed in the kitchen, and my muscles flexed in response.

"Who the fuck is there?"

The laughter came again, but nothing moved in the inky black. The front door slammed open with a bang, slapping against the hallway wall. The screen door squeaked and rattled like someone was trying to get inside.

The echo of my boots ran along the floor as I stomped to the door, but I hesitated when the chairs on the deck began rocking in synchronization. They stayed in perfect rhythm, although no one sat in them and goosebumps rose along my arms. A cool breeze brushed against my skin as a flick of movement in the glass had me whipping around. All I caught was the shadow of someone running along the back hallway and my lip curled up in a snarl.

I ran after whoever was in my house and found the cellar door open. The only glow was that of the phone still gripped in my other hand. Quickly, I hit the flashlight button, and the bright light illuminated the rickety old staircase.

"Show yourself. If I come down there, I will rip your fucking throat out through your asshole."

The screen banged, and a breeze snaked around my neck like it was trying to choke me. I didn't bother with some fucking stupid tippy-toeing down the stairs. I stomped down the wood, each step bending and groaning under my weight. Rounding the corner at the bottom, I was prepared and ready for an attack, but no one jumped out at me.

"What the fuck," I said under my breath as my eyes scanned every nook and cranny of the small space.

Using the phone, I shined the light around the room one more time and paused as it landed on a large skid with a canvas tarp over the top. Two large strides across the room I was ripping the tarp away, I raised the knife, but my hand stilled as I stared down at a pile of C4.

My arm slowly dropped as my eyes scanned over the old blocks stacked up like beautiful gold bricks.

"What the hell were you doing with this, you crazy old coot?" I picked up one of the bricks of C4 and held it out to examine it with the light of the phone.

My lips curled up, a maniacal giggle ripping from my mouth as I sat down on the large stack of my favorite version of Play-doh. Laying back, I laid my arms out to the side like I was making a clay angel.

"I fucking love you, Mr. Giltbert, you crazy old fuck!" I put the brick against my lips and kissed the thing like it was my lover. "I have big plans for you, very big plans indeed."

Not
even the
Devil could burn
the world like
I could

CHAPTER 13

Fuck, I hated bright fluorescent lights. The asylum was filled with the glaring things that hurt your eyes and made you want to slit your own throat. The fake glare and the hum that no one else noticed made me want to burn the convenience store down.

Hum, hum, hum.

My fists clenched, yet I didn't dare lift my head to keep my face adverted from the cameras.

I hated that everywhere I went, there were cameras staring me in the face. So much had changed in the nine years that I'd been locked up. The feeling of being trapped in a time capsule smacked me in the face with each passing day. The President was new, the technology was more advanced, and people talked using slang I could barely understand.

Case in point, there was the girl in the line behind me. She was on the phone, smacking on her fucking gum, saying, "I know" and "oh my god" at the end of each sentence, which made no fucking sense to me. And yes, I was seriously contemplating ripping her tongue out of her damn mouth.

"She was so salty. Did you see her face, like OMG." She laughed hard. "Yeah, I know she is so basic and cray. Right? Yup, of course, don't be so pushy bitch. I'll be there soon. I need all the deets, see ya bestie."

She hung up the phone and sighed loudly, her high-heeled toe incessantly tapping on the floor.

"This guy is so incompetent. Yo bro, can you hurry up? Some of us have a life and places to be," she yelled.

The kid behind the counter, who looked like he was ready to shit a brick, gave her a nervous smile before he smacked the side of the temperamental piece of equipment.

I looked over my shoulder at her, and she shrunk back as her eyes took in the scar on my cheek. The action immediately brought to the surface all the usual anger that accompanied being stared at like I was a freak. My jaw twitched as I pictured stringing her up and teaching her a lesson about manners.

The kid at the counter yelled, "next."

I moved up a step, glancing over everything the small store had to offer. It had a meager fruit selection and a ton of alcohol that took up half of the fridge area. There was even a variety of burner phones and cigarettes behind the counter, but what caught my eye was the newspaper. The headline read, "Manor Hill Asylum Fire."

A flush crept across my body as I stared at the image of the massive blaze and the numerous fire trucks that were lined up. My eyes flicked to the next newspaper stand, "Gas Leak Burns Down Apartment Building." A curl lifted the corner of my mouth as the kid yelled, "next," again. Stepping forward, I placed the few things I was purchasing on the counter.

"I'll take one of each of your newspapers as well," I said and pulled out the wad of cash from my pocket.

"Yeah, the cops think it was arson that burned down that asylum. Terrifying that someone could do that to another person," the kid said and shivered as he scanned the loaf of bread and container of milk.

"Definitely scary," I said, but the demon that lived in my mind smiled and loved the idea of being recognized for our hard work.

"Have a good night, Mister." The kid handed over the plastic bag, and I grabbed one of each of the different newspapers on my way out. Hopping on the bicycle, I peddled fast toward the farm, excited to get back and read my new treasure.

I could hear the roar of a motor coming up behind me before the headlights bathed me in a bright light, casting a long shadow along the road. Even though I was on the far edge of the shoulder, a horn sounded. The person made a dramatic swerve as if I'd been riding in the middle of the lane. The car's tires sent rocks flying in all directions, and the stones made little tinkling noises as they hit the bike.

The driver yelled, "asshole," from the open window.

Trying to ruin my nightly routine, I thought and had the urge to snarl at the back of the BMW.

The night bike rides were becoming a bit of a passion, and even when I didn't have a destination in mind, I'd take the bike out for a ride around the block after the sun had set. The air was cooler and seemed cleaner, and there was a lot less traffic. I worried less about being recognized by someone. Best of all, the rides seemed to calm the ghosts that visited like unwanted relatives that had overstayed their welcome. At least what I thought that would feel like.

My legs pumped hard, the muscles burning with the strain of the steep incline, and I savored the pain. It meant that I was free and alive and that I didn't have to eat crap food or take pills that made me feel like my body wasn't my own.

I couldn't deny that the rides were also getting me into better shape than I ever could've achieved from my small room in the asylum. The only sound was the thumping of my heart and my heavy breaths as I crested the top of the hill.

Spotting taillights off to the side of the road, I almost laughed aloud as I recognized the black BMW. The bike's tires rolled down the hill silently. I could've stopped and offered help, but I wasn't in the mood, so I peddled past the car.

"Hey!"

I looked over my shoulder, and as I did, I stared into the eyes of the same girl that had stood in line behind me at the store. I didn't believe in coincidences, and a little flutter took flight in my stomach as my earlier fantasy came surging up from the dark depths of my mind. It was like I could get it to go dormant for only so long before it needed to taste the sweet bite of death. This night was looking up.

Gripping the brakes on the handlebar, I stopped the bike. "What?"

"I need you to fix my tire. It's your fault that it has a leak, so you should fix it."

My eyebrows shot up. "Really? And how do you figure that?"

"I had to swerve around you, and that's when my tire started losing air."

She got out of the vehicle and began picking at something under her nail as her bottom lip pushed out in a dumb-looking pout. Didn't she know that pouting stopped being cute once you were no longer a kid?

"I'll help you," I said, the dark desire pressing in on my mind as I stared at her arrogant features.

She wasn't part of my plan, and I should stick to my plan, but there was no denying that a large part of me wanted to kill her. In theory, I knew it was wrong to enjoy the ideas of the screams of her death or the scent of her burning hair and her perfectly manicured nails.

Then again, I'd be doing the world a justice since she obviously didn't have any common sense or survival skills, and we didn't need any more humans like her breeding. I'd be saving her potential kids from turning into the same fucking pieces of shit she was.

I put the kickstand down, moved the bike to the edge of the road, and rounded the side of the car to take a look at the flat tire. It was right down on the rim. There was no way this happened because she supposedly had to swerve around me. She continued to stand on the other side of the car and glared at me over the trunk.

"Do you have a spare?"

"How would I know," she asked, my fist clenching at my side.

I was thankful for the darkness and lack of streetlights because I was positive my eyes would be showing exactly what I wanted to do to her and her smart mouth.

"Pop your trunk and turn off your car," I said, forcing my voice to remain calm.

"Why?"

"Do you want me to change the fucking tire or not," I asked through clenched teeth.

"Wow, no need to be an ass wipe about it." She stomped around to the driver's side of the car, leaned in the open door, and shut off her car before popping the trunk. There was an assortment of bags, and I pushed them aside to get at the spare tire access. "Hey, don't push those. They may wrinkle."

Keep talking. It gives me more reason to light you up.

I didn't say anything as she continued to complain and mumble about no cell service and stomped her foot.

"How long is this going to take? I'm late for a party, and I need to call my friend." I pulled the tire from the trunk and was happy it wasn't a stupid little spare tire.

I wanted so badly to tell her she didn't have to worry about her party or her friends anymore because she didn't have long to live, but that would've ruined the surprise, and we all deserved surprises in our lives.

"It takes as long as it takes," I said.

More groaning and annoyed mumbling reached my ears, but I ignored her whiny disdain. I was what you would call a self-taught professional when it came to blocking out all those that were annoying. I'd done it on more than one occasion when I was forced to endure Dr. Wallace's lectures. They usually entailed bullshit like 'I could be helped' and 'I would get out one day.' All I needed to do was get in touch with my feelings.

Well, I was in touch with my feelings, and my feelings told me that I didn't like Dr. Wallace and was looking forward to my plans of roasting his ass, but that wasn't really what he meant.

I got the car lifted up on the jack, and it took some elbow grease, but the nuts on the wheel finally loosened, and I was able to get the tire off. I made sure to put it in the trunk before putting on the spare.

"What's your name," she asked, the silence obviously too much for her.

"DW." I slipped the new tire into place.

"Oh, like Dwayne Johnson, that's cool."

Although I'd never met Dwayne Johnson, I was pretty sure he wouldn't be a fan of my extracurricular activities. He seemed to be more of a people lover, whereas I was only fond of them when they were cooking over an open flame. The thought made me smirk as I tightened the last bolt and lowered the car off the jack.

"That took you long enough," the bitch girl snarked at me. She stood arms crossed over her fancy top, with a little purse under her armpit.

I rounded the back of the car and looked down at her. "You really should be nicer to people."

"Oh really, and why's that?"

"Because you never know who you're going to piss off."

Bringing the jack up, I caught the bitch in the side of the face. The force of the blow not only knocked her ass out, but she delightfully landed face first in her trunk. She didn't even groan as she lay sprawled with her ass and legs hanging out of the trunk like she was inviting me to fuck her. I wouldn't, though, because rape wasn't my thing. I had standards.

Grabbing the glowing phone from her hand, I flipped her legs into the small space and slammed the door shut. After tossing the cell onto the passenger side seat, I quickly snatched my bike. It took some maneuvering, but I was able to get it in the back seat. Jumping behind the wheel, I searched the steering column for a place to put the key.

"How the fuck do you start this thing?" There was a glowing start button and my eyebrow raised as I stared at it. "Really?"

Reaching forward, I pushed the button, and a message flashed across the display to push the break. Doing as the car instructed, I then pressed the start button. Shock of all shocks, the thing started.

"What the fuck happened to keys?" I instantly hated the fancy car and everything it and its owner represented.

Pulling away from the edge of the gravelly shoulder, I flew along the stretch of open road—this car had a lot more get up and go than Dora's old car. I knew exactly where to take the bitch in the back. Twenty minutes later, I pulled onto the dead-end road that looked the same as it had when I was a kid.

At least some things hadn't changed.

The bottom of the car scraped loudly as it bounced along on the tough terrain. Pulling over, I grabbed the phone and read the slew of messages that had come in now that there was service.

Girl, where are you?

Did you get lost?

What the fuck? Did you stand me up?

This party is lit! Hurry up!

I rolled my eyes and made sure that she hadn't sent anything about me or taken any photos before wiping the phone clean and tossing it on the seat. Getting out of the car, I wanted to string her up, but I didn't have the supplies.

On the other hand, I did have the supplies to light the car on fire and that was just as much fun.

Smirking, I opened the trunk and pulled out the limp girl, who was still very passed out, put her in the driver's side of the car, and closed the door. I looked through the throngs of bags in the trunk and picked a top that would work perfectly, and proceeded to open the gas tank flap and frowned.

"What the fuck?" I growled out as I stared at the strange safety design. "I really hate this new fucking world, but you fuckers can't stop me."

Pulling the pocketknife from my jeans, I got down and found the gas tank and stabbed a healthy-sized hole in the fucker. Immediately gasoline began to pour out on the ground, and I pulled myself out of the way before any got on me.

Laying the shirt under the spray, I used my new lighter to light it on fire like my own little makeshift wick. Yanking my bike out of the back, I hopped on and only made it a couple hundred meters away when the car exploded behind me.

I paused and turned to stare at the tall inferno.

The flames were beautiful as they cast long shadows on the tall surrounding trees. The warmth of the flames bathed me as thoroughly as the light did, and I sucked it up. The experience recharged me and made my cock instantly hard. Like a wine connoisseur, I closed my eyes and sniffed. There was burning metal, rubber, leather, and just a hint of human flesh. Grabbing the front of my jeans, I gave my aching cock a squeeze and moaned.

A little shudder of sadness went through me as the flames transformed into Adalyn's face, and a whisper of her voice floated on the gentle breeze.

Avenge me.

Not
even the
Devil could burn
the world like
I could

Chapter 14

It had only been a couple of weeks since my mad escape, but I was realizing very quickly that in this new world, I needed to be a lot more careful than I had been. One of the newspapers had caught me in a photograph walking away from Dave's building. Luckily I had my hood up, and they hadn't said I was the killer, but that wasn't the point. It was too close. I had things to do before I died, and I would die before I was locked up again.

Unfortunately, that meant I had to deceive Dora, and the thought didn't sit well. Everything I needed was online, and a credit card had to be used. I couldn't very well use one of those with no fixed address, no identification, and a name that I would rather keep off of any computer system.

I tapped on the final item and added it to the cart to have shipped to her farm.

"Here you go, I'm all done, and here is the cash." I pulled out a wad of bills from my pocket.

"Nope, I don't want your money." Dora gave me a firm stare and crossed her slim arms over her chest. She would've been a force in her youth. She was still fiery as hell now, so I could only imagine. "I'd rather you do some work for me around here."

I looked around the small home that was as neat as a pin, and my face must have shown my confusion because she continued. "I mean outside. I have a leak in the roof, my garden fence needs fixing, and my chicken coop has seen better days. Some of these things are just too much for me anymore."

I pushed the money into my pocket.

"Alright, it's a deal. Write out a list of what you want done, and I'll take care of it."

Her elderly features lit up as she clasped her hands in front of her chest. "Thank you, Derek. I'll be right back with the list."

I'd never seen someone so happy to spend time with me other than Asher and Adalyn, but even with them, I wondered if they really wanted to be around me. Asher turned his back on me, and Adalyn and I hadn't really been given a chance to see how our relationship would grow. The mere thought of her sent a stabbing pain through my chest. If I hadn't been so quick to escape, then maybe, she'd still be alive.

Shaking off the thought, I turned to stare at the photograph that was above the mantle. It was of much younger Dora and a man with a young girl. This had to be Dora's family. She never mentioned anyone visiting, so I had to assume if the daughter was alive, she didn't visit. I guess if someone were desperate enough, that person would pay for the company even if it were with the likes of me.

"Here you go. The first couple of things are for inside the house. The rest are outside." Dora handed over a piece of paper. My eyes glanced at the list and then up at the wide smile on Dora's face. I didn't have the heart to tell her that half of the words were spelled wrong or missing lettings. I knew she had good days and bad, but her personality never let me know which kind of day it was. Her friendly and helpful mood never changed.

"I'll get right to it," I said and stuffed the paper into my pocket. As I made my way out to the garage to find the tools needed, I couldn't stop thinking about my newest purchases.

The fancy surveillance equipment was due to arrive tomorrow, and I was excited to try it. Dr. Wallace was my ultimate target, and Dave's phone had proved to be another goldmine of information, including access to all of Jim's social media accounts. People loved to share their lives, and Dr. Wallace was no exception. A smirk played along my lips as I thought about what I was going to do to that man. I wrote down all the needed information and decided it was time to get a burner phone as it wasn't safe for me to hang onto Dave's phone any longer.

It was late morning that I found myself under Dora's sink putting her pipes back together. She'd had a decent-sized clog in the old plumbing, but it was nothing that a little elbow grease and a new piece of pipe couldn't fix.

"Hey dear, did you want some fresh lemonade," Dora asked as I wiped my hands on an old rag.

"Thanks," I said and took the offered glass. I smacked my lips with the sweet and sour taste that hit my tongue.

"No good?"

"It's perfect actually, best I've ever tried."

"Now you're just flattering me." Dora patted my arm as she wandered past me to the fridge. "I was thinking...." She paused and turned to look at me with a brick of butter in her hands. She was in the process of making cookies. The first batch had already come out of the oven, and my mouth sang with the peanut butter goodness. Was she trying to bribe me?

"What is it, Dora?"

The look on her face made me a little concerned that she'd suddenly decided she wanted me to fuck her. I mean, she was still a good-looking woman for almost eighty, but she was more like the grandmother I never had.

She wandered over to the small kitchen table with the yellow sunflower tablecloth on it and picked up her purse. She rummaged around inside and pulled out a handful of plastic cards. The woman didn't seem to own a wallet, and I had no idea how she managed to find anything in there.

Watching her arm fish around in the bag reminded me of the big claw machine at the mall. The claw hand would reach into the pile of toys and pick out an item at random. I'd never played—only watched because I didn't have the money, but it was fun to watch others. Sometimes, I'd even pretend that I was one of those kids with the smiling dads that would want me to play the game with him. A normal family event, just once, that's all I asked for, and never got.

"Here," she said and held out a platinum credit card.

"What's this for?" I took the card from her outstretched hand.

"I have a feeling you're going to need it, and I have enough to keep you busy around here until the day I croak, so you might as well keep it."

I looked at the card and then up at Dora. "I can't take your card, Dora. I appreciate it, but...."

She held up her hands.

"No buts. Take the card. I have more than enough money. Unless you plan on purchasing a yacht, I can cover whatever you need."

Her narrow shoulders lifted and dropped.

"The only family I have is a granddaughter who doesn't even know I exist, and I can't take the money to my grave. I'll keep it paid off. You make a point of working through the list I gave you and then I will add more to it when you're done."

"I don't know what to say," I said and meant it. This strange woman had shown me more kindness than just about anyone ever had in my life, and I didn't understand why.

"Just say thank you and that you'll take the deal. I like the company, and I'm no dummy, Derek. I'm slowly losing my mind."

She put the purse down on the table, a shadow of sadness crossing her face.

"If I die, I'd like someone to know I'm gone. Someone that might miss this old face and maybe say a few words."

I gave her a small smile.

"Alright, then thank you." I took out the cheap wallet I'd purchased from the pawn shop and placed the platinum card inside.

"Also, if you go out to the shed, there's an old truck. It was my husband's, and I didn't have the heart to sell it when he passed. If you can get her to run, it's yours."

Stepping forward, I gripped the older woman in a hug, shocking myself with the need to show her affection.

"Thanks, Dora."

She was so thin. I didn't know how her clothes were not falling off her body. At that moment, a fierce protective instinct took a firm hold in my heart. If anyone hurt Dora, they'd have to deal with me.

Stepping back, she wiped a tear from her cheek. "Don't mention it. I'll be right back."

I watched her wander out of the kitchen and into the bathroom. The fates worked in mysterious ways. One thing was becoming very clear, whoever was pulling the strings on my life was helping me this time, and I intended not to waste this opportunity. Jason was next on my list, and as soon as I found his ass, he was going to meet his end.

I looked out the kitchen window toward the shed Dora mentioned. The sun glowed brightly through the window over the sink and decorative miniature vases that held dried flowers. A flicker caught my attention, and I took a step toward the sink. A warmth spread throughout my body as I caught sight of the shimmering image of Adalyn sitting in the garden, smiling at me. She raised her hand and waved, and I found myself walking to the back door. Moving outside, I looked around and couldn't see Adalyn.

Turning, I spotted her by the shed. She was wearing a pretty sundress with little flowers on it, her short hair blowing around her face. She laughed as she waved for me to follow her. Not hesitating, I jogged toward her image and let out a bark of a laugh as she stuck her tongue out at me, then stepped through the closed door.

Grabbing the rusted door lever, I pushed down and gave it a pull.

"Adalyn? Where are you?" I called out and stepped into the dank, dark space.

Waving my hand in front of my face at the thick dust floating in the air, I pulled the T-shirt I was wearing up over my nose to keep from coughing. It was obvious no one had been in here for years other than small creatures. Massive spiders hung from almost every rafter. The large shadows of their furry bodies blocked out the little bit of light trying to come in through the dirt-covered windows.

"Adalyn," I called out again, taking a step further into the darkness.

"Over here."

"Where are you? I can't see you." My eyes scanned the area.

Long threads stretched from floor to ceiling, and I had to push the white webs out of the way like I'd entered a heavily decorated haunted house.

"Over here."

"I don't see you."

"Who you lookin' for?"

I whipped around to see Dora slowly making her way toward the shed, her arm up to block the bright glare of the afternoon sun. I looked over my shoulder, and I could feel that Adalyn was gone.

"No one, Dora. I was just mumbling to myself. Is this the truck?" I pointed to the oil-stained tarp that was covering something large.

"Yup, go ahead and pull the tarp off. Annoying things, get off me," she grumbled and swatted away a spider that landed on her arm that looked big enough to cart the frail old woman away. "Guess I need to do some cleaning up in here."

"Don't worry about it, I'll fix it up." I looked around the space and smiled.

This spot had a lot of potential. The image of Dr. Wallace hanging from the ceiling by his feet crossed my mind making me want to laugh out loud.

"Once you get to the back of the space, you'll smile." She pointed toward the door. "There is an office of sorts, but it's air-conditioned. May take you a bit to get it going, but my Rupert loved to use this spot as his 'man cave.'"

She giggled, a forlorn grin gracing her lips.

"He'd putter around working on one project or another and then sit back there to cool off and have a beer." She looked around, her eyes seeing memories that were only in her mind. "I miss those days."

I could picture her younger. A spry woman in her twenties with a bright future ahead of her. "Dora, can I ask why you never talk about your family?"

She didn't answer me. She just made her way over to the loan corn broom leaning against the wall. Picking it up, she began swatting down cobwebs and slowly headed over to the long workbench. I watched as she sat the broom aside and picked up something that was so coated in dirt I couldn't make out what it was.

Dora slowly turned back toward me as she wiped off the item. Coming to a halt in front of me, she held out what I could now see was an old photograph. It was similar to the family photo I'd seen in the house, but this one was of a much older version of her daughter. She had a baby in her arms. Three generations all together.

"My daughter and I didn't see eye to eye very much about anything. We were just two very different spirits. I loved my life here on the farm, and I guess I tried to push that on her a bit too much."

She sighed and looked out the doors.

"But, we got along well enough until she got married. It's a long story, but I didn't approve of her choice for a husband. Guess it wasn't my place to say, but...."

Dora paused, waving her hand in the air as her eyes filled up with tears.

"I won't get into the whole story, but we both said a lot of things I regret. The last time I saw her was when my granddaughter turned seven. That was when my husband passed away, and she came to the funeral." Dora pointed to the picture. "That's my Anna and my husband Rupert when my granddaughter was first born."

"She's very pretty," I said, not sure what she wanted me to say, but it was obvious she was sharing a painful memory, and I should say something.

"Yeah, she is. I wonder how my granddaughter is a lot these days."

"Why don't you call?"

Dora laughed. "You'd think it was that simple, wouldn't you? Trust me, I've tried, but Anna refuses my calls, and I doubt my granddaughter would remember I exist. She would be twenty-three now."

Dora grabbed my arm and gave me a hard stare.

"Don't leave regret on the table, my boy. It's a terrible thing to live with, but it's worse to know your life is near the end and the weight is still hanging around your neck like an albatross." With that, she walked away.

"The keys are behind the sun visor if the critters haven't carried them away."

One thing I definitely planned on not doing was leaving regret on the table. Jason was next to taste my wrath, and then I would find my final prize.

Turning, I marched out of the shed. I'd deal with the cleanup later. As I slipped the latch into place with a clink, I rested my hand against the door.

"Thank you, Adalyn," I whispered.

Not
even the
Devil could burn
the world like
I could

CHAPTER 15

Wiping my hands on the rag, I walked around to the driver's door of the truck. It was the moment of truth. I had to either clean or replace every part on the 1959 Ford F-100 and had nothing left to repair at this point. Luckily, Rupert was a bit of a collector. He had extra parts for just about everything, and most had never been out of the package.

Slipping into the driver's seat, I pushed the clutch to the floor and held my breath as I turned the key. There was a moment of hesitation, but the old truck growled loudly and then roared to life with a few pumps of the gas pedal.

"Yes! Good girl," I yelled as I pressed my foot down harder on the gas. The truck rumbled as it shook slightly back and forth as the motor grumbled like an old bear rolling out of bed in the morning.

Hopping out, I released the hood and dropped the heavy weight into place before stepping back and looking at the classic truck. It was a true beauty. I'd grown to appreciate the classics living with the Giltberts.

Mr. Giltbert loved to take Asher and me to the car shows to see all the old cars and trucks. At first, I didn't like it and thought it was boring, just another place for people to gawk at my face.

The man's schedule ran like clockwork, and with the Giltberts giving us a place to live, I felt obligated to go. I can't even remember when the obligation turned to excitement. Just one day, I found myself excited every Thursday for the farm chores to be done so we could all head to the traveling car show. He'd buy the two of us ice cream, and sometimes they'd hold truck pulls to show off the old muscle engines. The roar and the smell of the gas and leather was the only time I understood true joy.

"I see you got the old girl running?" Dora stepped up beside me and handed over a glass of lemonade.

"Thanks." I gulped down the tall glass. The heat was oppressive this time of year. "She's a beaut, and once I clean up the paint job, she'll look as good as new."

Dora walked toward the truck and trailed her fingers along the hood, a forlorn expression haunting her light grey eyes.

"Thank you," Dora said, turning toward me. "This makes me so happy." She patted the truck like a lover. "Rupert took me on our first date in this truck."

"How would you like to get out for a little while," I asked, stuffing the rag in the back pocket of the coveralls I was wearing.

"Oh, I don't know." She stared at the truck, her hand laying on her chest over her heart.

There was something about Dora that made me want to help her as much as she was unwittingly helping me. She was like the loving family member I'd never known.

"I was planning on going to the farmer's market and picking some fresh oranges and lemons," I said, undoing the button on the coveralls and letting them pool on the floor. "I could use the company, and I'm not very good at choosing the best fruit."

Picking up the coveralls, I walked over to the wall and placed them on the hook. It had taken a solid two days of hard work to get the shed back into workable condition and a couple more to get the truck running, but it had been worth every minute.

"Oh, it's easy." Dora smiled. "Are you trying to trick me into going with you?"

I smirked. "I don't know. Is it working?"

Dora laughed and nodded.

"Alright, I'll meet you around front. I just need to get my purse." She shuffled out of the shed faster than I thought the woman could move, a smile plastered onto her frail-looking face.

Hopping in the truck, I let it roll out of the shed, then quickly jumped out to close the large wooden doors before pulling the truck around front. Dora was just locking the door, so I took the opportunity to pull on a hoodie. Placing the baseball cap on and pulling the hood into place, I jumped back into the truck at the same time Dora got in. She looked over at me and simply stared.

"What?" I thought she might be having another one of her episodes. It really was kinda creepy when she saw shit I couldn't. It was one thing to see shit others couldn't, but it was a whole different ballgame when the shoe was on the other foot.

"Why do you go out like that," Dora asked.

"What do you mean?"

She reached out and tugged on the hood I had in place. "Why are you wearing this? It's like a hundred degrees outside."

"The heat doesn't bother me, and this way, I don't scare all the little children," I teased, but Dora didn't laugh.

"Derek, you've never needed to hide your face."

"What?" My heart sped up as I searched her eyes.

"You don't recognize me, but I recognize you," she admitted. "You and your brother Asher lived with the Giltberts for three years before... well before." Dora didn't say the words, but I realized she knew I'd been locked up. My hand tightened on the steering wheel.

"You know who I am." I looked out the side window, trying to decide what to do with this information.

"And what you did, to the asylum. I'm assuming that was you?" My eyes swung back to hers, and she shrugged. "If I'd had to live there, I'd probably burn it down too."

"I don't understand. You should be horrified or scared to be near me. You should be worried I'll kill you next or calling the police."

One of her perfectly penciled eyebrows shot up.

"If I'd wanted to call the cops, I would've done it the first day you were on the Giltberts property. There is no way they hired you to do repairs when they are dead in their bed upstairs." My mouth fell open. I couldn't remember a time I'd been more shocked than in this moment.

"Derek, I've always thought you got the shit end of the crap stick. If the Giltberts couldn't keep the two of you, Rupert and I had already decided we'd take you two boys in. But then you were taken, and your brother was shipped off to wherever by social services. I didn't think I'd see you again."

She turned her head and looked out the front windshield.

"This is my opportunity to help you now. I mean, look at me. I'm a lonely old widow with no one left in my life. The way I see it, we're both lone rafts drifting in a big old sea that wants to swallow us up. I, for one, am happy that you came back."

"But, Dora..."

"No buts. Why are you throwing up arguments? A moment ago, you were fine with me being oblivious to who you are, so why is this different? I want to help you, Derek. I've always wanted to, and now the good Lord is helping make that right."

She reached out and grabbed my hand that was holding onto the stick shift.

"I understand your pain. That's all that needs to be said. Now you can choose to kill me to keep me quiet if you wish, or we can go get some fruit, and I'll make a fresh peach pie. I've had a real hankering for one of those."

Dora gave me a smile and then clutched her purse in her lap. I had no idea what to do or say. On one hand, it was dangerous for anyone to know who I was and where I was hiding, but Dora had weeks to turn me in and hadn't done it. Instead, she fed me, gave me this truck, allowed me to use her car, and gave me a freaking platinum credit card. She had to know that the shit I was purchasing wasn't for the farm, yet she played along.

Glancing at her, I was seeing her through an entirely different lens.

Putting the truck into gear, I slowly drove down the driveway, and as I turned in the direction of the farmer's market, I made the decision to let the old woman live. It could be a decision that might come back to bite me in the ass, but I had to give her credit. She was a fuck load smarter and clever than I'd realized. Plus, there were many benefits to having someone like that in your corner.

"Thanks, Dora," I said as we got to the main drag. Those grey eyes found mine, and she smiled and nodded.

"No need to thank me. I'm thinking that I'll also get some apples and do an apple crumble later in the week." She looked out the side window as she spoke next. "That was Rupert's favorite. I'd make it every Sunday for him."

The moment I chose to let Dora live, a sense of calm washed over me. Since escaping my small shoebox of hell, everything had come easy. It was like something bigger than myself was guiding my hand and helping me, and it was that little voice that said to let her live.

My gaze flicked to the older woman as she hummed to the tune on the old radio. Maybe Adalyn had guided my hand to this woman for more than a few meals and a truck.

Not
even the
Devil could burn
the world like
I could

Chapter 16

As soon as we arrived, I helped Dora get set up with a small scooter which she thought was fantastic, and took off like she was driving in a Nascar race. Grabbing a large basket, I wandered away from the areas with lots of people, weaving my way through the endless rows of trees that held bright plump fruit, ready for the taking. I closed my eyes and took a deep breath, a small smile curling up the corner of my mouth.

Adalyn always smelt like sweet citrus.

"What are you doing," she whispered as I sat on the simple bed and let her take my vitals. I leaned forward again and drew in a deep breath taking her scent into my body, and could almost taste how sweet her skin would be on my tongue.

"You smell fabulous. I could eat you up," I whispered low so the orderly keeping guard outside the door couldn't hear. Adalyn blushed, a soft pink spreading across her cheeks.

"I'd like that," she said and looked over her shoulder before leaning in, so her mouth hovered near my ear. *"I'll come back later."*

She placed a brief kiss on my cheek, but it had the same effect as if she'd grabbed my cock because it now stood at attention. Thoughts of her sneaking into my room were running rampant in my mind. I was extra well behaved in the session that day, the thought of Adalyn keeping me from trying to leap across the desk and rip out the throat of the doctor.

My eyes stayed closed as I feigned sleep with the sound of the door, much later than I anticipated. The lights were off, so the only light in the room came from the soft glow of the square window built into the door. It could be Jim and his fucker friends coming to teach me another lesson, or it was Adalyn. The problem with Jim and his friends was there was nothing that they could do that hadn't already been done to me by a man much worse than they could ever aspire to be.

"You awake?" Came the whispered question.

"For you, always." I sat up and smiled at the sound of Adalyn's voice.

"You still want to eat me up?" Her voice was breathy, the sexual innuendo loud and clear. My body flushed hot with just the thought of her touching me.

"You're so bad," I groaned and rubbed at my hard cock that was tenting my flimsy pants. I stood up.

"Bunch up your blanket and put the pillow under like you're sleeping. They can't see well in here, but it will look like you're curled up on your side if they check with a flashlight." Adalyn helped with the simple task, and I looked up just as the scrub pants she was wearing fell to the floor. My mouth dropped open as I stared at her naked flesh. Even in the darkened room, I could easily make out her pale legs and her hand disappearing between her legs as she rubbed at herself. *"Come here."*

Adalyn held out her hand for me to take, and my brain finally started working again. My hands shook as I reached for her hips, and a deep sigh left my lips as I touched her for the first time. She was so beautiful, and I *had no idea what she saw in my black soul and scarred face, but I felt different when I was near her.*

"Kiss me." Complying immediately, I dropped my head and captured her lips—lips that I'd fantasized about since she started working here. The rabid animal that was locked up inside my chest broke free of its cage. With a groan, I pushed her into the wall and deepened the kiss, swallowing down the desire that was threatening to burn me up like a piece of kindling. Adalyn took my hand and put it between her open legs, and we both moaned as my fingers made contact with her wet pussy.

I'd never had sex before coming here. I knew what you were to do, I knew what my body wanted to do, but teenage girls were not into a guy that looked like me. They would flirt when they could only see half my face, but they would run away as soon as they saw the other half.

My fingers explored Adalyn's softness, dipping into her body. She groaned as she shivered in my hold. Her feminine scent reached my nose and made the kiss between us frantic.

"Get on your knees," she quietly commanded as she broke the kiss. Lowering myself to the floor, I lifted the end of her top so I could admire the delicious-looking pussy up close.

"Have you eaten one before," Adalyn asked. I was embarrassed to say no, but I shook my head back and forth. "Good, I want to be your first."

The initial trepidation vanished with those few little words. Smiling, she stepped wider apart.

"Eat me like I'm your favorite dessert until I come on your face. And trust me, you'll know what I like," she said as if ready my mind.

Not holding back, I dove in with a feverish rush. Adalyn gasped as my tongue tasted pussy for the first time. Instinct and her soft moans of pleasure guided me as my tongue slipped in and out of her sweet spot. I swirled my tongue around, wanting every last drop of what she offered me, but I needed a better angle. Adalyn gasped and made a little disappointed noise that had me smirking. So, I stopped and leaned up against the wall.

"Sit on my face, grind that sweet pussy into my mouth." My voice was strangled, the words coming out in a desperate tone. My cock ached like it never had in my life, and was ready to break through the cotton material of my pants. As Adalyn stepped toward me to straddle me, I had to release it from the confines. Rubbing it helped to keep the throbbing at a dull roar.

"Oh, Derek," Adalyn panted out as I gripped her ass cheeks and forced her to sit more firmly on my face. A strangled growl ripped from my throat as Adalyn shifted her position, granting me better access, but my undoing was when her hand wrapped around my cock.

"Fuck, you're big. I can't wait to ride this one day," she said, but I barely understood the words. My tongue lashed out and twirled around the hard little nub that made her body shake as she stroked my cock with her hands.

I knew she was getting close to her orgasm. The shaking in her legs became more intense, and the little noises of pleasure and panting sped up. My fingers pressed into the soft flesh of her ass and pulled her harder into my face until I was able to suck on that luscious little button that drove her wild.

"Oh fuck, Derek, I'm coming," she moaned, her body shuddering as she frantically rubbed her pussy against my face.

A small gush of warm liquid hit me in the face, and I quickly wrapped my arms around her ass. My tongue darted up, not wanting to miss any of it. I sucked hard, and she whimpered, her body quaking in my grasp until she went limp.

"Fuck, that was the best. You're amazing," Adalyn whispered, making my pride swell along with my confidence.

She surprised me as she turned around on her knees and slid between my legs. I didn't have time to contemplate what was going to happen next when she leaned forward and took my raging cock into her mouth. I almost yelled out at the intense pleasure. Without thinking, I grabbed the back of her head and gripped her hair as she sucked.

The little moans and sucking sounds she made were intoxicating to my ears. My hips flexed up to greet her hot mouth, and she moaned around my cock. The vibration spread pleasure throughout my body.

"Oh shit...." I mumbled as my body dove headlong into an orgasm. My hands tightened more into her hair as my come slid down her throat. "Fuck me," I growled, as the last of the release shot from the tip of my cock.

I slumped against the wall, and Adalyn sat down beside me, both of us panting hard. She tapped the top of her watch that glowed in the dark. The light cast a shadow across her gorgeous face.

"I still have fifteen minutes until my lunch time is up, and they will be looking for me. Do you have it in you to try and make me come again?" she said.

I couldn't stop the smile from spreading across my face.

"Challenge accepted," I whispered as I grabbed her and laid her down on the floor. She covered her mouth as a little squeal escaped her lips. Laying down between her legs, I got to work. I was determined to make her come again. It felt like I could live on nothing but what she offered me.

I stumbled and grabbed one of the nearby orange trees. The memory had been so intense like she'd been right here with me. I could feel Adalyn's hands on my skin, and my heart was pounding loud in my ears.

"You okay?"

I jerked around at the sound of Dora's voice but stood straight, wiping away the heaviness that had settled on my chest.

"Yeah, I'm fine." Turning to face the woman, Dora's pursed lips and lifted brow called me a liar, but she didn't press. The basket on the front of the scooter was brimming with fruit. "Looks like you did well."

"I did. I'm heading over to the avocado trees, and then I think I'm done. I'll wait up front for you." She turned around and zoomed off before I could say another word.

Putting my basket down, I shook my head to clear it of the last lingering images that were stirring up desires I'd never have quenched again.

I quickly filled the basket and then held one of the oranges up to my nose. Daring the possible flashback to return, I sniffed the sweet fruit, but this time only a warmth spread over my body like a gentle hug.

"I'm going to plant orange and lemon trees on the farm, Adalyn. I want you to be comfortable there."

I spotted Dora sitting near the checkout area, sipping on a drink. She smiled and waved as I came closer.

"Here, I'll take those for you," I said, shifting the weight of the basket to one arm so I could grab the two bags Dora had sitting on the small table. I held out the keys to the truck. "I'll meet you there in a minute."

I made my way to the checkout and kept my head down, and turned slightly so that the cashier could see only the good side of my face.

"Hi, did you find everything you wanted?" Her voice was chipper as she pulled the basket onto the scale.

"Yup."

She blushed and smiled wide as she batted her eyes at me. I was used to this act. A while ago, I had fun scaring new people by showing the other side of my face, and I did it to prove a point. That there was nothing, anyone could do or say to fix the scars that ran so much deeper than the ones people could see on my face.

"That will be twenty-three dollars."

"Here." I handed over the small number of bills.

"Is that your grandmother? She's adorable and so sweet." I looked out the window at Dora, who was stepping into the truck.

"Why would you think that?"

"The bags." The girl pointed to the ones I'd sat off to the side. "Here's your change."

"Thanks." I didn't bother to wait for the receipt.

"Um, did you want to go out sometime?" She called after me, and I looked over my shoulder at her. This time I made sure she could see the scarred side of my face. Her eyes went wide, her face paling as she looked away.

"Don't worry, the answer is no," I said, unable to keep the bitterness out of my voice. I stomped out to the truck and placed all the items in the bed of the truck before getting in.

"What happened," Dora asked, her face concerned.

"Nothing. Why?"

"You mean other than the fact it looks like you just swallowed one of those lemons whole? Or the fact that you're gripping the steering wheel so hard that I'm afraid you're going to rip it right off."

Taking a deep breath, I pushed down the anger and resentment. My father had been dead for nine years, but every day I wished I could bring him back so that I could kill him again for turning me into this hideous monster.

"I'll be fine. It's nothing that hasn't happened a million times before." The truck started up on the first try, and within moments we were cruising down the road toward the farm.

Dora put the window down, and I looked over at her as she unclipped her seatbelt and got up to lean out the window.

"What are you doing," I asked, reaching for the back of her shirt in case the door opened.

"Woohoo! I love you, world!" She yelled like a lunatic as she hung out the window, the breeze blowing her hair back as she waved to random people.

"Have you lost your mind?" This question was ironic to me, considering it was me asking it.

"I love the beach and sweet tea. I love the sunset and little baby chicks. I loved my husband and life and feeling free," Dora called out and earned a few whistles as she continued on with her crazy rant.

All she needed to do now was to lift her top and show her tits off to those passing by to complete her escapade. Panting, she slipped back into the truck and smiled wide.

Reaching out, she grabbed my shoulder, and I couldn't help the concerned look from reaching my eyes.

"Boy, the first lesson you need to learn is to find the small joys in everything you do because the good Lord knows that this life is not fair, and it will push you to your limits and strip you of all your happiness if you let it." I gave her a little smile as she flicked on the radio and sang to the latest Ed Sheeran song, completely off-key.

She was right, and a part of me knew it, but it seemed like an unscalable obstacle. Maybe once my plans were complete, I could try for a semblance of a normal life. But for now, my demons frolicked in every part of my brain, and their claws were deeply embedded in my soul.

I slowed to pull into Dora's driveway. As soon as I could see the house I knew something was wrong. The front door was hanging open, and there were deeply grooved tire tracks in the driveway, the telltale sign that someone had peeled out of the place.

"Stay in the truck," I said, putting it into park.

Hopping out, I stomped up the steps to the open door and stuck my head inside, listening. Whoever had been here was gone, but they'd done a lot of damage. Anger burned in my gut as I looked at the smashed vases that had sat in the window with little decorative flowers from Dora's garden.

I did a quick search of the house to make sure that no one else was still lurking inside. By the time I got back to the front door, Dora was standing just inside on her welcome mat. It, too, was lying cockeyed. Her eyes, which had held so much happiness moments ago, were filled with tears as she stared around at the damage. It looked like a tornado had dropped inside the little home and had torn it apart.

Dora didn't say anything as she sat the bags down and walked over to the mangled picture frames lying on the floor.

She stifled a sob as she slowly bent down, picked up her wedding photo, and dusted off the remaining shards of glass.

"Why would someone do this?" She looked over at me, and I didn't have an answer for her. "I have nothing of worth. Why destroy my memories?"

"I'll help you clean up."

Dora shook her head no.

"I need to call the police. You better go home." Holding the image to her chest, she made her way into the kitchen and paused when she reached my side. "Thank you for the lovely day and for...." She looked around again. "I shudder to think what they would've done if I'd been here."

I hadn't even thought of that, but as the words sank in, the demon in my mind uncurled itself from where it had been resting and stood tall, wanting the lives of those that had dared to hurt Dora.

I cracked my neck as the darkness filled me. Whoever had done this was going to find out what kind of monster I really was. I could already hear their screams in my mind and taste the smoke on my tongue.

Their blood was mine.

Not
even the
Devil could burn
the world like
I could

Chapter 17

Not even the torrential downpour going on outside could tamp down the rage that was simmering in my veins. I refused to leave just in case the assholes that did this came back. So instead, I was reduced to hiding like a rat in the pantry listening to the cops as they talked and walked around. I knew it was a major risk, but it was one I was willing to take.

My hunch paid off when Dora went to the bedroom to get the officers something. They were currently parked at the small kitchen table with a coffee in hand. Dora insisted that they stay for a coffee since they had to come all the way out here to see her. I mean, it was their fucking job, but since I was stuck in the pantry, I didn't get a say.

"Do you think it's the same group we're always having trouble with at the football field near town?" the one I named Dick asked, who sat next to the one I deemed as Head.

I peeked through the very narrow slat in the door and watched as Head jotted down some notes.

"Most likely. Same MO as the other break-ins. They were most likely looking for drugs and just smashed the place up for fun." Head looked over his shoulder to make sure that Dora wasn't coming back and then spoke again. "I just wish we had enough to arrest them."

"Officers, can you come here for a moment?" Dora called out, and both Dick and Head left the kitchen. Seeing the opportunity, I pushed open the door and darted to the table, picking up the small notebook Head left behind.

I scanned over the notes until I found the scribble about the possible people involved. Using the new phone I'd ordered, I took a few pictures before sitting the book back on the table and making it inside the pantry just as their feet echoed along the hallway floor.

"If you think of anything else or notice anything else stolen, you let us know," Head said as he grabbed the notepad off the table and jotted down another note before turning to face Dora.

"Thank you for coming out. I'm sorry if I've caused any inconvenience."

Head, who seemed like the senior officer, commented on the statement. "No need to thank us, it's our job."

Fucking right, although you're not doing a very good job.

"We'll be asking your neighbors if they saw anything suspicious, and if we find anything, we will be sure to let you know."

"Don't worry about the farm down the road. The family is away, and they have someone coming in to do some maintenance, but he's only around on weekends," Dora said.

Smooth Dora, good thinking. I really was starting to like Dora as my accomplice. I didn't think she'd like to be my accomplice for what I had planned next, though. As soon as the front door closed, I stepped out of the pantry.

"Dora, I'm going to head out for the night. Do you mind if I take the car home?" I said to Dora as she walked into the kitchen. I watched the police car's lights flick on and drive around the small roundabout she had before disappearing down the driveway.

"Yes, of course, I'm off to bed." Dora looked worn out as she shuffled down the hall a lot slower than she normally walked.

Grabbing the keys, I walked out of the house and locked the door behind me before jumping into the small white car. Making sure that good old Dick and Head weren't sitting on the road first, I pulled out and flew along, sending little stones flying in every direction. Cranking the wheel hard, I drove up the Giltberts driveway and left the car running as I hopped out to get what I needed.

Ten minutes later, I was back on the road pushing the little white car to its limits as I went through the details I now had committed to memory. The large college football stadium was coming into view, and I slowed to do a lap and survey the landscape first. There were a couple of cars parked in the lot, but no one was standing around or sitting inside the cars.

The notes said that one of the guys was suspected of working at the stadium.

Perfect.

There was a main door that was at the back of the building near the loading dock for deliveries. Flicking the headlights off, I pulled into a spot that was between a large dumpster and a transport truck trailer. The area didn't have any lights and was shrouded in thick darkness.

The damp night air punched me in the face as I stepped outside, but I took a deep breath of the sticky air into my lungs.

It was a good night to die.

An emptiness was consuming me, the emotionless sensation was the same as the night I split open my father's skull with a crowbar, and I let it fill me and guide my hand. I could feel the long hunting knife strapped to my waist calling to me as a lover would. It wasn't identical to the one I always used to carry around, but it was close, and it was all I could find at the pawn shop. I had taken the time to sharpen the blade to a fine razor edge that would cut a sheet of silk with one slice.

Opening the car's trunk, I pulled out the ax that I'd just sharpened and a container of gasoline. Next was a long coiled blue rope that I tossed over my shoulder. My hand paused on the open lid of the trunk. Then I wrapped my hand around the crowbar.

I didn't expect the back door to be unlocked, but I was pleasantly surprised to see that the door was an old piece of shit. The metal lock gave a slight groan in protest but then cracked with the force of the crowbar.

Feeling like a rat slinking through the dark corridors and hallways of the quiet stadium, I paused as I heard a hoot and then a cheer. There was a soft glowing sign for the men's bathroom, and the light from inside pooled out into the darkened hall. Keeping to the darkness I stepped into the concession stand and sat down the gasoline and other toys I'd brought with me. I spun the ax handle in my hand, loving the feel of the polished wood and the weight of the weapon as I stared at the popcorn maker and pop machine. My mouth began to salivate with the memory of movie popcorn. I'd become very skilled at sneaking into the movie theater, and it was surprising how many people would leave behind half eaten bags of perfectly good popcorn. It was one of Asher's favorites and he would always light up whenever I'd sneak some into our room to share.

"Where the fuck are you going, man?" a male voice called out. I stepped deeper into the shadows behind the counter that was brimming with the assortment of candy.

"I need to take a piss. I'll be right back, and don't drink all the fucking beer on me," a different guy yelled his voice echoing as he started down the long corridor toward the concession area.

"Just piss on the grass," someone yelled.

"No, I work here, and don't you fucking dare either, or I'll kill you."

The sound of feet echoed off of the cement floor. He belched and then complained to himself about the stench.

Classy.

I had no idea which of these fucking assholes had broken into Dora's house. The only description in the officer's notes was a nickname, Hog. I guess it didn't really matter. As far as I was concerned, they'd all die by association alone.

A long shadow was cast out of the corridor into the hallway. When you were born into the dark you learned to blend and become one with it. He never even glanced my way, but I recorded everything about the man—the slight sway he had to his stride, the shaggy dark hair, and the chains rattling around his neck as they flopped against his bare chest. He also had a ridiculously large and gaudy tattoo of an eagle on the left side of his neck that a two-year-old could've colored in better.

As he moved, I moved. I was the thing parents warned their children about, the monster that hid in the dark and the harvester of souls.

I followed the piece of shit into the bathroom. He never heard me or saw me until the mop he called hair was being firmly gripped. I pressed the sharp blade to his throat. The hot streams of piss miraculously continued to land in the urinal despite the fact he was shaking. I'd always hated being the tall one in the class, the one that everyone called Big Foot or the Troll, but now being six-six had a very distinct advantage over the much smaller man.

"Do you want to live?" I whispered like a lover into his ear, and his body shivered.

I could feel his Adam's apple move against the blade before he nodded a slight yes."Then you're going to tell me what I want to know." Again, another nod. "First, put your cock away before I decide to cut it off."

I smirked as the guy gave it a hard shake and stuffed it into his jeans.

"Good," I growled in his ear and loved the sweat that formed on his skin.

I was tempted to fuck with him and lick it off, but I had a mission to complete. Fucking with this one pathetic piece of barbecue was only one small part. "Tell me, is your name, Hog?"

I elevated a small amount of pressure from his throat so he could speak.

"No," he whispered, and I mentally gave him a bonus point for not trying to scream.

"Is he here?"

"Yes."

"How many of you are there?"

"Four."

"Very good. Now tell me, did anyone in your group rob a farm tonight?"

Before the man opened his mouth, I knew the answer. His body quaked harder in my hold. The stench of fear emanated off his musky skin as my leather-clad hand tightened and yanked his head back enough so his eyes could see mine. His eyes shimmered with terror. I wanted him to see how much I wanted him to die, and there was a silent begging in his expression that excited me.

"Yes."

"Thank you," I said softly as I drew the knife with quick precision across this throat.

His eyes went wide, his body thrashing in my hold as his hand gripped at the gash. Blood sprayed all over the urinal wall with every pump of his pathetic heart. He went still in my hold, and I watched his eyes dim, savoring the moment that no life would be left inside his body.Pushing the corpse away, I snickered as his body went to his knees, and his face landed in the piss he had yet to flush. I never promised this man I would let him live.

I stepped out of the bathroom and made it back to the shadows just in time. The same voice that yelled earlier said, "Hurry the fuck up."

"Come on, man, you better not have passed out in there, you stupid fuck!" The man stomped along the concrete, and my muscles flexed as I prepared to spring.

As soon as asshole number two stepped out of the corridor, I grabbed him by his hair and hauled him into the darkness. Quickly, I wrapped my other arm around his neck like a thick python. This man struggled hard in my grasp, his hands smacking on my forearm, but his attempts at fighting back were equivalent to a human wrestling with a grizzly bear.

I could feel his resolve weakening as his air supply wasn't re-established, and I squeezed a little harder to make sure he knew who was in control, and there was no escape. Asshole number two went limp, and I let him sink to the floor and grabbed the blue rope and the roll of silver tape.

I was pretty sure this guy was Hog since he had a cartoon tattoo of a pig on his bare arm. Grabbing his face in my hand, I stared at the face that had hurt Dora by violating her home. She was a sweet woman who would've given him money if he'd asked, but instead, he damaged her house and made her feel unsafe. And from what the officers had said, this was not a single event of desperation. This was how this fucker got his kicks.

"Now you're going to see how I get my kicks, Hog." I let his head drop to the concrete with a thud.

As soon as his hands, feet, and mouth were secured, I picked up the ax and my knife. My body shuddered with adrenaline and excitement as I stepped into the corridor and marched toward the bright lights of the field. The two remaining Dickwads were sitting under one of the goal posts, their back to me as they sucked on the end of thick joints. A football was sitting between them, and a case of beer on either side.

"What the fuck do you want now," my dad bellowed from his recliner.

I held out my textbook and pointed to the math problem I'd been struggling with for over an hour. "I...I... need help with my math Dad."

My head rocked forward as a hand cracked across the back of my head, but I held back the tears that pricked my eyes.

"Can't you see I'm watching my football game, boy?"

My eyes flicked up to the television. The team he was watching was wearing red and white uniforms. I didn't see the excitement in the game, but Dad loved it.

"But, I have a test tomorrow," I said, my voice sounding weak.

"Does that look like it's my fucking problem? Go bug your mother!" My dad reached out, grabbed me by the T-shirt, and gave me a hard shove. Stumbling backward, I fell and hit my head on the wall, my tooth biting deep into my lip. It hurt so much, but I knew better than to cry. Crying meant I'd be punished.

My feet didn't make a sound as I stepped up behind the men. They had sprawled out with their eyes closed and seemed to be enjoying themselves. Probably from the effects of the weed they were smoking. The unmistakable skunk smell permeated the air.

"Hey man, don't be a fucker. You're blocking my rays," Dickwad Number One snickered as he opened his eyes and tried to stare up at my face.

I was using the lights at my back to shade my face from his gaze. Using the blunt end of the ax, I raised it over my head and dickwad's face twisted from humor to fear a moment before I brought the thick piece of metal down into the center of his face. As his skull caved inward, blood hit his buddy, who hadn't been paying attention. This should be a teaching moment to teens everywhere that drugs really did kill.

Dickwad Number Two yelled and wiped his face.

"What the fuck? Did you just spit on me?" His eyes snapped open, and he looked over at his friend.

It took a few seconds for his brain to register the carnage that greeted him. I could almost see the gears turning in his mind as his eyes went wide and his mouth fell open. As his drug-induced haze lifted enough for him to understand what had happened, he began hysterically screaming. That shit was like a lullaby to my ears.

Stepping over the body of Dickwad One, I stalked him. He tried to get up and run, but his impaired state, the shock of the situation, and the fucking stupid pants that were below his ass all held him to the turf floor.

"Go ahead and get up. I'll give you a head start," I said and stopped walking.

The guy, who seemed to be in his twenties and the youngest of the group, scrambled to his feet and started to run for the red exit sign. I pulled the knife attached to my belt and lined up the throw. With a loud heave, the knife flew end over end until it lodged itself in the man's back just below his ribs.

Fuckin yeah, bullseye.

Having nothing better to do on the farm other than throwing knives at wood blocks for entertainment actually paid off.

His legs comically froze mid-stride, and he crashed onto the fake grass face first. His body skidded along for a few feet until he came to a stop. He whimpered as I approached his hand, uselessly trying to grab the blade. It was a painful and debilitating spot to hit, especially when you were not accustomed to pain like I was, but it wouldn't kill him right away.

Reaching down, I grabbed Dickwad Two by the legs and dragged him like a cart behind me. Once I got his body across the field, he was once more lying beside his dead friend.

Pulling the blade roughly from his back, he screamed and then wailed as I brought the long hunting knife down with enough force that it stuck to the bone in his leg. It took a bit of wiggling, but I managed to jerk it free before repeating the action to the man's second leg. I made sure not to sever any major arteries. I didn't want him to bleed out. Yet. I'd already killed two of them much quicker than I'd wanted.

The song "Whistling Dixie" came to mind, and I proceeded to

whistle the tune as I made my way back down the tunnel to grab all my supplies. Then I quickly returned for the asshole that was just beginning to wake up.

It brought my heart joy to have Hog worm around and thrash as he tried to yell for help. I didn't stop walking until he was under the crossbar of the goal posts. I tossed the blue rope up and over, attached one end of the rope to his feet, and then crouched low as I hauled the fucker up, so he was hanging upside down.

Holding him in place and getting the rope tied took a few tries. Hog may have 'accidentally' hit his head off the ground a few times, making me smile. Once he was in position, I stalked toward Dickwad Number Two, who was crawling in different horror movie poses across the fake grass, leaving a red trail of blood in his wake.

"No, no, please," the guy begged as I once more dragged his ass back to the goal post. Using the leftover end of the rope, I tied it around his chest and between his legs, easily avoiding his wildly swinging arms. Man, he swore with a plethora of swear words I'd never heard. I was sweating by the time Dickwad was in position and wandered over to yank the tape off of Hog's mouth.

"Why the fuck are you doing this, man? I don't know you. I got no beef with you," Hog asked.

"Did you rob an old farmhouse tonight?" I said, and Hog tried to hide the reaction, but I saw it in his eyes.

It took him a few seconds too long to answer, but I wasn't surprised when he opened his mouth to spew a lie. "No, man. I didn't touch a farmhouse. I have stolen some shit, but nothing tonight."

I smiled at him and then walked around until I was behind him. He swung back and forth, trying to turn to keep an eye on me. Leaning down, I took the gold watch off his wrist and proceeded to walk around the man until he could see the watch. I knelt down and flipped the watch over.

"Rupert, I will love you until the end of time. Dora." I read aloud and loved that with each word of the inscription, his breathing quickened.

"That doesn't prove anything. I found that piece of junk at the pawn shop."

I sighed and stood. "Not only are you a piece of trash, you lie like one, and now you will also die like one."

"Come on, man! Don't do this!"

I looked at Dickwad whose head was bobbing to the side as he softly sobbed, and his jeans darkened with piss.

"You two make quite the sight, but your friend needs to be added to this picture."

Wrapping the last of the rope around the dead man's neck, I tied it into a thick knot, picked him up like he was nothing more than a heavy hay bale, and chucked his ass over the goal post.

I stood back for a moment to admire my work. It was quite the art piece—one by his neck, one by his feet, and the other like a baby swing.

Very creative.

The pièce de résistance was the garbage that I laid out under the three men like they were indeed piggies on a spit.

I paused in my preparation to turn and look at Hog as he told his friend to stop fucking crying like a baby. It was the most amusing thing I'd heard in a long time since it was going to be Hog that was wailing in a few short moments.

"Hog, what does it feel like when you rob a home? When you sneak into their private space and do whatever you want. Does it excite you?" I said.

I couldn't help wondering if Hog got the same level of satisfaction from stealing from people as I did from watching them burn.

"Fuck you, man, I'm not telling you shit. I didn't do it."

I shrugged, not really caring if I got the answer.

"Alright, have it your way." Grabbing the red can of gasoline, I sloshed a healthy dose on the dead guy first, and my cock twitched for the first time as I lit his jeans on fire.

It didn't take long for his body to burn bright, and Dickwad's screams and struggling as he watched made it all worthwhile. I sucked in a deep breath enjoying the scent of the burning flesh as the fire devoured his body.

"What do you think?" I stepped in close to Dickwad, who was in hysterics as he suddenly found a burst of energy and wiggled around like a worm on a hook. "Will it hurt more for you or for Hog to die?" Dickwad just continued to scream nonsense. "I'm curious to find out as well," I teased.

"Come on, man, don't do this. Okay, fine, I did it. Is that what you wanted to hear? I kicked in the door, stole some shit, and messed up that crappy home. That shithole had nothing of value in it, and robbing it was a waste of my time. Even that watch was worthless. Is that what you wanted to know?"

I paused while pouring the gasoline on the garbage to give Hog a grin. "Honestly, I didn't care, but thank you for confirming it for me."

"Fuck you," Hog yelled as I poured the remaining gasoline on Dickwad's legs and on Hog's shirt. "I told you what you wanted to know." He sputtered and spat as the liquid ran into his mouth.

"You seem to be under the misunderstanding that I came here to get you to confess." I knelt down so that I was looking into Hog's eyes. "This is where you've gone wrong, Hog. Do I look like a fucking priest or cop? I always planned on watching the skin slide from your body as you burned alive. The confession was simply icing on my extremely dark and delicious cake."

"No, no, no man. Please, please don't do this," he begged as my thumb hit the rowel on the lighter.

The sound was loud in my ears as the little flame danced before my eyes, and the sound of Hog and Dickwad screaming faded into nothingness. All that existed was the flame. I watched my arm as if someone else was reaching out to light the garbage first and then Dickwad's pants. Finally, that flame lit Hog's hair on fire.

I stood and took a few steps back to let my creation work its magic. It crawled over the bodies, and I was feeding it. The demon in my mind sighed and then had me gasping as my cock hardened to an unbearable length inside my jeans, my body begging for release. I held off, not wanting to leave any possible DNA behind, but I bit my lip and grabbed the hard length through my jeans as the men howled in pain. Even though it was dangerous I couldn't help taking a picture to saver later.

Taking a final shuddering breath, I walked away, the men forgotten, their lesson a warning to all those that fucked with what's mine.

Avenge me. The voice whispered in my ear.

Jason will be next, my love. I won't fail you again.

Not
even the
Devil could burn
the world like
I could

Chapter 18

I just finished mopping the floor when Dora walked out of the bedroom. The sun wasn't up yet, so I was surprised to hear her soft footsteps coming down the hall.

"Derek, you didn't have to do this," Dora said as she looked around at the room that was back in order. "Oh, my gosh, Derek," she exclaimed, her hands covering her mouth as she made her way to the fireplace and picked up the stolen watch. "Do I want to know?" She clutched the golden-colored watch to her chest.

I smirked as I picked up the bucket of soapy water.

"Probably not," I said honestly, but not expanding.

I dumped the water into the laundry room sink and put all the cleaning products away before heading out to the kitchen, where the scent of fresh coffee was already strong as it dripped into the pot.

"Did you want breakfast? It's the least I can do after you did all this for me," Dora offered, and I gave her a little smile, resting my hands on her center island. She mimicked the pose, and I laughed at the size difference in our hands.

I was tempted to say no, but my stomach growled, reminding me that I had skipped dinner to play last night. "Alright, maybe a quick bite. Lots to get done today."

"You should sleep. You look like something the cat dragged in."

Dora certainly didn't pull any punches. She had every reason to be terrified of me, but she simply smiled and went about making bacon and eggs like she didn't know I'd burnt down an asylum with a few hundred people inside. Kinda made me wonder which of us needed our head examined.

Breakfast was quiet, and I had just gotten up to put our dishes in the sink when a knock sounded at the door. Dora and I looked at one another, and I immediately took up residence in my hiding spot.

"Well, good morning, officers. I didn't expect to see you again so soon," I heard Dora say.

Immediately, I ran every second of last night through my mind, needing to know if I'd screwed up. If they were able to track me...but, no. There was nothing I could think of that would lead them to this house.

"Hi there, ma'am. Sorry to bother you so early, but we just wanted to let you know that those responsible for yesterday's break-in were in an unfortunate accident last night. Although we recovered these items from one of the suspect's home, we could not find the watch you mentioned. I'm afraid they might have already sold it."

"Oh my, I'm sorry to hear that, but I can't deny I'm happy to have my things back. They weren't worth a lot of money, but they meant so much to me."

"We just need you to sign here for the items."

There was the sound of rustling, and then Dora was saying goodbye. I was a little nervous about stepping out of the pantry. It felt strange to be nervous of a woman that I could snap in two, but she was the only real friend I'd ever had.

Pushing open the pantry door, I peeked out as Dora sat the box on the table.

"An unfortunate accident?" She looked over at me, and I couldn't help rubbing the back of my neck.

"It needed to be done," I said.

"Mmhmm. I guess it's a good thing then that by tomorrow I will have forgotten all about this conversation," she teased.

But Dora didn't fool me. I could see the terror she had over losing her mind, and I couldn't blame her. It was a terrible thing to have your own brain turn against you.

Heading to the door, I paused and looked back at the woman I barely knew and yet trusted more than I'd trusted my own mother.

"I'll make sure you never suffer, Dora. All you need to do is ask when the time comes."

She stared at me, the corner of her mouth curling up. "Thank you."

It was all Dora said, but there was weight to those two simple words, and I felt it in my soul. Nodding, I made sure the cops were gone before heading out. I needed to find Jason, and the only way that was going to happen was if I got my hands dirty differently since neither Jim's nor Dave's phone had given me anything useful.

An hour later, I was tucked away in a safe hiding place, watching an open concept backyard at work. Dr. Wallace was not my next target, but I wanted to build a daily schedule of his habits.

"And maybe you'll lead me to Jason's mysterious location," I mumbled as I watched.

It became glaringly obvious that Dr. Wallace either didn't know that Dave and Jim were dead or didn't care because he certainly didn't look spooked. I'd seen men scared for their lives, and the way he smiled and held up his beer to clink with his neighbors was certainly not it.

This whole open-concept thing was strange to me. I couldn't even picture having a backyard without a fence. The one I had growing up was like an overgrown shoebox with fences so tall that it wasn't until I turned twelve that I could even climb them. Dr. Wallace was currently barbequing while socializing like a rock star. Even from my hiding spot,

I could hear their laughter and voices, and each time he smiled, the urge to take everything from this man burned a little brighter.

More neighbors arrived, and it reminded me of a pack of dogs surrounding their source of food as they went straight to the large shiny barbeque and stood around it. It was kind of like a siren's call. Each one of them would lean over his shoulder and smile and then tap their drink to his like he was doing something miraculous.

As I watched them linger around like a flock of vultures, I realized that every human liked the smell of burning flesh on some level. However, these particular 'vultures' just decided that this smell was fine as long as it wasn't human. Dr. Wallace tried to say that I was crazy because I liked to smell human flesh burn, but to me, it was as tantalizing as the beef steak on that shiny barbeque.

Switching my position inside my hiding place, I looked around the small tool shed and decided that if I had to wait for someone to go inside for the night, this space was a comfy place to hang out. Admittedly, I was trying to figure out why he had the shed at all. The dirt had been so thick here that it was obvious he hadn't cracked the door open in months or maybe years.

Luckily the good Doctor liked to live the high life, and his home, along with the rest of the massive estate-style mansions on this road, all backed into an exclusive golf course. Sneaking onto the golf course had been easy, and for what I needed to do tonight, I didn't have to bring anything more than a single duffel bag.

Not only was the shed a perfect distance away to not be seen or noticed, but it was the type with little glass windows, and Dr. Wallace had been nice enough to have spare benches inside for me to lounge. Dr. Wallace was turning out to be quite the host, except for the stifling heat and the occasional annoying spider. I chugged the last of the water I had brought with me and stood to take a piss in the corner, all too happy to spray this asshole's walls with my golden shower.

When the man of the hour disappeared into his house, I paid close attention to the neighbors. Some seemed reluctant to leave and head back to their own homes. They kept staring longingly at the barbecue as if it would magically cook more meat.

I'd spent the better part of three days learning everything I could about the technology that was around these homes. Cameras were everywhere, and I quickly realized that I would need to find a way to evade them to get to my target. I'd found a few toys that would do the trick and still wasn't a fan, but the tech was growing on me like a bad fungus.

A slow smile spread across my face as I studied the paper and the location of all the cameras on my map. I even wrote down how long it took to walk to the road and how many steps it would take to reach each house.

As the setting sun cast long shadows on my hiding location, I got to work. First, I pulled out the black box with all the antennas on it. I was assured it would fritz out all the cameras in the area. I didn't know if I believed the sketchy guy I found selling this high-tech equipment, but I was willing to give it a shot.

Next, I pulled out the battery pack used to power the thing. It only took a few minutes to get it set up and turned on. Step two was to get inside the good Doctor's home. As if fate was driving my destiny, a teenage girl opened the sliding glass door, yelled, 'fuck off,' and slammed it closed. I watched the girl march away and then noticed that the door she slammed had bounced open a crack. The girl continued until she was out of sight, and I acted quickly as this might be the only chance I got.

Glancing up, I noticed the sky had turned dark grey.

"Shit," I muttered.

It was just after dusk and not nearly as dark as I would've liked, but I pulled my mask in place and grabbed my bag of tricks. I slipped out of the shed and jogged for the homes that no longer had anyone lingering outside. My head was on a swivel as I kept my eyes open for the girl, but she must have stormed off onto the golf course to vent her anger.

When I reached the door, it was easy to hear why she'd taken off. I understood her disgust as I heard Dr. Wallace and his wife fighting. The argument was loud, and I used the cover of their racket to slip inside.

Unlike the teen, I didn't forget to lock the door. Having her find me before I was set up wouldn't do. I pulled the tiny camera from my pocket and looked around, trying to find the ideal location. There was a plant hanging in the corner with an ornate holder. It had a great aerial point of view, so I quickly placed the small piece of tech up there. It fit perfectly because it was no bigger than the end of my baby finger.

The yelling got louder, and then there was thumping as the two went up the stairs to the bedrooms.

Could they make this any easier?

The second camera I placed in the living room, attaching it to a picture frame. Then I slipped down to the basement. The loud argument was echoing through all the metal vents, their voices as clear as if they were in the same room. Asher and I used to stuff our vent with a sweater to try and block out the noise when our parents fought. It didn't help, though. Nothing much helped the sound of a body slamming into the wall that was on the other side of where you laid your head.

Downstairs, I looked around the laundry room for a good spot to set up the booster for the signal of the camera scrambler. If this went well, then when the time was right, not one of the houses on this block would be safe. The thought made me as giddy as a kid in the candy store.

My eyes landed on the large mountain of laundry, and I wondered why people still built homes with the machines in the basement. I mean, I knew it was tradition to have the washer and dryer down here, but when you had this much money, why would you bother having to lug the shit up at least three flights of stairs.

Stupid if you asked me, but on the bright side, the place was a treasure trove of fun chemicals to play with if I wanted. A tingle started in the base of my spine as I thought about jumping the timeline and ending Dr. Wallace right now. I shook my head and clenched my fist to stop myself. I wanted to make sure that everything was in place first. I wanted Dr. Wallace's death to be front-page news for weeks, not just days.

Jogging back up the stairs, I made my way out of the house the same way I arrived and then ran to the next house. Each house had either a light, satellite, or stupid-looking wall art that made good hiding spots for another small booster.

Finished with my chore, I stuck to the long shadows and made my way through the trees around the golf course to get back to the little white car that was becoming quite the getaway vehicle. Pulling out the tablet I purchased, I hit the on-button, and there it was, as clear as day, the living room and the downstairs sitting area.

Dr. Wallace marched into the scene and threw his hands up in the air in obvious frustration. I didn't bother turning on the volume. It was a lot more entertaining making up the argument.

"But Alice, I can't go to Wonderland with you. I have too many lives to ruin," I mocked.

"I hate you, Wallace. You promised we'd go to the tea party." I grinned wide, enjoying this moment more than I should.

Dr. Wallace was shaking his finger at who I assumed was his wife. I'd never seen the man this worked up, and I'd gotten him worked up real good on occasion. All the times I'd spent with him in his office pushing his buttons, this was the first time I saw him red-faced and pulling his glasses off and shaking them as he argued. Then again, it was difficult to yell at someone like that when you're terrified of them. It took a level of guts that I knew this douchebag didn't have.

"Well, Dr. Wallace, you and I are going to get more intimately acquainted very soon."

Smirking, I turned off the tablet that made me want to sing with joy, but as I pulled away from the little hidden parking spot, I settled for whistling.

Soon Adalyn, very soon.

Not
even the
Devil could burn
the world like
I could

Chapter 19

I watched my prey for a couple of days, but the excitement was wearing off as I struggled to figure out how to get inside each of the homes. No matter which way I cut it, I needed to get into the homes to set my trap. My issue was the security systems. I needed them to let me in since breaking into all of these homes was not a viable option.

And then, in a moment of true brilliance, it came to me. Annoyingly it took another couple of days to acquire what I needed to make this a reality, but the night was finally here. I sat twiddling my thumbs as I waited for the cover of night to implement phase one. I had to admit this really was an ingenious plan.

The sun's final rays were setting, casting a dark orange and pink hue on everything it touched. Among the darkening sky, I could see Adalyn sitting on a bench reading a book. Leaning forward in my seat, I stared at the image in the clouds and smiled when she looked my way and blushed. She was so beautiful...and then it was dark.

Closing my eyes, I savored the image for a few moments, not wanting to let her go again, but I knew that what I did next, I did in honor of her. Getting out of the white van I'd stolen for the occasion, I grabbed my bag and sprinted like a dark spirit through the trees that lined the golf course.

Hunkering down at the edge of my cover, I watched for any signs of activity. Most people seemed to be out as their homes were completely dark. The people that remained were watching television, that harsh light glowing in the windows.

Satisfied that the coast was clear, I pulled the black mask down into place and jogged across the perfectly trimmed grass. I made sure to stick to the edge of the tall palm trees for as long as possible until I had to break away to get to the first home. Squatting by the dryer vent, I snapped off the protective covering and then unzipped my duffel bag.

Pulling out one of the premade glass containers, I held it up and smirked as I watched the inside move around like the jar was alive. Each one of my little packages was full of very pissed-off cockroaches. Cracking the lid, I lifted the dryer vent flap and turned the glass bottle to fit into the hole, and let the vent flap close around it. Running to the next house, I repeated the process, and of course, for the good doctor's home, I made sure that there were two bottles for the occasion.

I waited and glanced at the watch on my wrist. Once twenty minutes had passed, which gave plenty of time for my little pests to crawl out of the vent tube into each home, I doubled back the way I came to remove the bottles. Double-checking my work at my first stop, I opened the flap and smirked when the vent was empty. Pulling the bottle out of the vent, I put it into the bag and ran around to collect the rest of the glass jars.

Once more, I jogged back to the white minivan and slapped on the magnet that proudly stated, 'Ricky's Roach Removal.' Hopping in the back, I stripped out of the black clothes and pulled on the white uniform of my "new" profession. Kind of made me wonder if pest guys did this to get work. Now it was time to wait again. To do this job right, I couldn't be impatient. I had to be smart and cunning, and I was finding new layers and depths to reach for with each passing day.

Crawling into the front seat, I sipped my cooling coffee, munched on every snack I'd brought with me, and listened to the radio. Each minute was agonizing and thrilling at the same time.

I waited until the same rays I saw set, rising into the air before I put phase two into play. Right at eight, I drove around and parked at the furthest house from the doctor's. Pulling the white cap on and picking up the clipboard, I marched for the first home. Once by the front door, I kept my head down and my face turned away from the camera in the corner.

The name on the mail for this house said it belonged to the Michaels. A perky and very attractive blonde woman in a skintight exercise outfit answered the door on the second ring, her voice annoyed as she spoke. "I'm not interested in whatever you're selling, sorry." She went to close the door in my face.

"It's about the roaches in the homes in this area. I've gotten several calls about the infestation that has moved in and wanted to know if you'd like your home inspected and sprayed as well?"

The door paused halfway closed before she slowly pulled it open again. Her eyes stared at the van in her driveway. I flicked my eyes to the clipboard and the very professional-looking checklist I'd printed off on Dora's printer. I'd filled in a few of the home numbers on the street adjacent to this one and made sure that she could see the names and addresses.

"Did you say cockroaches?"

"Yes, ma'am, unfortunately, they are bad this time of year, and once they get into your home, they are hard to get rid of. Sometimes we have to spray two or three times to get rid of the eggs they lay. Once they start laying eggs, your home can quickly become overrun, and you will find them in everything from your food to your clothes. Have you seen any?"

My pen was ready to jot down all the useless information I had zero intention of actually addressing.

Mrs. Michaels opened her mouth when a high-pitched screech echoed down the hall, and a girl in her teens came running out of the kitchen as she continued to scream hysterically."Roaches!" It was the only word I could make out as she ran past and up the stairs, like hiding in her room would actually help.

Mrs. Michaels's eyes swung back to mine. "Oh my god, come in."

An hour later, I was fully geared up, my face and body hidden from all those that stood outside their homes as I walked into every single one and supposedly rid them of their problem. In reality, I sprayed around some smelly chemicals and sprinkled my little white phosphorus creation into at least four vents per floor. I wanted to make sure that the celebration I was creating went off without a hitch.

Finishing up at the last house on the street, I stood in the middle of the kitchen and laughed.

Rich people.

Shaking my head, I went outside and spoke to one of the men who seemed to have been appointed 'message relayer.' I told him there was a good chance all the homes would need to be done again and to call if that was the case. I handed over the business card and hopped into the back of the van to strip before driving away, with none of them being the wiser.

In celebration, I'd purchased myself an ice cream. Stuffing the last of the refreshing orange cream delight into my mouth, I watched the minivan burn in the abandoned industrial building parking lot.

I'd gotten to see the doctor up close. He had dark circles under his eyes, but other than that, the man looked exactly the same as the last time I'd seen him.

I couldn't help wondering if he had a sense that his time was coming to an end. Like an animal leaving the safety of its home or pack to die by itself. Did he feel me closing in? Did he feel the noose around his neck tightening into a stranglehold that he couldn't escape?

There were so many strange and mysterious things that happened in the world it was hard to determine which ones our minds made up and which ones were a product of something beyond our understanding. Adalyn visiting me from the dead as she helped and encouraged me in my task was something that I couldn't explain, and yet it was as real as the ground beneath my feet.

"It's going to happen, Adalyn. I'm closing in on him. You will be avenged, I promise you. I just need you to give me a little more time."

The fire of the van danced in my eyes, the roar and groan of the metal as intoxicating to my senses as any drug to an addict. As the flames found the gas tank, the van exploded. Most would have ducked or ran, but I smiled. The fire burned bright with the rainbow of reds, oranges, and yellows, but it was the blues and whites—the hottest parts of the flames that I found the most fascinating. My eyes were drawn to those sections as they swayed against the dark night sky.

My cock jerked as I trembled from the desire that flooded my system, but it was nothing compared to when screams were involved. I pictured someone struggling to get out from inside and smirked.

It was time to go. The longer I stayed, the higher my chances of getting caught.

Dr. Wallace, your time was almost up. I do hope you have your affairs in order.

This was a calling, it was my calling, and I had one obstacle left in my way before I'd be able to complete my task.

Grabbing my trusty bicycle from where it leaned against the crumbling brick wall, I pointed it toward home. Whistling softly, I pedaled off into the night.

Not
even the
Devil could burn
the world like
I could

Chapter 20

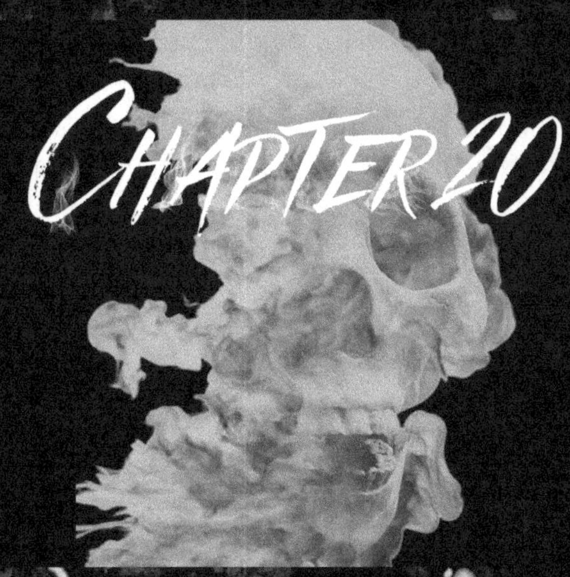

I finished patting down the dirt around the small orange trees I'd just planted when a metal trailer banged up the driveway. Pushing myself to my feet, I waved to the truck pulling the trailer, and pointed where I wanted him to go. There was lots of open space in the farmyard to turn the trailer around to back the doors up to the field.

"You're good there," I hollered and held up my hand with the universal sign to stop. Once in place, I opened the door and pulled it aside to let the cows walk out. The trailer rocked and thumped as the nervous animals hopped out and looked around at their new home. I couldn't stop the smile from spreading across my face as I watched the black animals make their way across the thick green pasture. I closed the gate and pulled the wad of cash from my pocket before heading to the driver's side door.

"Hey there," the man driving said. His name was Rob, a decent enough name, I guessed. He jumped out of the still-running truck. "Good looking herd you have there."

"Thanks." I made sure to keep looking toward the field and held out the cash so that he didn't see the ruined part of my face. As much as

Dora kept trying to tell me that I shouldn't be ashamed, I couldn't seem to break the habit.

The man thumbed through the thick wad of cash and smiled as he lit up a cigarette. My eyes instinctively flicked to the little flame as my tongue drew a wet line across my lips. My nostrils flared as he blew out the first puff of smoke, and I greedily breathed it in.

"If you plan on getting any more gimmie a call, I got more coming in the spring that I'll be happy to sell ya."

"Will do."

Rob jumped back into his truck, the sweet scent of smoke leaving with him. I watched my new addition for a little while to make sure they were going to settle in stress-free. There was something so peaceful with the way they wandered around and ate the tall grass.

Adalyn would've loved this spot. She'd mentioned more than once she wanted to move out of the suburbs and get a piece of property. Picking up the watering can, I finished taking care of my little trees that were only a few feet tall, but after a couple of years, they would start to produce fruit.

My phone dinged that there was movement in the good doctor's house, and I pulled the phone from my back pocket to take a look.

"Well, I'll be damned," I whispered at the sight of Jason's face as he walked into the doctor's living room.

I was on the run, stripping off the coveralls and grabbing my discarded hoodie off the porch before I jumped in the old truck. This was not the most ideal stalking vehicle in the world, but it would have to do. Illegal or not, I watched the men on the phone as I pulled the truck down the driveway and out onto the road. It was a solid twenty-minute drive, speeding and without traffic, to get to the doctor's. I only hoped that they talked long enough for me to get there.

Unable to help myself, I flicked on the sound of their conversation.

"Don't be an idiot, Jason. The man is dead. They found him in his room with the door locked," Dr. Wallace said.

Jason paced back and forth across the living room carpet, and I could see the beads of sweat on his brow. He was scared, I liked him scared, and Jason would be a hell of a lot sweatier when I got ahold of him.

"I'm telling you, doc, that crazy fuck is still alive. Jim is dead. The house mysteriously blew up. Do you want me to believe that Dave's apartment and almost the whole fucking building burning to the ground was also a coincidence? Never mind the fact that the entire fucking asylum burnt to the ground within minutes—who else would have that skill? I don't believe in that much bad luck."

"Smart man, I wouldn't either," I snickered at the phone.

"Yes, I agree it's odd, but they haven't even ruled the fire at the asylum as arson. I didn't know about Jim, but from what I read in the newspaper, they feel it was a gas leak at the apartment building. Derek didn't even know those other people at the apartment. Do you really think he'd blow up the whole thing to get to one man?"

"You underestimate my rage once more, Doctor. It's not a wise choice," I mumbled as I slowed the truck at a set of lights.

"Doc, I'm telling you that crazy son of a bitch is alive, and he is coming for us. Why did I ever listen to you in the first place? I told you when you had me drag him from his room the first time that he was dangerous and should be sent to prison, but you insisted on the asshole staying there so you could study him." Jason stomped across the carpet and pointed his finger at Dr. Wallace.

"Jason, get control of yourself. You're spiraling."

"We need to hide. We need to run. I've been staying at my sister's cabin to stay out of the city, and you should do the same. Shit, maybe we should leave the country." Jason broke away from Dr. Wallace and continued to pace.

I could tell it was irritating Dr. Wallace, bringing a warm tickle to my heart.

"If you're so worried about being seen, why are you here," Dr. Wallace asked.

"Good question, doc. Why are you there, Jason?" I mocked.

"Because everyone thinks I'm crazy, but I'm telling you, Derek West is alive, and he's coming for us like the fucking grim reaper. He's going to burn us to the ground for what we did to him, for what we did to Adalyn." Jason rubbed his face. "I regret that so much. Fucking Jim, if he weren't already dead, I'd kill him myself. I never should've listened and just walked out of the room. Shit, shit, shit."

"Too late, Jason. The verdict is already in, and I don't really care how you feel," I said, the anger burning bright, making me push the old truck a little faster down the final stretch of road.

"Jason, you need to calm down right now."

"Calm down? How do you expect me to calm down when a fucking maniac is on the loose and wants to burn me alive? This is all your fault. If you hadn't told us to go teach him a lesson, none of this would've happened." Jason pointed a finger at Dr. Wallace again, his face a mix of raw anger and wild fear. It was a good combination for me. In fact, I was loving it, and it was because of me that he was so worked up.

"He does have a very valid point, doc. How is he supposed to remain calm?" I was having way too much fun. I figured this was what a fly on the wall felt like, and I was totally enjoying it.

"I told you to teach him a lesson. I didn't tell you to rape a nurse, for fuck's sake. That was your stupidity." The doctor took a deep breath and held up his hand as he tried to remain calm. "This is what we will do. You're going to go back to your cabin, wherever that is, and you're going to stay there. Give me your number, and I'll text you if I hear anything about Derek or if I'm notified that the fires were arson. Does that sound reasonable?"

"I think we should leave the state—no, leave the fucking country," Jason mumbled again. "I don't know where I'd go, but anywhere is better than here. I could drive to Canada and then fly out." He was tapping his forehead as he thought out loud.

"Wouldn't matter, Jason, I'd find you," I said with a snarl curling my lip. "The devil can always find his mark."

"Fine, I'll do what you're asking." Jason relayed his phone number as the doc put it in his phone before heading for the door. His hand paused on the door handle, and he didn't turn around for the longest time. Dr. Wallace looked concerned and seemed ready to say something when Jason looked over his shoulder. "I worry that by the time you realize that Derek West is alive, it will be too late for the both of us."

Jason made a dramatic exit and slammed the door behind him. I continued to watch the Doctor as he rubbed his chin like he was contemplating what he'd just heard. He hit a number on his phone, but the image was too far to tell who he was calling.

"Hey, it's me. Listen, I want to bump up my vacation plans. Is it possible to leave next week on the cruise?" There was a long pause as Dr. Wallace listened to the person on the other end. A travel agent, maybe? "That's great. My wife will be thrilled we get to leave sooner. Thank you."

The doctor walked out of the room, discussing the other minimal decisions about the trip change. It was a shame he'd never get to the boat. He'd be dead long before then.

The golf course estates only had one entrance, and there was a fancy mall that sat at the corner. I wheeled the truck into the lot. It was one of those high-end spots with a spa, including a hair and nail salon. There were a couple of boutiques, a café, and a juice bar—the perfect place for all the rich yuppies to go. I could only hope that I made it to the parking lot in time to see Jason as he left. I tapped my fingers on the steering wheel as I kept my eyes peeled for the man.

"Thank you, Adalyn," I whispered.

I was certain her spirit was helping me on my journey as Jason pulled up to the set of lights. I slowly made my way out of the exit and was all too happy to have the four vehicles coming down the road slip between me and my prey. The guy was paranoid enough as it was. I didn't need him to think he saw me following him around.

The drive to the beach was tricky, and I thought I'd lost him more than once, but lady luck shone her light on me as I chose the right direction each time I lost sight of the red Civic. This end of the beach was not near the touristy area, and the cottages were on older property lots. Meaning they weren't crushed so closely together that there was no privacy.

Jason was a little larger than a dot in the distance when he turned into a driveway. A swell of joy flowed through me, and my blood pounded a little harder with the prospect of delivering the punishment to Jason that he so rightly deserved. As I drove past, I peered up the drive and spotted Jason heading from the cottage to the car to close the door as he carried some groceries inside.

Grabbing the phone, I pulled up a GPS of the area and smiled wide as I spotted the public parking lot not too far down the road. Maybe God had forsaken me, but the devil had taken this broken soul in and was helping me more than anyone else ever had.

Not
even the
Devil could burn
the world like
I could

Chapter 21

Fear was a relative term that meant many different things to different people. Some people were afraid of heights, and others were afraid of the dark. Some people were afraid of water or spiders. For me, I learned that fear came in the form of someone that was supposed to love and care for me. As hard as I tried, I couldn't remember a single memory that made me smile, other than hanging with my little brother. Asher was the only good thing in my life, but he turned on me in the end too.

The front door slammed, and I jumped up from the table with my textbooks in hand and ran. I made it to the bedroom just as the yelling started. The look on my father's face as he came through the door was enough for me to bolt. I'd seen it so many times that I knew what was coming.

Heart pounding, I leaned up against the bedroom door and tried to think.

"What's going on," Asher asked, pulling his feet up so he could hug his knees.

The mop of blond hair covering his eyes like that would hide him somehow. I wished it was that easy.

My father's voice echoed down the hallway as he yelled for Asher and me to come out of our room. I wasn't going out there. My arm was still in a cast from the last time he decided I was being bad. Running across the room, I opened the window. The old frame groaned, but I pushed the large panes out. I looked down at the ground, and it was possible for us to jump, but the sound of my dad's and mom's yelling was getting closer. There just wasn't enough time for both of us to get out. I couldn't leave Ash behind.

I ran over to my bed which was larger than Ash's. "What are you doing?"

I waved Asher over to the bed. "Come on, get under the bed," I whispered.

"But what about dad?"

"Forget him. Don't you dare go out there, or I'll never play with you again," I threatened as big tears filled his eyes. "Come on, get under, and I won't be angry." He unfolded himself and tiptoed across the room to get down and slip under the bed.

"Derek! You piece of shit, get out here! You better not be ignoring me, boy."

"They're studying. Just leave them alone."

"Get out of my way, woman." A thud hit the wall, and I knew it was my mother, but my father must have pushed her and kept walking. My heart hammered hard as the heavy boots thumped louder. I got down and slid under the bed in one single sliding motion. I pushed Asher as close to the wall as I could. My hands shook as I put a finger over my lips, silently telling him to be quiet."

The door slammed open, the sound echoing loudly with the heavy bang of the door handle smacking into the wall.

"Please, I'll get you dinner and a beer. Just leave the boys alone."

"That piece of shit needs to be taught a lesson. He skipped school! This behavior is your fault. You're too soft on him."

There was a loud crack, and my mother yelped.

"I had to take that call at work and then waste my time meeting with the principal."

"That's my fault, he had an appointment, but I didn't get the school called in time."

"Stupid bitch."

I sucked in a slow breath as the sinking feeling that had accompanied so many nights as this one rang in my ears. Asher's eyes filled with tears, and I slid my arm around his body and pressed his face into my chest, trying to comfort him and praying that he'd remain quiet a little longer.

The vibration of the heavy boots had me clenching my eyes shut as he stomped across the room. "The little fucker ran off and took Asher with him."

"Please, Phil, leave the boys alone. They were scared," my mother pleaded.

"That's because Derek is weak, and you encourage it."

A small scream made me dare to look over my shoulder at the two sets of feet that were toe-to-toe.

"He's gonna end up a faggot. No son of mine will be a weak little queer."

A loud smack made my body jerk a moment before my mom landed hard on the wooden floor. The side of her face was bright red and matched the dark bruise and open gash that was dripping blood. Our eyes locked, and I thought we were dead, but she didn't say anything.

"Phil! Stop, no," my mom yelled as she was dragged out of the room. I watched her slippers disappear around the corner. Tears filled my eyes, but there was no point in crying. Crying only made things worse. This could all be over if she would just leave. I'd begged her multiple times to

pack, and we'd go somewhere, anywhere she wanted, but she always refused.

Asher sniffled into my T-shirt.

"It's going to be okay. I'll protect you. You're my brother, so I'll always protect you," I whispered into Asher's ear as something crashed in the bedroom.

"I love you," Asher mumbled, his small shaking fists clung to my shirt.

I covered his ears as best as I could as the sound of the bed slammed into the wall, and the loud animal grunting noises started.

I softly hummed the Spiderman theme song in his ear as we clung to one another until the snoring started. It was the only time I took a deep breath, the only time I felt like I could breathe at all. Even then, I slept with one eye open and my clothes on, ready to run.

The sunset had been stunning tonight. A bright fireball orange with a pink hue made it look like it was a slow-moving fire. The brilliance was so pure that it warmed my cold heart to stare at it.

I nibbled on the stale bag of cheese puffs as I waited for it to be dark enough for me to make my move. The puff didn't crunch the way it was supposed to as I popped another one into my mouth. I'd missed these miniature cheesy snacks of pure heaven. I held another up before slipping it into my mouth, so many little things I'd missed while locked up. It was a marvel that they tasted the same, yet I was thankful because I could count on one hand the number of things that hadn't changed.

This beachfront view was truly stunning, another thing I thought I'd never see again. My eyes fell on a couple casually walking along the edge of the water. They had a dog following along with them, playing with a stick, and I wondered what that would be like to have that kind of companionship. To be so relaxed, to be in love, and to have something normal.

I looked around the public picnic area that was situated a half-mile away from my target. I'd managed to keep my anger at a simmer so far. But the thought of what my normal life could've been if Jason and the others hadn't entered my room that night was like a lighter creating a flame.

I watched as the water lapped onto the beach and washed away the footprints, leaving it unmarred, like humans had never been. I wished my memories were as easy to erase, but unfortunately, the tide never came in far enough to wipe mine away.

As the last of the setting sun disappeared on the horizon, I pushed open the truck door, the old hinges complaining with a loud squeak. I was going to need to fix that. It would never do to stalk someone only to be given away by a complaining door hinge. I grabbed my trusty duffel bag off the seat and made sure the black hood of my hoodie was hiding my face. There weren't any cameras that I could see, but one could never be too careful.

I stayed close to the edge of the tree line that fed out onto the beach. I wasn't a fan of stumbling across something in the bush that I didn't want to meet in the dark—human or otherwise.

Kneeling down as I reached my destination, my eyes searched for any sign of Jason and found him sitting on the back deck. The subtle glow of the little decorative lights hanging from the pergola gave off just enough light to show the man as he sat there drinking a beer. He put the bottle to his lips, and a small part of me hoped it tasted good because it would be his last. The next closest cottage was a good quarter mile down the beach, giving this place tons of privacy from prying eyes.

By the time Jason got up and went inside the small cabin, my knees and hips were locked in place from kneeling so long. I was kind of sad that this pretty little spot would be destroyed. I was tempted to drag him out into the woods to save the white cabin structure, but I wasn't one to change course once I had a good plan in place.

Hand clenched around the duffel like it might try and run, I slipped from the cover of the trees to jog across the grassy backyard. The deck was surprisingly quiet and only gave out a small groan as I made my way to the top. Grabbing the glass door, I gave it a tug and froze as it moved. Body ridged and senses on high alert, I searched the darkness inside, my eyes able to make out the furniture, but there didn't seem to be anything out of place.

Something wasn't right. The person I saw on the video at the doctor's house was a man that was in panic mode. If a person were that scared, he wouldn't forget to lock the door, especially if he feared for his life. I was tempted to leave, to rethink the strategy, but that seemed like a waste of time. I knew the man was inside, and I hadn't seen anyone leave from the front or the back unless he crawled out a window on the far side.

Hand twitching for the kill that was to come, the monster that fed my soul what it needed—encouraged me to walk in and take the risk. My boot stepped across the threshold, and as it did, a cool breeze rose the hair on my arms like a spirit had just passed through me. I sucked in a deep breath, comforted by its presence, and could picture Adalyn standing beside me.

I pulled the hunting knife from my belt as I sat the duffel down out of the way. The shadows that lurked in the corners were part of me. They were an extension of my black soul, the cloak that wrapped itself around the monster on the throne in my mind.

I'd been in graveyards that had more noise than this place. There was no fan or creak to be had—it felt like I'd stepped into a bubble of silence or a different world. As I crept along the hallway to inspect the rooms, I half expected to see the strange ghost thing of my father come crawling out at me. The eerie sensation was enough to make my hand tighten on the blade I held.

The knob of the first door turned as quietly as everything else in the house. Pushing the door open slowly, I scanned over the room's nautical-themed decorations. The only thing that stood out was a row of dolls that sat on the window's ledge across from the door. I moved a little from side to side, and I'd swear the things were watching me.

Fucking freaky.

I turned to make my way to the next room when something large tackled me around the waist and drove me to the floor with a crash. The knife banged as it fell from my hand and then slid under the bed. Fists rained down on my head, and I lifted my arms to protect myself from the heavy blows.

"You fucking prick, you won't get me." Jason's angry voice penetrated the silence.

As Jason lifted his arm for another swing, I gave his side a hard jab and pushed against his chest, but the man was like a damn squishy boulder. I didn't remember the man being this strong or heavy.

"Ahhhhh," he yelled as my fist made contact with his kidneys for a second time, but the little victory was short-lived as his elbow crashed down onto my nose.

"Fuck," I bit out as my vision went black from the initial blow.

The fury that fueled me soared up from the pit of my stomach and filled me. We were a mass of arms and legs as we each landed punches on our opponent. Like a pair of fighting octopuses, we rolled around on the floor. We crashed into the wall, and the creepy dolls decided to dive-bomb us as they fell off the shelf.

Two crashed, their faces breaking on impact, but one was left with part of a face and a creepy eye. That shit right there was right out of a horror movie. The third one smashed Jason in the back of the head and had him swearing. I laughed until a fourth of the eerie suicidal dolls cracked me in the forehead.

Fucking demon dolls.

Having enough of this entire situation, I pushed Jason off to the side, his back slamming into the bed leg. Rolling onto my side, I brought my knee up to try and stand, but in Jason's haste to get the upper hand, my knee drove right into his ball sac. I snickered as his body went slack and his hands grabbed at his junk. Any wrestler would be proud of this show we were creating. I stood and then dropped a knee down onto his chest, and the man gasped for air as he clutched at his sternum.

Standing upright, I growled as I brought the heel of my boot down onto Jason's jaw. An overwhelming frenzy erupted in my chest as my boot found one soft spot after another until Jason was a whimpering mass of human flesh.

Grabbing the man by the collar of his shirt, I dragged his fucking heavy ass out of the small bedroom door, slamming his head into the frame as I went.

"No," Jason suddenly said. Taking me by surprise, he grabbed my leg mid-stride, and with a yell, I fell forward and slammed off the round kitchenette table. My face crashed into the wood along with my side, and I knew that was going to leave a mark. The two chairs skittered across the floor and clattered onto their sides. My weight flipped over the table and had it rolling away. I jerked on my leg, but the fucker was hanging onto me like a damn ball and chain.

"You brought this on yourself, Jason."

"I never intended to hurt her."

"And yet you did."

Jason glared at me from where he clung to my jeans, his fists balled up into large fists. "You're not killing me, you crazy piece of shit."

A snarl lifted my lips like a hellhound had invaded my body as the words 'piece of shit' rang in my ears.

"Big fucking mistake, dad," I hollered as my foot found my father's face again and again. Panting hard, I collapsed back on the floor and made the decision to listen to my instincts next time.

Fuck, that hurt.

I touched my side, and it was definitely going to be badly bruised after this.

Groaning, I yanked my foot away from the prick's grasp and limped to my bag. I glanced behind me as Jason rolled over onto his back. I had to give him credit—he'd given me way more of a fight than I'd expected. Reaching into the duffel bag, I grabbed the black zip ties and made my way back to Jason.

He tried to pull his hands away from me, but I'd had enough of this shit and zip-tied him like I was hog-tying a cow. I did the same thing to his feet in record time.

"You know Jason, I didn't even know who the fuck you were until you showed up in my room that night. The few times you'd been forced to take me from my room, you always seemed like you didn't want to do it, and I gave you a pass in my mind. This really didn't have to go down like this, but what you did was unforgivable. You raped Adalyn, Jason. You say you didn't want to or didn't enjoy it, yet you managed to get it up more than once. So don't you fucking lie to me."

My hands were shaking as I turned around, holding onto a small propane tank with one of the bricks of C4 attached to it and a roll of silver duct tape.

Blood was running down my face, so I wiped it off, wincing as my arm ran over the cut above my eye. It was probably going to need stitches, but what the hell did it matter if I had one more scar when you had a face like mine.

"Please, man, I don't want to die. Jim ordered me to do it, or I'd be fired."

I paused and looked down at him.

"So, what you're saying is that your job was more important than doing the right thing? Then destroying a sweet woman's soul?"

Tears slid down Jason's face, and I felt nothing for this creature, this slob of a man that didn't deserve to continue breathing.

Squatting down, I took in the agony that was etched into his features, the fear that was tearing him up inside. Grabbing his face, I forced him to look at me. "Don't worry, Jason, it will all be over very quickly, which is generous considering the crime."

"You can't judge me. You killed four people. Your actions landed you in that place, and then you killed hundreds when you escaped." Spittle flew from Jason's mouth and landed on my sweater.

"I'm not going to waste my breath explaining the whys of my actions to you."

I smacked the small propane tank down hard onto his crotch and loved the instantaneous groan-whimper. His chest heaved as he continued to struggle. I had to give him credit. Most would've given up by now. I taped the thing in place and gave it a pat.

"So, you think you'll feel your dick being blown off before the rest of your body is ripped apart? Huh, interesting thought for later."

"What can I do? How can I make this right? I'll do anything, Derek, please."

My finger traced along the line of my chin as I contemplated the request, but nothing came to mind. The only thing he could do to make this right was to die.

"Sadly, Jason, there is simply nothing you can do. I have nothing left, so there is nothing you can do to make this better."

I smacked my hand off my leg.

"I almost forgot." I wandered around the space until I found his wallet and then got down on the floor in the small room to grab the knife.

Kneeling down, I stared under the bed. My hand froze as it slid over the handle of the blade. Asher's scared face floated in front of my eyes as the bang of the door in my mind made me jump. Closing my eyes, I braced my arm on the bed and tried to settle the racing in my heart.

Steeling myself from the memories and weak emotions that were threatening to take over, I pushed myself to my feet. Thumbing through his wallet, I found only cash. There was nothing else useful.

"Thanks," I said, holding up the wad of cash and dropping the empty wallet onto his chest.

Jason made one last valiant effort to wiggle out of this. I watched as he literally tried to inchworm his way across the floor on his side.

"You're a pain in my ass Jason," I grumbled. "Just accept this is going to happen. You were meant to die tonight. The spirits guide my hand."

"You're fucking crazy, man," Jason whined as I once more grabbed him by the feet and hauled his ass into the center of the room.

I quickly finished setting up the C4 by adding the blasting cap and attaching the detonation line that would be just long enough for me to get out of the cabin and far enough away from the deadly debris.

I strung out the line and wandered back over to the struggling man, giving him a hard right hook across the face. That did the trick, you annoying prick. I wandered over to the couch and groaned as I picked up the heavy wooden piece of furniture. It had to have a bed inside it because it weighed way too much. My muscles strained with every step, but I wanted to make sure Jason stayed put this time. He was proving to be a slippery one.

"Please...god...don't," he wheezed with the weight on his chest.

Arranging the couch over Jason, I let it go and then leaned on it as I stared into his eyes."This is what was always going to happen, Jason. Your master whispered in my ear, calling you home, but God is not his name." My lip curled up as I stood and grabbed my things before making my way to the sliding glass door.

"Goodbye, Jason. I'm sure I'll see you again. You all tend to visit me."

Pushing down on the rowel of the lighter, I lowered it to the line but kept my eyes on Jason's horror-filled face the entire time. I wanted to savor every second I could.

The loud hiss started a little flame that made its way across the floor like an animal sniffing out its prey. Grudgingly, I took off, ran for the spot I'd arrived at, and darted behind a large palm tree, getting low to the ground. The cabin blew, and the explosion had been a lot louder than normal. The added propane probably did the trick.

I peered around the tree. A smile spread across my face as the sparks and debris fluttered to the ground. What was remaining was burning bright, an unearthly beacon to those dark and twisted creatures that wanted Jason's soul.

I could almost see the wispy shapes sliding and crawling across the beach to reach what they desired. Not able to stay any longer, I tossed the pack over my shoulder and jogged for the truck.

Reaching my wheels, I quickly tossed the bag inside and hopped in. A shudder raced through my body as the image of the beach cottage and Jason's face danced erotically in my mind.

Grabbing the steering wheel, I squeezed, trying to hold back the violent sexual reaction that was coursing through my body.

"Aww," I groaned as my cock kicked inside my jeans. Frantic and unable to control the urge any longer, my hand shook as I unzipped the jeans and released my throbbing cock. I sighed as my still gloved hand with the smattering of blood on it gripped my hard length and stroked.

"Fuck," I groaned out.

Soft moans tumbled from my mouth as I closed in on the release I was after. I felt like I was standing on the edge of the cliff, sliding into something otherworldly. The rapture with each stroke was intense, and I had to grab the extra T-shirt on the seat to catch the explosion that was about to erupt from the tip of my cock. I slammed my head back into the headrest, my body flexing with the force of the climax, which felt as powerful as any C4.

"Ahhhhh!"

The scream was a mixed bag of pleasure and pain each time my hand slid from base to tip as my orgasm pounded through me. As the pulses ebbed, the emotional aftermath flowed through my body like a spiritual enlightening. It was as if I'd finally found what I'd been after for longer than I could remember.

Every fire, every lick of flame had been building me toward this moment, this awakening as the pleasure finally quenched what I'd been searching for and could never quite achieve. Even sweet Adalyn's arms couldn't compare to this moment. The guilt only added to the strange mix of emotions that were gripping me.

I wanted to do it again.

I could just see the glowing through the trees, but that was too dangerous. I needed to be smart. Quickly cleaning up, I pulled the truck out onto the road with a smile gracing my lips as my cock promised more pleasure when I got home.

The darkness had nothing on me.

Not
even the
Devil could burn
the world like
I could

CHAPTER 22

Silence is deadly for someone like me—deadly for my mind and most certainly deadly for others. *Click.* The lighter flared to life, and I stared at the tiny flame that wavered with the gentle breeze of the fan. The woosh of the fan blades spinning was the only other sound in the room as I stared at the peeling wallpaper.

The soft scent of the mold that I hadn't been able to get rid of fully was strong from the rain steadily assaulting the roof. My eyes flicked to the ceiling to watch another drop fall into the bucket waiting below with that signature *ping* sound. The dripping added to my little musical choir, compliments of the fan and lighter.

Whoosh, whoosh, rattle, click, ping.

An image of the asylum flashed through my mind and then was replaced with Jim as he and his girlfriend wailed. Seeing the apartment building where Dave met his end had me sucking in a breath before it was replaced with the men hanging from the football goal posts and that little bitch with her fancy car. But the one that kept my dick twitching was Jason's sister's beach cottage.

I wondered if she wept more for her brother or her cottage? I'd have bawled like a baby over the cottage and not shed a tear for the prick that got his just desserts inside. I had one more on my list. One more soul whose blood the demons in my mind screamed for, and then I hoped to be at peace. I hoped that Adalyn would finally be able to rest.

Avenge me. The words played on a constant loop in my mind like a broken record—Adalyn's sweet voice whispering to me from beyond and helping to guide my hand. *Avenge me.* The voice echoed again, and goosebumps rose across my skin, making me gasp as my eyes closed. *Avenge me.*

"I will, Adalyn, I will, but not tonight." My eyes looked to the darkness outside as the rain continued hitting the window. "I need it to stop raining first."

I wanted the good doctor's death to be special. Flicking on the little lighter again, I held up the cutout of the latest newspaper headline and grinned. I knew that the cops knew it wasn't a propane tank issue, but that's what the headline said. There was something so satisfying about seeing my work in print—to know that even if I was ever caught again, what I'd done would go down in history and stand the test of time as epic.

Digging around in my pocket, I pulled out my phone and swiped to my newest obsession. Dr. Wallace was looking a lot more stressed these days. His normally perfectly styled hair was a mess, his normally clean-shaven face definitely hadn't been touched by a razor in a number of days, and his clothes were stained with god only knew what.

"That's right, Doctor, feel the pressure of what it's like to live under someone's thumb. Have you reached that pressure cooker moment yet where you're just ready to snap? Ready to explode on the next person that walks through your door? I want you to feel what it's like not to know what the next day will bring and if it will be the last time you see the sun. That was every day for me for *nine years.*" I leaned forward and stared at the image of the man pacing his living room. "*You* wouldn't last nine years—you're barely keeping it together, and it's only been a day since Jason's unexpected demise."

Dr. Wallace began talking to someone I couldn't see, but as his wife and daughter came into view, both of them pulling a suitcase, I started laughing. She was leaving his sorry ass. I laughed even harder, stomping my feet on the ground as I clutched the phone a little tighter. His wife had just earned herself a free pass in my mind for walking away from that man.

"No, no, please don't go. I'll make this right. He'll never hurt you," I mocked in the doctor's voice. "I'm begging you, please, oh pretty please, with cherries on top."

"I can't stay here anymore. Whatever mess you made, you lay in it," I said, pretending to be his wife, and giggled again far louder than I should. It wasn't really that amusing, but I was getting a front-row seat to the doctor's life crumbling around him, and that made me happy. Very, very happy.

As a quiet knock sounded through the house, I whipped my head toward the door. I hadn't seen or heard a car pull in. Shutting off the phone, I set it down to fill my hand with a knife instead, rotating the handle around as I contemplated who it could be.

Using the knife, I peeled away a corner of the material covering the side window. The light was so bright I groaned and stumbled back, covering my eyes.

"Derek, I saw you moving in there. Come on, open up."

I recognized that voice, but it took a moment for it to register that it was Dora. I opened the door a foot, having to cover my eyes with my arm as the bright sun blinded me.

"Every time I see you, you look worse. Have you showered or eaten anything? And what the hell happened to your face? Open the door, boy, right this minute." Dora gave the door a little shove that had about as much effect as a bird hitting a window, but I moved back and let her in any way.

Striding up to me, Dora grabbed me by the chin and moved my head from side to side as she inspected me.

"Come on, come sit down," Dora demanded. I let the little gray-haired woman lead me to one of the chairs in the kitchen and sat when she pointed to a chair. "What in tarnation is going on in here?"

As Dora turned in a circle and looked around, I blinked and turned my head to do the same, and I had no idea what to say. Huh. Every window was now covered with cardboard and makeshift drapes made out of sheets. She didn't seem to care that I'd obviously done this on purpose, as she immediately marched over to the windows and ripped off the material. Groaning, I cringed away from the brightness like a vampire trying to escape from burning in the sun.

"Boy, I have no idea what is going on with you, but I'm taking this shit down, and then you're coming with me to my house so I can get you cleaned up and fed. Do you even remember what day it is? And why are you holding a knife? You planning on killin' me too, boy?" Dora fumed, her small hands ripping away all the cardboard that I couldn't remember putting up or why.

With each uncovered window, I could see more—the light broke through the darkness, puncturing holes in the fog that had settled in my brain. I looked down at the long hunting knife in my hand.

"I thought you were someone else," I said.

"Ever think the reason you don't have friends is 'cause of your sunny disposition?"

"I don't need friends." Standing, I slid the knife home into the holder on my belt. I pulled out the phone I'd been looking at a moment ago and saw that the battery was dead.

"What day is it?"

Dora stood with her small hands on her hips and shook her head.

"I'm not tellin' you nothin' until you agree to come with me and get cleaned up." I opened my mouth to argue that I had more important things to worry about than showering and eating, but the old woman poked me in the chest, cutting me off. "You will come with me right this moment, Derek. I'm not playing. I was a nurse, and that bump and cut on your head should've been seen by a doctor. We're seeing to it now. After that, if you want to run off and try to get yourself killed again, that's your choice."

"Okay." Once more, I let Dora lead me wherever she wanted, and as she pulled me outside, I stared around at the ground. Where was the rain? Why wasn't the ground wet? How did the sun come up so fast? "Dora, when did it stop raining?"

She paused as we reached the dusty driveway and looked up at me.

"Two days ago. Come on, Derek, get in the car. *I'm* the one going insane. We can't have both of us losing our damn mind—then who would look out for who?"

I had a new appreciation for the fear that I saw in Dora's eyes as I got into the car on the passenger side. As hard as I tried, I couldn't remember anything past right after arriving back at the house after killing Jason. I'd whacked off until my dick was raw, and then...nothing.

I stared at the cows in the field closest to the road and was thankful that I'd set up the automatic waterer, and they had three pastures' worth of fields to eat.

Pulling down the sun visor, I flipped open the little flap over the mirror and didn't recognize myself. Dark circles surrounded my eyes, and I now had the beginnings of a solid beard forming. My skin looked paler than normal, and I could tell I was very dehydrated with a quick pinch. I genuinely looked like a bag of shit, and that was before I took in the greenish bruise on the left side of my cheek, the still-weeping gash on my forehead, which I remembered getting at Jason's, and the lump beside the gash which announced I'd hit my head hard at some point that I didn't remember.

Flipping up the sun visor, I realized that the drive was already over. Dora got out of the car and came around as I opened my door. I didn't think I needed any assistance and had no idea what the little waif of a woman would do if I did fall, but she insisted on taking me by the arm to guide me into her home. It smelled like fresh baking, and as if my body were finally remembering what food was, my stomach let out a loud grumble as a sharp pain lanced my stomach.

"Sit at the table. I'll get you some food, and then we're taking care of that head of yours."

She reminded me of a little worker bee in the way she flitted around the kitchen, going from one thing to the next as if she were buzzing around looking for nectar. A plate seemed to magically appear in front of me piled high with roast beef on fresh bread, with a generous salad on the side.

As soon as I took the first bite, I turned into a ravenous dog. I may not be able to remember the last time I ate or drank anything, but my body was telling me it had been a while. Dora sat down a glass of water and a pitcher to refill it, and I grabbed the water, chugging the first glass down before pouring another.

"Hold up there, boy, you're going to make yourself sick." Dora placed her hand on my shoulder, the act comforting and calming.

I forced myself to sit the glass down and took another bite of the delicious sandwich. Dora sat down across from me and picked up what I thought might be some kind of needlepoint needle. She was quiet as I ate, her hands steady as she poked the needle and thread through the material and back again as she slowly created her art piece.

"Can I have another?"

"Not yet. You may throw up what you just ate. Let's see if it stays down first, and then you can have as many as you want. I also made lemon loaf and orange and cranberry cookies."

Setting down her crafting supplies, Dora stood up, but instead of going for the baked goods, she headed over to a drawer in the kitchen, returning with a small white box with a red cross on it. She nodded toward the phone I had placed on the table.

"Do you want that thing charged?"

"Yeah, please." I watched her as she picked up my phone and made her way over to a small table that held her phone to plug it in. "Why are you nice to me," I blurted out as she slowly made her way back. "I'm not a nice person, Dora. You should run as far away as you can get."

Her laugh was warm, her eyes teasing as she smiled at me. It was rare to have someone not be terrified of me, and yet this woman, who knew more about me than anyone else, seemed as content and comfortable as a cat lounging in the sun.

"And where exactly would I go, Derek?" She flipped open the lid of the first aid kit and began setting items out on the table. "This is my home, and I wouldn't leave it even if I did have another place to go to. Second, I'm pretty sure that you'd hunt me down wherever I ran off to and kill me if I tried."

She opened an antiseptic bottle and blotted some onto a square of gauze.

"Don't give me that look. You know it's true, and I know it's true. This is going to sting."

I sucked in a sharp breath as the cool little piece of material made contact with the cut, and it suddenly felt like someone was stabbing my head.

"But, that's my point. Why be nice to me? I know you said you feel like this is your second chance to help, but I hurt people, Dora. I hurt them, and I enjoy it. I know it's wrong, and yet I still crave going after the next person on my list."

Her hand slowed, her face becoming an emotionless mask.

"Did they deserve it?"

I took a deep breath and shrugged. "In a way, don't we all?"

"I guess you're right, but to answer your question, I don't have a logical answer for you, Derek. When I look into your eyes, I see a damaged soul and the boy I wanted to help. I don't see the man struggling with whatever is twisting you up inside." She pulled out a little white strip, some kind of bandage, and then pinched together the skin on my forehead as she put it in place. "What I see is that boy with immense potential and the man he could still become."

Dora made her way over to the freezer and pulled out a small bag of peas before handing it to me. "Put the peas on that egg you have on your head. It's most likely the cause of your loss of time, but you should really see a doctor."

The bag crinkled as I gripped it hard.

"No doctors. Never again with the doctors."

Dora sighed as she took my plate and began making me another sandwich.

"I figured you'd say that. Today is Saturday, Derek. I last saw you on Monday, and if you had anything to do with that beach home having an unfortunate accident with the propane tank, then that happened Tuesday.

"Four days? What the hell did I do for four days?"

"I don't know. I came by to check on you, but no one answered the door." Dora patted my shoulder as she set a second full plate down in front of me. "I'm worried about you. I'm worried about what will happen to you when I'm gone."

"Gone," I asked as I took a bite of the new sandwich.

"Yes, gone. Could be today, could be a year from now, but I'm an old broad now, and we both know my mind is not right. I could kick it anytime, and I don't want anything bad to happen to you."

Reaching out, I gripped her weathered hand lying on the table. It looked so small, absolutely dwarfed by mine.

"Don't worry about me. I'll be fine," I said, but what I didn't say was that I was worried for everyone else. These moments with her were oddly grounding, and I didn't feel like burning it all down when we sat and talked like this.

"Oh crap," I mumbled, then stood to go over to my phone.

"What's wrong?"

"I just had something to do, and now I'm hoping I didn't miss my window." I tapped on the app that controlled the cameras inside Dr. Wallace's place. I couldn't see anyone on either camera. Come on. He couldn't have taken off. Turning on the volume, I could make out the sound of a television and someone talking, but I couldn't determine who it was.

"I'm sorry to eat and run, but I need to go," I said as I went to unplug the phone.

"Like hell you are." I looked up to see Dora standing at the table with her fists on her hips. Her soft gray eyes glared at me as her mouth pinched together. "Whatever it is you have to do can wait a few hours."

"But...."

"No buts. I don't want to know who you're after this time but look outside. The sun is high in the sky—you have time."

"I can't stay."

"Yes you can, and yes you will. A couple hours, give your body a couple hours. For all you know, you haven't slept in four days."

I looked back down at the screen and the rooms that still didn't hold any actual humans and sighed. Everything in me was screaming to finish this and complete the task, but Dora was right. I was feeling weak and I needed to have my mind sharp. I hit the lock button and laid the phone down to finish charging.

"Okay, you win. I'll lay down for a couple hours, but that's it."

"Deal."

How did I get to a place where I was taking orders from an eighty-year-old woman that I could probably snap in half with one hand? Shaking my head, I laid down on the couch and was surprised to feel the steady pull of sleep as my lids got heavy. Perhaps sleep was a good idea.

Not
even the
Devil could burn
the world like
I could

CHAPTER 23

"**N**o, no, no, Dad, please," I begged. I grabbed his arm and snarled at the man—then my eyes snapped open.

"Ow! Derek, wake up. That hurts." I looked at my hand, which was crushing the life out of the fragile arm in my grasp and then into Dora's pain-filled face. She was on her knees beside the couch, fear in her eyes.

"I'm sorry." I let go of her arm, yanking my hand away like I was burnt. "Shit, Dora, I was dreaming I...." She cradled her arm to her chest, her kind eyes spilling tears.

"It's fine. I just need ice." When she made to stand, I jumped up to help, but she winced away from my touch, her eyes avoiding mine. She shuffled away, but instead of going to get ice, she walked down the hall to the bathroom.

"Shit." I looked down at the palm of my hand and shook my head before making my way to the bathroom. My knuckles rapped against the wood. "Dora, please let me see your arm. I feel really bad. You know I would never hurt you on purpose." I could hear her soft sobs on the other side of the door, and an emotion that I hadn't felt since Adalyn's death roared to the surface. Guilt. It gnawed at my gut, making me feel like the roast beef from earlier was about to come back up.

"It's okay, Derek. I'll be fine. I just need some time alone. You can go do what you need to get done."

"Are you sure?"

"I'm sure."

"I'm really sorry, Dora, like really, really sorry," I said before waiting for her to say something further, but when she didn't emerge or say anything else, I laid my head against the wood and sighed. Pushing away from the door, I made my way outside and hopped into the truck. I would make it up to Dora later. Right now, I had a doctor to visit.

Once back at the house, I settled into preparation mode. Though I'd slept longer than I had intended, I still had lots of time to get my go-bag organized. Today was a day of reckoning.

By midnight, I was stepping out of the tree line that I'd been to so many times now that it felt like home and slipping into the doctor's small shed. Turning on the surveillance app on my phone, I watched as the doctor came up from the basement carrying a basket of clean laundry before disappearing with it upstairs.

The four days hadn't done anything to improve Dr. Wallace's appearance. He looked just as disheveled as before, and his beard was a solid inch longer than the last time I remembered seeing it. I pinched the bridge of my nose, trying to recall anything from those four lost days, but it was a complete blank. Trying to remember just made me feel vaguely woozy.

Annoyed, I shook off the lingering effects of the fruitless attempt and checked the thermometer I'd brought to read the temperature of the air. I couldn't have my load going off prematurely—I snickered at the stupid joke.

In this area, it was normal for cool air to move in for the night only to be replaced by an oppressive heat that made it feel like you'd decided to leave the house wearing soaking wet clothes. I often wondered why the fuck anyone bothered to dry their clothes. We were all drenched after twenty minutes out in the heat of the day. Shaking my head, I refocused on the task at hand.

The temperature was a blissful seventy-nine outside. Perfect. Smiling widely, I checked the knife at my waist before pulling my mask in place and making sure that everyone in the neighborhood was asleep, or at least out of the way. A couple of the houses still had a single light on, but no one was wandering around outside. Darting out from my hiding spot, duffel bag in hand, I squatted down as I reached the air conditioner, which was sitting idle in the cool night air.

First, I needed to disable the cooling agent, and I pulled out pliers to snip the tube that supplied the cool air from the coils. The key to this was to have them blow only hot air—it was the only way that the present I'd left in the ductwork would get hot enough. If left running like this for very long, the whole thing would burn out, but it would run plenty long enough for what I had planned.

Job completed on the first unit, I put the side panel back on and ran over to the next house in line to do the same thing to that air conditioner. It didn't take too long for all the houses in the row to be ready for the final phase. I ran like a track star through the shadows until I was outside of Dr. Wallace's sliding back door.

I checked on the good doctor again, but the house was dark this time, and the only audible sound was the soft rumbling of what I assumed was snoring. The doctor most certainly didn't seem to care that Jason was dead despite his apparent panic right after Jason had spouted his theories. Maybe he somehow actually didn't know Jason was dead, though it would be hard not to unless they couldn't identify the body. I shook my head. I couldn't worry about that right now.

What if it's a trap? My hand stilled as I reached into the black bag at the whisper from the voice in my head. *What if it's a trap and they're going to take you to prison where you're trapped in a different cage?*

As long as Dr. Wallace died, I didn't really care if it was a trap. If I died inside with him, I would be at peace with that decision.

Pulling out the glass cutter and suction cup from the duffel bag made it feel a whole lot like I was in a spy movie. I'd found a place on the internet that had millions of videos with everything you could imagine. They showed you anything you'd ever wanted to know and many things you wished you never saw. A blessing and a burden on the creators, I'm sure. Truly a blessing for me.

Setting the suction cup, I did exactly what I'd practiced doing numerous times on the old glass panes that rested against the side of the barn. The sound of the cutter scoring the glass was sharp but didn't last long as I drew a circle around the suction cup. With a bit of pressure, the circle of glass popped free. Pulling the piece away, I stuck my hand inside the hole and unlocked the door.

Dr. Wallace probably thought he was safe with his fancy security equipment, but the problem was that I'd already been in the house, and that meant I'd already taken down the pin code for the security system. As soon as I pulled open the door, it started to beep, and I darted up the lower stairs to the front door to punch in the code to disarm the system.

Gripping my knife I listened for a sign of anyone moving in the house, but all was quiet. My heart pounded a little harder at the prospect of my goal being so close. I allowed the sensation of the hunt to fill, excite me, and push me toward my goal. I didn't leave the contents of any room to chance and slipped into each and every one to check for anyone unexpected before moving on.

The soft rumble I'd heard on the phone filtered down the stairs the closer I got to the bottom step. The carpet was plush and soft underfoot, exactly how I'd always pictured the carpet in a house like this would be. Numerous pictures of Dr. Wallace and his family hung from the walls. The trophy wife, with her wavy brunette hair and perfect tan, had a bright smile full of bright white teeth that practically glowed in every image. The daughter, on the other hand, didn't look as happy. She looked like her father and even had an identical scowl on her face.

The place was extremely large. There was absolutely no reason that a family of three needed a house with seven fucking bedrooms. Were they planning on renting the things out? If they got bored with the room they were in, did they move around from room to room? Everything was over the top, overdone, and, much like the man himself, a pretty lie on top of something ugly buried beneath the surface.

Each space I searched was empty. Nothing moved, yet the anticipation before entering each room had the blood pounding hard in my veins. Finally reaching the owner's suite, I stuck my head inside, and there he was. Dr. Wallace was lying face down on the bed, spread eagle in navy-colored sleep pants, with an empty bottle of whiskey in his hand.

I slunk across the room, tempted to use my blade and end the job this minute, but the darkness twisted around my soul and screamed that it wasn't punishment enough.

Kneeling, I stared directly into the face of the man that had controlled my every move for the last nine years. The man that had fed me drugs like they were fucking candy, and the man that had cost me the only precious thing in my life.

It was his fault that Jim had come to my room that night, and it was his fault that I'd gone to such extremes to escape. I may have added the fuel to the fire that stole Adalyn from me, but it was this man that lit the match.

I'd memorized everything about Wallace's face. I'd wanted to make sure I could recognize him even in a darkened room where only my hands could guide me. He'd played god with my life, and I knew exactly what I was going to do next. Instead of me doing it, it was far more entertaining to have Dr. Phil Wallace have to choose if he lived or died. At least he'd think he was getting a choice, but the result would be the same in the end.

Two orderlies were forcibly dragging me down the hall in leg restraints. I had no idea where they were taking me, but even at seventeen, I knew it was never a good thing when your first meeting with a doctor was before the sun came up.

I struggled in their strong grasp. The stupid straight jacket cinched tight around me, stealing all of my strength and ability to fight them off.

"Please, just let me go back to bed. I wasn't doing anything wrong."

"If you're in here, you've already done something wrong," one of the men said.

They'd dragged me into a part of this crazy fucking place I hadn't seen yet—the doors were much heavier, and I shivered as a cold breeze flowed over me. Even wearing scrubs and a straight jacket, all the hair stood up on my body. My heart felt like it was going to pound out of my chest.

"What is this," I asked as I was hauled into a room with a large chair with restraints and a bathtub.

My struggling became more insistent as the men tugged me toward the tub, which was filled with water and ice cubes.

"Welcome, Mr. West. I'm Dr. Philip Wallace, but you can simply call me Doctor. I'll be treating you while you're here with us."

I hadn't noticed the doctor standing in the corner until he spoke, my eyes seeking and finding his behind a pair of wireframe glasses. The name alone was enough to make my blood freeze and my stomach flip. My father's name was Phil, and that name had never meant anything good for me. I had the scars on my body to prove it.

"No greeting? Manners are important, Mr. West. It's customary to say 'hello' or 'how are you,' maybe even 'nice to meet you' when you are meeting someone new," he drawled, sounding far older than he looked. I guessed his age to be in his early forties, which seemed young for a head doctor at a hospital for the mentally ill, but who the fuck was I to judge?

"Why should I bother? Being nice landed me here."

The doctor stepped forward and tapped his chin. It was an action I instantly found irritating.

"Interesting. So, you feel that murdering four people is being nice?"

"Ridding the world of fucktards is," I said before yanking again on my arms, which the men had yet to release.

"Well, I'm not here to hurt you, Mr. West. I'm here to help you." I searched the doctor's simple features. He had one of those forgettable faces that you'd lose in a crowd—and maybe you'd want to. His face was a little too long for his jaw to be considered strong, and his eyes were a little too narrow, making him seem rattish. I'd already met enough liars in my life to know that this man genuinely believed what he was saying. The fact that he didn't look like or consider himself a monster, and yet I was still standing in what could only be some sort of old-ass therapy room, screamed just how fucked up this place really was.

"Yeah? Prove it. Let me go."

"As in, let you out of the hospital to roam the world free?" The doctor laughed, and the orderlies snickered behind me, which sent blood racing through my body.

"I've been assigned to help you so that you won't be a threat to others once you're rehabilitated and freed into the world. Simply letting you go so you can continue to build on your skills and kill more people is not the way to accomplish that."

"I don't want to kill more people. I tried to tell the guy that came to speak to me that I killed the ones I did for a reason, but I don't want to hurt anyone else."

Dr. Wallace took another step closer, his eyes searching my face.

"I believe that you believe that, but someone like you, a firebug—that seed only sprouts with time. No, this is the right thing to do so that you don't end up a blooming flower of chaos and destruction."

I couldn't help but raise an eyebrow at the man. To date, that had been the strangest description I'd ever heard used to talk about someone.

"A flower doesn't sound all that bad."

"I'm not here to quip with you, Derek," he said, drawing out my name like it was disgusting to say. His eyes suddenly flashed with an evil that I'd also seen way too much of in my seventeen years, and I realized there was no way I was getting out of this place, not ever, and especially not alive. "I'm here to help cure your obvious dark desires and manic behavior."

"Um, how do you know I have anything like that? We've never spoken," I asked, and Dr. Wallace rolled his eyes at me.

"Jason, get him in the tub, and then we will see how the new electrotherapy machine works." Dr. Wallace's eyes found mine again, and this time when he smiled, I could see the sadism shining back at me. My father always had that look in varying degrees—the biggest difference was that my father was like a raging bull while the doctor here was far more cunning. He was a snake in the grass, lying quietly until his moment to strike presented itself.

The one thing I could tell they had in common was that as long as you were suffering some form of mental or physical pain, they were happy.

"Please don't do this," I begged and then started to struggle as he nodded to the men behind me, who simply picked me up off the ground. "No, no, please don't do this!"

"It's for your own good, and for the good of the world, that we reset your brain and your thinking, Derek. We need to make sure you never want to start a fire again."

I fought as hard as I could, but it was no use, and within moments I was submerged in the ice-cold water. Water had to be flying around the room as I kicked hard, but they held me firmly down until I almost passed out. The men lifted me just enough that my head rose above the water and let me take a couple of breaths before shoving me back under the surface. I looked up from under the clear, freezing water full of chunks of ice at Dr. Wallace's distorted face as he smiled at me.

I knew at that moment that one day if I lived, I'd kill him too.

I shook off the memory. Not making a sound, I wandered back down the stairs to finish my prep. Then I'd wait. If the fucker had gotten too drunk...well, then I'd make sure he was awake for the surprise.

As I suspected, Dr. Wallace was still very passed out by the time I was through with the prep, but it was time. He needed to wake up. He was the star of the show, after all—it wouldn't do any good at all if he slept through his solo performance.

Making my way up the stairs, I walked into the en suite bathroom, which was as big as a high school locker room, and stared down at the oversized tub. This thing was going to take forever to fill, but it didn't matter. I had the time to wait. Turning on the cold water, I paced the hall and stared at the man on the bed, who had yet to move, as I waited. My impatience got the better of me once it reached half full, and I turned the water off.

"Time to return the favor," I said, marching into the bedroom. With a heave, I tossed him over my shoulder, and though he groaned, he didn't stir awake as we entered the bathroom. "Time to wake up, Doc." With a bounce of my shoulder, I flicked the man up and off, stepping back as he fell into the whirlpool tub.

"What the fuck!" Dr. Wallace swung his arms around wildly, his eyes wide as the shock of the cold acted like a shot of adrenaline to his alcohol-laced system. I waited until his eyes found mine and recognition registered in their shit-brown depths before snatching up a handful of his thinning hair and pushing hard. His hands grabbed for the sides of the tub but slid down the slick acrylic, making a high-pitched squeaking sound.

Hauling his head up out of the water, I watched gleefully as he gasped and spit.

"So, tell me, Doc, does this make you feel better? The medical community would like to know if it makes you feel cleansed and cured of what ails you." Not giving him time to answer, I pushed him under and waited until his eyes screamed that he was about to pass out before pulling him up again.

The little sputtering and blubbering noises he made were delightful, and suddenly I wished that I could play with him all day—repay the man by doing all the sick little tests on him that had taken an emotionally abused teen and turned him into me. He was not the first in line to mold me into this thing or to cause my soul to darken further. He wasn't even the first to stir up the demons in my head and encourage them to stand up and roar, but he would be the last to hurt me.

The part of me that was still human, that loved beyond reproach, had died at the hands of this man.

Using his hair as a handle, I yanked up hard on his head, pulling him from the tub with enough force that his back and ass made a loud smacking sound as they hit the tiled floor.

"Derek...please."

I never slowed my stride as I marched on to the chair I had set up for him for this discussion. I'd even made a pot of coffee, both because I was a fucking nice guy like that and because it was an expensive roast that I was eager to try before I burnt the house to the ground. Why let the beans go to waste?

His ass thumped loudly on the stairs as I dragged him down them by the hair, his yells and weak slaps at my hand comical rather than annoying.

"West, put me down right this second."

"It's Mr. West now, and I no longer take orders from you." The anger and adrenaline riding my body made it easy to throw the doctor into the large reclining chair currently in the middle of the living room. The force of his weight and the momentum from my throw almost tipped the large, comfortable-looking chair over backward. "I don't think you're in a position to issue orders, Doc. In fact, I don't think you're in a position to do anything other than listen."

His eyes were wide and terrified, which was great, but I wanted to talk to the darkness that lived in him. The only thing was, I had a feeling that his darkness was born from feeling supreme over others, while mine was from watching them scream as they died—two very different demons at the same poker table.

I slipped my leg over the seat of the dining room chair that I'd placed backward and across from the good doctor and rested my arms on the chair's tall wooden back.

"Come out, come out wherever you are," I whispered as I stared into the doctor's eyes.

He looked around the room like he was expecting someone else to join the party.

"Who are you talking to?"

"I'm talking to the thing that lives inside of you." Reaching into my pocket, I pulled out my lighter and flipped back the lid to flick the little spark wheel. The doctor licked his lips and stared at the small glowing flame. "The thing that enjoys watching others suffer. The thing that likes to manipulate others and use your authority and position of power to inflict your will onto their body, mind, and soul."

"I don't know what you're talking about."

"Come now, Phil, there is only the two of us here, and no matter what, you're not leaving unless I let you, so you might as well be honest in these last moments of yours." I hit the spark wheel again on the lighter, let the flame burn out, and then hit it again, and again, and again until the doctor's hands clenched on the chair.

"Okay, fine," he yelled as he leaned forward. "I enjoyed hurting you. I enjoyed hurting all of you sick fucks that the courts deemed in need of healing. There is no healing you. You're a sick piece of worthless shit that should've been killed by your father," the doctor spit out before he sucked in a deep breath and slammed a hand over his mouth.

"And there he is. The real Dr. Wallace, please stand up." He went to stand, and I laughed. "Sit your fucking ass down. You wouldn't make it two strides."

Dr. Wallace did as I asked and slowly lowered himself into the chair once more.

"What do you want?"

"I thought that would be self-explanatory. I want you to die, and I want you to suffer, and most of all, I want you to have to choose death for yourself." I bit my lip to keep the twinge in my groin in check. It wouldn't do to have to pull out my cock and rub one out right now. Mind you, the prospect of coming all over his chest while all he could do was sit there being marked like a dog had its appeal.

"You want me to kill myself?" He crossed his arms over his chest and let out a huff. "That's not going to happen. You might as well get it over with, I'm ready."

I smiled widely and tapped on the back of the chair.

"In such a hurry to die, I have to admit that only makes me want to see you suffer longer, but we will see what you say once I'm done explaining your options." I stood up and strolled around the living room, making sure to take a good, long look at the family portrait that hung as the centerpiece of the room. "Nice looking family. Tell me, Doctor, did they decide to leave because of me, or did they decide to leave because you were cheating on your wife with her best friend?"

I let my words sink in as I slowly turned around to face the man or the useless excuse for one, anyway.

"How do you know about that?"

"You mean, how do I know that you've been having an affair with one woman or another for years? Or do you mean how do I know that you've gotten your wife's best friend pregnant, and she's finally left you and your sorry ass? You *do* know that she would've most likely taken you for all the money you have, right? And I have to say, good on you for getting the friend knocked up. Not only did you cheat, and do it in the worst way possible by destroying two relationships, but you couldn't even be bothered to put on a condom so that your pathetic-ass sperm didn't get the woman knocked up. Not so bright there, were ya?" I let out a soft chuckle and held up my finger as his mouth fell open.

"How the hell do you know any of this? They were all private conversations." Dr. Wallace was very obviously starting to panic.

My head tilted, and my lips curled as the malicious part of my personality cheered at the extra victory over the man that had caused me so much pain.

"Because, Doctor, you've underestimated me from the moment I landed in your lap. You thought I was just some weak kid, something you could pick the legs off of like a science experiment—something that would break and fall into line." I hit the little spark wheel again and loved how he shivered in the chair. "But you see, the moment you had those men touch me was the beginning of the end for you." I looked around the living room. "I've always been here, listening to you, watching you. You were always so arrogant, but I could've killed you so many times while you slept or while you ate your fancy steaks, but I chose not to. You're only alive right now because I let you continue breathing."

It was a total exaggeration, but the bulging pulse in Dr. Wallace's neck told me he was buying every word.

"It really is a shame that your very pretty teenage daughter hates your guts for being a cheating piece of dickless meat." I held up the little flame and looked through the orange hue at the portrait on the far wall. "Gotta tell ya, I'm not surprised that she never wants to talk to you again. It's also a shame that this is what your life has come to. Dirty clothes, microwavable dinners, and heavier drinking with each passing day."

Walking over to the portrait, I turned to lean against the wall and ran my finger down the daughter's cheek.

"She really is beautiful. I wonder how beautiful she'll look when I melt the flesh from her bones."

"Don't you dare touch my daughter," Wallace growled out.

"Ah...you didn't mention your wife. That is very telling." I made my way over to the dining room chair that I'd been sitting on and placed my foot on the seat so that I could lean my arms against my knee. "What I do next, and to whom, is going to depend solely on you."

"I don't get it. You're free, and everyone thinks you're dead. Just go, and no one will ever know that you were here or that you're alive."

I laughed hard until tears were streaming down my cheeks and my stomach hurt, but then my face sobered, and I stared him dead in the eyes as I let him see all the hatred and death that swam in their ice-blue depths.

"That will happen anyway." I let the weight of my words fill the room. The only noise was that of the tall grandfather clock as the pendulum ticked back and forth. "You know this whole thing could've been avoided if you'd just never sent Jim and his goons to my room that night. It's your fault that all those people are dead and that the sweetest soul I'd ever met died. Adalyn didn't have to die. Her death is on you."

The doctor shook his head.

"What are you talking about?"

Now it was my turn to stare at the doctor like he'd lost his mind. Had I not burned the asylum down? I wracked my brain to make sure that I was remembering correctly. How else would I have escaped? There is no way that was some big, elaborate dream.

"The hospital. I burnt it down."

"I know that. I mean, what are you talking about with Adalyn? She's not dead."

All the blood in my body sank to the floor as my heart stopped beating in my chest. Narrowing my eyes at Dr. Wallace, I search his face for the lie. He'd spent too many nights manipulating me for me to believe him and yet I wasn't able to help the little bit of hope that flickered to life.

"What the fuck do you mean she's alive?" My voice was gruff when I spoke.

Dr. Wallace shrugged his shoulders. "Just what I said. She wasn't at the asylum. She was at home when it burnt."

"But how is that possible? Her car was in the parking lot." I sat down before I fell from the sudden lightheadedness.

"Her car was in the parking lot because she was taken to the hospital in an ambulance, and she hadn't picked her car up yet."

If she wasn't dead, then who was speaking to me? Who was encouraging me to avenge them? None of this even made sense, and I wouldn't believe it unless I saw her with my own two eyes. Out of my peripheral vision, I spotted Dr. Wallace slowly start to stand.

"I wouldn't if I were you." I turned my head in his direction, and he froze, looking like a mime in the middle of an act. "Sit your ass in the fucking chair." The movement was slow, but the doctor lowered himself into the seat. "Don't worry. You'll have a chance to run."

"I don't understand what you want, Derek. The girl is alive. Go. Run away and be with her. You don't need to kill me."

I hung my head in disbelief. It was like trying to explain logic to someone while bashing my head against a brick wall.

"Do you really think that I'm doing this just because of Adalyn? You're not just a sadist, you're an idiot. Not a great combination." I stood in a rush, and Dr. Wallace pushed himself back into the large chair. "Here's the deal. I'm going to give you a choice of whether you die and do so as a solo performance, or whether you live, which will invite more actors to the stage."

Gripping the back of the wooden chair, I gave it a squeeze, the wood whining from my fingers digging in. It was either the chair or his throat, and I didn't want to kill him just yet.

"I don't know what that means."

"The house is going to go up in flames no matter what you do in—," I said, looking at my watch, "half an hour, give or take a few minutes. The question is whether you die or your family dies." Dr. Wallace didn't say anything further, and I didn't blame him. I wouldn't either if the roles were reversed. "But first, let's make sure we are saving this for prosperity."

I pulled the cellphone out of my pocket and turned on the video app before making my way around the chair and holding the thing, so the screen clearly showed Dr. Wallace's face but nothing more than my arm.

"What are you doing?"

"Don't be so impatient." I hit the voice distortion option I'd downloaded and pressed record. "Ladies, this video is for you. Will your husband and father choose your lives over his own? I don't know. The suspense is killing me. We should ask." I turned to look at the side of the doctor's head as he stared straight into the camera like a deer caught in headlights.

"So, Dr. Wallace, here are your choices. Option A is for you to live. You can run off with your new baby mama and have a happily ever after with your new woman, but if you choose option A with the new woman, then I'll hunt down and kill your wife and daughter. Sorry ladies, but someone has to pay for Dr. Wallace's naughty behavior. Now Doctor, if you choose option B, then you will die here in this house, but your family and new baby mama will remain safe. I'll never go near them, as your debt will be paid in full. Here is the twist to option B. If you choose to stay, then you will have to detonate the house yourself. You will have to kill yourself."

I paused to let the information filter into his pathetic brain.

"Your beautiful daughter doesn't have to die, nor the wife that has loved you all these years that you have treated so poorly—this is your chance to prove that you really did love her more than the ass that you accidentally knocked up. So, Doctor, this is the moment of truth. What is the verdict? Which option will you choose?"

It was total bullshit. The house was going to go up in flames with him inside no matter what, but I wanted him to think there was a choice. It was part of the game, part of the fun, part of the emotional turmoil I planned on putting him through before the fire ate away his life.

"Don't make me do this, please, I'm begging you," he pleaded.

"Doctor, this is a straightforward yes or no question. Did you stop torturing any of your patients when they begged? When they pleaded for you to help them rather than hurt them?" Dr. Wallace swallowed, and the sound was audible. "I'm waiting for an answer, Doctor."

"No, I didn't." Tears rolled down his cheeks, and he removed his glasses to wipe away the crocodile tears. "I'm so sorry. I'm so sorry for so much."

"This is not a confessional, Doctor, this is your sentencing for all of the pain you've caused your family and patients all these years while you smiled with your friends and ate fancy food. It's payment for your part in creating monster after monster while you fucked pretty girls and played golf with colleagues. So let's get on with it, shall we? Option A— run away with your baby mama, or option B—die, but save your wife and daughter? Tick, tock."

The man looked away, and I knew which he'd choose. He was a weak man and an even weaker soul that would sacrifice his own mother to save his skin. Then again, I killed my own mother, so that wasn't a great comparison.

As the seconds ticked on, my patience crumbled.

"Choose," I screamed, and the doctor jumped in his seat and cowered into the corner of the chair.

"A," he whispered with his head lowered.

"I didn't hear you, and neither did your family. Again, and louder this time."

As the doctor glared at me as he lifted his head, the evil that was squirreled away in the recesses of his brain stared out at me.

"I choose option A." He looked at the camera. "I choose A."

"Sorry ladies, I guess we know how much he really loved you, and it's not very much." I turned the video recorder off and stood up straight.

Stuffing the phone into my pocket, I smiled. "Thanks for that. It's going to make this next part so much sweeter."

"What are you...."

The crack from delivering the punch to his face was like a miniature explosion in the silence of the room. The doctor's head snapped back and to the side as he was knocked out cold. I'd already prepped all the ropes, and after kneeling down, I slid them out from under the chair and wrapped them in place, each one rendering the doctor more useless. Gripping his hands, I tied them together and then weaved a longer strand between them, wrapping it around to the back of the chair where it could be secured with a knot. That way, the fucker couldn't wiggle out like Houdini, or at least not too quickly. I smirked, knowing full well he was going to try.

I finished tying the last rope into place and turned the man's chair around so that he had to stare at the large family portrait on the wall. Pulling the packet of smelling salts from my pocket, I held it under his nose, and his eyes snapped open.

"What the hell?" He shook his head. "Ow, fuck." Dr. Wallace went to shift in the seat and only then realized he was tied. I loved watching the recognition of his predicament register in his brain. His breathing became loud as the panic set in. "What is this? You said you'd let me go if I chose."

"I did, didn't I." Turning to jog up the stairs, I snickered as Dr. Wallace yelled for help. In the bedroom, I ruffled through all his drawers and pulled everything out, tossing anything worth money into the duffel bag. Jewelry and cash were the big things, but anything small that I thought could bring in a dollar I took. Pulling out a cigar box, I found a fancy Rolex and gold cufflinks, as well as a grand in cash.

Marching into the closet, I pulled out a box that had a bunch of paperwork from the hospital in it. I was going to leave it, but on a whim, I grabbed a folder and opened the red cover. The name was one that I didn't recognize, but my eyes still scanned over the report. It clearly stated that the person was not in need of psychiatric help, only outpatient therapy.

Placing the folder back, I grabbed the next one, and this time I did recognize the name of a patient that had shown up around the same time I had. The words that stood out were depression and chronic fatigue. There was nothing that said this guy needed to be locked up. What the hell had he been doing in the max security wing of an asylum?

Each folder I pulled out, I quickly looked over before tossing it aside for the next. One thing was identical for every one of these patients—they had no family and no friends. They made the perfect prey.

Reaching into the box, I pulled out another stack, and just like magic, there it was—my name in black and white. I didn't bother reading the entire report, but I found the recommendation on page six.

Mr. West exhibits signs of extreme abuse and trauma. The patient is not criminally insane but a product of his environment of continual abuse at the hands of his father and mother. After a complete and thorough exam of Mr. West, it is my conclusion that although his actions were extreme and resulted in the brutal deaths of four people, those deaths came about from a crime of passion for protecting himself and his younger brother.

Mr. West was in a state of deep emotional angst, which I feel can be helped with therapy. He will require patience to build up his trust in human contact due to the excessive abuse Mr. West has suffered at the hands of his father, the late Mr. West, and the justice system that did not remove him and his brother from the abusive environment.

It is my professional recommendation that Mr. West stay for a maximum of five years in a minimum-security facility where he can still attend school and build relationships in a healthy and safe manner. At such time, he will be reevaluated, and a hearing will be set to see if he is ready to assimilate into society.

Dr. Miller

My hands shook as I read the recommendation from the doctor I'd first spoken to when I was arrested over and over again, my brain trying to comprehend what the words meant. My body trembled with the rage that was consuming me, but my mind was calm. Dr. Wallace knew I wasn't supposed to be there—he knew, and he'd still tortured me, and kept me like a pet lab rat. The man was more of a monster than I'd given him credit for, and I'd considered him to be pretty monstrous.

I quickly stuffed all the files back into the box. Standing, I picked up the box under one arm and the duffel bag under the other as I made my way downstairs, my booted feet landing hard and even on the plush carpet. It caused a thump like a giant was coming.

"Why did you do it?" I asked quietly as I entered the living room.

Dr. Wallace had stopped screaming at some point, and his face was flushed red from his obvious struggles.

"Do what?"

Sitting the box down, I picked up my folder and held it up for him to see. Once more, he licked his lips and didn't say anything.

"Let me guess. I had no living relatives, my younger brother was lost to the system, and I was the perfect prey to play all of your games with, to test out your theories on." I screamed the last part. My body was as hot as any fire, with the fury of the situation running rampant in my brain. I knew the soul crushing sadness would be next, but for now I fed off the anger. "You paid for all this crap off of the backs of people that never should've been in your ward."

I wanted to tear apart the home with my bare hands, but that would draw too much attention from the noise. Even with the houses spaced so far apart, I didn't want to take a chance on the cops being called too early.

"I needed to do research. You were sick, Derek. You still are." He tugged on the ropes. "This is proof of that. And, yes, you're correct that I chose you because no one would miss you."

It took every ounce of self-control I had to not leap across the short distance separating them and choke the man to death. I wanted to rip out his still-beating heart and make him watch as I took a bite out of the fucking thing.

Instead, I kept to my plan. No matter what this piece of shit said, I wouldn't ruin what I had put into place, and with a quick glance outside, I knew I had to get moving. The sun wasn't up yet, but the night sky had shifted from black to gray, which meant I didn't have much time.

"I guess it's fitting, then, that almost no one will remember you, and the few that do will hate you. I'll make sure that all these files are found and that your wife and daughter see that you chose their deaths over yours. That's quite the legacy to leave behind."

"Let me go, you crazy fucker!" Anger was taking over from fear, but I knew the next stage for him would be acceptance, and I didn't want to miss the show from the safety of my hiding spot.

"For the first time I'm realizing that I wasn't the one whose been crazy all this time. Goodbye, Phil Wallace. I'd say it was a pleasure, but we both know that would be a lie." I marched away, ignoring the yelling and screaming. I easily snuck across the grass to the shed and slipped inside. Sitting, I dropped my head into my hands and cried. As the tears streamed out, it felt like something vital was being ripped from my chest, and my mouth opened wide with the force of my silent screams. Truly grasping what I'd lost and the life I could've had—the life that was *stolen* from me—tore away the last fragments of my soul until I felt completely empty.

Dr. Miller had believed me. He'd believed in me and my ability to turn my life around, but Wallace had stolen it all. I was now nothing more than a damaged piece of moving flesh fumbling through life alone and lost. I was officially dead to the world, and only one eighty-year-old woman cared. This was what it truly felt like to be no one.

Taking out my phone, I turned on the app that controlled the little camera inside Dr. Wallace's living room. He was in the same position, but he was thrashing back and forth against the tight constraints. Pulling forward hard, he roared, and I turned on the volume so I could listen to his wails of fear. He reminded me of an animal caught in a trap. Now, if he *really* had balls, he'd chew off his own arm. I checked my watch and the corners of my mouth turned up. The time was drawing closer.

As the hands ticked to seven o'clock, I stood to watch through the window, anticipating what was to come. For a moment, all the houses remained quiet, and then there it was—a flicker of orange flared in the window of one of the houses on the far end of the row. With a resounding boom, the house practically exploded. Windows blew out, and smoke shot from the chimney like a torrent of exquisite destruction. A house in the middle was next, and this time, the fire was instant, all the rooms lighting up and glowing before the home acted like a bomb and detonated with such ferocity that it shook the little shed.

"Well, that is certainly going to wake a few people up." I tore my eyes away from the destruction to see what Dr. Wallace was doing and realized that he was missing. Shit, did he free himself too soon? A brief surge of panic ripped through me as I stared at the empty chair and then back up at his house. And there he was at the back of the house, trying to get out the sliding glass door.

Oh, this was even better. I hadn't expected to watch him in real-time. Reaching down, I squeezed my cock hard through the black fatigues I was wearing as the rat scampered back and forth as he tried to understand why the door wouldn't open. He yanked hard against the handle, but the door jamb I'd set up to keep the door from sliding was holding.

Another house exploded, and he plastered his face to the glass to look down the row. His expression morphed into sheer terror as a neighbor that had wandered outside to check out the commotion was impaled by a fiery piece of debris. The man ran a few strides and then landed face-first on the ground near Dr. Wallace and his uncooperative sliding door.

Dr. Wallace stared at the man and then looked up. As he did, I waved at the good doctor from the window of the small shed. The orange flames suddenly bursting from his air ducts had the appearance of liquid streams of deadly fire. They climbed the walls and spread across the floor so quickly that Dr. Wallace didn't even have time to contemplate his next move before the flames found the edges of his sleep pants and crawled their way up his body.

My cock strained beneath my hand, and I had to grip it hard to keep it from taking over my actions as my eyes took in every detail of the display. I could hear his screams—they filled me with ecstasy. It was the same feeling from Jason's death, but stronger. It was revenge for what he'd done to me, what he'd done to so many, but it was more than that. This glorious moment was enlightening. I felt euphoric as I watched the man suck in his final breaths.

Fuck, I wanted to stroke off to this, but I couldn't leave my DNA behind, so instead, I panted hard as the doctor's struggling form stilled. His body fell and leaned up against the glass.

"Pure rapture," I whispered as his body slid down the glass, leaving streaks of red and flesh behind it. The camera fizzled out and burned up just as the doctor's house vibrated, and then, with the loudest boom yet, it exploded. Brick, shingles, glass, and wood all sailed into the air, some of it raining down on the small shed.

Peeling my eyes away from the sight that filled me with joy, I stuffed my remaining items into the duffel bag and then slipped out of the shed, leaving the box of folders behind. Except for one folder. Mine was mine, and it was coming with me.

I turned as I reached the entrance to the trees to watch the chaos. People ran screaming, some on fire, others simply consumed by fear. This was my calling. This was what I was good at, and this was what made me happy now. As the sound of sirens got closer, I slipped into the shadows. Darkness was the place I was born. It only made sense that I'd return to the darkened shadows as a man.

Not
even the
Devil could burn
the world like
I could

Chapter 24

I couldn't go home, not until I knew if what the doctor had said about Adalyn was true or if he was simply feeding me a line. Could she really have been alive all this time that I'd been out? Could we have been together rather than me being holed up in an old farmhouse alone?

The truck rumbled along down the street, and I made sure to leave the windows open to enjoy the sound of the sirens. I sadly couldn't see the flames from where I was, but I knew they were to my right and over the rise. Multiple sirens of different kinds filled the air, and as I pulled up to a traffic light, a pair of fire trucks, as well as an ambulance and a couple of police cars, flew through the intersection heading in the oppo- site direction—none of them the wiser that they'd just driven past the man responsible for their early morning call.

"Fuck, this is fun," I said, looking in the rearview mirror to watch the lights a little longer. I flicked on a local broadcast station to see if anything was being said yet, but so far, it was still just sports highlights and the usual morning talk that the radio hosts did.

Adalyn had never told me where she lived, and I hadn't paid any attention to her street address when I looked at her registration the night of my escape. However, I did remember that she'd said she loved a particular little market near her home, and the name had stuck in my head. Food Harmony—it sounded like the name of a song when she said it. There was only one in the whole city, which made it easy to track down.

I followed the little GPS on my phone to the location of the market and pulled into the parking lot, but her yellow car was nowhere to be seen. Then again, she could easily have traded it in by now...or she could just not be shopping...heck, she could've switched stores or moved for all I knew. In fact, the only thing I did know was that she said she liked to pick up food for the night and the next day around lunchtime.

Adalyn was big into whole foods that were fresh and local. She always complained consistently about the crap they fed us at the hospital. She'd even gone so far as to sneak in the odd healthy snack for me to have. I didn't have the heart to tell her they tasted worse than the crap they fed us at the asylum because the thought behind it was what had made those nasty snacks taste sweet on my tongue.

This could be a completely fruitless mission, but I had to try. If there was even a chance that my Adalyn was alive, I couldn't walk away. I left the truck turned off but rolled down the windows for my little surveillance mission. I sat a little straighter as the radio hosts switched to the news. Smacking my hand against the steering wheel in jubilation, I had to stop myself from cheering out loud as they gave a blow-by-blow account of the fire and the actions of those trying to contain it. Apparently, it was spreading to the next street over.

Awe, such a fucking shame...not.

I closed my eyes for a few moments to visualize the blaze as I continued listening to the radio. Doctors, lying lawyers, and judges all lived along that road. It didn't take much digging to find that not one of them, for all their smiles and laughter around a barbecue, was a very nice person. One was up on charges for tax evasion reaching into the hundreds of thousands. Another, a pediatrician, had charges brought against him for touching girls inappropriately during physical exams. I didn't really care who lived in the homes, but it sure made it sweeter to know that I'd done a good thing.

I was a monster with a mission. Each one of those men and women had been born of the same sort of evil and then molded from a different clay to become the shining beacons we saw. I'd make those beacons light up a different way.

The bright green of the digital clock in the market's sign drew my eye as I sighed. The time read that it was well into the afternoon, and if Adalyn were coming, I would have expected her to be here by now. I reached for the ignition before freezing as a yellow bug drove into the parking lot. It pulled down the same aisle I was parked in, leading me to scoot down low into my seat, but I kept my eyes up high enough to see.

It was hard to see over the hood of the truck to see who was getting out of the small car from this angle, but then, like some miracle from the spirit world, she walked directly in front of my line of sight as she headed towards the market. Adalyn. My heart drummed in my chest at an erratic pace. She was a mirage of grace and beauty, she was my Adalyn...and she just disappeared into the store to buy food.

The doctor hadn't been lying about this. He may have been a fucknut about everything else, but he hadn't lied about this. I was so tempted to follow her, to find her in the store and wrap my arms around her, but I didn't want to terrify her. Like everyone else, she probably assumed I was dead.

I banished my nervousness away and allowed my mind to daydream about what our life was going to be like once we were blissfully reunited.

It was one of those rare moments where all the staff was in a meeting and Adalyn was able to slip away. Even though we were fully clothed, just to have her body pressed against mine, to feel her hand on my heart, made my spirits soar. These brief moments were so rare and highly coveted.

"What are you thinking about," I asked quietly. My hand pressed against her lower back as we lay on the small bed together.

"How I'd love to do this with you outside of this place without the fear of being caught hanging over our heads." Her voice was soft as she said the sweet words into my chest.

"You mean that?"

Adalyn lifted her head and rested her chin on her hand as she stared at me.

"Of course I mean that. I'd love nothing more than to have a real future with you, which is why I keep bugging you to behave in your sessions with Dr. Wallace."

I let out a snort.

"That man is never letting me out of here. I'm either going to die inside this place, or I'm going to die in prison, but either way, I'm never getting out of here alive unless I escape."

"But if you escape, Derek, what kind of life could we have?"

I thought about her question for a moment. It was a good one. What would a future on the run look like?

"I'd have to make it look like I died so no one would be looking for me, and then we could move to a different state, whichever one you want, and settle down. I'd love to live by the mountains, maybe someplace where a stream ran through the property. We could go hiking or fishing and no one would know us. We would be free of all of this."

The prettiest smile I'd ever seen graced her sweet, angelic features, and my heart swelled.

"Do you really think you can make that happen? Escape and be free of this place for real? I mean, they have a lot of security."

"If I have your help, I can do anything." Raising my head, I kissed the end of her button nose, making her giggle.

"I think I'm falling for you, Derek."

. . .

The flash of a light blue sweater coming out of the store caught my attention, and my pulse skyrocketed as she walked in my direction. I waited, hunched low in the truck, until she passed, slipping out of the truck as she stared down at her keys.

She was bending down to put the armload of grocery bags into the car when I rounded the edge of the vehicle beside hers and stared at her back.

"I've missed you," I said, and she let out a yelp and jumped away from the sound of my voice.

Adalyn's head whipped up in my direction, and even with my hood up and her sunglasses on, I could feel our eyes lock.

"Derek?" That one breathy word sent a shiver racing over my skin.

"Yeah, it's me." I stepped a little closer but stopped as she took a step back. She looked me up and down and then removed her sunglasses. The fear I saw embedded in them pulled at my heart.

"What are you doing here?" she asked, looking around the parking lot.

My mouth fell open, not sure what to say. I'd figured that would be the self-explanatory part. I'd assumed she'd be happy to see me and run into my arms for us to be reunited.

"I'm here because I just learned that you're still alive, and I wanted to see you. We always planned to run away together. I...I guess I thought you'd want to see me."

I crossed my arms over my chest and looked down at the black army-style boots I was wearing. The range of emotions flowing through my body was all over the map as my earlier enthusiasm had a big bucket of water poured on it.

"I'm happy to see that you're alive, Derek, of course I am, but to be honest, I figured you were alive," she said, and I lifted my head to look her in the eyes.

"You knew I was alive?"

"No, but I guessed you were. All these strange fires going on around town—they're you, aren't they?"

I looked away from her and nodded. I didn't feel ashamed of what I'd done, but at the same time, the look of disbelief on her face made the enthusiasm I'd experienced earlier over my wonderful plan working feel tarnished.

"I did them for you," I said.

Her hands went to her chest as her mouth dropped open.

"What do you mean, you did this for me?"

I stepped in closer and took some encouragement from the fact she didn't step away this time. I leaned closer, lowering my voice.

"They were all the people that hurt us. That hurt you," I whispered. "Jim and the men that attacked you that night, and today, I completed the task by making sure that Dr. Wallace never hurts anyone ever again. You knew what he was like, what he was doing to his patients. You hated it, and it was time for him to pay for all the terrible shit he'd done to me." Adalyn shook her head as she stared at me. This was so not how I pictured this conversation going. "You were encouraging me. I could hear you telling me to avenge your death."

"My death?"

"I thought you were dead. I thought you'd died in the hospital fire."

She leaned in close, her face darkening.

"Don't say that like it was some random act of God. *You* did that, *you* set that, and if I'd been in there, you would've killed me too."

I swallowed hard.

"I know, and I cried, and I grieved and...I didn't mean to. I didn't think you were back at work. I mean, you weren't, and I know that now. You know what I'm trying to say."

Adalyn sucked in a deep breath and crossed her arms over her chest.

"Oh, I know exactly what it is you're trying to say. You didn't think I was there, so that was why you did what you did, but then, for whatever reason, you thought I was...." She stopped talking and hit her forehead with her palm. "My car. You saw my car. That's why you thought I was dead. I was wondering why someone would break into my car and only take my car's registration papers. It made no sense, but it does now."

"Adalyn, I escaped to be with you. I escaped so we could have the life we always talked about together." I reached for her and laid my hands on her shoulders, and even though she didn't cringe at my touch, she looked sad and disappointed. "What is it? I don't understand."

"What about all the other people?"

"What other people?"

A soft chuckle left her lips before she covered her eyes and shook her head like she was disgusted with me.

"All the other people that died in those fires—the people that never hurt you, the people that were trapped in a terrible situation just like you. Or how about the people that unwittingly died in the apartment fire you set? Did you know that a firefighter died trying to save a little girl from falling debris as the building collapsed? The girl lived, but he didn't." She lifted her arm to point in the direction of the fires that, to the best of my knowledge, were still raging. "What about that entire neighborhood of homes with families inside, or whatever it is you torched this time? Why? I can't even wrap my head around it, Derek."

"I...I...," I struggled to explain, but Adalyn stepped back until my hands had to fall from her shoulders.

"First of all, I did love you, Derek. I still care for you but I also always knew we'd never have a future. I never thought we'd actually run off into the sunset together, that was a fantasy. I have a whole other life, and also a boyfriend I've been seeing for awhile that I like." She shook her head.

"But, because I do care for you and know you had a shit deal handed to you, I'm not going to turn you in. I'm going to go home and pretend that this conversation never happened...because, Derek, I can't be with you. I can't be with someone that purposely kills people, guilty or otherwise. I also don't want to move to another state or constantly be on the run from the authorities my whole life." She lifted her shoulders in a shrug. "It's just not the life I want for myself."

"I don't understand. A boyfriend? You just moved on? You never really loved me? It was all a fantasy that I made up? You said you loved me, you don't just throw words like that around."

"Love can look many different ways, Derek. It doesn't always mean that there is a white picket fence at the end of it."

"Then why were you okay with me killing before? You knew what I did to land me in the hospital, and you didn't care." I crossed my arms over my chest protectively as the hope that had been soaring only a few moments ago turned to curdled milk in my veins. A woman walking past on the sidewalk glanced over, and I glared at her until she looked away.

"I wasn't fine with it, Derek, but I understood what happened. I understood the trauma you'd been through and the lashing out, but I thought you regretted your rash actions. I thought you wanted to be different and that those that worked at the asylum pushed your buttons. I never thought you'd do all this. I just...I can't be with someone who enjoys hurting others and don't you try and tell me you don't. You wouldn't have gotten more creative with each and every fire if you didn't enjoy the kill and the theatrics."

Adalyn stepped past me and slipped into the driver's seat of her car.

"Adalyn, please don't do this. I can make things right between us."

"Derek, I have a whole other life. I want something you can't give me, and what's been done has already been done as far as...." She waved her hand in the direction of the fires. "All that is concerned. Now please, step back so I can close my door. I don't want to see you again, and so that I'm clear, I never contemplated an actual life with you." She gave me a sad little smile like she was pitying my stupidity and my body began to tremble. "But, now you're free, it's what you always wanted. Just go and live your new life, out there, doing what you want. I won't stop you." She waved her hand like she was shooing a dog that was begging for food.

I stepped back like I'd been punched in the gut and leaned against the vehicle behind me. I couldn't catch a breath as her car started. She didn't even look at me as she pulled out of the parking space.

In a weird fog of befuddlement, I stumbled back to my truck and hopped inside. The confusion was morphing into something else—something dark that was uncoiling in my gut and growing with each breath. I looked up to see Adalyn turn out of the parking lot. The world narrowed in as the anger took over.

I'd done all of this for her—for us—for what we lost. How the hell could she not see that? How could she not be happy about getting justice? How had she moved on so fast? How could she say she never really wanted a future with me? I'd held her close to my body and told her all my deepest fears and insecurities. I showed her a side to my soul that no one had seen before. How could she simply close her door and drive away like she was dropping off an unwanted pet?

The truck roared to life, and I slammed her into gear and stomped on the gas as I flew toward the exit, almost hitting a man and his shopping cart on the way. I'd have mowed his ass down if he'd taken one more step, but I ignored him as he yelled and gave me the finger. At any other time, that would've bought him a one-way ticket to hell, but I had bigger issues at the moment.

I could see the roof of the little yellow car down the road, and the darkness in me gripped the steering wheel and turned the truck in the same direction. By keeping my distance, it was easy to discretely follow her for the five-minute drive to an adorable dollhouse-like home with a robin egg-blue door.

I pulled over on her street and watched her disappear inside the little bungalow-style home, which had matching hanging baskets full of blue flowers framing the front entrance. I sucked in air and breathed it out in long streams like I was a dragon. The engine was still running, with me frozen inside the cab with my hands on the steering wheel and eyes focused on the front door of the home as night descended and blanketed the truck.

Unable to sit there any longer, I pulled the hood low over my face and slipped on the black leather gloves. Blissfully, the street was quiet, and as I jogged across the street and through her yard, there wasn't a single soul around. Putting my back against the siding, I slid along the side of the home until I could see a window ahead. I couldn't see anything from that vantage point, but I could hear music playing. Reaching out, I silently opened the gate of the chain-link fence surrounding her backyard.

A lone dog barked further down the street, and a cat was yowling loudly somewhere, looking for a mate. The two animals reminded me of my current predicament. It was like Adalyn, and I were speaking two different languages and couldn't understand one another.

Drawing closer, I peeked into the next window and ducked as Adalyn walked past a door leading to a room in the back end of the house. I was a shadow as I followed her around her home. My eyes glued themselves to a mirror hanging on the wall as her reflection appeared in it. As she pulled her shirt off, my body shivered with desire. She disappeared once more from sight, and I searched until I found her again behind the mosaic-patterned glass framing the window. The image was distorted, but she was definitely undressing. My cock stood at attention, pissed off that it didn't get a release earlier.

I looked up as the fan turned on, and the sound of what had to be a shower reached my ears. Moving around to the back door, I looked at the lock through the small pane of glass. There was no security system, but I didn't have any tools with me.

No simple door was stopping me from getting inside her home. Marching to the garage door, I tried that handle and smiled as the handle turned. I found a lot of useful tools as I wandered around inspecting the place, which would never fit a car because it was so jammed full of boxes and other items. Tall, towering columns of flower-pots rose toward the ceiling. There had to be at least a dozen boxes marked 'clothes' in another pile. She had four bicycles, a pile of tires, two cabinets that looked to be falling apart, a small rocking horse, boxes labeled 'decorations' that filled an entire quarter of the space, and every type of outdoor equipment that you could imagine.

I had no idea how she lived with all this shit in here. It would've driven me crazy. I hated clutter, and I didn't like disorganized, and this one room was both. I made my way over to the single table that had a random mess of tools piled on top, and as I picked up what was needed to get the job done, I spied some of my other favorite tools. A roll of tape, a length of rope, and, of course, my personal favorite—a jerry can. I picked it up, gave it a shake, and sighed. It was only half full, but it would do if need be. I grabbed a few more items that looked like they might have potential and made my way to the back door once more.

I'd never understood the obsession with collecting this much stuff. Why did one person need so many things that they never looked at and didn't touch, admire, or use? What was the point? Was it a competition to see who could collect the most useless crap? The doctor's house had been the same way. Each room was filled with items that those who'd been living there never paid attention to, never even appreciated, and yet they continued to add to the mass of items with better, newer, and shinier items.

I quickly checked the bathroom window to confirm that Adalyn was still in the shower, which should mask most of the noise I was about to make. Selecting a crowbar, I placed it by the crappy lock and stuffed it into the thin gap between door and frame. The old wood gave easily as I pushed on the end of the crowbar, and the door groaned with the assault. The temperature had dipped lower since the sun had set, and a fresh-smelling breeze off the ocean, which was not far off, cooled off my heated skin as I worked.

One final wedge and push and the lock gave way. I had to jump and grab the swinging door quickly before it banged into the wall, which would most certainly alert Adalyn. I slipped the jerry can and other treasures inside and hid them all in the back hall closet. Doing a quick survey of my surroundings, I found the place to be just as disastrous as the garage. Dirty clothes and dishes were strewn about and the television had been left on but muted.

This woman, orderly and seemingly perfect at work, was the complete opposite in her home. Shaking my head, I skulked down the hall until I was near enough to stand and watch the last of her shower through the cracked-open door. My cock gave another jerk in my jeans like it was trying to remind me it was attached to my body and needed to be attended to, but I ignored it for now. I had time.

Standing there, I wanted to close my eyes and breathe the heady citrus scent of Adalyn's body wash in and never stop. The heat of the shower only accentuated the delicious aroma. It wasn't as good as the scent of burning flesh, but I had to admit it was up there on my list of favorite smells. It screamed *clean* and *fresh* and *sweet,* just like the fruit it mimicked. The water shut off, and after a moment, Adalyn's hand emerged from the steamy shower to feel around for a towel.

I stepped away from the door and hid among the shadows, melding in with them as a lover would. I'd been born a monster, or maybe a creature from Hell, if it existed. It had taken me time to realize that, but I did now. I saw myself for what I was, and I embraced it rather than pretending to be something else.

Adalyn stepped into the hall with one towel wrapped around her body and a second towel on her head in a fancy twist thing. She didn't notice me even though I stood only fifteen feet away. As she moved, so did I. I loved how the towel draped over her curvy ass and showed off those shapely legs I craved to have wrapped around my head once more. I loved seeing her bare shoulders and slender neck, which was prime for sucking. Fuck the boyfriend. When I was done with her, she'd always remember me.

She turned into her bedroom, and I knew I would never forget the look of surprise and terror in her eyes as she looked up and saw me behind her in the tall mirror. As she froze, so did I. Our eyes locked in the mirror—scared met ravenous. Her body shook instantly, goosebumps rising all along her skin. Adalyn's hand went to her mouth, and I knew she'd been tempted to scream but managed to swallow it down.

"Go ahead and scream, see what happens next."

I grabbed her by the shoulders and slowly turned her around to face me. She was like a petrified little bunny looking up at me. Bunnies always got eaten by the wolf.

"Derek." She said my name, the word coming out as a long stutter.

"Adalyn," I said, mocking her fear. "I told you I avenged you, and you told me to go away. You told me that you've moved on after feeding me lines for years and professing love. I don't think so. That's not how you treat the people you claim to love."

The murky thing that lived in my soul filled my body with a feeling that I'd never been able to describe. Maybe it was anger, or maybe it was betrayal, or sadness—I really couldn't tell, but it wanted her blood. It wanted her flesh. It wanted to see the light fade from her eyes the same way the light had disappeared from the eyes of the only other bitch that had turned against me in my life. My mother deserved to die that night, and so did Adalyn now. Women couldn't be trusted.

"I trusted you, and you turn your back on me?"

"Ahhhh," Adalyn screamed as I picked her up around the waist and tossed her down on the bed. Her body bounced and the towel splayed open, showing off the body she'd handed over willingly only a few months ago. "Derek, what are you doing?"

She tried to crawl off the bed, but I grabbed her ankle and hauled her back as she now tried to scream. The houses were way too close together for her screams to go unnoticed. My large palm looked huge wrapped around her face as I clamped it down to muffle the sound.

Her eyes were wide as she smacked my hand. I leaned down and sniffed her skin that was so sweet. She was as soft and stunning as I remembered.

"If you scream, it will only make things worse," I said. She nodded, so I removed my hand.

"I don't understand, Derek." Tears welled in her eyes, and a little of the dark shadow that floated around inside of me lightened. "I didn't lie, I did love...."

I cut her off.

"Stop saying that. You didn't love me. You never loved me." Grabbing together both of her hands in one of mine, I held up the piece of rope and gave her a suspicious look when she didn't struggle to get away. "Why aren't you fighting?" I asked, the anger morphing into confusion.

"Would it do me any good?"

I mulled that question around. She had a point. I'd overpower her and kill her no matter what she did, but there was still something off about her reaction. It was too casual, too...I couldn't put my finger on it.

"No, I guess it wouldn't. Is your boyfriend on the way?" Adalyn yelped as I gave the rope a hard tug and tied her with her hands above her head to the long, white metal bar that acted as a headboard.

"No."

"You swear?" I grabbed her chin, and she sucked in a deep breath.

"I swear," she whispered, and then the stupid towel slipped completely open, and I couldn't stop staring at her heaving breasts. Her nipples were hard and stood out from the beautiful peaks, heaving in rhythm to her breathing.

One finger at a time, I pulled off the black leather gloves until I could slip my hands out and laid the gloves on her nightstand, loving how she watched my every movement.

"Derek, please try to understand that I do love you, but sometimes love is not enough. We have very different views on life, our future, and the world. Like, the situation with Jim and the others should've been handled differently in my mind."

"Oh, and how were you planning on solving the problem?"

"I was suing them. I had pressed charges against the men and the hospital, but my case went up in smoke with the asylum itself before it even got started."

Unable to help myself, I trailed the back of my finger down the side of her body, loving the silky softness of her skin. She shivered under my touch, a small gasp leaving her mouth.

"Do you really think that would've gone somewhere? The hospital would've paid you off to keep you quiet, and the guys would've continued on with their lives. They'd eventually get work somewhere else because the system is that broken, and in the end, they'd hurt someone else."

Adalyn shook her head, her eyes narrowing at me.

"Even so, I would've been compensated. I could've gone anywhere in the world with that money and left this place behind. Or, maybe they would've ended up in prison, and either way would've been fine."

Staring at her was like staring into the center of a whirlpool. I knew I should stand up and walk away, burn the house down with her in it, and yet I couldn't stop staring. The craving to taste her once more had my tongue tingling in my mouth. My eyes traveled from her sweet face to the breasts I'd sucked on in my dreams and then further still to her pussy. Despite Adalyn's obvious fear, she had her legs splayed open wide.

In a daze of swirling emotions and needs, my fingertips drew soft lines from her belly button up to her breasts. I rolled one hard nipple between my thumb and finger and then gave it a hard squeeze. A yelp that ended in a moan left her lips. I glanced at her face and saw she was biting her lip even as she glared.

"Stop it, Derek."

"Why," I asked, repeating the action on the other nipple.

"Because I don't want you to touch me," she said, but the bite of anger that had accompanied her earlier words was missing from her tone.

"Is that so?" I slowly drew a line down the center of her body and watched it quiver more with each inch lower that my finger traveled. Her legs snapped together, but I was easily able to slide a single digit between her tightly clenched legs and into her folds.

"I said stop it," she said, her voice husky. The sound had the same effect on my body as the screams of those in my fires.

"I don't think you want me to." She wasn't just a little damp, she was soaking wet, and my body responded with another flush of heat and desire that went straight to my throbbing cock. Adalyn sucked in a sharp breath as my finger slid up and down her wet folds and circled around her clit, which was so engorged that I was able to grab it with two fingers and stroke it like a tiny cock.

"I said stop," Adalyn said, but her legs opened wider, and her hips pressed up into my hand, demanding more. The cock in my pants had yet to lay down fully from when I'd started the fires that morning. I could be in the running for some Kamasutra challenge at this point, but I wasn't going to resist the urge any longer.

"You really want me to stop?" I asked, dipping my finger deep into her sopping wet pussy. Adalyn moaned, the sound loud, as I started thrusting my finger into her. Using one hand, I got the zipper undone on my pants and pulled my raging length out of the confines of the boxers I'd been wearing. The head was already coated with shiny pre-come, and another droplet formed on the tip as I watched. "I don't think you want me to stop. In fact, I think you like the fear."

Adalyn moaned as she bit her lip, her walls clenching around my finger.

"I'm right, aren't I?" She pushed her hips up into the air, giving me better access as my finger continued to press in and out at a quicker pace. "You don't know if I'm going to fuck you or kill you, and you love that. In fact, I think that's what you always loved about me."

Both my hands continued to work, one sliding up and down my hard cock to smear the wet, slippery pre-cum all over the hard shaft. The other diving in and out of her pussy, which was now fully humping my finger as I slowed my pace.

Adalyn splayed open the leg closest to me, giving my hand better access between her legs. I looked up at her face and saw it was now a mask of pure pleasure. The fear was still there in her eyes, but a darker desire was overriding it. Adalyn's eyes were trained on my cock, and I knew she wanted it. She wanted me to give her my virginity and slam the raging cock deep inside of her.

"Isn't that right, Adalyn? All those nights that you snuck into my room so I could suck on your pussy and dip my tongue into your sweet folds, you worried I might snap and kill you, but that was why you were there." I added a second finger to the mix, and Adalyn's back arched off the bed. "Just like how right now, you're terrified to be in the same room with me, but it makes you wet. It makes you want to come all over my fingers as the fear of possible death heightens your desire."

The sounds of her eager moaning and the soft squeaks of the bed shifting as my fingers dove between her legs, rocking her body in time to the sensation, filled the room. I stopped fingering her and pulled out, collecting as much of the wetness that she'd produced as possible, and used it to coat my cock.

"I...I...don't want this," she said, but her back arched, and her ass wiggled back and forth as she silently begged for more. As her desperate eyes found mine, she licked her lips, then shifted her gaze back to watch the cock moving between my closed fist. My cock looked angry with the distinct shade of red-purple it had become. The throbbing need to come was so strong that I groaned loudly every time my hand slid up to the sensitive head. I looked over at Adalyn writhing on the bed. She was thrusting her hips in my direction in time to my hand's movements.

"Tell me the truth, Adalyn. The fear is what draws you to me. You're a kinky little slut, and you try to hide it, but you only wanted me then, and you only want me now because I terrify you, which feeds the darker demands of your body."

I reached between her legs and gathered more of the wetness steadily leaking from her body like a little stream. I made sure not to give her any satisfaction as I brought it to my cock.

Pulling the boxers down a little further, I was able to hook them under my balls, which pushed them up for her to see as well. The heavy sacs were pulled up tight and throbbing in time to my strokes. I may have been a virgin, but I also knew that I was on the large side, and the hungry look burning in her eyes screamed how much she wanted what I had to offer.

"That's also why you took a job working as a nurse with the most dangerous and deranged that humanity has to offer. Every person in that place fed the sick darkness in you that craves anxiety as much as the release. You'd come all over me right now if I wrapped my hand around your throat and choked you out while I shoved this thick cock into your pussy, wouldn't you? Tell me the truth, Adalyn. Tell me now," I demanded.

She thrashed on the bed like she'd been possessed as she fought back the emotions racing through her body and the argument over what was proper raging in her head.

"Say it! Say the words."

"Yes," she finally yelled on a pant. "Yes, to it all."

My hand stilled as a thought occurred to me, and my eyes snapped up to hers.

"Jim and the others. They raped you, but did you like it? Did you like being used like a slut to be passed around by them? Some gang bang, nonconsensual orgy fetish you'd always secretly wanted?"

She closed her eyes and looked away, and that was all the confirmation I needed. Why had I not seen it until now, what with the way she snuck into the room—the way she'd ask me to push her up against the wall and not be gentle with her. It wasn't love she felt. It was a carnal lust that attracted her to me like a magnet.

"If they'd wanted to, you'd have let them do it again. Fuck you hard and use you. Wouldn't you have?"

Tears streamed down her cheeks, and though she sucked in a gasp, she nodded her head yes.

"God help me, yes." Her eyes locked with mine. "I didn't want it at first, I swear. I only wanted you when I was at work, but I couldn't stop myself from enjoying it. I never wanted them to stop."

The realization was like having ice water dumped on my head at the same time as that raging anger inside me flared back to life. All those people died because I'd thought I was avenging her, and all this time she was not only alive, she'd liked it?

Standing in a rush, I backed away, clenching my fists. I wanted to scream as the pain settled in my chest. Nothing in my life was ever real. It was always a lie—fake family, fake doctor, fake love, fake concern. My eyes snapped up to Adalyn's, and she was still in the throes of a toxic combination of desire and terror, her body a writhing mess on the bed as she tried to relieve the building pressure inside.

I no longer had anything, and a man that had nothing to live for was the most dangerous.

"I was going to give you this," I said as I stood to show off the large cock standing tall against my stomach. "I was going to let you be my first real fuck, slam this cock into you hard, and make you scream my name."

"Oh god, yes, please Derek, please fuck me hard. Use me for your pleasure. I want to be used."

I was tempted to shove the fucking thing back in my fatigues and walk away, but why shouldn't I have something that I enjoyed first? Walking around to the foot of the bed, I grabbed the frame from underneath and gave it a heave. It scraped easily across the wooden floor as I pulled it away from the wall. I stood at the foot of the bed and made sure that Adalyn's eyes were trained on the cock between my legs as I stroked it fast.

Her breathing had picked up and was coming out in pants even though I wasn't touching her. Yes, I knew what I wanted to do now. I leaned over the foot of the bed and practically dove between her legs to get a taste of that pussy. It was still so tempting. She groaned and thrashed around as I sucked at the juices and the sensitive folds until the whimpering changed pitch and I knew she was close to coming all over my face. Standing, I walked around to the head of the bed and pushed the fatigues down enough that I could straddle her chest.

"What about your boyfriend? Won't he be upset that you fucked this cock?" I asked, bouncing it off her face. She turned her head to try to lick at it, but I made sure to stay just out of reach.

"I don't care."

I lifted an eyebrow at her. Had she been like this away from the asylum? Had she sought out wild sex with whoever and then cuddled with her monster when she could? It was an answer I didn't dare ask for fear of killing her immediately. If she said the word 'yes,' there was no telling what I'd do.

"You want your monster?" I stroked the thick length right in front of her eyes but just out of reach. My hand slowly ran from base to tip to squeeze out a drop of clear liquid that dripped onto her face. "Is this what you crave?"

"Yes! Fuck! Yes!"

"Are you sure, Adalyn? I can't tell with the stench of lies in the room," I asked, smacking her in the face with my cock hard enough that the sound could've been mistaken for the slap of my hand. As the quick sharp sting of pain registered, I learned something new about myself—I liked the pain. I quickly smacked her again, harder this time, and a red mark appeared on her cheek. This time, I left it sitting on the side of her face and admired the view.

"Yes, oh yes." Her tongue snaked out of her mouth, and I groaned, the sound more like a growl as she traced wet lines along the shaft. "Give it to me. Shove it in my mouth," she begged, turning to latch her lips onto the throbbing shaft. The warm sucking sensation, even in just the one small spot, was incredible. I wanted more, so I was going to take it.

Grabbing her chin, I pulled her mouth away from my cock and stared down into her eyes, feral with need. "Then you're going to take it all, and you're not going to complain."

She nodded her head furiously in my grasp, and my muscles flexed as my own shudder of desire flowed through my body faster than any accelerant. Releasing her face, I rose up and leaned on the headboard's metal rail until I could align my cock with her mouth. In that position, Adalyn's tongue could just reach the tip, swirling around the engorged head. The rage was as strong as the longing to finally find release as I rammed my cock into her mouth without any warm-up or hesitation. Her eyes opened in surprise as she instantly gagged on the large invasion.

"You're going to take it, slut," I growled out as I lifted my hips and then pushed back into the hot mouth. She was no longer a person. She was no longer Adalyn. She was simply a hot hole that was satisfying my body's needs. I leaned over the rail of the bed and thrust hard in and out of her mouth. The bed bounced, the springs squeaking loudly with the force of me fucking her face.

A few times, she tried to turn her head or say something, but I didn't care what she wanted to say. I had one goal, and that was to release this hot load of come down her throat and make her swallow or choke on it. I didn't care which one happened.

"Fuck yeah," I moaned, picking up the pace. My thrusts were hard and fast as I rammed home into her mouth and deeper into her throat, using her the way she said she wanted. I used her the way she always saw me.

I was the monster. I was the thing that snuck into your home. I was going to scare her and scar her for life. She'd never look at another cock the same way, as I'd forever be burned into her mind. She was getting what she'd always wanted now because I wasn't holding back. I wasn't acting like a lover that thought about their partner, and I sure as hell wasn't stopping.

"Oh, fuck, yes," I growled as my cock expanded, giving me just a moment of warning before the first stream of come shot from the tip.

Adalyn began sucking hard and moaning as each thrust brought another load from the depths of my balls into her waiting mouth. The last stream shot out, and my body shuddered with the violent final release. Pulling my softening cock from Adalyn's mouth, I looked down at her for the first time since I started fucking her face. She was soaked with tears, her eyes red, and streams of my come that she couldn't swallow trickled from either side of her mouth. I grabbed my semi-hard cock and rubbed it on her face like it was a caress. The wet, sloppy sound alone already had me starting to get hard again.

"You're a good slut." I smacked her hard on the left cheek with my cock, making her wince. "Did you like that?" A smack on her right cheek, one that got a little harder with the sting. "Do you want me to do it again?" A smack on her swollen and puffy lips.

"No," she said hoarsely, but her eyes flared with desire.

"Well, you're not going to get a choice because look at this," I said, once more making her stare at the hand traveling over my shaft. She never took her eyes off what I was doing, and her body flexed as she moaned beneath me. "I'm hard again already." I grabbed her hair and yanked her head back to force her to look up at me. "Isn't this what you wanted? For your monster to take his pleasure by using you? Fuck you hard in all your holes?"

"Ah," she yelled as I reached back with my right hand to tease her pussy. I pinched that rock-hard clit between my fingers and stroked it hard and fast, making her cry out and squirm as she panted like an animal. I'd never heard noises like the guttural ones slipping from her lips, not even listening to the nympho at the asylum get fucked multiple times a week. I liked the sound. I wanted her to continue to beg me and to want more—to feel the need to come and be so close, only to be denied.

"Yes, oh yes, I'm so close," Adalyn panted, bucking her hips into my hand hard. "Put your fingers in. Oh please, fuck me with your fingers."

I let go of her pleasure button and slid my cock between her breasts.

"Now stop denying it, Adalyn. Do you want me to fuck your face again?"

"I need to come! Oh god, don't stop. Let me come." She pulled hard on the rope, and I smiled as her hips bounced on the bed, making my cock bounce between her tits like a kid on a ride. I had the sudden urge to yell 'ye ha' as she continued to cry out. Leaning forward slightly, I let her erratic movement stroke the base of my cock and balls, getting me extremely hard again.

"Oh, you'll get what's yours in due time, but first, the monster is going to take what he needs. You owe me that." Getting back into position, I stared down at her and smiled. "I can usually go three times a session, so it's a real good thing that throat of yours is loosened up." With a hard shove, I again entered her mouth with a groan.

Oh yes, she was going to get what she deserved, but not before I took what I wanted from her. To me, she was the monster, not the other way around. She used me for my cock, feeding off me like a succubus of fear, and after tonight, I'd never see her again.

But I wasn't going to burn her house down, and I wasn't going to burn her alive. That was too easy. That was too nice for the mind fuck she gave me. No, this little slut was going to get a different punishment for fucking with me, one that she'd have to carry around with her for life.

Burn

I'd surprised myself and managed to make it four times with very little break between, which was a new record for me. Pulling my cock from Adalyn's mouth for the last time, I slowly stood from the bed and stared at her well-used body. She was crying now, but the tears were mixed with needy moans. I could only imagine how on fire her body must feel, how badly she must want to come by now.

I glanced at her legs, spread wide on the bed, and the distinct wet spot between them stained her sheets. Adalyn was covered in sweat. The bit of makeup she'd applied after her shower had run or been wiped off by my cock long ago, and dried come caked her face. If it had been under any other circumstance, I'd say it was the sexiest thing I'd ever seen, but I just felt dead inside.

It had brought me some measure of satisfaction to know that no matter how much she squirmed as I teased her to the point of insanity, I was going to refuse her the release she was after. She didn't deserve to come by my hand or by any other part of my body. Kill her or let her live? These questions swirled like a storm in my mind.

Making my decision I walked out of the room and left her panting, a shaking mess on the bed to go and get my tools. I came back after a second trip to the garage. Marching into the room, I dropped the items I'd collected on the floor and stood still, staring down at Adalyn. She really was beautiful.

For the briefest of moments, I toyed with the idea of simply using her for this, of making another deal with the Devil to come into town to fuck her when I wanted, but I couldn't do it. I'd lived through multiple versions of a fucked-up relationship my entire life. As emotionally damaged as I was, I couldn't willingly put myself into a similar situation of being used and using another like that. I already had nothing—adding more emptiness on top of it was not what I wanted, even if it had felt amazing.

Grabbing the wide roll of duct tape, I tore off a healthy piece. The tearing noise finally got Adalyn's attention, and she flinched away.

"What are you doing?"

"Making sure you always remember me." I slapped the tape onto her mouth. Leaning over her, I grinned, the gesture not reaching my eyes. "You made me lose the last threads of my sanity. What I just did was only half of your punishment. I plan on scarring your soul and your mind, just like what you did to me."

Her body shivered as she stared up at me, her eyes now filling with real fear—not the kind that fed her soul, but the kind that screamed at her to run away from the monster under the bed. I closed my eyes and took a long sniff of her skin, the aroma a combination of that citrus scent and my sex, committing it to memory. Standing, I once more pulled on my black gloves.

Reaching down, I grabbed the rest of the rope and made a quick hogtie knot around her ankles before tying them down to the legs of the bed. No one would ever hurt me again. Not anyone. I picked up the small propane mag-torch and slowly turned on the fuel. With a simple click of the button, the bright blue flame whooshed to life.

Adalyn tried to scream behind the wide tape, and she really struggled this time.

"Just so you know, I would've burned for you," I said.

Leaning over the bed, I ignored her struggles and, making sure that my hand was at the perfect height, aligned the flame with her collarbone. Her high-pitched wails were muffled as I drew one agonizing line down her body to the opposite hipbone. I needed to make sure that it wasn't so deep that it would do too much damage while still allowing my blue flame to eat away enough flesh that it would leave a permanent scar on her body—something that she could never erase.

If it weren't for the fact my cock was beyond well-spent, it would've stood at attention from the rich smell of her burnt flesh filling my nose. I sucked the scent deep into my body like it was life's blood. Satisfied with the first line, I repeated the action on the other side. Tears streamed down Adalyn's cheeks as she whimpered behind the tape covering her mouth.

Finished, I stood back and looked down at my work—a perfect X that now graced her body. It ruined her formerly smooth skin with a mark that would always remind her of me. Every time she tried on clothes, it would be there. Every time she looked in the mirror, there I'd be. And every time she fucked another man, they would see my mark.

I flicked off the torch and put it in my bag along with everything else that I'd touched. The very last thing I did was rip the tape from her mouth, allowing the room to fill with her sobs.

"It goes without saying that if I see my name in the news, Adalyn, then I will be back, and no one you know or love will be safe. If I have to burn the world down to flush you out of whatever hole you've crawled into, I'll do it." I grabbed her face and squeezed hard. "You will always remember me, and the only thing I wish I could see is how you'll explain this to every lover you ever have from this moment on." Releasing her face, I glared down at her. "You like fear? Now you really know what it is, and you can live forever with the fear of me deciding to come back and finish the job. This is how you properly say goodbye, Adalyn."

With a quick tug, I freed her hands and then did the same to her feet before tossing her phone on the bed.

"I'd call an ambulance and have a good story ready if I were you—but remember, I'm the monster under your bed and I'm always watching." I leaned in close, and she shook harder. "Even while you sleep." I glanced at my work once more and was satisfied. "I was never here."

As I walked out the broken back door and strode over to my truck, I knew I'd taken another step closer to a ledge from which there was no coming back.

Not
even the
Devil could burn
the world like
I could

Chapter 25

I drove aimlessly around town for hours, barely noticing my surroundings, before finding myself in this rundown part of the city where there were more motorcycles than cars. Most of the streetlights were burnt out, and the walls of the surrounding buildings looked like they were being held up by dirt, spray paint, and bags of garbage—yet, they still looked better than I felt.

Pulling over in front of a bar, I turned my head to stare at the half-lit sign above it. I'd never had a drink for obvious reasons, but I didn't want to go home to the farm and sit there alone, and I certainly didn't want to face Dora yet.

So, this lonely, sad fucking place seemed to be the option for the night. Pushing open the truck's door, I put my hood up and made my way to the front entrance. The smell of cigarette smoke was already strong before I opened the door, so not surprisingly, a smoky haze punched me in the face as soon as I gave it an escape route. I breathed it all in like I was sucking it from the room and envisioned a dragon in my mind getting ready to roar with a bellow of fire.

Stepping inside, I surveyed my surroundings. There was a total of eleven people in the bar, including the bartender. Two were at a pool table, one was tending the bar, and another was sitting on a stool. The rest were scattered among the booths in varying stages of disarray and drunkenness. They all looked at me, and I suddenly felt like I'd just walked into a saloon from one of those old western movies that Asher liked to watch. After a moment, they all turned back to what they'd been doing.

The music playing was a rock song I didn't recognize. As it played softly, the colorful lights on the jukebox flashed. The walls were dark wood, along with the booths, flanked with what I assumed were red seats at one time. My eyes flicked over the pictures of motorcycles hanging on the walls with women in different stages of naked lying on them.

Hood up, face down, I made my way toward the bar and picked a stool three away from the only other person sitting on one of the tall chairs.

"What do ya want?" the bartender asked, sounding more annoyed than interested in making a buck.

I didn't have a fucking clue what to get and looked over the man's shoulder at the selection that lined the mirrored shelves.

"Give 'em one of these," the guy sitting a few stools down said, holding up a brown bottle of beer. "The rest of the shit in this place tastes like watered-down piss. I've had my share of both piss and alcohol, and trust me, this is the only good thing here."

I glanced over and saw a man that looked like he'd been sitting on the stool long enough for it to become part of his ass. The dark circles under his eyes screamed that he needed sleep instead of the cigarette caught between his lips and the beer he was drinking.

The bartender plunked a beer bottle down in front of me, and a little bit of foam seeped out of the top, reminding me of what I'd been doing with Adalyn. Picking up the bottle, I gave the liquid a sniff. It smelt like shit.

"What in the ever-loving fuck are you doin', man?" I looked over at the man on the stool, his own beer bottle frozen halfway to his lips as he stared at me.

"Do you have a problem?"

"That's a fucking loaded question these days," he said before looking away, his eyes going to the television that was on mute above the bar. I followed his gaze up to the newscaster, and my mood perked up a little as I realized that emergency crews were still at the residential area trying to get the fires under control. Oh, I'd really been a naughty boy this time —the small stir in my gut at the thought had the corners of my mouth curving up.

Putting the bottle to my lips, I took my first sip of beer and then almost spit it back out. It tasted worse than it smelled. My face must have said exactly what I was thinking because the guy on the stool started to laugh, his hand smacking the top of the bar.

"What's with that face? You never had a drink before?"

I shook my head back and forth.

"First time. How do you drink that crap?" I set the bottle down and shoved it away. How the hell my father drank those like water was beyond me.

"Holy fuck, a virgin," the man yelled, not realizing that had a double meaning for me. I watched as he stood and got everyone's attention. "Hey boys, we got a drinking virgin in our midst."

A loud round of whoops rose behind me as the man on the stool picked up his beer and shifted closer.

"Name's Spider," he said, holding out his hand. I just stared at it.

"Spider? What kind of fucked up parent names their kid after an arachnid," I asked, finally placing my hand in his. The man didn't say anything and just stared at me before bursting out into laughter, shaking my hand roughly.

"Spider is what I go by now, but my name is Chase. Call me which- ever you like."

"Well, I don't like spiders, so Chase it is. I'm DW."

"What, your mama couldn't think of a real name, so she just put two letters together?" Chase shot back, one-upping my momma joke. I shot the man a glare but then laughed.

"Like you, it's what I prefer."

"But you're not going to tell me what it stands for, are you?" I shook my head no. "Well, alright then, DW, let's get you some real drinks. I'm not letting you leave here still a virgin. Let's get him one shot of everything you have, and it's on me," Chase said before grabbing my shoulder. "So, what brings you into a shithole like this?"

"I heard that," the bartender mumbled under his breath.

"I can't help it if it's the fucking truth." Chase leaned in a little closer—I could smell the scent of beer, cigarettes, and weed coming off him like it was his own personal cologne. "Woman issues?"

I shrugged, giving him a noncommittal answer as the first shot was laid on the bar top before me.

"Hey, where the fuck is mine?" Chase demanded, glaring at the bartender. The bartender rolled his eyes and slammed a second small glass down in front of Chase before filling it up with a brown liquid. "Alright, let's get the cherry popping started." Chase held up the shot glass. "This is whiskey. Ready?"

"Are you serious?"

"Fuckin' right, I'm serious. Pick up the glass and swallow it in one go. On the count of three." Not sure exactly why I was indulging the man, I picked up the glass. "One, two...three." I tossed my head back and downed it, brown liquid burning as I swallowed.

I shook my head and squeezed my eyes closed as the hot burn of the alcohol slid down my throat and made my stomach feel like I'd just swallowed a ball of fire.

"Woo," Chase said, shaking his head, obviously feeling the same sensation I was. "Damn, that shit will burn the hairs right off your ball sac."

Two more shots, this time a lighter-colored drink, were poured into glasses and slid over.

"To misery loves company," I toasted, raising up the next glass.

A twisted grin crept across Chase's face.

"To misery loves company," he repeated before holding out his own small glass so we could clink our glasses together. "This one is fireball whiskey—hope you like cinnamon." He didn't bother with the count-down this time, and with a nod, we tossed the shots back.

"Fuck, wow." I smacked my lips together and looked at the little glass in wonder. "The answer is yes, I do," I said. "I could drink more of that."

"In due time. We need to get you acclimated to all the bounty there is to offer first."

A third drink was set down in front of me, this one as clear as water.

"To answer your earlier question, the answer is yes," I offered.

"Yeah, figured it was a fucking woman. Only the opposite sex can fuck with a guy's brain that much. I'm going through my own shit, a fucking Princess. Fucking hot ass, and those legs...." Chase shook his head and picked up the shot.

"Huh?"

Chase waved off the question and pointed to the shot I still had yet to pick up.

"Ready? This is vodka, and the shit will really mess you up, so don't drink too much. Unless, of course, you want to get messed up." Not waiting any longer, we swallowed the shots down. I stuck my tongue out at the taste, making Chase laugh hard.

"I fuckin' like you, man." Chase clapped me on the shoulder.

"That's only 'cause you don't know me," I said, my eyes going back up to the image of smoke and flashing lights that were front and center on the screen. With the black night sky as the backdrop to my work, it really did look stunning.

"Most would say the same about me." Chase gave me a wink as the fourth shot was laid on the bar. I stared at the dark brown liquid, my head already getting a touch woozy.

Chase grabbed the little glass.

"This is Kahlua, and you'll like it. I'll race ya?"

Smiling, I nodded, laughing as we knocked the drink back on the count of three. I slammed the little glass down a second before Chase.

"Beginner's luck," Chase snorted before pointing to a bottle that was a pale golden shade. "That one is the best. Hey Mike, give us the whole bottle, three more shot glasses each, and the salt." I watched in eager fascination as Chase reached over the bar and grabbed a dish of sliced lemons. "You're gonna love this." I let out a barking laugh.

"You keep saying so."

"Shut the fuck up. I'm trying to unvirginize you." Chase paused as the two of us stared at each other before we both roared with laughter. After lining up the shot glasses on the bar in front of us, Chase rubbed his hands together.

"Okay, so you lick your hand like this." My eyebrow rose up as I watched Chase's tongue lick the back of his hand like he was a fucking cat cleaning himself. "Then you put salt on your hand where you licked, so it sticks." He picked up the shaker and shook some of the white granules onto the back of his hand. "So then, you're going to lick the salt off. Then you take the shot, put the lemon in your mouth, and suck hard. Got it?"

Reaching down the bar, I grabbed a second salt shaker.

"Ready." I smiled as Chase rubbed his hands together and cracked his neck like he was getting ready for a fight.

I followed Chase's lead and licked the back of my hand. Waiting until Chase said, 'go,' I shook salt onto my hand, grabbed the first glass, tossed it back, and then laughed as we both grabbed for a lemon at the same time. The little container tumbled, leaving a trail of lemons on the bar. My stomach was churning like I'd swallowed a volcano that was about to erupt by the time we finished the three shots that had been set up for the challenge.

Chase let out a belch and shook his head as he reached into his jacket and pulled out a small container. Opening it, he tapped some white powder onto a small, dry section of the bar.

"You wanna try some, man?" Chase asked, holding out the container. I stared at the white lines of cocaine that Chase had set up and was tempted, but ultimately I shook my head. I was already feeling woozy. I didn't need to add that shit to my system.

"More for me, then," he replied. I watched in fascination as Chase rolled up a one-dollar bill and snorted the shit up his nose before lighting up another cigarette. I stared at the glowing cherry before he moved his hand down and blew a stream of smoke up into the air. "So, why are ya wearing a hood inside?"

I peered at him from under the hood.

"You don't want to look at my face. I'm simply sparing you."

"Do I look like I get disturbed easily?" He sucked in another drag, and I couldn't stop myself as I took a deep breath in, the fresh scent mixing with the hellfire that was bubbling in my gut and making me feel warm and cozy all over.

Reaching up, I paused for a moment and then decided to say 'fuck it' as I pulled the hood back and showed Chase the scarred side of my face.

"Well fuck, what asshole did that to ya?"

"How do you know I didn't do it to myself?"

Chase made a snorting sound.

" 'Cause you don't look like the kind of idiot that would purposely burn their face."

"Fair." I grabbed the beer bottle I'd pushed away and took a sip.

"My father, he liked to hear me scream," I said, staring up at the screen.

"Huh. That's hardcore." An oddly comfortable silence fell between us. "So, what you're sayin' is that you have mommy and daddy issues," he added, and I looked over at him as he snickered and hit my arm before laughing along with him.

"Asshole."

"Speaking of parents of the year, I grew up in a motorcycle club. Things like drugs, random sex with random women, and murder were second nature all before I knew what a fucking hard-on was. Had its perks, though. I got my cock sucked off a lot, once I knew what it meant when it stood straight, by whatever sweetbutt would let me shove it in their mouth."

I nodded toward the leather vest he was wearing.

"I like that." I pointed to the logo of the scythe on his vest.

He pet the front of the patch.

"This cut is a blessing and a curse."

"I doubt you know the meaning of a curse, man, no offense."

"Alright, let's give it a go. I almost committed suicide, but my niece saved my fucking life. She doesn't know she did, but I was gonna leap off a cliff that night. I owe her my life, and instead, I almost let her get killed."

I turned the stool to look at him.

"My father beat the shit out of me daily. I protected my younger brother, but when I killed our parents, he turned me in, and I was tossed into an asylum with a fucking psychotic doctor that enjoyed doing experiments on me for the last nine years of my life."

Chase blinked at me.

"Yeah, okay, you win that round." Chase took a shot, and we started the strange game again. "Your turn to start first."

"I thought that I was in love, and that she died in a fire I set, only find out she's still alive but has a boyfriend, and has decided that me avenging her by killing off the men that raped her was '*too much*' for her to handle. Oh, and the only reason she actually liked me was because I was a scary but locked-up monster. She didn't actually want me, so she tossed me out on my ass."

Chase looked down at the bar, his fingers drawing random shapes.

"My wife and kid were blown up in a car bomb, and my brother killed them," he finally said.

My eyes grew wide. Reaching out, I gripped his shoulder in a silent gesture of support. Picking up one of the small glasses, I refilled it from the mostly empty bottle and took the shot before speaking.

"That's cold, man. My brother was a dick for turning his back on me, but that is next-level family fucked up."

"Yeah." Chase rubbed at a spot over his heart, and I knew that he still carried their deaths around with him.

"At least with a bomb, they wouldn't have known what happened. Not much consolation, but it would've been quick, like a blink. I'm alive, and then I'm dead. Fast."

Chase's bloodshot eyes found mine.

"What the fuck do you know about it?"

"Your wife? Nothing. But I'm a bit of an expert in the explosions and burning department. Be back—I need to take a leak." I stood up from the stool, and the entire room spun. I had to grab for the bar to stay upright and not fall over. I could hear Chase laughing at me as I stumbled to the bathroom to relieve myself. I now understood the phrase 'walking like a drunken sailor' and found myself whistling a stupid tune as I pissed.

I'd always been annoyed at the mess and wondered how my father could miss the toilet when he was taking a piss, but as I swayed back and forth on my feet, I suddenly comprehended the predicament. It was like trying to hit the center of a moving donut. The small bathroom smelt like I wasn't the first one to have this issue and also like no one ever bothered to clean it.

I shook my head, not sure if I was into this fuzzy-around-the-edges sensation or if I hated the not being in control part. I'd spent my entire life being controlled by one thing or another, but this was one night to let it all hang out there, so I was fucking going with it.

Making it to the sink, I leaned over to wash my hands, which took a shit load longer than it normally did, before I reached up to grab for a paper towel—and there weren't any. I tapped the plastic dispenser like that would help, but none magically appeared.

"For fucks sake," I mumbled before just staring at myself in the mirror. The glare of the fluorescent bulbs overhead made the rippled skin of the scar on my cheek look more haggard than normal, and my fists balled up as I leaned harder onto the sink to stare at my reflection.

Nothing I ever did alleviated or washed away the pain of what my father had done to me. My face was a constant reminder of the thing that I'd become—of what he'd forced me to become. I was nothing more than a hideous beast on the outside, and now, I was the monster everyone thought I was on the inside too. The demons that had wormed their way into my mind were firmly planted on their dark thrones and calling me family.

With one wavering hand, I touched the rough skin and shuddered. The residual pain of my childhood was like the shots I'd just taken. Shots burn the worst when you first put one in your mouth and swallow it down, but then the numbness takes over. You've still swallowed it, though, even if you're numb now, and the aftertaste makes your mouth taste like shit unless you can wipe it away somehow. My pain was something I'd never be able to wipe away.

Pushing away from the sink, I gave my head a bit of a shake to clear it enough to make it back to the bar without falling on my fucking ass.

As I entered the main part of the bar, I spotted Chase sitting in a booth with his feet up on the opposite bench, and as soon as he saw me, he waved me over. As I flopped down onto the bench, Chase pulled the toothpick he was chewing on from his mouth and pointed to the television. I looked up and saw that the scene had changed to show a rundown on a rash of recent murders in the area that they thought was a targeted attack on a motorcycle gang. The most recent had taken place in a bar where multiple people had been shot and a woman raped.

Chase snickered and then full-on laughed as he continued to point at the screen.

"I did that," he gasped out at the end of a laugh before dropping his head down to continue laughing.

I gave in to the hysterical laughing and joined in, my dark mood shifting slightly.

"Ha! You think that shit is impressive?" As I leaned back in the booth, Chase lifted his head, eyes narrowing.

"Among other things, yes. I killed the fuck out of those guys, and many other guys, and raped their women, fucking sluts, and I did other shit that I'm having trouble remembering at the moment, but it was all bad. Very, very bad." He smiled and laughed, and once more, I found myself laughing over nothing.

"Wow, that sounded so terrible. So very, very terrible." We were laughing so hard at that point that tears were running down our cheeks, and I clutched at my stomach, unable to breathe. It felt incredible. Sobering up a bit, I wiped the tears off my cheeks. For a moment, I stared at the wetness on my hand before looking back up at Chase, who was once more staring at the television with an evil look burning in his eyes.

I leaned on the sticky table and dropped my voice.

"You know that asylum that burnt?" I pointed to myself and got an appreciative nod from Chase. "You know that apartment building where an entire floor went *boom* and the building collapsed?" This time, Chase pointed toward me, and I nodded. "You know that explosion at the beach where the home astonishingly burned to a crisp with no leads a few weeks back?" Chase's eyes went wide, and I looked around before lowering my voice further. "Did you see that oh-so-sad story about the Richie Rich college girl in the burned-out car? All me."

"Fuck, man, you weren't kidding when you said you were not a nice guy."

The channel switched again, and this time, it showed a glimpse of the residential area and how most of the homes had been reduced to charred lumps of debris. Chase looked up at the screen and then back at me. An evil curl lifted the corners of my mouth.

"Wait...no...fuck...that too?" Chase pointed to the television, and my lips pulled up into a lopsided smile. He let out a low whistle. "I like your fuckin' style, man, no messin' around. You just took out like thirty people today."

"They all had it coming."

"Don't they all." Chase tapped his chin. "I have an idea. Do you want to play?" He leaned on the table and smiled like he was a fucking teen about to watch a porno for the first time.

"What you got in mind?" I crossed my arms over my chest.

"I kinda got a girl tied up out back. A rival club's sweetbutt that decided to wander into my path. I was planning on shooting her in the head when I was done with my drink, but I think we should make this a real party." Before I could answer, Chase stood and walked out the door.

I had no idea how he managed to walk a straight line. My head was swimming around and doing the backstroke in an alcohol-induced haze. I felt like I should be asking my brain if it needed a floaty, so it didn't drown in there.

Chase wandered in a few moments later, pushing a little redhead along in front of him. The girl looked to be in her late twenties, maybe early thirties. It was hard to tell with the streaks of mascara running down her face making her look like a crying clown. He picked the girl up, who squealed, and put her on the table like she was a hood ornament.

"What she do?" I asked, pointing a finger at the girl.

"You remember the wife and kid I mentioned? This one belongs to the group that killed them."

I looked her up and down and couldn't picture her killing anything, so this had to be a 'by association' type of thing. I lifted a shoulder and let it drop.

"Okay, so what do you want to do?"

"I'm thinking we put her to use sucking our cocks, and if she's any good, I'll see about letting her go free," Chase said, smirking.

There was no way this girl was getting the chance to go free. Chase was feeding her a line just like I'd fed one to Adalyn. The dark glint in his eye said he wanted to have some fun, and this was his latest toy.

My chin dipped as I looked down at my fatigues and the well-used and flaccid dick that I knew lay under the material. My head shook slowly back and forth.

"If she can get this thing to get up and go off again tonight, she'll need a fucking trophy to go along with her freedom."

"I can do it," she suddenly said. Her eyes were wide as she stared at me, but her voice was full of conviction.

Chase reached around and grabbed one of her boobs, giving the large mound of flesh a squeeze.

"I like them eager," he said. "But first, I need another line." He pulled out the container of cocaine again, and I raised an eyebrow at him. "I fucking see that judgy look on your puss."

"Not sayin' a word, man. It's not my brain you're fucking with. What the fuck do I care if you make yourself a vegetable?"

Chase paused as he was about to do the line he'd cut and looked up at me.

"Way to fucking ruin a good high, prick—and here I thought I liked you." Chase turned to the girl. "You do the line, then. You're gonna need it."

The girl's face lit up like it was her birthday, excitement evident in her hazel eyes as she grinned and turned around to lay on the table. Her short jean skirt pulled up until her ass was completely exposed, showing off that she had nothing on underneath. Not even a thong. Chase had set up two lines, and she took the little rolled-up dollar from Chase's fingers to eagerly sniff each one up before smiling widely.

I'd never touched another woman before and watched my hand

move like it belonged to someone else as it reached for the bare skin in front of my face. The girl giggled and wiggled her ass back and forth like a dog wagging its tail as my hand stroked the soft skin.

"Mmm, I like that," she said, placing her head on the table and lifting her ass a little higher into the air.

Chase's hand joined in on the exploration, but he was far rougher as he groped at the skin and then smacked her ass hard, leaving a handprint behind. Sliding my finger between her legs, I explored what she had to offer. She moaned as my finger slipped inside her tight hole until I couldn't push it in any farther. She was so wet that it made a little squelching sound when I pulled my finger out and thrust it back inside of her.

"Oh fuck, you've got big hands. I wonder if your cock is just as big," she purred before yelping as Chase cracked her ass again with another smack. Pulling my finger free, I held it up to her mouth. Her eyes locked with mine as she pulled the finger into her mouth to suck off her own juices.

"You down for this?" Chase asked me, and I knew he meant the blowjob and the killing. I found that neither idea excited me so much as fascinated me. I wasn't disgusted by the thought of the girl trying to suck me off—I'd been faithful to one woman, and she didn't want me, so what the fuck did I care anymore? I nodded, and Chase's eyes shone with a look I'd seen on myself when I got excited. The demons were rampant in his mind tonight.

"Here, last two in the bottle." Chase poured the tequila, though we no longer had any salt or lemons left. It didn't matter. That alcohol was all going down smooth now.

"To new friends," Chase said, holding up his small glass to clink it with mine.

"To new friends," I said.

"To new friends," the girl chimed in, and we both stared at her like she'd lost her mind. Stupidity had no limits, it seemed.

As soon as we swallowed down the alcohol, Chase jumped up and grabbed the girl, tossing her over his shoulder. She giggled, her red hair swaying back and forth like Chase had a horse's tail, as he carried her to the back exit and took her out into the alley behind the bar. He unceremoniously plunked her on the ground once we were in the alley, but she only laughed a little harder. He looked at me and rolled his eyes, which said it all. This girl had no idea that Chase was still planning on killing her no matter if she got them off in record time or not.

The alley was not the place I would've chosen to do this, what with the piles of garbage and the stench of stale piss and puke. I had to admit that the stray cats watching while rats stood guard over bits of trash was odd as well, but this was Chase's show, and he didn't seem to mind it as he whipped his dick out for the girl to suck. Unlike myself, he was already hard and stroking his cock as the girl shifted closer to her task.

"Come here, man. Get closer—unless you're freaked out by seeing my sexy-ass dick." He waved it up and down and barked out a laugh as the tip hit the redhead on the nose. He did it again and yelled, "Boop."

I had zero idea what the fuck that meant.

"I couldn't care less about your dick, man. Just wasn't sure of the protocol. This is my first random alley fuck," I shot back, stepping up beside him as the girl positioned herself between the two of us.

"Do you need me to tell you what to do next, then, rook?" Chase teased as he lit up another cigarette, took a long drag, and sighed as the girl slipped his cock into her mouth. Her hand reached out, groping for my pants. I couldn't believe I was actually going to do this, but the alcohol made it easy to wash away any of the negative thoughts.

I pushed her hand away, which was being about as useless as a wet noodle at trying to unzip my pants, and undid them for her. My cock had seen more attention tonight than it ever had, and after it got pulled out, it hung loosely between my legs. Even as her cool hand wrapped around the base and she switched over to sucking on the head, it lay heavy and dormant. She switched back and forth between Chase and I, but it didn't matter how much attention she paid to my cock—it just didn't want to stand.

"You got a problem or something, you know, getting it up?" the girl asked me.

The crack from Chase's hand hitting her face was loud in the quiet alley. She yelped and grabbed for her cheek.

"Don't you fucking ask that. If his dick's not hard, then it's your fault, not his. Got it, sweetbutt?" She nodded vigorously. "You have one job in this whole fucking world, and that is to swallow our come or to let us fuck you and come in another hole, and don't you forget it." She licked her lips and immediately started sucking on my cock again.

Taking a deep breath, I closed my eyes and pictured what this pretty little redhead would look like laid out on the ground naked and screaming as I slowly burned parts of her body to ash as she watched it happen. I could almost see the white bone left behind in the darkness of the char and the look of unbridled terror in her eyes as the missing body part didn't kill her. Imagining the smoke rising around me and coating my clothes in the rich scent of her burning flesh made me shiver and my hips rock forward. Anyone else would've thought that the scent was as horrible as a rotting corpse, but not me. It was a sweet heaven that I wanted to roll around in forever.

"Oh, yeah," I groaned out as the scene continued to play out behind my eyes and my cock repeatedly slid down the girl's throat.

My eyes snapped open as a seemingly impossible orgasm ripped from my body. I reached over the girl's head to lean on the wall, taking the girl by surprise as I splashed her in the face in the middle of switching to Chase's cock. She squealed but smiled, quickly slipping my cock into her mouth to suck out the remaining spurts of the load to swallow it down. She moaned and sucked hard.

As the last drops fell from the tip and her tongue licked them up, I panted hard, resting my head on my arm against the disgusting brick wall to catch my breath.

"Mmm, you taste good. It was worth the extra effort."

She still had a hold of my cock as it deflated, but I was too spent to be bothered about forcing her to let go. She took my dick along for the ride as she rocked back and forth, continuing to suck Chase into her mouth.

"Oh fuck, yeah, take it, bitch. Take it all," Chase said, his voice gruff. I glanced over to see his face contorted in pleasure as he grabbed her head and jammed his cock into her mouth hard while his fingers pulled on handfuls of her hair. "That's it, yes! Fucking slut!"

As I watched, Chase started to come down her throat, but on the second spray of his release, he yanked his cock from her mouth and showered the girl on her face, with one last spurt aimed at her tits. She giggled and held her mouth open while rubbing the liquid around on her cleavage, which at some point had gotten pulled out of the top of her shirt.

There was this brief moment where I couldn't help thinking how fucked up this all was, and how ironic that thought was coming from me.

"Can we do it again? I want my pussy fucked," the girl said, slowly stroking the two softening cocks in her hands.

"No," Chase said, pulling his cock away. I followed suit, both of us stuffing ourselves back into our pants. Chase leaned down and gripped the girl's chin. "You ready for your reward?" She nodded, one hand dipping between her legs to rub at herself under her short skirt. She had way too much enthusiasm for what the situation warranted. "Very good. My friend here is going to have some fun with you, and I get to watch."

The girl looked into my eyes—murderous eyes—and swallowed hard as she shrank away.

"I'll be right back," I said before making my way over to the truck and my duffel bag of toys inside of it. I paused as I passed the truck bed and then decided to grab the red jerry can I'd taken from Adalyn's.

I marched my way back up the alley to where Chase was leaning casually against the wall. The girl had finally caught on that her life was still in danger and was begging for her life. She was offering all sorts of depraved favors along with promises to turn against her gang for him. Apparently, loyalty only ran so deep.

"Grab her," I said, and the girl screamed as Chase bent down, easily picked her up, and held her in a vise-like hold. "Do you want to be able to hear her scream?" I asked.

Chase looked at me, a malicious smirk pulling up one side of his face.

"Oh, fuck yeah, I do."

Grabbing the rope that I'd used to tie Adalyn down to the bed earlier, I managed to tie her hands together even though she put up a valiant effort to fight off Chase. There was no getting out of this. The Reaper had found her this night.

Her feet were next, and I gripped her legs hard to get the rope wrapped around her ankles so she could stand but not walk or run. The best she could do was bunny hop around, and the image that created in my mind made me laugh. I looked around the alley and spotted a large dumpster. Pulling on the black leather gloves of my trade, I marched over to the dumpster and pulled out a half dozen bags so there would be just enough room for her to stand in the middle of the big box of rotting trash.

"Put her in here," I said, pointing to the hole I'd just made. I liked the fact that Chase didn't question—he seemed to be genuinely curious about the entire process and was an eager student.

"Please, no. Spider, don't do this. I can help you. I can be useful, I promise. I can fuck you whenever you want, and I'm good at stealing things. You name it, and I can get it. Please, please, please," she begged as more tears and makeup continued to trail down her face. At this point, I had no idea where the makeup was even coming from and had to wonder if her eyes were simply producing it at this point.

"You're a Reaper. I don't make deals with Reapers," Chase said as he tossed her into the hole feet first. The steel dumpster came up to her shoulders, so all we could easily see was her head poking out of the top of the bin like a comical little gopher.

"What if I switch to your club? What if I get you valuable information about the Reapers to help you destroy them?"

Even I knew that was a stupid question without Chase having to say anything. Chase shook his head, glaring at the girl.

"Last fucking thing I need is a disloyal piece of shit like you in my club. If you can turn against them so easily, what would stop you from doing the same thing to me?"

I opened the gasoline can and poured it all over the trash in the dumpster as her screams for help echoed down the alley. A smattering of fuel landed on the girl in a few places, but for the most part, I tried to make sure it didn't hit her—it would prolong the process that way. This would cause the most fear and suffering possible, and that was exactly what Chase was looking to see.

"Please," she whimpered, her eyes finding mine.

"You're begging the wrong devil. I live to see you burn." Clicking on the same propane torch as earlier, I tossed it onto the pile of trash. It was almost as therapeutic as what I'd done to Adalyn. To kill this random woman while destroying all the items I'd used to hurt Adalyn—it was like she'd stepped in to become the final sacrifice.

There was a sudden whoosh as the flames all around the girl rose high into the air. I noticed Chase step away from the extreme heat, but for me, it felt like home. The flames and the fire were my only family, and I watched them dance and waver as they looked for their promised feast.

Her hair caught fire first, and the horror in her eyes became frantic as all of that bright red hair stood up and wavered like billowing curtains in the wind as it was wreathed in flames. When the screams turned into shrieks of pain, my cock twitched again even though it had no business even bothering to try to get hard. She thrashed around inside the dumpster, her limbs banging into the steel walls until her body finally fell silent. I became transfixed by her eyes as they liquified and were eaten away, leaving nothing more than two blackened sockets.

I couldn't tell you how long it was until the fire dimmed and Chase laid his hand on my shoulder. My gaze slowly tore away from the sight of the crackling embers and the smoke rising into the night to look at my new friend.

"First, man, that shit stinks, so I'm gonna stick with bullets," Chase said before nodding to the dumpster. "Second, I've seen some sick shit, but the look in your eyes right now is terrifying, so you officially take the cake on 'most fucked' up with extra icing on top, and yet I really fucking like you."

I smiled at him, the strange comment filling me with a tingling of joy.

"Thank you."

Chase sniffed my shoulder and made a face.

"Damn, you reek. Come on. We got the rest of the night to party."

I gathered up the meager bits of equipment left into my bag and tossed it in the truck before following Chase back inside the shitty little bar. Somewhere in the far reaches of my mind, I knew that the last remaining threads of sanity that I was hanging on to were being threatened by this man. Chase was like a vast expanse of unstable ground filled with quicksand and sinkholes, yet I found myself laughing and happily following him inside for another round of craziness.

I had no reason to ask for forgiveness anymore. Truthfully, I don't know if I ever had one, but the world was about to see what the monster in me could really do once set free.

Not
even the
Devil could burn
the world like
I could

CHAPTER 26

I startled awake and sat up straight like I was emerging from a bad dream.

"Ow, fuck," I swore as I slammed my head off the steering wheel and then had to contend with the sun shining in the windshield. Covering my eyes like a vampire, I groped around for my sunglasses and, finding them, slid them into place as I flicked down the sun visor.

"Oh shit," I groaned as my stomach rolled, giving just a second's notice that I was going to be sick. I barely got the door open and myself out of the truck before I was puking my guts out until my stomach felt like it had turned inside out. My hand squeezed the shit out of the side of the truck bed, my arm shaking as the puking turned into dry heaves that left me gasping for air. If it wasn't for the truck, I would've landed in my own puke as my knees shook.

Everything fucking hurt. My eyes hurt, my body hurt, and of special note, my mind felt like it was screaming hysterically as it tried to bang its way out of my skull. What the hell had happened last night?

I slowly straightened up and looked around and found that I had no clue where the fuck I was. The parking lot was empty, and there were no other buildings in the strange location, just the one behind me. As I turned around, I stared up at the black-painted building. The neon sign was off, but it read 'Foxy Rail' and sported an image of a girl hanging on to a pole.

"How did I end up at a strip club?" At this point, the better question was probably asking what day it was. I dug out my phone and tried to get it to work, but my thumbs acted like they belonged to someone else, and as a result, it took like ten tries and both hands to get it to turn on.

I sighed and leaned back against the truck as it said it was only the next morning. It felt like I'd lost months—everything was either a blur or completely blank. Pulling up the map on my phone, I leaned more against the truck and looked to see where the hell I was.

"Son of a bitch," I mumbled as my eyes focused on the map, which said I had over an hour's drive to get home. With a great deal of effort, I got myself back into the truck, where I noticed a bottle of water with a sticky note on it. Picking the bottle up, I realized there was a baggie with two white pills inside attached to it with some tape.

Hey Man, take this to stop the bongo drums. C. Mathers.

"Fucker." I cracked the bottle and took a swig before tossing the pills in my mouth, preparing myself for what came next. The sound of the truck starting up was enough to make me want to run away from my own body. The loud engine and vibration of the seat made it feel like I'd hopped on a loud roller coaster full of people screaming, but in my head.

The drive home was blessedly light on traffic, and after arriving, I sat staring up at the farmhouse and groaned. I needed a shower, and yet it seemed like an insurmountable effort to make it up the stairs to the front door and then up another flight to the bathroom. Just thinking about it was making my head pound. The sound of the door of the truck opening was like someone screaming into my ear all over again, and I winced, grabbing for my temple.

I slid more gingerly than hopped out of the cab, and then immediately and ungracefully threw up on the grass. This time, it was all clear-colored as the bottle of water made a reappearance. Nope. I was never drinking again, at least not with Chase. That fucking asshole was a one-way ticket to a hell I had no interest in visiting again anytime soon.

I was purposely avoiding Dora. I knew she wouldn't be happy with me over the residential area, and I had this strange, self-destructive urge to tell her what I did to Adalyn. That was not a good idea for either of us.

I didn't want her to see me as the monster I knew I was. She was the last remaining human on this god-forsaken rock that actually liked me—Chase didn't count. I certainly couldn't ruin the last bit of faith she had in me by showing up looking and acting like this after hurting her the way I had. Accident or not, I'd scared her, and that bothered me.

Seeing her without pulling myself together first, without clawing my way back into a better headspace, would be a disaster. It wasn't going to happen overnight, either—it would take some time, maybe even days. After all the shit that had been happening recently, I needed some time when nothing was happening.

So, other than doing the daily things that needed to get done, like tending to my cows, making sure the lawn was cut or fixing whatever decided to break, I spent a solid week not doing anything else. The week went painfully slow, and after the first few days, the silence in the empty farmhouse became deafening. I'd never longed for the ghosts of the dead from my past to speak to me, but as I found myself staring down at that one frayed hole in the carpet that looked kind of like a dog, again, I realized I'd even take that instead.

The cuckoo clock on the wall began singing annoyingly to announce the time. If it wasn't for the fact that Dora had given it to me as a house-warming gift, I would've pulled out a shotgun and shot the fucking thing off the wall by now. No matter how many times I listened to that little bird and its stupid chirp, I couldn't get used to it.

I sniffed the air and tried to pick out the scent of whatever I had cooking in the oven over the pervasive smell of dust and mildew. It was still a mystery ten minutes in—maybe something with mushrooms? Dora seemed like a mushroom lover.

Dora had dropped by earlier to knock on the door, and I had felt like one of those people online that threw themselves to the floor to hide as I dove out of the front window's line of sight.

"Derek, I know you're in there. You have to speak to me sometime," she'd called through the door as I stood around the corner out of view. The handle had rattled, but she didn't use the key I knew she had. "When you're ready to talk, you know where these old bones live." With that, she'd shuffled away from the door and was gone, with only the covered casserole dish she left behind to show that she'd been there at all.

Was hiding out childish? Most certainly, but I just needed a couple more days to get my head right. Now, thanks to Dora, I'd even have something to eat during them. She hadn't labeled what she left, so at the moment, it was a mystery and the only real excitement in my day. Leaning back into the couch, eyes closed, and arm flopped over my face, I waited for dinner to be done.

Suddenly, my phone vibrated. No one had my number...I didn't think.

Pulling the phone out of my jeans pocket, I saw it said I had a text message from 'Cherry Popper.' Who the fuck was *Cherry Popper*? I opened the message and smirked.

It's Mathers. I need some chickens deep-fried.

I stared at the strange message. To the best of my shaky memories of that night, we hadn't eaten any fried chicken that I'd made. I mean, I couldn't remember enough to say for certain, but it didn't sound like something I'd do, so I could only assume he meant the girl from the dumpster.

I'm not in the chicken business anymore.

I'd make it worth your while. No one makes chicken like you do.

I tapped the phone against my chin as I thought. On the one hand, the demons in my head had been remarkably quiet while tucked away on this dusty little farm. On the other hand, that morning, I'd caught myself talking to a large spider that had moved into the shed until it had gotten sick of me standing there and taken off up into the rafters. That was a low moment, even for me.

How well do you want them? I asked.

Extra crispy.

I sat up on the couch, a spark of excitement coursing through me.

How many chickens are we talking about?

Consider it an extermination.

I'll think about it.

After typing back, I stood up to pace around the small living room. I couldn't stay here doing nothing all the time, and I also couldn't be normal—that was becoming clearer with each passing day. I took another lap around the living room while my brain mulled over the pros and cons. Giving in, I sighed.

I'll cook for you.

I'll leave you a list at our favorite spot. Just ask the bartender for Sam's list. It will be there in a couple of hours.

Okie dokie.

I knew that response would throw him for a loop. I could picture the look on his fucking face now. I was only mildly disappointed when he didn't send anything back.

It was wrong to be filled with this much excitement over the thought of killing who knew how many people, but I couldn't deny that I wanted to do it. I never would've thought that one drunken night would lead me down this path again, but if I was going to jump into the deep end of the pool once more, I might as well do it for a cause.

Peeking at the timer, I saw that it had forty minutes left, which gave me just enough time to go and check my supplies. Then, I could pick up the list.

Burn

Three hours later, I was pulling into the same spot on the side of the road that I'd parked in when I'd decided to walk into the dingy bar the first time. My stomach rolled as I looked up at the sign, and I had to quickly swallow back down my dinner. Apparently, my stomach remembered being here. Hopping out of the truck, I made my way inside.

The patrons sitting around didn't stare this time—in fact, they quickly turned away like they were worried that looking at me might draw my attention. I walked up to the bar and the bartender, who had his back to me.

"One second," he said gruffly, and as he slowly turned around, his eyes stayed fixed on the beer mug he was drying. When the bartender looked up and his eyes found mine, he sucked in a deep breath, his eyes going wide. The guy swallowed hard, the beer mug stilling in his hands, which were noticeably shaking. He looked as frozen as if the mother fucking Medusa had just wandered in.

I'd been stared at a lot. I'd even gotten used to receiving terrified stares, but that was usually because of the burn on my face. This was new. I felt like Al Capone or something.

When the man didn't move and simply continued to stare, I decided to prompt him.

"I'm here for Sam's list," I said.

Like I'd shot the man out of a fucking cannon, he bolted to the far end of the bar before sprinting back like he was doing a hundred-meter dash, white envelope in hand. He held it out with just the tips of his fingers. So *this* was how a tiger in a cage felt.

I had no idea what all that was about, but I wasn't about to ask— some things you didn't really want to know. I wandered back out to the truck, opening the envelope on the way. Hopping in, I scanned over the addresses. I didn't know these locations, but if this had anything to do with the motorcycle club Chase was at odds with, then they needed to be destroyed in close succession. Days or weeks in between wouldn't work, or they would scatter like ants and reform somewhere else.

I hoped he knew what he was asking, because once I started this, there wouldn't be any turning back.

Opening my phone, I mapped out where all of the targets were and then pulled away from the curb to go and have a look for myself. I needed to know where the buildings were and what the surroundings were like. The hardest part was going to be figuring out the best way to get inside, and of course, what was going to be the best and most efficient way to burn them down.

I wiggled in my seat as I pulled up in front of the first target—what looked to be as rat-laden of a bar like the one I'd just left. I was getting excited. There was no way around it, as thoughts of what this place would look like burning made my cock stand straight.

I didn't have time for a little rub down—that would have to wait until after I was finished. Chase had mentioned that he needed this done as quickly as possible. The fucker didn't ask for much. There were seventeen locations to hit. He either thought I was some sort of super villain with a fire ability, or I'd talked myself up a little too much the other night.

The next target was not far down the road from a college campus. Go figure. Not where I would've looked for a motorcycle club, but then again, that was probably the point. I was marking down the size of the building when movement in the rearview mirror caught my attention. I glanced up, away, and then immediately back again as I wondered what in the ever-loving fuck was happening.

A tiny blonde was running down the street in my direction. That in and of itself was not the issue—it was the giant Care Bear on the apron she was wearing, making it look like the bear was skipping down the street, and the metal strainer she was wearing on her head that was the issue. The girl was being closely followed by a guy that was leaping into the air while grabbing at nothing.

My window was down, and as they closed in on the truck's location, I could understand what they were yelling.

"Stop! Gimme back the cookies," the girl yelled, swatting wildly at the air with a spatula.

The guy was right on her heels.

"You bitch, Tinkerbell! I fucking see you, and I'm not wearing that fucking dress." He leaped in the air, and I watched out of morbid curiosity as the guy landed, tripped, rolled, and jumped back up to continue running like nothing had happened.

I glanced around at the buildings again.

"What the fuck do they put in the water around here?" I looked at the bottle of water I'd purchased at the convenience store down the road and tossed the closed bottle on the floor. "Nope. Already had enough of not knowing what the fuck was going on for the year," I mumbled, pulling away from the curb as the pair turned and came running back up the sidewalk toward me.

"And they fucking locked *my* ass up." I shook my head in wonder.

Each target was given a code that told me what I needed to accomplish the task. Most were going to be easy, but two were more challenging due to the number of cameras and people in the area.

I smirked as I jotted down my notes for the last location and decided that I was going to make good use of the C4, the electrical panels, and a few burner phones. I felt like a kid at Halloween, or at least like a normal kid at Halloween. I'd never had a normal Halloween unless it was considered normal to hide all night like the monster lived in your home —because in my house, the monster was real and he didn't wear a costume other than the face of my father.

On Halloween, my brother and I had sometimes eaten dinner in an eerie silence before being forced to listen to our parents have sex until my father passed out. Candy, costumes, laughter, family parties, or seeing friends was out of the question. Sometimes, I'd steal a small toy or handful of candy from one of the kids at school that had so much they never noticed the loss and gave it to Asher. His face would light up and he'd hug me hard.

I love you, Derek.

I love you too, Ash.

As my phone vibrated, I got pulled out of the old memory. Picking it up, I smiled at the message.

Money transferred to the account I set up for you as payment. If you need anything else for the chickens, let me know. I have cooking supplies.

Righty-ho. I'll send you a list of what I need and a locale for where to leave the barbecue items.

There was a long pause where the little typing bubble appeared and disappeared several times.

Righty-ho? WTF Man?

I couldn't contain the snort of laughter as I pulled away from the last location and made my way out of town to do a little shopping. Was it sad that my only amusement was seeing if I could freak Chase out? I was going to owe him a beer at some point for getting me out of the house. I hadn't realized how much I'd needed this until this moment.

Not
even the
Devil could burn
the world like
I could

CHAPTER 27

It had taken forty-eight hours to get everything I needed in place. It also took a few phone calls and favors from Chase to make sure the targets were distracted enough that I could sneak inside and set the rat traps. He hadn't been joking when he said this was an extermination. If the fires took out everyone they should, it would reach the high double digits for sure, and more if others were inside.

It was finally time, and an insatiable eagerness rushed through my body. I cracked my neck and rolled out my shoulders as I got ready for the show.

The first explosion was smaller. It was meant to maim and trap—it was the other explosions that were intended to kill. As the secondary explosions started, they sent a shockwave through the streets, and I was mesmerized as the nearby store windows shattered, the glass becoming miniature projectiles. I smiled as a black cloud of smoke, and orange flames rose into the night sky. I would never grow tired of staring at the beauty of a blaze when it was in its full glory.

"Our God comes and will not be silent; a fire devours before Him, and around Him a tempest rages," I whispered the bible verse as I stared at the third building bursting into flames in the rearview mirror. "If we confess our sins, he is faithful and just to forgive us our sins and to cleanse us from all unrighteousness."

I had to wonder if John meant that God would forgive and absolve me of my sins? I doubted any kind of god could see past what I'd become.

According to Chase, this was the best time of day to hit to make sure that as many people were inside drunk and passed out as possible. It was a lull in the morning where everything was blissfully quiet, like everything in the world had pushed pause at the same time. As I passed the closed stores and dark windows of homes, I realized that this was my favorite time of day. This was when I was at my most peaceful.

I glanced at the timer on my wrist. Each target had an hour interval, but a few locations were being taken out at the same time since they were on the same street. This made it very difficult for the firefighters to get control of the burns, and the police would be thinned as more fires started and more roads became closed and blocked off.

The second target was two stores sitting side by side that looked like a simple pawn shop and a dry cleaner's shop. I held the burner phone out like a television remote and pressed the detonation button. The explosion was instantaneous, and the truck vibrated and shook from the shockwave as the buildings erupted. There was nothing sweeter than the sound of the rumble and roar of a fire coming to life.

Car alarms up and down the street blared, lights flashing and winking as if trying to summon help as I slowly drove away. I could imagine the panic and fear that those inside the buildings experienced for the few seconds before they died and loved the idea of them trying to run from the fire like it was a beast on their heels.

I repeated the process at a couple more locations and smiled as I noted that I was right on time. The GPS showed that emergency services had blocked off the roads I suspected they would. Using the back alleys, I rolled into the parking area near the next location. The sun was starting to rise and brighten the sky, making the last couple of targets the most dangerous.

The radio broadcasts were about the fires, how the police were at a loss, and how off-duty emergency crews were being called in to help control the spread. Within me, there was a calm satisfaction that I only found when sitting within a mass of chaos. It was nature's way to create chaos, just as it was a human desire to create order, but I'd never been one to feel calm within the confines of order like others. My skin would itch, and a restlessness would take hold of my body. It wasn't until I'd broken the sociological chains wrapped around my throat that I'd finally felt free.

I smoothly parked the truck in a corner spot that was just shy of a ten-minute walk from the next target. For this one, it was better if I walked. I didn't want to take a chance on the truck being spotted on camera again so soon, so that meant I was going to have to sneak in close enough on foot for the signal from the cell to work.

I grabbed the burner phone labeled 'college road' and stuffed it in my pocket as I stepped out into the early morning light. If I listened hard, I could almost hear the scream of sirens in the distance. Sticking to the darkness of the alleys, I wove my way toward a long building posing as a nightclub, smirking as I spotted the long line of motorcycles neatly parked in a row down the side of the building. Looked like a full house. Wasn't that just a shame?

My thumb rubbed over the little button in my pocket as I stood in the alley hidden among the shadows with the other dangerous things that like to lurk in the dark.

My thumb hovered over the button for a moment longer. Then, with a sharp intake of breath, I pressed the button. It was like having a wet mouth around my cock as the building roared like a dragon. The ground shook with the first explosion in the back of the building, and then, like a deadly game of dominos, the rest detonated in succession.

I couldn't take my eyes off the sight and watched with evil glee as someone tried to escape the mouth of the beast by running out the front door. Their daring escape was short-lived, however, as the hungry fire, angered by the person's attempt to escape, reached out with the last of the explosions to wrap itself around the person like a hug.

Leaning against the wall, I could only wish for a bag of popcorn and someone to suck me off as I watched the man run around in circles while screaming hysterically. The fire ate away at his skin and nerve endings before sliding down his throat, which was what ultimately killed him. He stood still for several seconds, frozen in death like a beautiful work of art, before finally collapsing. His skin continued crackling, turning blackened and wrinkled.

When I closed my eyes and concentrated, I could smell the sweet scent of his charred flesh from where I stood. The heat of the immense blaze warmed my skin as I glanced down at the timer. I had time to watch this one a little longer—it was magnificent.

"It's a bonfire. I need a stick!" My head jerked up at the sudden yell that pulled me out of my reverie. A small, pink, fluffy ball of unicorns and Care Bears trailed by a bobbing blonde ponytail sprinted past the mouth of the alley where I was standing.

What the fuck?

I peeked around the corner of the alley to watch where the glittering ball of crazy was heading.

"Anyone have chocolate? I can't make s'mores without chocolate," she called out to the people starting to gather on the street to gawk as she held up a bag of marshmallows. When she turned in a circle, I realized it was the same girl who'd been running around with a strainer on her head. You didn't forget something like that. I watched in fascination as she skipped off down the alley beside the burning building like she was out for a day at the local amusement park.

Another girl was now heading down the street—she just looked annoyed as she marched toward the scene, like all the dying people were being the biggest inconvenience in the world. The people on this street were the strangest I'd ever encountered, and yet, like a trainwreck, I couldn't look away. My eyes roamed all over her features as she got closer. She seemed familiar. A quick flash of Chase showing me a picture of his girl that he called Princess crossed my mind.

Huh? Chase didn't mention she was practically jailbait.

"You dirty old bastard. Good for you," I snickered.

Peering around the corner at the growing crowd, I saw a group of guys had started talking to Chase's girl, but it was the strange little blonde near them that had me laughing unexpectedly. She was back after having found a stick somewhere and was currently roasting a marshmallow over the still-steaming dead guy. I had no idea who she was, but she was my kind of crazy.

A few cop cars screeched to a halt at the scene, and that was my cue to get going. Slipping from the shadows of the alley, I walked down the street away from the fire with my hood up and head down.

The pitter-patter of feet running up behind me had me tensing up, and my fists clenched as I prepared to be attacked. Instead, I received a hard poke in the back that had me turning around and looking down into the eyes of the crazy girl. Her lips were covered with white marshmallows, her mouth full of the same sticky substance.

Why was that look fucking hot on her? I shook my head at the weird girl.

"What?" I asked when she just continued to stare as she rocked back and forth on her slippered feet.

She smiled widely, and there was a glimmer in her eyes that I recognized. I saw the same look when I stared in a mirror. Someone had hurt her, and at some point, her mind had protected itself by creating this odd form of her personality. It was like she viewed the world around her like it was a book with continually flipping pages, only catching glimpses at a time of a story that wandered between fairytale land and reality.

"You're the dragon," she said, pushing out her chest.

"I'm what?"

She pointed at the fire and then looked closer at her fingers as if just realizing there was sticky stuff on them. She proceeded to suck them all into her mouth while trying to talk around them. For just a moment, I wondered if she was going to put the whole fist in her mouth. The imagery was oddly fucking hot.

"You da dwagon," she mumbled with a little bit of drool dripping down her chin.

I didn't know if I should be more concerned that she knew I'd set the fire or that I understood what the fuck she meant and was still enjoying watching her suck on her hand like that. The thing was, now I had to decide if I needed to kill her.

A thought occurred to me, and I narrowed my glare as the other blonde kept glancing our way.

"Do you know Mathers?" I asked.

Her eyes went wide.

"I don't know, do *you* know Mathers?" she asked, whispering like we were talking state conspiracies. Her eyes darted around as her tongue slipped between two of her fingers. Before I could have any more inappropriate thoughts about the girl, the other blonde yelled for her.

"Ava! Get back here now! I'm not chasing you all over the city. I have better things to do," the girl I was pretty sure was Princess yelled, hands on her hips and lips puckered so tight she looked like she'd just sucked on a lemon.

The dragon girl looked over her shoulder and sighed as she pulled her hand out of her mouth with a sucking sound.

"She probably wants spring rolls." Shrugging, the little blonde turned and skipped off. One of the top ten strangest interactions I'd had in my life, hands down, and I'd fucking lived in an asylum for nine years. Turning, I pulled the hood low over my face and made my slow, deliberate escape.

I'd gotten behind in my timing for the last couple of stops, and it wasn't until the sun was fully up that I reached my last target. The cops had blocked off a much larger area than I'd anticipated, which caused delays getting to the required locations.

The truck rumbled to a halt down the street from the last target, which happened to be a small house in a low-income subdivision. I stared at the home before realizing that it looked exactly the same as my childhood home. My hands squeezed the steering wheel hard, the leather gloves covering them squeaking in response.

Smack.

The hand had come out of nowhere, cracking me across the face.

"You didn't cut the grass," my father yelled. I could feel the eyes of neighbors staring at us, but no one told him to stop. No one came over and offered to help me. Instead, they all looked away as I looked around.

"I'm talking to you, boy." My father's hand grabbed my arm, fingers digging deep into my skin. "Answer me."

"It was too hot all day, dad. It would burn the grass up. I was going to do it once it cooled off," I said, trying to reason. He shook my arm hard in response.

"Don't you lie to me. You're a worthless piece of shit. Can't even do a simple task."

My dad raised his hand to smack me again.

"Dad! Look what I got," Asher called out as he pedaled up the sidewalk. A large smile stretched across his face as he held up a football. My father let go of my arm with a shove and smiled at Asher.

"That's my boy! Where did you find that?"

"Tommy gave it to me. He said that we can join the school team together, and one day, I can join the NFL. His dad is the school's coach, and I'm a shoo-in if I can throw. I tried a few passes already, and he said I was a natural." Asher hopped off his bike, which clattered to the ground as he left it behind. If I'd done that, I would've gotten a beating.

"Well, at least one of my sons is going to do something with their life."

My father glared at me. "Cut the fucking grass and put your brother's bike away. I hate clutter on the lawn." He wrapped his arm around Asher's shoulders as he listened to him happily talking about trying out for the school team. I watched them walk away and couldn't help but wonder why I was the child he'd chosen to hate.

I loved my brother, but in that moment, I hated him for having something I'd never experience. Even if it was short-lived, even if it was a fleeting thing, Asher had our father's love and pride.

Grabbing the last remote, I snarled as I slammed my thumb down on the button. As the house erupted in flames, I turned the truck around and turned on the radio. The song "Flowers on the Wall" was playing. My left foot and hands tapped in time to the catchy song, and as I watched the fire rise into the sky behind me, I smiled.

My only wish was that I hadn't killed my father so quickly. I would've liked to see him scream as he burned.

Not
even the
Devil could burn
the world like
I could

Chapter 28

The smile stretched across my face from the last seventy-two hours of adventure slipped as I turned onto my road. I needed to go see Dora. I hadn't made sure she didn't need anything for a week now, and the little knot in my stomach was yelling at me that I was being a pussy for staying away so long. She'd been nothing but kind to me, and I had promised to help out around her property. After everything she'd done, I had to suck up my fear and pride and go see her before I did anything else.

I drew in a deep breath and then smiled as I pulled up beside her white car before jumping out of the truck. The place really was in a stunning spot, I hadn't taken the time to appreciate it before, but the layout of the large property combined with the small pond, naturally rolling fields, and old bank barn, which still looked new, all added to the mystique of the place. It was as if someone had waved a magic wand and frozen everything in time.

I made it to the front door and took a second deep breath as I readied myself to be greeted with Dora's grandmotherly concern. Opening the door, I stepped inside, but only silence greeted me. I looked back out the door, and yup, the car was still there.

"Dora? Dora, it's me, Derek," I called out. Everything seemed to be in place, yet I couldn't help feeling like something wasn't right. "Dora?"

I marched down the hallway toward her bedroom, poking my head into every open doorway along the way. Nothing. I looked into her bedroom—the bed was perfectly made, but she wasn't in the room.

"Dora," I called out again into the quiet home as I made my way to the kitchen. Bowls and ingredients were laid out on top of the island like she was in the middle of baking.

My foot faltered as I spotted the hand on the floor.

"No, Dora." I darted around the island, the pounding in my head forgotten as I took in her still form lying on the floor. Going to my knees, I touched the side of her neck only to find that her body was cold to the touch. I couldn't find a pulse.

"Dora," I whispered as I slowly turned the woman over and pulled her into my lap. This little old woman had been the closest thing I'd ever had to a loving mother, and with a howl of pain, the tears came as I realized I was truly alone.

I rocked her body back and forth as the tears spiraled into a torrent of pain I couldn't explain. I'd barely known this woman. We weren't family, yet it had felt like we were, and the last memory I had of seeing her alive was watching her back away with fear in her eyes when I'd grabbed her arm.

Guilt tore at my heart, ripping away the scabs from all the other old wounds it had suffered. If I'd been here with her, maybe I could've helped her. I dropped my head to the cotton material of her flower-patterned dress and let all the emotion I'd bottled up pour out. The memories started flowing, starting with the cruelties of my father and not stopping until that moment when I'd stared at Adalyn's face and realized I'd only been used.

By the time the tears stopped, I felt exhausted and beaten down. It was the same way I'd felt so many other times, but this time felt different. I was being given a message—I couldn't hang on to any part of my past, the good or the bad, if I were going to be reborn into what I was destined to become. I wasn't one hundred percent sure what that was yet, but nothing in my life that was good ever lasted, and there had to be a reason for that. There simply had to be a logical explanation for why any glimmer of hope or joy was always stolen from me.

Pulling a semblance of myself together, I stood with Dora in my arms. As a flash of color caught my eye, I turned my head and couldn't help but stare at the little cross stitch she'd been working on that'd been left lying on the counter. 'You are who you are, not who you used to be,' it read. As I read and re-read the words over and over, the pain in my chest thumped in time with the pain in my head.

Tearing my eyes away from the little piece of artwork, I walked out into the backyard to bury not only the rest of my past, but also the body of the one person that had shown me true kindness.

Burn

Many hours and bottles of water later, I stumbled back into the house. My hands were blistered from the shovel and now just as dirty as my blackened soul. I couldn't call the cops to come and take her body away, and I knew she knew that, but it didn't ease the guilt of tossing her body into a hole in the yard like she was a random dead animal.

I collapsed onto a kitchen chair, unable to find the motivation to drag myself to the shower, and looked down at the paperwork that she'd laid out. It looked like she'd been in the middle of paying some bills, and I found myself lifting the pages a piece at a time to read what each one was and then lay it back down.

I was about to stand and leave the rest for later, if ever when the corner of a notepad sticking out of the pile caught my attention. I pushed the paperwork sitting on top of it off and stared at the handwritten note.

My Dear Boy Derek,

I wanted to write you this letter so that there is nothing I've left unsaid to you, and with my muddled brain, I can barely remember the day, let alone a conversation, anymore. I know we're not family, but I feel like you're my son, and although I never said it out loud, I want you to know I love you as if you were my own flesh and blood.

I'd always seen you, the shy boy in pain living under the rude teen protecting himself with harsh words and a harsher attitude. There are only two things I regret in this world. The first one is not pushing harder to find you when you were taken from the Giltberts. You needed someone to fight for you, and it will haunt me until the day I die that I didn't push. The little you've told me about your time at the hospital breaks my heart, but I still see you, and you're still that little boy lashing out at an unjust world. I won't tell you to stop because you wouldn't listen even if I did, but I want you to know that there is another way, and that one day, someone is going to pull you out of the pain you are in. Just don't let others define you or tell you who or what you are. You're so much more than that.

The only other thing I regret in this life is not reconnecting with my daughter and my granddaughter, Rebecca. For all my big talk, it has taken me a long time to stop being scared to reach out to others and get over my own ego, and I guess I don't want you to make the same mistakes that I have. Find your brother, reach out to him, and heal the wounds that lie between you. You are each other's only family now, and all you have left. Don't make light of that.

I wish I had great pearls of wisdom to pass on to you, but I think you already know what path you must walk. I just hope that whatever time we have left together, you know that knowing you has brought some of the happiest and most special moments of my life to me.

If you're reading this, I'm most likely already dead and gone or my brain is so lost that I no longer know my own name. I know you promised not to let me live like that, and I thank you for that. It meant the world to me to know that I wouldn't end up staring at a wall with shit in my pants. Don't laugh. I know you just pictured that.

You will find on the next page all the information you will ever need to get into my bank accounts and make it look like I'm still alive. Yes, I know it's wrong, but I can't just put your name on the accounts when everyone thinks you're dead, my boy, now can I? Besides, by this point, I'm pretty sure you are past caring what is right and wrong.

If you happen to see this before I die, then please bury me by the lemon trees and visit me often, for I will miss you, and you will always be able to find me there. Take care of yourself, Derek.

Love, Dora

P.S. I've been making extra meals every day and freezing them for you because the Good Lord knows you would go without otherwise. You will find the freezer in the basement full, and yes, there's lemon pie.

Droplets landed on the page, and I looked up at the ceiling to check for a leak before realizing it was my own tears dripping onto the page. I hadn't cried as much in my life as I had since my escape from the asylum, and I had to wonder what exactly they'd done to me there. After lifting the page to look at the next one and see the list of accounts and passwords, I laid the top page back down. I didn't want to see those right now.

In my life, I'd experienced sadness, loss, betrayal, fear, and of course, pain, but the grief and guilt I felt over losing Dora was new. The ache in my chest was worse than when I thought Adalyn had died in the asylum. That sweet little old woman had been the only good thing in my life, and I hadn't spent the last few days with her out of my own cowardly fear.

I was pathetic. I was weak. I'd chosen to focus on killing dozens of people for a man I barely knew rather than taking care of the one responsibility that actually meant something to me. I didn't deserve her money, and I certainly hadn't deserved her kindness.

Standing from the table, I made my way to the bathroom, the last place I'd spoken to Dora. Her last moments of being with me had scared her enough to lock herself in a bathroom. I looked around the small space filled with her things and collapsed to my knees on the floor. I couldn't breathe as the sobs wracked my body with wave after shuddering wave of aching regret.

"I'm so sorry," I gasped out. "I'm so sorry I wasn't here." I balled the small mat on the floor into my fists and wanted to trash the small space, but as I looked up at the pretty dried flowers and decorative jars of soap, I couldn't do it. I couldn't destroy the last remnants of the kind soul that had touched mine.

"Stop trying to follow me," I growled at my brother. He was being extra clingy tonight, and I had things that needed to be taken care of that couldn't involve him. When I'd seen the couple in the store, I'd been tempted to push the tall food rack over on top of them, but Asher had been with me, and besides, they would've lived—they needed to die for what they did.

"No. I know you're up to something, and I don't want you to go," Asher said, pulling on my hoodie.

I yanked my arm away and glared at my younger brother.

"I told you that I'm not up to anything. I just need some time alone. Maybe I'll try and connect with a friend, or hell, get us a meal from that fried chicken place you like."

"Chicken? That's your big secret?" Asher stood with his fists balled as he glared at me. He was way too perceptive for his age, and normally, I'd say that was a great life skill. At the moment, it was just annoying.

"Why do you think I'm up to something?" I held out my hands the way magicians did when they wanted to show they didn't have any cards up their sleeves. Totally trustworthy. "Have I said something that would make you think that? Have I done something to make you not trust me?"

"It's your energy."

I raised an eyebrow at my eleven-year-old brother. Where the hell did he learn this crap? My energy? Please, spare me. My energy was just fine.

"You've been hanging around Mrs. Giltbert and her lady friends too much, bro."

He rolled his eyes at me like I was the one being unreasonable, but his face softened as he looked down at the dirt floor of the barn.

"I can't lose you, D. You're all I have. We are all that each other has, and I know you want to go after mum and dad. I hear you mumble about how much you want them to die in your sleep."

I stood up straight. I hadn't realized I talked in my sleep, let alone about our parents.

"What do I say?"

Asher shrugged his shoulders, doing that thing where he didn't really say anything.

"Just stuff. You say they need to go, that dad needs to pay." Asher shook his head and crossed his arms over his chest. "And then you started acting all weird at the store, and I just know you're not going to let this go."

"How can you expect me to let what they did to us go?" I stepped away from my brother, my anger boiling to the point where I had to haul off and punch the wooden post that supported the rafters. The immediate bite of pain gave me a sliver of relief from the anger and pain churning in my chest.

"We're living out of a barn, Asher. Look around. We are in constant *fear that they will find us, and you know that will not go well. Look at my face."* I pointed to the ragged scar that lined the right side of my face and officially classified me as a freak. *"It's been two years since this happened, and the pain in my face is still like it just happened. I can't take the chance of ending up back there, Asher. I just can't. This spot may not be fancy, but we have food and a roof and a little bit of money."*

"But, that's my point. If you run off and punish mum and dad, something could happen to you. I don't want anything to happen to you. I don't want us to be separated. The Giltberts are nice. I don't want to leave."

Walking forward, I placed my hands on Asher's shoulders.

"That's not going to happen, Ash. We have too much unfinished business."

Burn

The wind picked up, and somewhere, a wind chime tingled softly. I slowly lifted my head, not sure where I'd walked to until my eyes landed on my childhood home. I stood in the shadows of the large tree in the front yard, my eyes fixed on the warm glow coming from the window. The home had been re-built and looked brand new with its fresh paint job and the flowers hanging from baskets over the small stoop, but all I saw when I looked at it was the hell it had been and the charred skeleton it had become.

My nose flared as I pictured my father stomping across the living room floor, his hand cracking my mother across her face as I ran into the room screaming to try and stop him. All I'd ever wanted was to protect myself and my brother, but I'd loved my mother until I was old enough to understand that she chose to stay. She chose to remain in that fucking hell even though my father hurt me in front of her. After realizing that, I could no longer find love for her. Maybe that was unfair, maybe she'd been too scared. Fuck, for all I knew, maybe she even tried to leave, but her unsuccessful attempts didn't stop the broken bones and the sleepless nights. It certainly didn't stop the crack of my father's belt or.... I touched the side of my face that was the visible reminder of the scars that marred my soul. No, she got what she deserved.

Asher was the only person that meant everything to me, and he'd turned me in to the cops. He had me arrested and carted away for looking out for him. Why didn't he just stay in the barn like he was told? Why did he have to follow me? Why did he fucking care what I did to them? How many times had I protected him from being turned into the same kind of punching bag that I'd been? They were evil people, and they deserved worse than what I'd given them. My hand balled into a fist, and my knuckles cracked with the force of the squeeze.

The breeze picked up again, and a fluttering piece of newspaper rolling along the sidewalk tumbled toward me before fluttering straight into my leg. I stared down at the large page as it clung to my leg before reaching down to pull it off so it could continue on its way, but as I did, a glimpse of an image caught my attention.

Standing up straight with the black and white paper in my hand, I stared at the full-page picture of one of the warehouse fires. The fire was in full burn, the flames reaching up into the sky, caught like that for all time by the photographer that had snapped the shot. It was beautiful.

However, it was the back of a man wearing a firefighter's jacket in the foreground that drew my attention. The man was pointing toward the flame, his face mostly hidden from the camera, but the jacket clearly read 'A. West.' My heart pounded hard in my chest as I took in everything about the man and knew with certainty that it was my brother. It struck me as ironic that I'd set that fire, and here *he* was putting it out.

Still trying to stop me, little brother?

Maybe Dora was right. Maybe it was time for me to arrange a little family reunion. My gaze found the yellow front door of the home that used to be my personal hell and then looked back down at the image of Asher. Folding the piece of paper, I put it in my pocket.

Yes, a reunion was in order, but I didn't think it was going to be what Dora had intended.

Not
even the
Devil could burn
the world like
I could

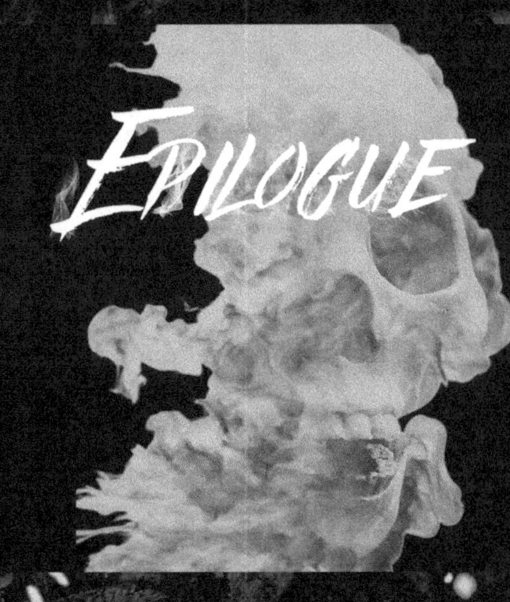

Epilogue

Tick Tock, the mouse ran up the clock. It had taken more time than I'd ever imagined it would to find my younger brother. He didn't have a listed number or address, and I'd resorted to starting small fires to see where he'd show up in the Miami area. My luck changed a month after the fires Chase had commissioned. Over a hundred had died in those fires, and they were calling it the worst tragedy the city had ever seen. It was only second to the asylum fire in casualties.

I'd followed the fire truck back to the station where he worked, and now I had nothing to do but patiently sit along a side street and watch. I wanted to know everything about him—what he ate, and where, who his friends were, where he lived, and even who he fucked. The key to hurting him the way he'd hurt me was not simply killing him but ripping everything he loved out from underneath him.

I wanted to create a fault line in his world and rip out his heart like he'd so callously done to me. He was my brother, yet for nine years, he never even came to see me. He wrote me off like a terrible secret and moved on with his perfect life. Here he was now, a firefighter focused on once more destroying the thing I loved. I could almost imagine the pained wails of the flames as the water crushed them out, and if it was even possible, I hated him a little more at the thought.

He emerged from the fire station, his golden hair picture-perfect even after a long shift. Was there anything my brother couldn't do? The old annoyances from our childhood surfaced with a vengeance as he got into a fancy pickup truck that glistened a bright cherry red in the late afternoon sun. As Asher pulled out of the parking lot, I crept the old truck out from the shade of the side street I'd been waiting in to follow along.

The game of cat and mouse was about to begin. There was some business you couldn't leave unfinished.

Book 2
Chapter 1

BROOKLYN CROSS

CHAPTER 1

I'd waited as long as I could, but as the second pebble hit my window, I knew I needed to get going or not go at all. Stuffing pillows under my comforter, I waved to Becky, who was waiting on the back lawn. I could just make her out, standing in the shadow of the pool house. As quietly as I could, I pulled up on the window and froze as it made a squeaking noise. For this being a relatively new home, it sure made a ton of strange noises.

I looked back toward the door that proudly had my name, Violet, hanging over the top in bright purple letters. My parents thought I just really liked the stupid thing I made in shop class when in reality, it was my little alarm system. Anytime someone was walking down the hall, it rattled back and forth.

As the sign remained silent, I smiled and slipped out the window to the overhang that traveled the entire length of the back porch. I thought about closing the window but didn't want to risk it making any more noise. I scooted to the edge of the overhang. Getting onto my knees, I reached over, my fingers brushing the top of the lattice for my mother's climbing roses.

"Come down backward. It's easier," Becky whisper-yelled at me.

"I can't. I hate heights."

"Just do it."

"Shh, don't wake my parents, or I'm so dead."

"Fine, do it your way, just hurry up."

Getting a grip on the white ladder-like wall, I swung one leg and then the other over the side of the roof.

"Ouch," I whispered and shook my hand as it landed directly on a thorn. "Stupid roses."

Carefully, I made my way down. When close enough, I jumped to the grass below.

"What took you so long anyway?" Becky asked as she ran her fingers through her mane of wavey brunette hair. "I was beginning to think you weren't coming at all."

I stared at my best friend for a moment. She'd put on make-up and was wearing a cute sun dress. She never did either of these things. I had no idea why she suddenly wanted to try and impress a stupid boy—they were all jerks.

"My parents were being dick-wads about my grades and other shit. They went to bed late." I dusted off my jeans and grabbed the backpack I'd stashed earlier in the day from the pool house. "Come on, let's go," I said and headed across the large backyard toward the woods. Becky remained standing in the same spot. "What is it? I thought you were wanting to get going?"

"I do."

"Well then?"

"Maybe we shouldn't. You know what will happen if we're caught— you are going to be so grounded."

I smiled wide. "I'm already grounded. Now come on." I held out my hand to my best friend. As soon as our hands clasped, we were off.

It didn't take long to get to the small beach cove. It was a hidden gem that rarely anyone ventured to, and we could hear the music before we exited the narrow path that opened up to the small sandy area. A bonfire was well under way as people talked and danced. I raised my hands in the air and wiggled my hips back and forth to the Eminem song that was playing.

"Isn't this awesome?" I asked Becky. She didn't look so certain now that we were here. Her eyes were darting from side to side as she stood, arms wrapped around her body. "What's wrong?"

She nodded off toward the far side of the beach. I narrowed my eyes, my hands balling into fists as I recognized Tyler locking lips with Jenny. "That jerk. Weren't you to meet him tonight?" Becky nodded, her big blue eyes glistening with unshed tears. "What is he doing locking lips with that slut?

I took a step in their direction, and Becky grabbed my arm. "No, Vi. Don't."

I glared at my best friend. "He's not getting away with this. I can do it here, or I can do it at school, take your pick."

"Vi, please leave it. He's not worth it," Becky begged. Her eyes held so much hurt, even though she tried to cover it up. I couldn't let it go.

Grabbing her face, I kissed her forehead. "Trust me—this is going to be good." I smiled wickedly and walked away. I marched across the grass, rolling up the sleeves of my shirt. Those that I passed stared. I'm sure they were wondering who I was after now. To say I had a bit of a reputation would've been an understatement. I had an affinity for getting into trouble. What could I say? It found me, and I liked it.

"Hey, Ass-munch," I said as I reached the couple in the process of feeling each other up. I got to see way more of Jenny's naked boob than I ever wanted.

Tyler broke off the kiss and stepped back from Jenny. His eyes were glazed—he'd obviously already had some of the alcohol. "Vi-Vi, what do—"

He didn't get any further before I smiled and stepped in, kneeing him hard in the crotch. The look of pain on his face was instantaneous. He slumped forward and grabbed at his precious cargo.

"Aww, did that hurt?" Making a pout face, I hauled back and gave him a hard right hook across the jaw. He crumpled to the ground, blood seeping from his nose as he cried out in pain.

"Bitch, what the hell is your problem?" Jenny wailed as she dropped to her knees beside Tyler. I kicked sand at the two of them, a good portion of it going into her mouth.

"Call me that again, Jenny, and you'll join Tyler."

"There's something wrong with you," Jenny said as she spat sand out.

Ignoring her, I pointed my finger at Tyler. "You stay away from Becky. If I even see you look in her direction or ask for help with home-work again, this will be the least of what I do to you. Understand?"

His eyes were a mix of anger and fear, but the fear was winning out as I stood over him. He nodded, and I smiled. "Now that we have that settled. Have a great night, you two."

I skipped away and found Becky sitting on the log, covering her eyes. "Oh, come on, Beck, you know you loved to see him get what he deserved."

She slowly shook her head back and forth. "Honestly, I just want to go home. I only came to see him. The night is kinda ruined for me. Do you mind if we go?"

I sighed dramatically. "Two songs." I held up my fingers and stuck out my bottom lip. "Please, pretty please, for me?"

"Only if you stop making that stupid face."

"Deal," I grabbed her arm and dragged her to the dance area.

I don't know how many songs it was, but it was definitely more than two when we made our way out of the cove, heading for home. We laughed and giggled as we walked the quiet road that led to the lush golf estates. We had both moved into the neighborhood the same summer and had become instant best friends. She was the Bat Woman to my Cat Woman—we have been inseparable ever since.

Becky grabbed my arm, pulling me to a halt. "Do you smell that? It smells like smoke." She looked around.

"No, it's probably just the bonfire smell in your nose."

"No, Vi, look." Becky pointed through the gap in the trees, and there was a bright orange glow. "That's a...."

"Fire," I yelled as I ran for the opening toward my home. I skidded to a halt as I burst from the small patch of woods. My house was completely engulfed in flames, the orange dancing high into the sky and billowing out my window. My eyes searched the yard, but I didn't see my parents.

"Mom, Dad," I screamed at the top of my lungs. "Mom! Dad!" I ran around the house, covering my face from the thick smoke. I couldn't see a way in, there was fire at every window. It was hot, so very hot.

"Violet!" I could make out my father's face in the bedroom window.

"No." I ran toward the house but was pushed back by the searing heat. I looked around for any way to help. He was frantically trying to pull up on the window, but it seemed stuck. He slammed his fists against the glass, but it didn't break.

"Dad!" I ran to the garden and grabbed one of the decorative statues, hurling it at the window. It made contact but didn't even make a scratch. Frantic, I grabbed another and threw it again with a loud grunt.

"Vi." I looked up and stared into my father's eyes. "I love you, Vi." He covered his mouth and coughed, the smoke so thick I could barely make him out now. His hand pressed against the window, and ever so slowly, he disappeared down into the room.

"Dad, no!" I grabbed more rocks and threw them at that stupid window until I couldn't lift my arm. Not caring, I reached for another when movement caught my attention. I looked up to see a boy, who was about my age, dressed in all black. He had a hood up hiding his face but,

I could feel his stare. As soon as I looked directly at him, he turned and ran.

"Vi, we're coming." I looked over and realized that Becky had gone to get her parents. Other neighbors were now jogging my way. I'd been so focused I hadn't heard the firetruck until the flashing lights were driving up the lane.

"They're up there." I pointed to the window as the firefighters ran my way. They reached me and looked up to see where I was pointing when the whole upper floor exploded. I screamed as the firefighter jumped on me and took me to the ground covering me with his much larger body.

I didn't realize I was still screaming until Becky grabbed me and shook me. My eyes found hers, tears streaming down both our faces. She wrapped her arms around me and held me tight as I cried into her shoulder.

"I told them I hated them," I mumbled through the tears. "I didn't hate them. They died thinking I hated them."

Thank You

Thank you to all those that decided to pick up this book and read it. It is only with readers continued support that Indie authors, such as myself, are able to keep writing which is why your reviews mean so much to us. If you enjoyed this book, please consider leaving me a review.

ABOUT THE AUTHOR

Writing is not just a passion for me. It is a lifeline to my sanity.

I have always loved writing but suffer from severe dyslexia and short-term memory retention issues. I struggled in school while I worked every night on re-training my brain.

I was frequently treated like I would never succeed, and I found myself putting my love for writing on a shelf.

Even at the age of six, I found it easier to communicate with animals than people, which was a big reason why I was drawn to dressage horseback riding. I remained focused on my passion for riding until I had to step away from the competition world for personal reasons.

Today, my desire for writing and storytelling has been rekindled. I have published multiple books and will never let anyone or anything hold me back again.
I am a proud romance author who offers my readers morally grey heroes, a ton of spice, epic journeys, and redemption stories.

-Follow Your Dreams-

Brooklyn Cross

BookBub: www.bookbub.com/profile/brooklyn-cross

Goodreads: Brooklyn Cross (Author of Dark Side of the Cloth) | Goodreads

TikTok: Author Brooklyn Cross (@authorbrooklyncross) TikTok | Watch Author Brooklyn Cross's Newest TikTok Videos

IG: Brooklyn Cross (@author_brooklyncross) • Instagram photos and videos

FB Group: Crossfire - A Brooklyn Cross Reader Group | Facebook

www.ingramcontent.com/pod-product-compliance
Lightning Source LLC
Chambersburg PA
CBHW071938210726
48293CB00001BA/235